NEVER A HERO

Also by Vanessa Len

Only a Monster

NEVER A HERO

VANESSA LEN

HARPER TEEN
An Imprint of HarperCollinsPublishers

NEVER A
HERO

ONE

"Don't you slow down!" the coach shouted. One of the boys had turned up late, and now the whole football team was suffering for it. From the fence line, Joan watched them stumble past in yet another lap. Most of the boys were gasping, but at the front of the pack, Nick's pace was steady, as if he could have kept this up for days.

Go home, Joan told herself. She'd been weak today. She'd walked down here after school, hoping for a glimpse of him. Well, now she'd had it, and as always it felt like a punch to the gut. *He doesn't remember you. He doesn't know you anymore.*

"All right!" the coach shouted. "I think you've had enough."

There were groans of relief, and the boys staggered to a stop. Some dropped to the ground, exhausted. Others grasped their knees, trying to catch their breath. Still a few strides ahead, Nick slowed to a jog, and then turned to walk back to his teammates.

He glanced idly toward the fence. Joan's heart stuttered as his gaze skated over and beyond her without interest or recognition.

"Nick!" one of the boys panted from the ground. "You gotta keep up, mate. Team captain can't be trailing behind us all the time."

Nick laughed and went over to help the boy up. "Need a hand, Jameson?"

"I need a defibrillator," the boy grumbled. But he gripped Nick's offered hand and struggled up.

Joan's breath caught at Nick's unguarded smile. He'd always been so solemn when she'd known him. He'd had the world on his shoulders. It occurred to Joan now that she didn't know him anymore either—not this Nick.

She felt that familiar pang of longing for the boy who wasn't here. She suppressed it ruthlessly. That Nick was gone, and she shouldn't want him back. This was Nick as he *should* have been. A guy with an ordinary life.

Go home, she told herself again. And this time, she hefted her schoolbag higher and turned away from the fence.

It was mid-November, and the trees were nearly bare. Cold cut through Joan's trousers as she walked across the empty school grounds. After hours, the whole place had an abandoned quality. The teachers' parking lot was desolate—all concrete and patchy weeds. Joan made her way through it, past the library and down to the back field.

Joan's phone buzzed: a message from Dad. *Nearly home? I made pineapple tarts.* A photo arrived. Flaky pastries cooling on a rack. *Look professional, huh?!*

He'd been checking in on Joan a lot lately; he knew something was wrong. "You seem really quiet," he'd said to her last night. "Everything okay at school? With your friends?"

Sometimes, Joan wished she could just tell him the truth.

Gran died, Dad. They all died. Gran and Aunt Ada and Uncle Gus and Bertie.

But she couldn't tell him that. Because they *hadn't* died. Only Joan remembered that night. Only she remembered Gran's last desperate moments and the thick warmth of Gran's blood; the metallic smell of it. Joan had pressed against the wound, trying to hold Gran's body together, and Gran's breaths had rattled, further and further apart until they'd stopped.

Joan breathed in now, letting the cold air catch in her lungs. None of that had happened, she reminded herself. Gran and the rest of the Hunts were in London—just an hour away by train. They were *fine*.

Joan messaged Dad back. *Looks great! Be home soon.* Then she shoved her hands into her pockets. It was getting colder. Above, the sky was heavy with darkening clouds. There was a storm coming.

She fought the wind as she crossed the field. Her hair whipped around her face, and her blue blazer billowed. She shouldn't have stayed back for that glimpse of Nick. Seeing him—being unseen by him—had thrown her back into that first shock of being in the world without him. There was no place or time she could go to find him. He was gone.

Lightning flashed and the air sharpened. Joan walked faster, absently counting the seconds. *One one thousand, two one thousand, three one thousand* . . . Thunder rolled at the count of five. The storm was maybe fifteen minutes away. She shrugged out of her blazer and shoved it into her bag. She didn't mind the rain, but she only had the one school blazer, and she didn't fancy wearing it again tomorrow, damp.

She was near the gate when the next flash of lightning came. *One one thousand, two—*

A familiar voice sounded behind her, startling her. "Excuse me, I have—" The rest of his words were drowned out by thunder. Joan's heartbeat sounded even louder in her ears. *Nick.*

It wasn't him, she told herself. She was just hearing what she wanted to hear.

But when she turned, it *was* Nick, alone on the field with her, his pace easy and smooth, as familiar as his voice. His dark hair was cut differently now—swept over his brow—but his eyes were just as they'd always been: as sincere and honest as an old-fashioned hero, the kind who rescued cats from trees and people from burning buildings.

For a moment, Joan could almost imagine it really was him— *her* Nick, with all his memories intact, coming after her because he'd remembered her. Her feelings were a tangled skein of trepidation, fear, and a horrible hope.

He stopped, just out of arm's reach. Joan hadn't been this close to him since the night in the library when they'd kissed. That night, the other Nick's existence had ended. No, she corrected herself. That night *she'd* ended him. She'd chosen her family over him. Monsters over the hero.

Whatever was on her face, it made Nick's expression change to apologetic. "Sorry, I didn't mean to scare you." He held out her phone. "I saw you drop this back there."

Joan searched his face. Now that he was closer, she couldn't fool herself. He was looking right at her, and there was no recognition in his eyes at all. This version of him even held himself differently. The other Nick had carried himself with a certain dangerous tension: the understanding that he might have to fight and kill. This Nick's stance was open and untrained. Joan should have felt relieved, she knew, but she was hit with an ache of grief like a physical wound.

She accepted the phone from him, trying not to feel anything when his fingers brushed hers. "Thank you," she heard herself say.

Nick smiled, small and so familiar that Joan could hardly bear it. "I'm always losing mine," he said.

"Really?" Joan was surprised into asking. He'd always been careful with details. She'd never known him to lose anything.

"Well—" Nick's smile warmed into something more relaxed than Joan had ever seen on him. "Really, my little brothers are always stealing it."

"Brothers?" Joan echoed. She heard the wonder in her own voice. His brothers were alive. Joan had known it, but somehow hearing him say it felt like a miracle. The Nick she'd known had been tortured over and over, his whole family murdered in front of him. Joan had seen the recordings. She'd never forget them—not one second of them. All those bodies on the kitchen floor.

"Brothers and sisters," Nick said, still smiling. "Six of us, if you can believe it." And Joan heard an echo of that other Nick telling her, with shadows in his eyes: *Three brothers and two sisters. My brothers and I all slept in the TV room until I was seven.*

"Big family," Joan said. They'd had this conversation before, alone in a house in London, curled up next to each other as darkness had fallen.

Lightning illuminated the field. It shook Joan out of herself, and she was horrified to realize that she'd been about to talk about herself too. *I'm an only child, but I have a big extended family.* What was she thinking? A minute alone with him, and she'd forgotten herself.

She made herself start walking again and felt a twinge of disquiet when Nick fell into easy step beside her. It was too comfortable, a worn groove from a different lifetime.

"I think I've seen you around," Nick said, and Joan looked at him, surprised. "You're in the year below me, right?"

"Yeah," Joan managed, trying to ignore the warm glow it gave her. He'd noticed her. She'd thought . . . Well, it didn't matter what she'd thought. There couldn't be anything between them— not this time, and not last time. Not ever.

Nick ducked his head shyly. "I'm still pretty new at this school."

This time, Joan didn't trust her voice. She'd never forget her first day back at school after the terrible summer, when her body had still been telling her that she was on the run. She'd jumped at every raised voice, every slam of a locker door. Sitting in her stuffy little classrooms, with their single exits, had been close to unbearable.

That first day, she'd walked up the school corridor with her friend Margie.

Holy shit, Margie had said. *Have you seen that new guy yet?*

New guy? Joan had asked.

So hot, Margie had said. *And not just normal hot. I mean proper Hollywood hot.*

And then they'd turned the corner, and there he'd been. Nick.

In their school uniform. Tall and square-jawed and perfect. And Joan hadn't known whether she wanted to run toward him or the other way.

Now, a few months later in November, he was already about fifteen rungs more popular at school than Joan had ever been. Nick Ward, the new football captain. The hottest guy in school. The smartest guy in school. Most of Joan's year had a hopeless crush on him.

"Do you have far to go?" Nick said now. Joan shook her head. She was just a few streets from home. He smiled then—the smile that made half the school weak at the knees. "I'm just here." He pointed at one of the houses across the road.

Oh. So this was it, then. *Remember this*, Joan told herself. Because there wouldn't be any more conversations like this. She couldn't let this happen again.

Nick's dark hair was falling over his eyes. There was a stray leaf on his collar—a red rowan leaf, the last of the season. Joan let herself wonder just one more time. *Nick, don't you remember who you are?*

"You have a leaf—" She gestured at her own neck.

"Oh no, really?" He laughed. A flush climbed his throat. "Not very smooth." He brushed at his collar. "Gone?"

It was still there, hooked to the shoulder of his green-and-gray football jersey. Joan shook her head. "Can I?" She tried not to notice how his flush deepened. He nodded.

Joan reached up. Her own breath hitched, and she could tell that he'd registered it. His eyes darkened. She half expected him to stop her—to catch her wrist. But he didn't flinch, not even when she brushed her knuckles against the back of his neck, just touching the soft bristles at his nape.

"Gone?" he asked. His voice deepened, like just before he'd kissed her.

Joan made herself smile back at him. "Yeah," she said. She snagged the leaf and took her hand away, very careful not to take any life from him. "All gone."

He was gone. He was really gone. Joan felt empty suddenly. And so lonely. She was the only one who remembered him as he'd once been. A boy who could walk unarmed into a room full of monsters and have them flee in fear. A boy who'd protected humans from the predators among them. Not even he remembered.

He didn't even know that monsters existed anymore.

There was still a tinge of red along Nick's cheekbones. Joan told herself that it was from the cold. "Maybe I'll see you around?" he said.

Joan was rescued from answering by shouts from the house. Two kids came bounding across the road—two miniature Nicks, a boy and girl of about six. They had Nick's dark hair and dark eyes. The boy had thick black-rimmed glasses that made him look like a tiny professor.

Nick jumped to meet them, corralling them onto the pavement. "Hey, hey!" he said to them. "What do we do when we cross the road? We wait, don't we? We wait and we look both ways!" He tucked them close, an arm around each of them.

Another girl came hurrying after the kids. She was older than Nick. Maybe nineteen. "Careful!" she said to them, echoing

Nick. "Be careful, now!" She had lighter brown hair than the other three, and her northern accent was more pronounced than Nick's.

"We're helping Mary make chicken!" the boy announced to Nick.

"Robbie dropped it!" the girl said. "On the floor!"

The boy scowled at her behind rain-speckled glasses. "You weren't supposed to say!" he said. He turned to the older girl: Mary. "*She* licked the skin! The raw skin!"

Mary sighed. "Come on," she said. "Holding hands this time." She held out her own hand. Unexpectedly, she threw a wry smile at Joan. "Hi!" she said. "Sorry to interrupt your chat."

"Hi." Joan made herself smile back.

Mary returned her attention to the children, beckoning them, and Joan's eyes caught on her ring. It was plain black with no shine. Joan had seen it before. Nick had worn it on a chain, tucked under his shirt. Joan had never known it had belonged to his sister.

"See you at school?" Nick said to Joan. He'd taken the little boy's hand.

Joan nodded. Mary. Robbie. The little girl must be Alice. Nick had talked about them—just a bit. Joan hadn't known it at the time, but he'd been grieving their loss for as long as she'd known him.

She had a flash again of the kitchen in the videos. Of all three of them—Mary, Robbie, and Alice—lying still and dead. And Nick . . . Joan's heart clenched at the way he was smiling down at the little ones now. He'd shoved a knife into their killer's neck, face contorted with misery and horror. Joan would never forget the sound he'd made.

Joan couldn't hold the smile. "See you," she managed. She turned fast.

She walked up the steep slope of the hill, pushing herself until the physical exertion overrode the tightness in her chest. Gusts of wind stirred up sticks and stray leaves. Heavy drops of rain began to fall. The wind carried fragments of conversation up the hill.

"—that pretty girl?" That was Nick's older sister, her tone teasing and fond.

"*Mary!*" Nick said, sounding so much like an embarrassed younger brother that Joan found herself almost smiling for real.

High laughs and shrieks from the kids, and then Joan was too far away to hear anything more. Safely out of sight, she squeezed her eyes shut.

She took a deep breath and let it out slowly. It was okay, she told herself. She shouldn't have spoken to him, but it wouldn't happen again. She'd make sure of that. And the stuff she was feeling right now—she could handle it. Heavy rain hit her face like tears. She could handle this. She'd been handling it.

She was back here in the real world. No monster slayers. No monsters. Just her normal life at home. And that was how it would be from now on.

"I'm home!" she called to Dad. She was hit with warmth and sweet pastry smells: butter and pineapple jam and ginger.

"Hi!" Dad called from the kitchen. As Joan kicked off her shoes, he emerged with a plate of pineapple tarts. "I've already eaten five!" he said. He saw her then and frowned. "Where's your blazer?"

Joan slid her shoes under the rack with the side of her foot and grabbed a tart from the plate. "Didn't want it all rained on." She bit into the pastry, cupping her free hand underneath to catch flaky crumbs as she followed Dad to the kitchen.

"It's supposed to be rained on," Dad said. "It's supposed to stop you from being rained on."

"This is really good," Joan said with her mouth full. "Oh my God! How many did you make?" she added as she saw the kitchen. There were dozens of tarts cooling on racks—on the stove, on the bench, on top of the fridge.

"You give some to your friends!" Dad said. "And we'll take some tomorrow!"

"Tomorrow?" Joan said. "What's happening—" She stopped. There was a sticky note on the kitchen bench, in Dad's handwriting. *Hunt family dinner 6 p.m.* The jam turned sour at the back of Joan's throat. "What's that?"

"Hmm? Oh. Your gran phoned this afternoon."

"She did?"

"She's invited us to dinner tomorrow." Dad rummaged in the drawer. "Down in London with the whole Hunt family."

Joan's stomach tightened. She hadn't spoken to any of the Hunts since she'd come home. Her cousin Ruth had messaged her a few times.

Hey, if you ever want to talk about the whole being-a-monster thing, we can do that.

Even if you don't want to talk about it, we should. You might think you can shut it out, but you can't.

Joan had told herself she'd reply, but weeks and now months had passed, and Ruth's messages were still unanswered.

"I got the feeling that your gran wanted to talk to you about something," Dad added.

"About what?" Joan said.

"Oh, you know your gran," Dad said, sounding distracted. "She doesn't like to say much on the phone. *There* you are!" He produced a pair of black oven mitts from the drawer.

Joan found herself remembering a different kitchen—Gran's kitchen in London, cocoa bubbling on the stove. Joan had had a strange encounter with Gran's neighbor. He'd pushed her into a wall one morning, and then night had abruptly fallen.

Joan had run back to Gran's place, terrified. *He did something to me,* she'd told Gran.

Gran's green eyes had been luminous in the low kitchen light. *He didn't do something to you,* she'd told Joan. *You did something to him.* She'd leaned close. *You're a monster, Joan.*

A few months ago, Joan had learned what the rest of the Hunts had always known. Her mum's side of the family were monsters: *real* monsters. They stole life from humans. They used that life to travel in time.

Now, in Joan's own kitchen, there was a slight stirring as if from a breeze, although nothing in the room moved. Dad didn't react. Joan had felt it with her monster sense. The wave came again, rippling through the world without actually disturbing anything.

Sometimes the timeline seemed like a living thing—a creature with a will of its own. Tonight, Joan perceived it as a natural force, as if the storm itself had come inside.

Dad closed the oven door with his elbow. "So tomorrow night?"

You might think you can shut it out, but you can't. Joan folded her arms across her chest. "I don't know," she said. "I'm working tomorrow."

"Don't you finish up at four?"

"I've got an essay."

"Can you do that on Sunday?" Dad asked. "The thing is, your gran reminded me . . ." He hesitated. "Tomorrow is the fifteenth anniversary of your mum's death. I think your gran wants to spend some time with you." He looked down at his oven mitts. *"I should have remembered it was a special day,"* he said. "I suppose you and I always celebrate your mum's birthday instead."

A familiar pressure of emotion started. Joan shoved it down. She hadn't expected Dad to say that. Dad talked about Mum all the time, but Gran *never* talked about her.

"Is that okay with you?" Dad said. When Joan didn't answer immediately, he said, softer: "Joan, are *you* okay?"

He'd been asking that question in different ways for weeks. *You seem so quiet lately. Is anything going on? Have you had a fight with your friends?*

Joan tried out the truth in her head.

I found out that I'm a monster, Dad. The Hunt side of the family are all monsters.

Or another truth.

The boy I loved was a monster slayer. He killed Gran and the rest of the family. But I unmade him. I unraveled his life. And now the Hunts are alive again. But they don't remember.

He doesn't remember me.

The hollow grief of it hit her again. She couldn't tell Dad any of it. He wouldn't believe her. She didn't *want* him to believe her. She wanted him safe, here at home, far away from the world of monsters.

"I'm fine," she said. She tried to make it sound real. "Just. You know. Stuff."

Dad searched her face. "What stuff?"

"Normal stuff." Joan needed to keep the emotion out of her voice. "Nothing stuff. Everyone's stressed about school this year—*you* know that."

"Joan—"

"You don't have to keep asking, Dad. I'm really fine!" It came out frustrated. Joan pressed her lips shut. She didn't want to fight about it. She didn't want to tell Dad more lies than she already had.

In the silence, the wind rattled the windows. Dad's sigh was barely audible over it.

Joan looked past the kitchen's open-plan arch to the photos on the living room wall. Joan and Dad. Joan as a baby. Mum. The three of them together in a park, Mum and Dad holding Joan's hands. As a kid, Joan had stared at those photos for hours, trying to match her own features to Mum's. Joan had always looked more like Dad than Mum. More Chinese than European.

"You remind me so much of her," Dad said. He'd followed her gaze. "More and more every day. She'd have been so proud of you."

That pressure of emotion again. There were things about Mum that Joan *really* didn't want to think about. Mum had died when Joan was a baby. Her death had always been a fact—one that Joan had learned before anything else, before she'd learned to count or read. An immutable fact. A foundational fact of her life.

"Gran never talks about her," Joan pushed out. "Like, never. Don't you think that's weird?"

Dad was silent, his eyes still on the photos. "I didn't understand that either for a long time," he said. "But . . . your gran and your mum didn't always get on. They had an argument just before your mum died. I think your gran felt very guilty about that. I think she blamed herself for your mum's death in some strange way." He took off the oven mitts. Mum must have bought those ones. All the dark stuff in the house was hers; Dad preferred bright colors.

"I think this dinner is a big step for your gran." Behind his glasses, Dad's eyes were wet.

He wanted to go to this dinner, Joan realized. He wanted to see the Hunts tomorrow. He wanted to remember Mum with Mum's family on this anniversary.

Joan took a deep breath. "We'll both go together?" she said. Dad would be at this dinner, she reminded herself. The Hunts wouldn't be able to talk about monster things in front of him.

"Of *course*," Dad said. "It's a family thing."

"A family thing," Joan echoed. Not a dinner with monsters, but a dinner with Mum's family and Dad. "Right," she said. "A family dinner." And after their dinner, Joan and Dad would go home to their normal lives. It wasn't like Joan would be pulled back into the monster world.

TWO

It was a hot morning, but the path to Holland House was cool in the shifting shade of trees. Joan could hear the sounds of the garden already: kids laughing, peacocks cawing, the booming voices of the tour guides.

She emerged onto the lush lawn. It wasn't even noon, but the place was already packed. It seemed that everyone had had the same idea: to take advantage of the good weather at the park. Costumed guides led groups of tourists toward the maze. Kids kicked up water in the shallows of the pond.

Beyond them, glints of glass reflected the morning sun. Holland House was always beautiful, but this was its best time of day. The redbrick facade glowed.

Joan was struck with a pang of grief out of nowhere. It didn't look like this anymore, she remembered suddenly.

It had *burned*.

She woke with a start.

Light showed through cracks in her bedroom blinds. Outside, it was still raining heavily, a relentless roar. Joan tried to slow her breathing. The ache of loss hit her again. In her memory, Holland House had been one of London's most popular tourist attractions; people had visited from all over the world.

In this timeline, it lay in ruins. People didn't even remember its name.

Joan rubbed her eyes. The dream had been so vivid that this actual rainy morning seemed surreal. She glanced at the clock. Still pretty early. She had a vague feeling that something difficult was happening later today. A math exam? No, it was Saturday.

Then she remembered. She was seeing the Hunts tonight. *I got the feeling that your gran wanted to talk to you about something*, Dad had said. Joan's empty stomach turned over. What was Gran going to say? Joan half wished that she could step back into that dream—go back to that sunny day, so far from here, to that long-gone house.

Too late, she registered that she'd veered into dangerous emotional territory.

The morning light dimmed, as if night were falling again. The patter of rain muted. Even Joan's own growing panic felt far away from where she was. She had a flash of Aaron touching her, his gray eyes alarmed. *Hey, stay with me.*

Still half-asleep, Joan fought to ground herself in the present moment, as Aaron had taught her. She focused on the details of her physical surroundings. The sound of rain. Shadows of striped morning light on the wall. The rough embroidery of her quilt. She clawed back each sense, one by one. It felt like forever before morning dawned again and the rain rose back to a roar. Joan's next breath was a choke of relief. She sat up and gripped her knees. *I'm here*, she told herself. *I'm here and I don't want to be anywhere else.*

These fade-outs were getting worse, she knew. She'd done her best to stop them. Her bedroom walls had once been covered with old maps and illustrations of ancient places, but now they were bare. She'd dropped history at school. She'd tried to remove everything from her life that might trigger her desire to travel in time.

She remembered Aaron's words. *You nearly died. You tried to travel without taking time first.*

She should have told Gran about this problem weeks ago, she knew. She shouldn't have been avoiding the Hunts for so long. *Tonight*, she told herself. She'd tell Gran tonight.

She forced herself from her warm bed. The floorboards were cold, even through her socks, and the chill helped to ground her. She found her work uniform and pulled it on. Then she went to brush her teeth.

In the kitchen, Dad was working on his laptop, specs on, phone to his ear. Tupperware boxes of pineapple tarts were stacked up beside him, labeled in his neat handwriting. *The Hunts*, one of them said.

He pressed mute as Joan headed past him for the front door. "Aren't you having breakfast?"

Joan scrubbed a hand over her face. Controlling the fade-out had taken longer than she'd wanted. "Slept in," she said. "I'll grab something at the bakery."

"We should eat more fruit," Dad said, a bit absently. Joan could tell the client was saying something to him on the phone. He called to Joan as she left. "Have a good day!"

Joan worked every Wednesday evening and all day Saturday at an old-fashioned cake shop with a window full of scones and fondant fancies. Inside, the owner had packed ten tables into the small space between the counter and the door, and all day long, people scraped their chairs back and forth on the wooden floorboards to allow servers and other customers to pass.

Joan barely had time to think between spooning thick cream into ramekins for scones and cutting slices of Victoria sponge. It was eleven a.m. and then one forty-five p.m. and then two thirty p.m.

By three thirty, most of the cakes were gone, and the bakery was empty except for Joan and her friend Margie. Joan wiped off the chalkboard and wrote: *50% off everything.*

"Have we sold any of these meringues?" Margie said. She held one up—a blobby white thing with a dip in the middle. "What even is this?"

"Maybe a snowman?" Joan suggested. It was November. "Like a festive thing?"

Margie took a bite, and her expression turned thoughtful. "Huh." She offered the rest of it to Joan, stretching over the counter.

Joan had picked up a tray to clear the tables, and so she leaned to take a bite from Margie's hand. Meringue crumbled in her mouth, an airy candy cane. She raised her eyebrows.

"*Right?*" Margie popped the rest into her own mouth. "They're *good*. Why aren't they selling?"

"Maybe they need faces."

"Maybe little arms," Margie said. "Little chocolate arms . . ." She held out her own arms, hands starred to demonstrate, and Joan grinned. "You started that English essay yet?" Margie asked.

"You haven't?" Joan was surprised. Margie was so organized that she kept the calendar for their whole friendship group. If Joan wanted to know when Chris was free, she'd ask Margie, not Chris.

"I can't even look at it!" Margie said. "Remember how nice Mrs. Shah was last year? What's going on with her? She's the *worst* now."

Joan paused, laden tray in hand, not sure if she'd heard right. "How nice she was *last* year?"

"Guess she prefers teaching history to English."

"Mrs. Shah taught us history last year?"

Margie gave her a funny look. "Why are you saying it like it's a question?"

It was one of those unsettling moments when Joan's memory didn't align with other people's. Joan's history teacher last year had been Mr. Larch, a short man with a booming laugh that bellowed from his whole chest.

Joan went into the kitchen to stack the dishwasher. It was a big industrial thing that Margie called RoboCop because the top half had a thin visor-like screen, and the bottom half opened up like a mouth. When she closed RoboCop again, there was a dark mark at the edge of its silver door—the size and shape of Joan's thumbprint. She rubbed it idly and was surprised to find that it was rough like a burn mark.

Her mind, though, was on Mr. Larch. When had she last seen him? He was usually on uniform duty, standing at the school gate to call out people wearing sneakers or the wrong socks. But he hadn't been there in months.

"Hey, where's Mr. Larch these days?" she called over her shoulder to Margie. "He on holiday or what?"

"Who?" Margie called back.

"Mr. Larch from school," Joan said, but when she came back out, Margie looked blank.

"Who's Mr. Larch?"

Margie used to do impressions of Mr. Larch all the time. "*You* know," Joan said. "Big glasses. Always banging on about uniforms." She mimicked: "*What color are those shoes, Margie Channing!*"

"What are *you* banging on about?" Margie said, her smile half-amused, half-confused. "There's a Mr. Larch Reading Garden behind the library. Is that what you mean?"

Joan felt a curl of unease. There was nothing behind the library—just a big weedy stretch of ground up to the fence. When had she last gone back there, though? Not in the last few months. Not since she'd returned after the summer.

"That's not your guy, though," Margie said. "It's dedicated to some teacher who died ten years ago—way before our time."

"That's not him," Joan agreed. Mr. Larch was definitely alive. He was short and loud and kind. When Joan had struggled with the order of prime ministers, he'd made up a song on the spot for her. The tune still got in Joan's head sometimes. *Then John Major took the stage, and—*

Margie popped another meringue into her mouth. "I'm going to hand-sell the hell out of these," she said with her mouth full. "I'm not letting them go off the menu." She grabbed the tongs. "Hey, you doing anything tonight? We could get those essays over early."

"Tonight?" Joan echoed. She'd noticed things wrong with this timeline—big things, like the destruction of Holland House.

Small things, like Nick going to her school now. But . . . *No.* Mr. Larch wasn't dead. He was just teaching somewhere else. For sure.

"Dad's making that pasta you like with the tomato and mint."

"Yeah," Joan said absently. "Sounds good. Oh, wait." Her heart sank. "I'm having dinner with my gran tonight. Dad and I are going down to London."

"Why are you making that face?" Margie squashed her mouth. "I thought you loved going there."

"I do, but—" Joan stopped as Margie gripped her arm painfully. "What's wrong?" Joan said, and then she realized that Margie's face was pink with excitement.

Margie nodded at the window. "Is that who I think it is?" she hissed.

Outside, a familiar muscled figure examined the display cakes, black T-shirt riding up as he bent. Joan swallowed. It was Nick.

Margie grabbed for her phone. "Is he coming into the *shop*? No. *Yes.* He's—"

Nick walked around to the bakery door and pushed it open. Behind the counter, Joan's phone lit up. A message from Margie.

Stop everything nick ward just walked in

Then one from their friend Chris:

in where?? In the bakery???

Margie: he looks SO good

Chris: NO IM SO JEALOUS

A rush of emotions hit Joan. She'd promised herself that yesterday was an aberration—that she'd stay away from him. But here he was, and some stupid part of her was glad of it. Standing here, in Joan's ordinary world, he seemed larger-than-life. The school football star. The hottest guy in school.

Hollywood hot, Margie had said about him. He was classically handsome, with soft dark hair and a square jaw. He could have been the lead in a movie: the hero. It seemed absurd suddenly that any version of him had ever been into Joan, let alone that they'd been soul mates in a kind of way.

Nick's gaze swept over them, and his face lit up. It took Joan a second to understand that he was smiling like that because he'd seen *her.*

"Hi," he said. The *hi* encompassed Margie and Joan both, but his eyes returned to Joan as if he were compelled. "Did your phone survive the adventure?"

Joan could see Margie at the edge of her vision, staring at her, and she felt strangely on display. She nodded, and his smile warmed.

Joan's phone lit up again. Another message from Margie— just from her to Joan.

Since when do you know nick ward??

Joan shook her head. *Please don't say anything*, she willed Margie. She needed to get Nick out of here. "You came in at the right time," she said to him out loud. "Everything's fifty percent off for the end of the day."

"I *did* come at the right time," Nick said, still smiling, and then he reddened, as if he hadn't meant to say it aloud.

Joan's whole body felt too warm suddenly, like she'd been standing in the sun. In her peripheral vision, Margie's smile was turning Cheshire cat.

Joan's phone lit up again. She glanced down, expecting

another message from Margie, but to her surprise, it was an incoming call from Gran.

Joan hesitated. She should answer it, she knew. But . . . she was at work. She'd see Gran in a couple of hours anyway. She hit the red decline button.

"Well, that's me done," Margie announced. "Going to take this lot to the charity."

"What?" Joan said. Margie had only boxed up the meringues. And she and Margie always took the leftovers down together. "But we haven't—"

"Back in ten." Margie was already slipping the loop of her apron over her head. She turned her back to Nick and gave Joan an exaggerated wink.

"Margie," Joan said. All she needed to say was: *There's more to box up.* Margie wouldn't question it; she'd stay. Joan opened her mouth, but no words came out. Her face felt like it was on fire. Margie's grin widened. *You're welcome*, she mouthed. And then she was walking out of the shop.

Nick met Joan's eyes, and Joan was suddenly aware of his size: how he'd hunched a bit to make himself less imposing. He bit his lip, but he couldn't hide his amusement. Margie hadn't exactly been subtle. "Hi," he said again.

Joan's chest constricted. She wasn't used to these unshadowed smiles from him. "Hi," she said stupidly. His hair was curling a bit at the ends. "See anything you like?"

Nick blinked at her, and Joan gestured at the cakes.

"Oh," he said, and for some reason, he flushed even redder. "Uh . . . I'm not sure. What can I get for ten pounds if . . . Well, there's a lot of us at home."

He could get plain iced buns for that, but Joan suddenly wanted him to have the really nice ones. "We're doing chocolate chip buns this week. For ten pounds, you can get ten." Not quite true, but Joan could add her own discount to the half off.

And then he was smiling again. And suddenly it *hurt*—this fantasy that they'd just met; that they might run into each other at school next week; that he'd come into the bakery again. That this could be the start of something rather than the end.

Joan concentrated on folding up a couple of cardboard boxes. In two minutes, he'd be on his way home. She could bear this feeling for two minutes—you could bear anything for two minutes, and then for two more minutes after that. She'd been learning that since getting home. Five sets of two, and then Margie would be back.

Joan put six buns into one box, and four into another. Then, knowing she shouldn't, she added two mini Bakewell tarts to fill the space. "On the house," she said, not looking at him. She'd have done it for any customer, she told herself. They wouldn't keep.

"They're my favorite." Nick sounded surprised and grateful.

I know, Joan thought. She knew he liked almonds and cherries. Just like she knew he'd want quantity over the big Bakewell tart in the window so that the kids would get a whole bun each. She knew him so well. Except that she didn't. Not this Nick. *This isn't him*, she reminded herself. *He looks like him, but he isn't him.*

She could bear this. Nick would finish up school this year, and she would next year. Maybe he'd move away. She'd move away. She could handle this for a year. And then . . . maybe her feelings for him would eventually fade. Maybe, one day, she'd be able to think of him without this yearning.

Another notification flew up on Joan's phone. She glanced down, expecting more messages from Margie and Chris, but it was a voice mail from Gran.

That was weird. Gran never left casual messages—not ever. Not even scrawled notes on the kitchen table. She always said: *Don't leave words lying around. The wrong people might find them.*

The bakery door opened, bell jangling. *Margie*, Joan thought, and she wasn't sure if she was relieved or disappointed that she and Nick had only had a moment alone. *Relieved*, she told herself firmly.

"Did you forget your coat—" Joan started to say, and then stopped.

It wasn't Margie. The new arrival was a man of about thirty. He'd dropped a duffel bag outside, and now he stood just beyond the threshold like a vampire waiting for an invitation. He was tall, with narrow catlike eyes and hair the color of burnt butter. His mustache was thin and sharp as a pencil mark—a shade darker than his hair. And there was something *wrong* about him. The cut of his suit; his hairstyle. He could have stepped out of a photo from the 1920s.

Or stepped out of the actual 1920s.

Joan's heart thudded once, twice. He was a time traveler. A monster. She'd never seen a monster in Milton Keynes before. "What do you want?" she said. It came out hard.

Nick looked puzzled as he registered Joan's rudeness. And then his eyes narrowed, and he shifted between Joan and the man, instinctively protective.

"You've been remarkably difficult to find," the man said to Joan. He frowned at Nick. "And you shouldn't be here at all. We were told there'd be two girls alone." And that made Nick's fists clench, still instinctive. The man stepped across the threshold, and Nick took a warning step of his own. The man sighed like someone who'd arrived to do a small job and had found a bigger one waiting.

And then Nick was frowning too, as if he wasn't sure what he was seeing. "What . . ." His voice trailed off.

Something made Joan look again at the duffel bag.

It wasn't a bag. Joan lurched forward. "Margie?" Her voice came out strained and thin. "What did you do?" she blurted to the man. "What did you *do*?"

Margie had fallen at an angle, legs tucked under her like she was curled up on the sofa at home. The boxes of meringues had fallen beside her, spilling out over the wet ground. Around her face, wisps of golden hair lifted in the breeze. The rain had stopped, but water dripped from the eaves, striking her face. She didn't flinch. Her eyes were wide and blank.

"Little butterfly of a thing," the man said contemptuously. "Guess she would have died in a few months anyway."

Joan couldn't take it in. She shook her head disbelievingly, picturing the man lifting his hand to Margie's neck, and then siphoning all her life with one touch. "*No*," she breathed, as if by saying it she could make it untrue. That Margie would again just be walking up to the charity. That she'd be back in ten minutes.

"Get back," Nick murmured to Joan, his posture dangerous

suddenly, and calm fell over her. This man didn't know who he was dealing with.

Almost as quickly, her understanding reframed. Nick couldn't fight this guy. Not anymore. Not after what Joan had done to him.

She scrambled around the counter and grabbed Nick's arm before he could take another step.

"It's okay," Nick told Joan softly. "Just get back behind the counter." He hadn't taken his eyes off the man. "I'm going to—" He stopped, eyes widening.

A few paces from him, another man was stepping out of thin air, striding into the world as if through an invisible door. And now more people were materializing all around the room—men and women in anachronistic clothes: heavy 1940s suits and 1920s gowns. *Monsters.*

The man in the doorway spoke: "Take the girl. Kill the boy." He barely raised his voice, but the new arrivals scrambled into motion.

As if a switch had been flicked, Joan's numb shock at seeing Margie vanished. If she and Nick didn't get out of here, they were both going to end up dead too.

She shoved over the nearest table, full of uncleared plates and cups. A man in pale linen startled back from the smashing china. "Through the kitchen!" she said to Nick.

Nick didn't hesitate. Together, they dove around the counter and into the kitchen. Nick slammed the door behind him, and Joan grabbed a heavy cart stacked with baking trays. Nick caught the other side, and they toppled it with a loud clatter of metal, blocking the door.

"What's going *on*?" Nick gasped out as they sprinted for the back door. "They appeared out of thin air! *How?*"

Joan shook her head. They were monsters. More than that, she didn't know. "As soon as we're out, get to the alleyway on the right and *run!*" she gabbled. *Take the girl,* the man had said. *Kill the boy.* But Joan *knew* that if she and Nick split up, the attackers would go after her, not Nick. They hadn't even expected Nick to be here. "Just get away from me! They'll follow me, not you!"

Confusion flashed across Nick's face. "You mean let them *have* you?"

"Just *do* it! Just—" Joan reached the back door and flung it open. She gasped. More monsters were materializing in the courtyard, filling the tiny space. She hesitated, staring.

Nick grabbed her hand. "Come on!" he said. And there was no time to think. Together they tumbled out the door. They dodged around the materializing monsters, and they *ran.*

THREE

Joan didn't make it out of the courtyard. A man caught her around the waist, the heavy belt of his arm knocking the air from her. Her knees sagged, and the man squeezed her into a bear hug.

Ahead, Nick passed the gauntlet of monsters and was almost out on the street. Joan felt weak with relief. He was going to make it.

But Nick turned, apparently realizing that he'd lost his grip on Joan's hand.

"No!" Joan croaked out. "*Go!*"

A monster grabbed at him, but Nick shook off the grip with irritated ease. He threw one punch, and then another, fighting to get back to Joan. And then the other monsters converged.

Joan struggled, trying to break the iron band around her chest. She couldn't breathe. Her vision spotted and faded. From the grunts and gasps, Nick was holding his own, but all it would take was a single touch to his neck. Clawing, Joan dug her fingers under her attacker's arm. He shifted, and her lungs reinflated with a sudden rush. She forced out: "Nick, *run!*"

"*Corvin!*" someone snapped. "What are you waiting for?"

The man holding Joan raised his voice in command. "Stop! Stop fighting!" His chest rumbled against Joan's back. "Be quiet. Be still."

The command was so ridiculous that Joan almost laughed.

Did he think they'd stop just because he'd told them to? She wrenched and kicked at her attacker—*Corvin*, someone had called him. Her heel impacted with his shin, and he swore.

For a long moment, the only sounds were Joan's feet scuffing and slipping against the wet cobblestones and Corvin's grunts as he tried to hold her still.

They really were the only sounds, Joan realized slowly. . . . She couldn't hear Nick. She twisted, searching desperately, already imagining her worst nightmare—Nick, dead on the ground, like Margie.

But Nick was still standing. Joan barely had a moment to feel relief, though, because his posture was strange. He was in the middle of the courtyard, still as a stone, his eyes on Joan. The attackers had pulled away from him, but Nick wasn't taking the opportunity to fight. His arms were stiff by his sides.

And his eyes . . . His eyes were so eerily blank that Joan had a horrible flash of Margie's lifeless face. Of Gran's. Of Lucien's. The eyes of the dead.

"Nick?" Joan said. It came out scared and uncertain. He didn't move. "*Nick?*" she said again. What was wrong with him? "What did you do to him?" she said shakily to Corvin.

Instead of answering, Corvin raised his voice in an order: "Hand me the cuff!"

A woman advanced on Joan. Her neat bob of hair and flared 1950s dress made her look like a black-and-white advertisement come to life. Her lipstick was a touch asymmetrical, giving her mouth a cruel twist. From her breast pocket, she plucked a slim golden cylinder. She handed it to Corvin, and he flicked it with his thumb. It unrolled into a short length of paper-thin gold, cut into lacework.

"What are you *doing*?" Joan managed. What *was* that thing? "Who *are* you?" She kicked at the woman to keep her back.

"Steady her," Corvin said, and someone seized Joan's right arm and shoved her shirtsleeve up, popping the button.

Joan struggled. "Nick!" she gasped out. He was still just standing there. What was going on? "*Nick!*"

Corvin draped the lacework onto Joan's forearm, just below the wrist. For a moment, it lay there like a pretty golden arm cuff. And then it seemed to shiver and writhe and burn, burrowing into Joan's skin like a live thing. Joan gasped—it hurt like a splash of molten metal.

"She's anchored to me," Corvin said. "We can go."

Go? Were they taking her somewhere? "Who are you? Why—" Joan's voice cracked, and she blurted, "Why did you kill Margie?" She couldn't believe Margie was dead. "Why didn't you let her go?" Margie's little sister, Sammy, was turning six on Wednesday. Margie had been planning to make a smash cake in the shape of a rock with dinosaurs inside. And now . . . "She was *leaving*. She was on her way out!"

"Oh, stop," Corvin snapped, as if Joan had questioned his professionalism. "There was barely half a year left in her."

Little butterfly of a thing, he'd called Margie earlier. Was he saying that Margie would have died soon anyway? Joan shook her head. She couldn't bear it.

Corvin raised his voice. "Someone stay back and clean up!" he ordered. "Deal with the body and the boy!"

Kill the boy, he'd said before. Joan lost it then. She elbowed and kicked, trying to get out of Corvin's grip. Nick was still standing there, statue-still. Had he even blinked? "Nick, *fight!*" Joan begged him. "Fight! You have to get out of here! They'll *kill* you!" And it would be Joan's fault. The other version of Nick could have stopped them all, but Joan had stripped him of his memories and abilities. She'd made him helpless against monsters. Even he didn't know what he'd once been.

In the distance, a siren started up. "Head out!" Corvin said. "Quickly now!"

Joan was peripherally aware that the courtyard was emptying as monsters vanished into thin air.

Out of nowhere, the desire to time-travel hit her too—a punched-gut yearning so strong that for a second, it overwhelmed every other feeling, even her fear for Nick. But it wasn't her own desire. *She's anchored to me,* Corvin had said. He'd put that thing on her—that *cuff*—and now he was trying to drag her out of this time.

"Come *on!*" Corvin said to her.

The feeling of forced yearning increased. Joan needed to follow him—more than she wanted to breathe. It was primal.

Joan fought on the same primal level to stay here, in this time. Monsters time-traveled by thinking of a time and yearning for it. Joan filled herself with a yearning for home. For here. For the place they already were.

Joan fought it like she'd fought the fade-out this morning, focusing on her senses. It was cold. She could smell wet cobblestones and baked bread and chimney smoke. *I'm home,* she thought. *I don't want to be anywhere but here.*

"Do you have her or not?" This was said by a thin man with

a pointed face and spare gray hair. He sounded dubious, almost condescendingly so.

Corvin's response was irritated. "Course I have her." He grunted, though, as if he were struggling with a heavy weight.

The forced desire became desperate. Joan could feel herself losing her grip. *I don't want to be anywhere but here,* she told herself again. But her internal voice seemed weak in comparison with the desperate need to travel. She twisted again in Corvin's arms until she could see Nick, and only him.

Corvin growled with effort. Joan couldn't breathe. *Nick,* she thought, letting herself yearn for *him* rather than pushing her feelings away for once. *I want to stay here with you.* But Corvin was too strong. Around her, the sound of the siren faded to nothing. The sharp smell of rain disappeared.

Nick . . . Nick . . .

In the growing darkness of her vision, Joan glimpsed movement where there'd been none. Nick's hands were clenching slowly into fists. His face took on expression like water filling a cup.

"Run!" Joan gritted out. Her own voice sounded tinny and far away.

But instead of running, Nick turned toward Corvin with grim purpose. In one stride, he was there. He did something hard and fast that made Corvin croak with pain and stagger back, pulling Joan with him.

"Kill him!" Corvin called, looking over his shoulder for help. "Stop him!"

But there was no one to help.

The other monsters had vanished, leaving him alone in the courtyard with Joan and Nick.

FOUR

⌐•¬

The feeling of yearning had stopped. Joan gasped in relief, sagging in Corvin's grip. It had worked. She'd managed to stay here in this time.

"Where is everyone?" Corvin sounded irritated. It seemed to dawn on him that he hadn't traveled out with the others. "What the hell?" He turned his catlike eyes on Joan, pale brows drawing together. "How did you fight that cuff?"

His grip had loosened as he'd looked around. Joan took the chance to twist and wrench away.

Corvin reached for her, but then Nick was there. Nick slammed a fist into Corvin's face, making him stagger back. Corvin drew a breath to speak, and Nick punched him again, hard in the jaw, and then Corvin was down, unconscious on the courtyard's wet cobblestones.

Nick stared down at him, his broad shoulders rising and falling. Joan struggled to catch her own breath. The neighborhood sounds had returned. Birds chirped and distant cars rumbled. The air smelled of wet stone.

Nick turned to her. "Did he hurt you?" His eyes roved over her.

Joan shook her head. And then déjà vu hit her hard. An image overlaid her vision: Nick standing over Lucien Oliver's body, blood dripping from a sword. *Are you all right?* he'd asked her.

"I'm really sorry," Nick said now. He ran a hand over his face.

"I don't know why I froze up like that."

"What?" Why was he sorry? He'd just saved her from being abducted by monsters.

Nick's brow creased. "You were struggling, and I just stood there while you fought them. I'm sorry."

"No." That wasn't right. "No, you—" Joan stopped. What exactly *had* happened? She'd never seen anything like it. Nick had been fighting, and then Corvin had commanded him: *Be quiet, be still*, and Nick had stopped in place as if Corvin had hit pause, blank as a doll.

Joan looked down at Corvin now, sprawled unconscious on the wet stone ground, hair darkening to clumped black in the puddled rainwater. The fight had lifted one of his sleeves, exposing a tattoo of a tree. The trunk started near his elbow, twisted branches crawling up the palm of his hand, their withered ends reaching to the tip of each finger.

A burnt elm tree, Joan's memory supplied. The Argent family sigil. Argents could sway humans to their will. Her stomach lurched. "*You* didn't freeze up. That wasn't you." Nick had come back for her. He could have escaped, and he'd saved her life. "It was *him*," she said. "He used a power on you."

"A power?" Nick's dark eyes fixed on her.

Joan opened her mouth to answer, and then stopped. She'd wanted to take that look from Nick's face, to ease his misplaced guilt, but she remembered again who she was talking to—a boy who'd once been a figure of terror in the monster world. A slayer so dangerous that myths had been created around him. He'd led the massacre of her family last time, and that couldn't happen again. She shouldn't be telling him anything about monster powers.

Nick said slowly: "He told me to be quiet. To be still. And it was like . . . It was like I *wanted* to obey him. Like I had to." His gaze on Joan was sharpening. "Who *are* these people? How did they appear out of thin air?"

All those questions were dangerous, and Joan didn't know how to answer them. There wasn't time to answer them, she reminded herself. "We need to get out of here," she said. "He's going to wake up soon." And then he'd be able to use that power again.

On impulse, though, Joan spared a moment to kneel on the cold cobblestones and rifle through Corvin's pockets. Left jacket pocket. Right pocket. *There.* A wallet. And inside his jacket, a chain hanging from a buttonhole. Joan drew it out and found a black pendant at one end—a burnt tree with withered branches. It was a chop—the monster version of an ID card. She pocketed the wallet and pendant. She might not know who'd sent these monsters after her, but she was going to find out.

She looked up and found Nick's honest, square-jawed gaze on her still. She felt strangely ashamed, as if he'd caught her picking over the man like a vulture. The Hunt side of the family were thieves, and through Nick's eyes, she suddenly felt like one too. "I just want to know who he is," she said.

Nick seemed surprised by her defensiveness. "Of course," he said. "Does he have a phone too? Might as well delay him if we can." And now it was Joan's turn to be surprised. She couldn't imagine the other version of him condoning theft.

She hunted through the rest of Corvin's pockets. "I can't find one."

"That's okay." Nick offered his hand. "Let's just go."

Joan let him help her up, her mind more off-balance than her body. *I don't even know how many people I've killed*, he'd told her once. Had the previous version of him adopted his strict moral compass as a way of dealing with monster slaying? It was strange to think that this new Nick might have a slightly different morality than the boy she'd known.

There was a narrow brick-walled passage leading to the street. Joan braced herself as they reached the corner, knowing Margie would be crumpled in the doorway. *Careful*, she mouthed to Nick.

"I think the cops have arrived," Nick murmured back—barely a breath of sound. "That siren was getting close when those people"—he hesitated and felt out the strange word slowly—*"vanished."*

Siren? Joan had forgotten about the siren. Without it, the passage seemed very quiet. Even the rain had stopped dripping from the eaves. She peered around the corner. "The street's *empty*," she whispered, surprised.

The bakery was one of a strip of ten shops. On a late Saturday afternoon like this, she'd have expected to see cars parked along the street; familiar faces ducking into the greengrocer. But there was no one around at all. The parking spaces were empty. No police.

"Your friend . . . ," Nick said slowly.

"What?" Joan jerked her gaze to the bakery's front door.

Margie wasn't there. The attackers had moved her body? Joan stumbled up to the bakery window. All the chairs were neatly stacked. The table that Joan had upturned had been tidied up. There was no sign of Margie in the room. No sign of the attack at all.

"When did they have time to clean up?" Nick said.

Unease hit Joan then. She took a step back. The air seemed warmer than it had been a few minutes ago. *Much* warmer.

She turned.

When she'd arrived at work today, the big tree out front had just been gray branches with tattered-rag leaves. Now it was heavy with white blossoms. Their faint sweet scent drifted over on a breeze.

Joan had a vivid flash of struggling with Corvin as he'd tried to drag her through time. Joan had thought she'd stopped him, but what if she'd only disrupted his landing? What if he *had* taken her somewhere?

Some*when.*

Another vivid flash—this time of Nick trying to break Corvin's grip on her. He'd grasped Joan's arm, right where that gold cuff was. Joan pictured Corvin dragging her through time, with Nick pulled in their wake. "Nick . . . ," she said.

Nick didn't reply. He'd moved to the next window, as if changing the angle might change what was inside. His face had a grayish cast.

There was a small brass plaque bolted under the window. *Margaret Marie Channing. Nicholas Arthur Ward. Missing and deeply missed.*

Nick backed up from it fast, stumbling, uncharacteristically off-balance.

"Nick." Joan didn't know what to say. *Missing and deeply missed.* The names looked permanent there. Not even a missing poster but a plaque, as if Margie's body had never been found; as if Nick had been gone long enough to warrant remembrance rather than a phone number to report sightings.

How big had that jump been? How long had they been gone? Months? A *year*? And where was Joan's name? Why wasn't *she* on the plaque?

Joan fumbled for her phone, suddenly desperate to talk to Dad. Did he think she was missing too?

There was no sound from the phone. Joan blinked at the screen. The carrier icon was missing, and she wasn't connected to the internet—not even the bakery's Wi-Fi. Had her phone plan been canceled? Had the bakery's password changed?

Joan's vision was turning hazy. She took a deep breath. She couldn't panic. There were notifications on the screen: the voice mail from Gran. She pressed play.

"Joan, my love," Gran said. Her usual no-nonsense voice was rushed. Joan's heart thumped. "You must listen to me. You are no longer safe in Milton Keynes. You must leave immediately *without* your father. Convince him to stay home tonight. You have to keep him safe."

There was a strange note in Gran's voice. It took Joan a moment to register it as fear. She'd never heard Gran afraid before—not even when she'd been dying.

"I know you have questions," Gran said. "I'll explain when I see you. For now, just get to Euston Station. I'll wait for you all night if needed." A click. The message ended.

Joan kept the phone against her ear, as if Gran might start talking again. But there was nothing more.

Nick's eyes hadn't left the plaque. "I don't understand," he said. "Why would someone put that there? Is this some kind of messed-up prank?" He shook his head, though, as if he didn't really believe it was a prank.

Joan dragged her thoughts back to the present moment. Only one thing mattered right now. She had to get Nick out of here before Corvin Argent woke up. Because as soon as he did, he'd be able to control him again. "We need to leave!" But where could they go?

"This is wrong," Nick said. "This is all wrong. The shops . . ."

Gran. Joan had to get to Gran. But how? There was no way to know where the Hunts were now; they moved constantly. *Get to Euston Station,* Gran had said. *I'll wait for you all night.* But Joan had jumped into the future. That night was long gone.

"The florist next door," Nick said, frowning. "It's different."

"Different?" Joan said. The sign above the door said *Fresh Blooms.* This morning, it had been *Laurie's Wildflowers.* "What?" Joan mumbled. Laurie had owned that shop for years—longer than Joan had been alive.

"And this bakery . . . ," Nick said. "The color is wrong. It was a different green a few minutes ago." He touched the door. "Paint's dry," he murmured, as if to himself. He rubbed his thumb and forefinger together. "Dirt on top of dry paint." He touched the plaque. "Dust on this too . . ."

It was a subtle color difference, but he was right—about the paint and the name of the florist. And now Joan could see other changes. The café opposite had become a bookshop. The pizza shop was a salad place.

How long would it have taken for all these changes to happen? Joan tried to quiet the babble of panic starting in her. How far had they jumped? Could it have been *more* than a year? How long had they been gone?

"It doesn't make sense," Nick murmured. "This can't be real." His eyes shifted back and forth as he reread the memorial plaque. "Because if it's real . . ." He took another step back.

"Nick," Joan said.

Nick didn't seem to hear her. He backed up more.

Joan realized his intention too late. "*No!*" she said. "Wait!"

But Nick was already running—out into that unknown time.

FIVE

Joan sprinted after Nick. She lost him within a few minutes—he was faster than she was—but she knew where he was going. He'd pointed out his house yesterday.

She tried to take in details as she ran. Were the cars different? Maybe a little. Near the church on the corner, she passed a girl her own age walking the other way and an elderly couple hand in hand. Their clothes looked . . . Joan didn't know. Like clothes. The girl's phone looked like a phone.

Out of nowhere, Joan remembered Aaron taking one sweeping look at a park and declaring it was 1993. She wished he were here. He'd glance at one car and announce the exact date. Then he'd say something cutting, and Joan could push back at him and feel better for it.

Joan shoved the thought away. Aaron *wasn't* here—Joan could never see him again. Right now, she just had to get to Nick. She had horrifying visions of the attackers waiting for him; of him arriving home to find his family much older. She put her head down and *ran*, pushing herself until her legs shook.

Nick's place was about fifteen minutes from the bakery. Joan's lungs were burning by the time she reached his street, but she sucked in a painful, relieved breath when she saw him, standing alone and unharmed on the path outside his house.

And then she saw what he was looking at. There was a *Sold* sign in his front garden.

"*Mary! Robbie!*" he shouted. He was suddenly in motion, running to the front door. "Mary!"

Joan sprinted after him. When she got to the door, he already had a key in the lock. "Nick!" Joan tried to catch his hands as he twisted and twisted the key fruitlessly. The house was empty, wide-open curtains framing rooms without furniture. "They're not here! They're not here!"

Nick didn't seem to hear her. He gave up on the key and pounded on the door with his fist. "Mary!" he shouted. "Alice! *Ally!* Where are you?" His voice cracked, and Joan could hardly bear it. His expression was too familiar—too much like those terrible recordings after his family had been murdered.

A few houses up, a door flew open. "Hey!" a man called out. "What's all this noise?"

"*Nick*," Joan said. "*Please.* We can't be here!" The attackers could be back at any moment.

Nick peered into the window beside the door and made a broken sound. He'd come to the same conclusion Joan had. The house was empty. He dropped his head against the door, breathing unsteadily. "What's going *on?*"

Joan shook her head. How long had she and Nick been gone? How long would his family have waited for him before moving away?

"I don't understand," he said to Joan. "Where's my *family?*"

"I don't know." Joan's own voice cracked. She wanted to run home too—Dad was just a few streets away. But she couldn't draw those attackers to him. Margie had already died, and Joan couldn't hurt anyone else she loved.

"You do know *something*, though," Nick said to her, his dark eyes wide. "Back at the bakery, you knew that man had a power!"

Oh God. Joan opened her mouth—not even sure what she was going to say. But as she did, she registered a faint sound. A siren. She looked over her shoulder. Nick's neighbor stood in his doorway, arms folded. "Did that guy call the cops on us?"

"Did he?" Nick's breath rushed out in relief. "Maybe they can find my family!"

In the distance, another siren joined the first, and then another. Three police cars for a noise complaint? Unease surged in Joan. Some instinct made her think of Corvin's words. *Cuff her.*

She turned over her arm. Her green work shirt was loose at her wrist, a tendriled cotton thread where the button had popped. In the parting, Joan made out a glimmer of gold: the tip of a wing. Her heart started to pound.

She shoved her sleeve up. There was a golden mark on her inner wrist: a winged lion, posed as if stalking the viewer. Joan's breath stopped as if she'd been punched.

It was the sigil of the Monster Court.

"What is that?" Nick said. "I saw them put it on you."

A flash of remembered pain. Of delicate lacework turning to molten gold, bubbling into her skin. "I don't know." *Cuff her,* Corvin had said, and he'd used the sigil of the Court to do it.

Joan wasn't sure what was going on here, but she knew one thing. "We can't be here when those cars arrive!"

"But we were attacked!" Nick sounded confused. "We should talk to the police!"

As he spoke, the sirens slowed. They'd hit the roundabout on the other side of the school.

Joan's throat was so tight, it was hard to get the words out.

"That is not the police! They're *not* going to help us! Nick, I'll explain things later, but right now, we have to *go*! We have to—"

"Hey." Nick's voice gentled. He was searching her face, forehead creasing. Joan wondered just how scared she looked. He scanned the front garden. Joan wasn't sure if he'd believed her, but her urgency seemed to have cut through. "*There*," he said. He nodded at the wooden fence by the house. A thick boxwood stood in front of it, tall and unkempt. Joan could see that it had once been a high hedge, but the outline was blurred now by overgrown tendrils. "If you push behind the hedge, a space opens up," Nick said. "My little brother and sister use it as a cubbyhole."

Even standing by the door—at a perfect viewing angle— there was no hint of a hollow in the hedge. It would be a perfect hiding spot. But . . . Joan shook her head reluctantly. "If they find us there, we'll be trapped." There was only one good choice from here. "We have to get to the school." It was just across the road. There'd be more places to hide and more ways out. And they both knew the grounds. They had to go *now*.

"There's a hole in the fence," Nick said steadily, as Joan turned.

"What?" Joan said.

"There's a hole in the fence behind that bush," he said. "It leads to the garden behind the house. And behind *that*, there's a back street. We'll hear anything they say, and we'll have a way out unseen."

That was a good plan—a better plan than her own. Joan found herself looking at him for an extra beat. He'd pulled himself out of fear and confusion faster than she would have in the same circumstances. Faster than she'd have expected anyone to.

The sirens blared. Too close. Joan nodded quickly.

They jogged to the fence. Joan craned her neck, looking for Nick's neighbor. She couldn't see him from here; she hoped that meant he couldn't see them either.

"Here." Nick pushed aside the spiky branches so that Joan could slide between the boxwood and the fence. Joan squeezed herself in and dropped to her hands and knees. The fence palings were broken at the base, leaving a jagged gap.

Joan shimmied through and emerged into a small back garden with weed-filled flower beds. She turned to help Nick out. It was a much tighter fit for him. He grunted, trying to flatten enough to army crawl. Joan grabbed for his hands and pulled. And then Nick must have found purchase with his sneakers because to Joan's relief his big body abruptly surged out.

They only just made it. The boxwood was still rustling back into place as the cars drew up. Two engines cut out, and doors opened and slammed, slightly asynchronous. And then footsteps padded across the grass.

After a long moment, a voice cut through the silence, unnervingly clear—as if the speaker was standing just in front of the hedge. "What do we have?"

Joan's heart thumped, and Nick shot her a wide-eyed look of recognition. It was Corvin Argent—the man they'd left unconscious in the courtyard. Joan had been right. The attackers *had* been in those police cars.

A second voice rose, curt and military. "Noise complaint at the boy's house. Neighbors saw two teenagers running here from the bakery. The girl was wearing an apron, possibly the bakery uniform."

Joan glanced down at her apron, bright white and conspicuous. *Damn.* She'd need to dump it—but not here. If she left it here, it would practically be a calling card.

Corvin spoke again, sounding less formal and more frustrated: "A *noise* complaint?"

The military voice was bland. "If you'd just pinpointed where you landed—"

"I *did!*" Corvin said—with even more frustration. Joan had the impression that it wasn't the first time they'd had the exchange. "So just the noise complaint and local reports?" An audible breath. "Don't tell me. The cameras failed again. And none of our own observers have managed to spot them. Again."

"If you're not happy with the intelligence—"

"What *intelligence*?" Corvin said. "Broken equipment? Misattributed sightings?" He paused. "Don't you think there's something very strange going on here?"

"Strange?"

"Why have they been so difficult to find?" Corvin said. His voice lowered. "I think the rumors of unusual fluctuations are true."

The military man was silent for long enough that Joan wondered if he'd answer at all. When he finally spoke, his voice was lower, matching Corvin's. "Listen. You lost the girl. That's bad enough. You'll only make things worse by reaching for farfetched excuses."

"*Is* it farfetched? It would explain why she was so difficult to find the first time. Why I missed the rendezvous. Why we haven't been able to find them since."

Joan crouched to peer through the hole in the fence. She

couldn't make out much from this angle. The leaves were thicker at the base of the bush. What had the military man meant by "pinpointed where you landed"? They'd landed in *this* place with Corvin, barely fifteen minutes ago. And what about "unusual fluctuations"? What did *that* mean?

A *click*, and Joan recoiled as bright white light illuminated Nick's front garden. Someone had turned car headlights on. Joan hadn't realized it was getting so dark. She squinted into the glare and made out two pairs of shoes: big military boots.

Were they guards of the Court? They'd put that winged-lion sigil onto Joan's arm, but none of them had been wearing the sigil themselves. Joan had never seen a guard without one.

As she watched, a third pair of shoes appeared as their wearer stepped out of thin air. These weren't military boots but black dress shoes, so shiny that they might never have touched grass before tonight.

Joan hesitated. She was tempted to stay and hear more, but she and Nick needed to keep moving. She didn't know how the Argent power worked. Could Corvin instruct Nick from where he was standing? What if he suspected Nick was nearby and raised his voice?

She touched Nick's arm. *Let's go*, she mouthed.

But then the third person spoke. The voice was a boy's, posh and precise.

"Let me guess," the boy said. "We've been given another wild goose to chase. How many of these vague reports must we waste our time on?"

Joan's breath stopped in her throat. Barely conscious of her own actions, she scrambled to her feet. Just above eye height, there was a small hole in the fence. She stood on tiptoe to peer through. A breeze rippled the leaves, allowing brief glimpses of the illuminated front garden. Corvin stood by a tall man with a crew cut—the military voice, Joan guessed. But the third figure was too obscured to see.

Nick stepped closer. Joan registered, peripherally, that his head was tilted in question. But she couldn't focus on anything but the indistinct shape through the leaves. She peered, straining. She needed to *know*.

Then there was another surge of wind. The branches and leaves parted, revealing the third person in full.

Joan's heart thundered back to life—louder than the voices, louder than the rustle of the wind.

It was Aaron Oliver.

Joan had conjured his voice and face every time she'd had a fade-out recently. She'd imagined him with her, helping her, almost every morning this week.

But her memory of him hadn't done him justice. Illuminated by the headlights, he looked like he'd walked off a red carpet. His hair was a crown of gold, and his heather-gray suit was perfectly tailored. It was the same color as his eyes, Joan knew. He had the kind of beauty that made people stumble over their words and stop in the street and stare. In this mundane setting, he seemed incongruous: a da Vinci in a suburban supermarket.

Joan's heart beat painfully. *Aaron.* The shape of his name started inside her mouth. She held it there, silent. She hadn't said it since the last time she'd seen him. That day, he'd brushed his hand against her cheek and told her: *If you change the timeline, you can't ever meet me. You can't ever trust me. I won't remember what you mean to me.*

And Joan had followed his wishes. She hadn't gone looking for him. She hadn't let herself believe she could ever see him again.

Corvin's scowl was familiar—Aaron had a knack for getting under people's skin. "You'll *waste your time* whenever we call you," he snapped, as if he himself hadn't been complaining moments before Aaron had arrived. "I'm told you can identify her, and until you do that, your time is mine."

"Believe me," Aaron said, "nothing would please me more than identifying that girl. That *filth.*" His beautiful face twisted as he said *filth*, as if he was thinking of a much harsher word. "But I do have to actually see her to identify her."

A heavy weight settled in Joan's chest, making her next breath hurt. *That filth.* Aaron had never spoken about her like that. His father had, but never Aaron.

"And now I hear you've dragged a human boy into it," Aaron said, tipping his head so that his blond hair shone from the headlights. "Quite the mess."

"The intelligence was flawed," Corvin ground out. "That boy wasn't even supposed to be there." He took an intimidating step toward Aaron, and Aaron's haughty expression faltered. "You'd do well to remember your place," Corvin told him. "Your father is a great man, but *you* . . . I'd have thought you'd seize this opportunity to demonstrate your deep, abiding, passionate—dare I say, *sniveling*—obedience to the task. From what I hear, you need the redemption in his eyes."

Joan waited for Aaron to say something biting like *flawed*

intelligence says it all. But his mouth stayed shut, and a flush crawled up his neck.

A touch on Joan's wrist. She jumped, almost startled into making a sound. With a shock of belated horror, she realized Aaron had said the words *human boy*. Nick had to have registered it.

Nick's expression, though, was very gentle. He inclined his head toward the gate.

Joan took a step and registered distantly that she was shaking. *That filth.* She'd never imagined Aaron saying that about her. Nick's hand closed over hers, strong and reassuring. *Let's go*, he mouthed.

As they reached the gate, a radio crackled. The military man's voice rose. "We believe they're still together. They're both mired—the girl's wearing a cuff."

Mired. It seemed the cuff would prevent Joan from time-traveling—unless, perhaps, someone was dragging her with it.

Another radio crackle. "I want eyes on every route out of here. Every bus stop, every train station, every road. If they're in the vicinity, I want them found!"

Nick released Joan's hand so that he could open the gate. He nodded for Joan to slip through, and followed her. She reached back to set the latch, holding it all the way down, careful not to make a sound.

Nick's shoulders dropped as if he'd been holding his breath. Joan released her own. She still couldn't believe that Aaron was back there, working with the attackers to hunt her down. That he'd said—

No. She couldn't think about what Aaron had said or how he'd said it. If she didn't keep her head right now, she and Nick would end up captured or dead.

She looked around. They'd ended up in a narrow walkway between back gardens—the kind of path that only locals used. It was so narrow that Joan wondered if it even appeared on maps. From the front, the houses had looked immaculate; but here, at the back, people had relaxed. Overgrown trees hung over leaning fences; weeds stuck out underneath them. The ground itself was a simple strip of cobblestones, with dips for drainage on either side.

This whole path was too exposed. It stretched the entire length of Nick's street, as empty as a bowling lane. Joan judged the distance to the nearest crossroad. Too far.

Inside Nick's house, lights flicked on. Any second now, people would swarm out into that back garden, and then they'd see that gate.

Joan sought a sturdy enough fence. Nick was already nodding when she pointed at it. They hurried over, and Nick bent with cupped hands. Joan stepped into the offered boost, gripping his shoulder for balance. A moment later, she was at the top. Nick leaped to join her, hoisting his big body up as easily as he'd lifted Joan. He dropped to the ground in near silence and held out his arms for her.

Joan's chest swooped with fear as she jumped—the fence looked higher from up here. But Nick caught her easily around the waist and set her down.

Joan took a deep breath, trying not to feel the lingering echo of his touch as she looked around. She'd expected to find herself in someone's back garden, but they'd landed in a dark concrete yard.

"Back of that little gym," Nick breathed, and Joan recognized it then too. Dad worked out here sometimes. The owner's daughter, Melanie, was in Joan's English class at school.

The gym's lights were on. Joan couldn't see inside—the windows were long rectangles high up near the roof—but she could hear the *thunk* of weights and rhythmic punches against heavy leather. So strange to think that people were going about their ordinary lives, unaware of the monsters lurking outside.

"Your apron," Nick whispered.

Joan nodded and untied it quickly, slipping the loop over her head. Nick knotted it into a rough ball, and then threw it onto the roof in a basketball toss. It vanished behind an air filtration box. Joan doubted even time travelers would find *that*. And her green work shirt should be dark enough to be unremarkable—at night at least.

Nick touched her arm before she could start for the road. Light leaked from the gym windows, but not enough to show his expression. "Back at the house, you told me that you could explain," he murmured. "*Can* you?"

Behind him, the sky had turned the purple of a bruise. Trepidation ran down Joan's spine. Nick didn't know it, but she'd been on the run like this before—from *him*. He had no idea how dangerous he was; how deeply embedded he'd once been in this world. What could Joan risk telling him? What might he figure out himself? The thought of explaining anything to him made her stomach turn.

But . . . Nick had been caught up in an attack by monsters. They were trying to kill him still. He was back in the monster world, whether Joan liked it or not.

She swallowed hard, and then nodded. "As soon as we're safe, let's talk."

SIX

The gym fronted onto a busy road. There, tucked into the deep shadow of the building, Joan saw the full scope of the search. Cars passed in slow procession. At the roundabout, on the top of the hill, they peeled left and right. Joan imagined checkpoints being set up all over town.

And somewhere, among all this, Aaron was here. A bubble of misery rose in her. She bit the inside of her cheek until it hurt enough to counter it. She really, *really* couldn't think about Aaron right now.

Nick moved to jog across the road, and Joan put a hand on his arm. "Not here," she murmured. She pointed at the camera on the gym's eave; another clamped to the streetlight across the road. "We can't get caught on camera—they'll use it to track us down." Nick himself had found Joan like that last time.

Nick gave the camera a long look. "These people have a lot of resources."

He had no idea.

Truth was, Joan didn't understand how she and Nick had escaped at all. They were being pursued by time travelers. Shouldn't there have been people waiting in that courtyard when they'd jumped? And Joan had worked at the bakery twice a week for months. Couldn't someone have gone back to a previous Saturday and tried again—or gotten to her at home or at school?

Or was that not allowed by the timeline? Maybe, having

picked one moment to capture her, the attackers could only try again in her personal future. There was so much she still didn't know about being a monster.

As she thought that, though, she remembered Corvin's words in the garden. *I think the rumors of unusual fluctuations are true.*

What did *that* mean?

Joan bit her lip. She had to focus. They hadn't actually escaped yet.

Joan's own neighborhood had never seemed so alien. The round-abouts usually made traffic flow in regular rhythms; tonight cars stopped and stalled and crawled.

Monsters were *everywhere.* On the next street, two men materialized, barely ten paces away. Joan grabbed Nick's arm and dragged him down behind a parked car. She pressed her lips tight, trying to quiet her breaths. Beside her, Nick had a hand on the cold pavement, ready to push himself up and fight. Bare-armed in his T-shirt with muscles coiled, he looked as dangerous as his old self.

Joan strained, listening. After a long moment, Nick lifted a hand and made a walking gesture with two fingers. *Walking away,* he mouthed. Joan risked peering around the side of the car. The men were at the far end of the street already, oblivious to how close they'd gotten to their prey. As she watched, they turned the corner and vanished from sight.

Nick stood slowly, hands still in fists for the fight that hadn't happened. With his dark hair and handsome face, he reminded Joan unnervingly of a superhero in ordinary-man disguise. She wondered if he might actually have won that fight. If, untamed, he might have won the fight in the courtyard.

"They look like they're in costume for a period drama," he murmured.

Joan's heart had been slowing, but it quickened again at his observation. The men had been in 1920s suits and newsboy caps. Nick had barely been in this world an hour, and he was already figuring out how to spot monsters.

A few streets up, Joan gestured to a cul-de-sac—a few houses and a patch of trees. At first glance, it looked like a dead end, but between the trees there was a dirt path, almost occluded by leaves. A hidden bike track.

Inside, the track was overgrown and disused, tree roots pushing up the ground. An old lamppost drooped, unlit. Joan tried not to think about how the last time she'd been here, Margie and Chris had been with her. Chris had begged for a cycling day, and Margie had fallen almost straightaway, laughing as her bike had crashed, and then finding it even funnier when Joan and Chris had rushed to fuss over her.

Behind them on the street, cars droned, but the track itself was quiet and very still. No crackling radios. No bobbing lights. No voices ahead.

Nick broke the silence first. "Where to from here?" he whispered.

"We need to find my gran," Joan whispered back. The problem was, the Hunts were impossible to find at the best of times—they gave Joan new addresses and new phone numbers every year, sometimes every few months. Joan sometimes wondered if they were running from something.

She ran a hand over her mouth, thinking. How could she get a message to Gran? Maybe at a monster inn—she knew of one in Covent Garden. . . .

At the thought, a memory came to her. The Hunts were thieves and forgers and fences. Growing up, Joan had never been allowed into the shadier parts of the family trade, but she'd heard things. *If anything goes wrong*, Gran had always said, *get to the Wyvern Inn at the Queenhithe Dock. We have friends there.*

"Have you ever heard of the Queenhithe Dock?" Joan whispered to Nick now.

"Queenhithe near Blackfriars?" Nick said. "I think there *is* an old dock there."

That had to be it. "My family in London can help us," Joan whispered. "But these people will have eyes everywhere. Checkpoints on roads . . ." She'd seen a search like this before.

"And our phones aren't working," Nick murmured. "No rideshare."

"They'll be all over," Joan whispered. "Bletchley. Wolverton."

Nick lifted his head. "What about Bedford?"

"Bedford?" Joan repeated. That was a whole other town, half an hour away by car—and not in the direction of London. "Why would we . . ." She trailed off as she saw his thought process. "It's a different train line."

With any luck, the searchers' attention would be on the route from Milton Keynes to Euston. They wouldn't be looking at Bedford to Blackfriars at all.

Joan kept playing out the scenario. She and Nick had been dragged forward into spring, and the sun had set maybe half an hour ago. That would make it around nine or ten o'clock right now. About eight hours until dawn. If they stayed on foot, it would be a long walk to Bedford. And then an hour or two on the train to London . . . but they could do most of it under cover of night.

She nodded. "All right, let's go," she whispered. "Best keep moving." She started on the path again, but behind her, there was silence. Nick hadn't followed her. She turned back to him.

"Please," Nick said. "Just tell me what's going on."

Joan's stomach dropped. He stood in the shadow of the laurels, a broad-shouldered shape in the darkness. The moon offered a little light, but not enough for Joan to make out his expression. "We can't talk yet," she whispered. "It isn't safe."

Nick glanced around. They were alone here—no cars, no lights from surveillance cameras. They *could* spare a minute, Joan knew.

"Nick." Joan could hear the strain in her own voice. It was so hard to be this close to him. She could feel the familiar pull of him. It wasn't just how her body reacted to him—it was how she felt every time she looked at him. Like she'd come home, and she never wanted to leave. "You need to trust me," she whispered. "We *have* to go."

He was silent for a long moment. "You know . . . you keep saying my name," he said. "We didn't properly introduce ourselves yesterday, though."

"What do you mean?" Introduce themselves? They'd talked yesterday and again at the bakery.

"I don't know *your* name," he said.

It hurt like someone had reached into her chest and squeezed her heart. She'd been talking to him—thinking about him—as someone she knew; she'd forgotten that he'd only just met her. *Soul mates,* Jamie had once said of them. And now . . . *I don't know your name.*

"I'm—" Joan's voice failed her for a moment. "My name is Joan."

He tilted his head, maybe hearing the emotion in her voice and not knowing what to make of it. "I'm Nick," he said. "Nick Ward."

Joan couldn't look away from his shadowed face. She remembered the first time they'd actually met. He'd walked into the library at Holland House—a boy with dark hair and kind eyes.

For weeks, they'd shared early-morning conversations, just the two of them in the quiet of the house. She remembered his huffed laugh against her mouth when they'd kissed.

I don't know your name.

"Joan . . . ," Nick said. It was careful and intentional—the way you'd say a name new to you. Joan hoped that it was too dark for him to see her face clearly. "This afternoon, I went for a walk to the shops," he said, "and then the whole world stopped making sense. I saw people appear out of thin air. A man froze my body. A girl *died.*" A harsh hiss of air at that. "And when I went home, my family was gone. My house wasn't mine anymore. And you said you could explain."

A girl died. Margie had *died.* Joan folded her arms around herself, trying to keep it together. She couldn't believe this was happening. And Nick was looking at her like she could explain it all.

She couldn't, though. He'd been a monster slayer in the

previous timeline—a legend, whispered about in stories. If Joan said the wrong thing, she could put him on that path again. And last time, that path had led to her family dying.

But . . . if she didn't tell him *something*, she could lose him right here. Maybe he'd figure it all out anyway. Maybe he'd find that path again by himself.

Nick shifted, all contained strength, reminding Joan again of a superhero. Or maybe something more old-fashioned. An old-school knight. A king. The kind who got crowned because people wanted to follow him. The kind who could raise armies.

She looked down and saw that her hands were shaking. *Careful*, she told herself. *Only tell him enough to satisfy him.* She started slowly. "There's a—a world," she said. "Hidden within our own. A world of people with . . ." She searched for the right word. "Powers."

"Powers?" Nick's eyes sharpened with interest. "Like the ability to appear and disappear?"

Joan wet her dry lips and nodded. She'd just broken a taboo. *You must never tell anyone about monsters*, Gran had always said. It was the most fundamental monster law. And here Joan was, telling the most dangerous person she'd ever known.

"Like the ability to command people?" Nick asked.

"Well . . ." Joan's stomach churned. She'd never seen the Argent power before today. "Some people can do that." She felt sick remembering how Nick's eyes had blanked and his body had stilled.

"Can *you*?" Nick said. His voice lowered to a pitch that Joan felt in her bones. "Can *you* control people's minds? Can you control mine?"

"What?" Joan whispered. *"No."* This conversation already felt wrong: a train that had jumped the tracks.

Nick took a step forward, his face falling deeper into shadow. "You're one of them, though, aren't you? The guy at my house called *me* human, but not you."

Joan couldn't stop her flinch. *I never thought you were one of them*, he'd told her after his massacre of monsters at Holland House. She had a flash of him plunging a sword into a man's heart, throwing that same sword across a room as easily as if it had been a dart. He'd once been a bedtime story to frighten monster children. And he was already thinking of *them* and *him*—of her and the attackers on one side, of him on the other.

But then he took one more step into the moonlight, and his face was gentler than she was expecting. Joan had conjured his old self in the shadows, a predator full of suspicion. But now that she could see him properly again, he didn't look like that at all. "I phrased that poorly," he said slowly. "I'm sorry." His next words were careful. He watched her, taking in her response. "Can you tell me how you know about this world?"

This wasn't *him*, she thought, with one of those strange tugs of grief and relief. This wasn't a slayer, probing for weaknesses. This was a boy who'd been attacked; who'd saved her life; who'd lost his family and was trying to make sense of it all.

Joan tried to find an answer. "My mum was a—" She stopped again before she said *monster*. "My mum was like the people in the courtyard, but she died when I was a baby. My dad is human. I didn't know that this world existed until last summer."

"You're new to this too," he said. Joan heard him shift his weight and realized she'd dropped her gaze. She lifted her head, still half expecting suspicion, but his eyes were soft. "I'm sorry about your mum," he said. "My dad died a few years ago."

"Your dad died?" Joan whispered, shaken. In the other time-line, his father had been murdered by a monster when Nick was much younger; Joan had assumed his whole family was still alive in this timeline.

"He had a heart attack at home," Nick said. "It's been . . . It's been hard."

"I'm so sorry." Joan had imagined him happy, his eyes unshadowed. But grief had still been part of his life here too. She found herself looking at him properly for what felt like the first time—not the hero and warrior he'd been, and not even the school football star, but the boy in front of her right now. He was shivering a little in the growing chill. He'd arrived in this time in a thin T-shirt—far too cold for the November day they'd left behind and still too cold for spring. The kind of clothes you'd wear when you thought you'd be home again in fifteen minutes. "I'm *so* sorry I got you into this," she whispered. He should have been home, safe with his family—not on this dark path, being hunted by monsters.

Nick tilted his head as if he'd heard a sound that Joan hadn't. "You didn't get me into it."

Joan wished that were true. "They came for *me*."

"You were *attacked*," Nick countered. "I was there. Nothing about that was your fault."

Joan didn't want to have a whole back-and-forth with him about what was her fault and what wasn't—he didn't know enough. *She'd* stripped him of his knowledge. She felt sick.

"Do you know what they wanted with you?" Nick whispered.

"I . . ." Joan had once overheard a Court Guard describe her power in a hushed voice: *Something forbidden. Something* wrong.

Before she could answer, Nick's head lifted. For a second, Joan was sure he was going to press harder. But then he murmured, "Do you hear that?"

Joan strained, listening. She couldn't hear anything at first but distant traffic. Then a sound rose above the others, one engine louder than the rest. A car—maybe as close as the cul-de-sac. Time to go.

"We need to keep away from cameras," Joan reminded him.

"And people with strange clothes and haircuts."

Joan had already turned away, but now she jerked her gaze back to him. "Right," she said, unsettled. Not all the attackers had been in strange clothes, but now that Joan thought about it, they'd almost all sported haircuts that weren't quite of this time. She hadn't noticed that until now. "That's . . . that's right."

He didn't have his training anymore, she told herself as they started walking, Nick's soft steps belying his muscled frame. But could some of it have remained? Small things did linger from timeline to timeline. The first time she'd met him, his voice had been as familiar as her own. Could some echo of his training have carried over like that?

Joan knew from experience how little would be left and how intangible it would be. For her, those remnants had been more like instinct than knowledge; like déjà vu that had never resolved into true memory.

But still . . .

Suppressing her unease, Joan walked with Nick through the trees.

Bedford Station was a flat-topped glass box that made Joan think of the municipal center where she'd learned to swim. She tried not to relax. She'd worked a full day's shift and then walked for hours, and the long, long day and night were catching up to her. She squeezed her eyes shut and opened them. *Don't let your guard down*, she told herself. They weren't in London yet. They weren't even on a train yet.

Beside her, Nick's pace was steady. He still seemed fresh. They hadn't talked much as they'd walked—at first it hadn't felt safe, and then Joan had lapsed into exhausted silence.

They stopped at the edge of the station's parking lot and surveyed the low brick walls, scattered cars, and trees.

"Looks quiet enough," Nick whispered.

It wasn't just quiet; it seemed safe—which wasn't how Joan would normally have felt on a dark street. But she couldn't imagine many muggers going up against Nick.

"Should we finish that conversation now?" he murmured. "Or do you want to have it on the train?"

"Conversation?" Joan whispered. She tried to clear the fog in her head enough to make sense of the questions. What conversation? Hadn't they already talked?

"Well . . ." Nick stood beside her, in profile, hands in his pockets and his eyes on the station entrance. "My phone says it's two a.m., but it looks closer to dawn, don't you think?"

That woke Joan up. He was right. The sky had shifted from black to deep blue. In a nearby tree, wrens chittered in high staccato. It couldn't have been more than an hour before dawn.

Nick met her gaze now, his dark eyes very steady. "I keep replaying that attack," he said softly. "How I wanted to help you, but I couldn't move. I thought I'd frozen in fear. I didn't understand until you told me later that that man was controlling my mind."

The horror of the moment swept over Joan again—he'd been awake and aware while his body had been frozen. He could have died so easily today—like Margie had. All it would have taken was a touch to his neck.

Nick registered her reaction, gaze flicking down to her shoulders and then back to her face. "You kept begging them for my life, like what they were doing to you didn't even matter. You fought so hard," he whispered, "that I think that man lost control of me. He couldn't fight you and hold me at the same time. And then . . . I grabbed you and . . ." He frowned, his voice softening with the memory. "The temperature shifted—the air was suddenly warmer. And then we walked out onto the street . . ."

And all the shops had changed.

The first time Joan had time-traveled, she'd been terrified. Day had turned to night in a blink. She'd thought she'd been knocked out or maybe drugged.

"What *really* happened in that attack?" Nick whispered. "What didn't you have a chance to tell me back there?"

Don't, Joan imagined Gran warning her. Joan knew she shouldn't tell him. If she did, he'd be barely a step from figuring out the entire truth of monsters. And he'd already demonstrated how effortlessly he could put information together.

But . . . *He's already figured it out*, Joan imagined telling Gran. *He's already guessed.* Joan suspected he'd half known as soon as he'd touched the bakery wall, its new green paint dry under a layer of grime. And if she didn't confirm what he already knew, she was going to lose his trust.

She took a deep breath. "We traveled in time," she said. "That man dragged us into the future."

Nick might have already guessed, but hearing it still hit him. He took a step back, shaken. "I saw flowers on those winter trees."

"I think it's spring now," Joan said, nodding.

He ran a hand through his thick hair. "When those attackers appeared out of the air, I thought they'd teleported in from another place," he murmured, almost to himself. "But they came from another time, didn't they?"

And *this* was why he was still dangerous—trained or not. It wasn't just because he was strong, but because if you told him two things, he'd connect them together, and then figure out two more.

"How long have we been gone?" It sounded like it was all hitting him now. "That plaque . . . My family thinks I'm missing, don't they? Or *dead*!"

"I'm sorry," Joan managed. "I don't know." She still didn't understand why only he and Margie had been on that plaque. "I thought we'd jumped a few months, but . . ." She shook her head and admitted the truth to herself. There'd been too many changes for months. "I think it must have been years."

"*Years?*" Nick looked really shaken now. "I need to get my phone working," he said. "I have to call my family."

"You *can't!*" Joan forced herself to say. He stared at her wildly. "You can't tell them you're alive." And she couldn't tell Dad either. It hurt to say it. Ever since Mum had died, it had just been Joan and Dad. He got worried anytime she came home late without telling him in advance. Joan couldn't bear the thought of him all on his own, scared for her for *years*.

Nick stared at her, disbelieving. Joan could see him trying to understand. "Is it because I'll look too young to them? I know this world is a secret, but . . . *my* family won't tell!"

Joan wanted to cry. Dad wouldn't tell either. God, how long had she and Nick been *gone*? "We can't bring them into this," she said, willing him to understand. "We *have* to keep them safe. The people after us are *ruthless*."

Nick shook his head again, but Joan could see that her words had cut through.

"My gran will help us," Joan said. "My *mum's* mum. She'll know what to do. We just have to get to Queenhithe to find her."

Nick's eyes cleared slightly. "She can help?"

Joan nodded. "She *will*."

Gran would be angry with her, of course, for telling Nick all this stuff. But when Joan explained, Gran would understand. Gran loved Joan, and she'd look after Nick if Joan asked her to. Joan *knew* she would.

Inside the station, only one ticket booth was open. A bored man in a red beanie yawned, eyes on his phone. He'd propped it up against the service window so that he could flick his gaze from screen to customer without moving his head. Joan guessed he was watching cricket or rugby—the phone emanated the faint roar of a crowd and Australian-accented commentators.

"Two tickets to Blackfriars," Joan said. She kept her head down, wishing she had a cap to hide her face. Train stations always had cameras.

"Ninety-nine pounds eighty." The guy's name tag said *Mark*.

"*What?*" Nick interjected. He'd been scanning the station, alert for anyone entering, but now he turned to Mark, sounding more shocked than he'd been about any of the other changes so far. "A hundred *pounds* for two tickets to London?"

Mark shrugged. "That's how much it costs."

Joan didn't have that kind of cash. She had a debit card, and Dad had put an emergency credit card on her phone, but there was no way she could use those without drawing *someone's* attention—even if the things still worked.

Wait . . . she'd taken Corvin's wallet. She dug it from her pocket and rifled through it, glimpsing transparent-and-gold monster currency. To her relief, there was a sheaf of familiar banknotes too, paper-clipped together like a tourist might have done. Joan plucked out four twenties, a ten, and two fives.

Mark took the notes and printed off their tickets, still yawning. He started to slide over twenty pence in change and then paused. He sat up straighter. "What's this?"

"What's what?" Joan said, and then her stomach dropped.

Mark was staring at a crisp ten-pound note with an unfamiliar queen's face on it. "*Who* is this?" He turned it over, frowning. Was that Emily Brontë on the other side? *Shit.* That had to be a banknote from the future.

"Here." Nick snagged the note from Mark's hand, leaving behind a more recognizable one. His cake money, Joan remembered.

"Wait." Mark didn't look bored anymore. "Give us another look at that note. What *was* that?"

"Nothing. Sorry. Just got back from overseas," Joan lied. "Malaysian money." She hoped Mark hadn't noticed the giant letters at the top of the note: *Bank of England.*

Mark looked like he wanted to argue, but then his phone roared—someone had scored a goal or taken a wicket. His eyes flicked back to the match, and Joan grabbed the tickets before his attention could return. "Thanks!"

She cursed at herself as she and Nick sped to the platform. A banknote from the future would have been a clear announcement that she'd been here. She couldn't make mistakes like that. Nick's life was on the line as much as hers.

It was still more nighttime than morning. The platform's lights were on, making the sky look darker than it was. There didn't seem to be anyone around.

"Train'll be here soon," Nick murmured, and Joan nodded, trying to relax.

The minutes ticked down on the screen. Eventually, the train arrived in a slow-motion rumble. Through the windows, Joan spotted sleepy commuters and no obvious guards. The last carriage was empty.

A wave of exhaustion hit her as she boarded. She found a window seat, and Nick settled beside her, his body a solid wall blocking the rest of the world. In Joan's tired state, she felt almost safe, even knowing who he'd been. Even knowing they were still on the run.

"Just over an hour to Blackfriars," he murmured, and Joan nodded again. "And then we'll find your grandmother," he added.

His voice was even and matter-of-fact. There was nothing off about his tone. But Joan found herself tensing. It occurred to her that she was about to guide Nick right into the monster world—to *Gran*.

In her mind's eye, she saw him knock Corvin out without any seeming effort. One strike to Corvin's jaw, and Corvin had slumped. Then Nick had punched him again as he was falling. Precise. Expert. Could someone untrained have done that?

What if Joan *was* wrong about Nick? What if he *was* playing her? What if he was still the hero, and she was leading him to her family?

"You should sleep," Nick said. There was gravel in his voice. "We've been on the run all night, and you worked a shift before that."

Joan searched for any clue that he was something other than he seemed, but his expression was guileless. This wasn't *him*, Joan thought with a hollow ache of grief. If he were here with her, she'd know. She'd surely feel it. Right now, all she felt was his absence. He was nowhere in the world. He was just gone.

"I should check my messages," she whispered back. Maybe Gran had left one that she'd missed. She unlocked her phone. There was only the one voice mail, but there were unread text messages.

Joan thumbed open the app automatically and realized it was the group exchange.

Margie: Stop everything nick ward just walked in

Chris: in where?? In the bakery???

Margie: he looks SO good

Chris: NO IM SO JEALOUS

Chris: someone take a sneaky pic

Chris: selfie with the pecs

Chris: WHATS GOING ON IS HOT NICK STILL THERE

Chris: TELL ME TELL ME

Chris: SOMEONE REPLY!!!!

Joan stared at Margie's last message.

"Margie was your friend from the bakery?" Nick said softly.

Mortification merged with grief. Nick had been the subject of those messages—Joan hadn't been thinking when she'd opened the app. She'd forgotten that they'd all been talking about him. "I—I'm sorry," she said roughly. "Those messages were just—"

"*I'm* sorry," Nick said, low. His dark eyes were grave. "I'm so sorry about what happened to her."

Joan clenched her teeth. It wasn't safe to feel these feelings yet. But she couldn't stop the hitch of her breath.

"You don't have to . . ." There was a small crease between Nick's eyes. "Hey." He shifted. "Can I?" he said.

Don't, she told herself. But she found herself nodding. He put a warm hand on her back. It was heavy and almost unbearably comforting. She turned toward him. And then, to her agony and desperate solace, he pulled her to his chest and tucked her close.

This wasn't *him*, she told herself. He wasn't here with her. He felt like him, though—his hard chest against her cheek. And he smelled *so good*. Joan took a deep breath as if she could fill herself with him.

"I'm so sorry you lost your friend," Nick whispered. "I'm so sorry she died."

"I can't believe—" Her voice failed, and she squeezed her hands into fists. She tried again. "I can't believe she's dead." Margie had died because those people had been after Joan, and Nick had been dragged into this too.

Nick's arm tightened, and it felt like everything Joan had needed forever and shouldn't need. She missed his other self so much. It was messed up how much she missed him.

"Why don't you sleep for a little while?" Nick said, his voice rumbling against Joan's cheek.

Joan shook her head. They needed to be alert. They weren't safe here. *He* might be dangerous. What if she dropped her guard and he remembered who he was?

"I'll keep watch," Nick said. "I'll wake you up if they come back."

She shouldn't give in to how safe she felt with him holding her like this. She shouldn't feel anything for him at all. "I'm tired," Joan admitted hoarsely. *I'm so sorry you lost your friend.* She was so tired of losing people. Gran. Bertie. Uncle Gus. Aunt Ada. Margie. Nick. Aaron. Dad. Mum, so long ago. She was so tired of fighting how it felt.

"You can sleep," Nick said. "I'm right here. I'm not going anywhere, I promise."

Joan's breath hitched. She tried to slow her breathing, to push it all down. It had been working since she'd come home after the summer, but this time a sob spasmed painfully from her chest, tearing from her. He *wasn't* here. He wasn't anywhere, and he'd never be anywhere again. Distantly, she heard Nick murmuring. And then she was crying against his chest.

He put his other arm around her, and Joan knew she shouldn't be touching him like this. It was wrong. This wasn't him.

But it didn't feel wrong. He felt like home. He smelled like home. And she found herself clinging to him instead of pulling away.

SEVEN

Joan ran desperately through the hedge maze of Holland House, breath burning in her throat. Her clothes caught on twigs and leaves. Someone was chasing her, someone just a few paces behind. She put on a burst of speed, and the sharp edges of the hedge scratched at her face and hands. There was a turn ahead. Left or right? No time to think; she went left.

In front of her, the path ended abruptly in a high wall of dense leaves, forcing her to stumble to a stop.

"*Joan*," someone said behind her. She turned, panicked breaths cutting into her lungs like knives.

It was Nick. His body filled the path like another wall, trapping her. He held a sword in one hand, as if it weighed no more than the plastic souvenir swords in the Holland House gift shop.

"*Please*," Joan whispered. There was a stitch in her side, and her chest hurt more with each heaved breath.

"You stole human life," he said. His voice was sad. He wasn't here for vengeance. He was an executioner, carrying out his duty. "I can't allow you to harm anyone else."

"We wanted to make peace between humans and monsters!" Joan said pleadingly. It had seemed possible, once upon a time. "Remember? We were going to make peace!"

"You didn't choose peace, though." He raised the sword. It was the one he'd used to kill Lucien and Edmund. Last time, he'd used it to protect her. "You killed the person protecting humans. You chose monsters."

"*No!*" she begged him. "*Nick!*"

The blade flashed toward her.

Joan woke with a gasp, heart pounding.

"Joan?"

Nick was *here*, looming over her. Joan heard herself make a terrified sound. She tried to scramble away, but her back struck something hard and smooth. He had her trapped in a tiny corralled space. She searched for a weapon and, finding nothing, kicked out at him. He dodged easily, clambering to his feet, eyes wide.

Joan looked around frantically. Had he hurt the others? Where was Ruth? Where was Aaron?

"Joan, you're safe. It's okay." Nick's voice was very soft—the tone you might use to soothe a frightened animal. "You're on the train. We're going to London, remember? It's just you and me here. No one's going to hurt you. I won't let anyone hurt you."

Joan's vision adjusted slowly. He wasn't standing among hedge leaves but in a narrow aisle. Behind him, long windows showed a rushing view: red-roofed houses and trees. They were on a train. And Nick . . . Joan gulped in air. This was the *other* Nick.

"They didn't find us," Nick reassured her. "We escaped."

"I had a nightmare," Joan murmured numbly. She'd kicked at him, she remembered. Thank God, she hadn't used her hands. She could have killed him with a touch. She could have drained all his life from him. "Did I hurt you?"

"Of course not," Nick said gently, and Joan saw in her mind's eye how easily he'd dodged. "I didn't mean to crowd you when you woke up. I thought . . ." He hesitated. "I thought you called my name."

Joan's breathing had been evening out, but the next one caught. "What?"

"You called out to me when you woke up. Or maybe . . ." Puzzlement passed over his face. "Just before you woke up . . ."

Outside, the blur of green reminded Joan too much, suddenly, of the hedge walls from the dream. She shivered hard, and Nick saw it, forehead creasing. Joan struggled out of the seat. "I just need to—" she said, and Nick shuffled back quickly, giving her room to pass him down the aisle.

Joan put her back to the train's glass door. The cold seeped through her shirt, grounding her. She looked around the carriage. It was still empty.

She realized with a start that she'd been looking for Aaron since she'd woken; the dream had felt too much like the time they'd fled through the maze together. She'd needed to see for herself that he was okay too. But he wasn't here. He was somewhere out there, hunting her down. Joan felt that weight settle again in her chest.

"Last stop was Leagrave," Nick said. "You barely slept."

Joan folded her arms around herself. She felt groggy with exhaustion, but there was no way she'd get to sleep again. Not after that dream. She focused on Nick and saw now how pale he was. He was still standing in the aisle, a hand on a backrest for balance. That need for a crutch told Joan how tired he must be too.

"Why don't *you* sleep?" Joan said. They were only half an hour out of London, but he could at least close his eyes.

"Don't think I can," he said. "Too much in my head, you know?" And then, so quietly she could hardly hear him over the drone of the train: "I know how long we've been missing."

"What?" Joan straightened. "You got your phone working?"

"No." He fished his train ticket from his pocket.

Oh. They'd had the date on them since Bedford. Joan suddenly didn't want to know.

"It's been six years," Nick said. "We've been missing for six years."

"Six years," Joan echoed numbly. Margie had been dead for six years. Dad hadn't seen her for six *years*. . . .

"I knew it had to be a couple of years at least," Nick said. "All those changes to the shops couldn't have happened in a few months. But . . . six *years* . . . I keep thinking how my little sister, Alice, would be twelve years old now. Robbie would be eleven. Do they even remember me? They don't remember my dad. . . ."

"Nick . . ." Joan couldn't bear the thought of that. "I'm so sorry." It sounded completely inadequate out loud. She didn't know how to express how sorry she was. He was only here because of her. Because he'd come back to help her when he could have run.

"If it was possible," Nick said slowly, "I know you would have said, but . . . I have to ask. Can't we go back? Can't we stop that attack from happening?"

Last time, Joan *had* circumvented the timeline's restrictions. She'd undone Nick's massacres by unmaking Nick himself— reverting him from a trained hero back to the ordinary boy he'd once been. But . . . when she'd used that power, she'd known instinctively that reverting Nick would bring her family back. Even if she'd still had access to her power, that same instinct was telling her that there was nothing to unmake here. Nothing that she could undo to bring Margie back. And just that thought sent a wave of grief through her.

It must have been in her expression because Nick took a sharp breath. His free hand curled into a fist. He was clearly trying to hold it together. Joan knew how that felt. "It's just . . . ," he said. "My family needs me. Ever since my dad died, I . . . I help out a lot at home."

She'd do anything for him, she thought. Anything she could. If there was any way to fix this, she would. "There's a lot I don't know about this world," she said. "When we find my gran, she'll know more, but . . ." She shook her head. "It's really hard to change an event. There's a . . . a *force* that pushes back against changes we make."

She could feel the timeline even now. The other night, it had seemed like a storm, but this morning her impression was of an animal—for once, purringly content, as if it was satisfied that it had finally put Joan and Nick into extended proximity. *Just stop*, Joan wanted to tell it. *Leave us alone. You're trying to mend a rift that can't be healed.*

"It's hard to change an event," Nick echoed. "But not impossible?"

Joan hesitated. She only knew of the timeline being changed twice. Legend had it that the monster King had erased the original timeline to create a new one in his own image. And Joan herself had changed the timeline again, in a much smaller way, to unmake Nick.

"We should talk to my gran," she said. They weren't far from Queenhithe now. If anyone would know a way to bring Margie back, to get Nick home, it would be Gran.

The train rattled on the tracks. Outside, a platform slid into view: *Welcome to Luton*, the sign said. Commuters leaned sleepily against the station's brown brick wall, some scrolling on their phones, some staring at nothing, earbuds in.

Nick went back to their seats, and Joan joined him, squeezing close to allow the new arrivals to walk down the narrow aisle. Joan watched each person pass. Could any of them be monsters? They didn't seem to be, but for the first time, she wished she had the Oliver power—the ability to know for sure.

The train started. Joan began to shift away from Nick again, and she felt him take an unsteady breath. There'd been a time when she'd wanted to see him in pain. He'd taken her family from her, and she'd wanted him to suffer for it.

Since then, though, she'd seen him in enough pain for a thousand lifetimes. She'd seen recordings of him being tortured; of him having to watch his family being murdered. Over and over and over. She couldn't bear the thought of him hurting more now. She pressed closer to him, and it seemed to help a little. His shoulders went down, and he took a deeper breath.

"Why don't you close your eyes for a little while," she suggested.

Nick shook his head. He glanced around the carriage, still checking for the attackers.

Ever since my dad died, he'd said, *I help out a lot at home.* Joan could imagine that he'd taken on a lot of responsibility.

"I can keep watch," she said. "You don't have to do it all yourself."

To her surprise, he met her gaze and quirked his mouth up, a little self-deprecating. Butterflies fluttered in Joan's stomach as he closed his eyes.

This had to stop, Joan told herself—these feelings she kept having. They had to stop. The boy she loved didn't exist anymore. And *this* Nick would loathe her if he ever learned the truth.

The dream had been a reminder of that.

EIGHT

By the time they got to Blackfriars, the train was packed with bright-eyed early-bird tourists and yawning people on the way to work. Nick couldn't have slept more than half an hour, but when Joan woke him, there was some color in his face. He surveyed the platform as he exited the train. Even tired, he was methodical about it. After he'd checked and dismissed people, he didn't look at them again.

Joan imagined him filing away the details. When they'd volunteered at Holland House, his memory hadn't been as perfect as a Liu's, but it had been close. In the first week, the head curator had asked them to take all the tours. *It'll give you a feel for the place, even if you don't remember it all*, she'd said.

But Nick had remembered it *all*. Every fact from every tour— every name and date.

Good memory runs in my family, he'd told Joan once. They'd just started an early shift. They'd been mopping the foyer, sunlight slanting in through the shutters, making stripes on the floor so that it was hard to tell what was water and what was shadow. At the word *family*, the rhythmic swish of Nick's mop had paused, and Joan had turned to find his head ducked, his nape exposed above his collar. Nick had never liked to talk about his family. That morning, though, his guard had seemed down. When he'd spoken again, it was with the northern burr that always came out when he was tired. *But I was trained to notice things too.*

Trained? Joan had said, confused.

Taught, Nick had corrected himself quickly. And before Joan could ask who had taught him *that,* he'd changed the subject and the moment had been gone.

Now, in the station, Joan scanned the crowd too. People's clothing and technology seemed subtly different, although she couldn't have said what had changed. Maybe the cuts were more tailored; maybe the phone screens were brighter and sharper. If anyone was a monster, Joan couldn't pick them out.

"I remember all the people who attacked us at the bakery," Nick murmured as they made their way to the exit. "But there were a couple more attackers I didn't see."

"Hmm?"

"At my house," Nick said. He hesitated, and Joan suddenly knew what he was about to say. "Did you . . . recognize one of them?"

His eyes were still on the crowd. Around them, the sounds of the station clamored: trains, near and distant; people hurrying; tourists chatting. He wasn't aware of the cat-and-mouse game they were in, Joan told herself. He just wanted to know more about the attack that had upended his life.

"His—his name is Aaron." It felt strange to say his name aloud. She hadn't said it since the last time she'd seen him. It was her turn to hesitate. "I met him over the summer."

"They said they brought him in because he could identify you," Nick said. He looked curious. "Who is he?"

"Just . . . someone I knew for a while." It felt wrong to phrase it like that. Aaron had meant something to her by the end. He *still* meant something to her. She couldn't believe he'd been in that garden. That he was working to hunt her down. She put a hand to her cheek where Aaron had touched her on their last day together. *Joan, if you somehow remember this, remember what I'm saying now. You have to stay far away from me. From me and from my family. Never let me close enough to see the color of your eyes.*

Joan hadn't felt a glimmer of her power since she'd burned it out on Nick. She'd never even used it in this timeline. Someone knew about it, though. If Aaron had been called in to assist with the search, they surely knew.

Nick's dark eyes turned to her with the same intense attention he'd given to the crowd. "Why do I get the feeling," he said slowly, "that whatever happened to you over the summer, it was bad?"

Joan opened her mouth, feeling off-balance. She'd expected him to ask about the attack again. To ask how exactly she knew one of the attackers. She didn't have an answer for this. *You happened*, she thought. *You happened to me, and I happened to you.* But it had been more than that. Edmund Oliver had tried to kill her. The Monster Court had tried to kill her. And now someone was after her again. *That* was what Nick had been caught up in this time.

"What does he look like?" Nick nodded at the crowd.

Joan took a breath. "Blond with gray eyes," she said. "He isn't here." She'd have known if he were—Aaron Oliver turned heads. Crowds rippled around him like he was a stone thrown into water.

She braced herself for the next question, but instead there was a flicker of measurement in Nick's expression. She watched him make the decision not to push. He *knew*, she thought. He knew she was keeping something from him. Not unintentionally. Not *I didn't get the chance to tell you.* But deliberately. He knew.

They emerged from the station into a clouded London morning. The glass-and-steel monolith of Blackfriars Station was exactly as Joan had remembered it. There was no sign of the six years that had passed without them.

Cars and trucks crawled past as they made their way along Blackfriars Bridge, heading for the staircase down to the riverside walk. Scaffolding to the east and west blocked most of the view, but on the other side of the bridge, the One Blackfriars building looked just as it always did, pale and sail-like under the white sky.

Nick's vigilance began to ease slightly. They hadn't seen a single monster since Milton Keynes. Joan loosened a little too. Maybe they really had escaped.

"I thought there'd be more differences," he said, looking over the railing at the cars streaming by on the underpass.

"Six years isn't so long, I suppose," Joan said. "On a city scale." On a personal scale, though . . .

Nick gave a crooked smile, acknowledging the unsaid part of it. "You know what's weird? I keep thinking I'm late for Sunday football. I get up at six on Sundays to coach my brother's team. And then I've got my own match after that."

"I know what you mean," Joan said, half on autopilot. And then she properly heard what he'd said. "Except about waking up early."

Nick chuckled, two lifting notes of surprise, as if he hadn't expected to laugh. "Not an early riser?"

"*No*," Joan said. "I'm usually the last one up."

Nick's answering smile was unguarded, and something heavy eased in Joan's chest. "What about you?" she said. She tried to picture Nick lounging about but couldn't. He'd always arrived early for shifts at Holland House, even the punitive seven a.m. ones. Joan used to imagine him going to bed at dusk and rising at dawn, Spartan-like. "Do you ever sleep in?" she asked.

Nick's handsome face scrunched, as if he had to really think about it, and something dangerously fond started in Joan's chest, easing the weight a little more.

"I—" Nick broke off, his gaze snapping to something ahead.

Joan turned fast. Had he seen one of the attackers?

No, he'd seen something else. . . . To the right, the scaffolding had ended, and a swath of the south bank had come into view. Joan gasped.

Near the London Eye, there was a new landmark: a half pyramid with a low-sloping side that sparkled, diamond-like. And beyond that, an unfinished tower—a narrow column with jutting pieces that almost looked climbable from this vantage.

Back in 1993, there'd been too few buildings, but this skyline was just as uncanny: a mouth with too many teeth.

Joan imagined scrambling to the top of the new tower for a better view of the city. She'd been thinking of the world as largely unchanged. Now, she was struck with the feeling she'd had when she'd jumped into the past. This wasn't her London anymore.

"We traveled in time," Nick breathed, shaken. "I mean, I knew that we did, but . . ."

"Now it feels real." Joan understood. It was one thing to suspect it—to see a date on a train ticket—but a new skyline was undeniable.

"This is real," Nick agreed. His eyes returned to the strange view over and over until they found the staircase and descended. Until the new buildings vanished from sight.

On the riverside walk, between the two Blackfriars bridges, London looked momentarily like its old self again. The great red pillars of the old bridge were still here, rising from the water in their familiar lines: ghosts of Victorian London.

It was more crowded here, and the narrow path slowed their pace. As they walked, Joan began to notice Nick's effect on people.

Back at Blackfriars Station, Joan had thought about how crowds reacted to Aaron. Now she saw for the first time that they reacted to Nick too. He didn't ask for it, didn't take up more of the pavement than anyone else—but he seemed to command the space around him. People's heads lifted as he passed, as if they'd sensed some charismatic presence among them. Their gazes weren't the admiring desire often directed at Aaron, but something just as primal. People looked at Nick the way a compass pointed north. Joan watched the ripple of it: how it affected everyone, from schoolboys to joggers to briskly walking office workers.

Had Nick always had this quality, she wondered. Or could people somehow sense who he'd once been?

"You coach your brother's team?" Joan asked. She should have been keeping more distance between them, but she was curious about his life. Her own Nick had only mentioned his family a few times and had always tensed when speaking of them.

This new Nick actually relaxed. "I coach my little brother's and sister's teams." His eyes softened. "They're both really good," he said. "Better than I was at their age."

"*You're* really good," Joan blurted. The team won all the time now.

"You've seen me play?" Nick said, sounding a little surprised.

Joan felt herself start to flush. "Well . . ."

Nick's gaze roved over her for a moment as he took in the flush. He bit his lip, the corner of his mouth quirking up. He started to say something self-deprecating. But then he hesitated and said instead, a bit shyly, "I love the game. I love playing with the team." He said it like a confession. Like he'd never told anyone that before.

Joan's chest constricted. She'd never heard the other Nick express pure enjoyment of anything. *I've always put the mission first*, he'd told her once. *I never allowed myself anything more.*

"What about you?" Nick asked. "What do you like?" He sounded as curious about Joan as she was about him.

Joan concentrated on the path in front of them. Her face still felt warm. "I'm kind of a history nerd," she said without thinking. "I like the really old stuff." As soon as she heard herself, she tensed, but to her relief, her senses stayed sharp and unmuted.

"I wanted to be an archaeologist when I was small."

"You did?" Joan said, surprised. They'd met volunteering at a historic house in Kensington, but he'd been undercover at the time. She'd assumed later that he'd had no actual interest in the work they'd been doing.

"There was a dig near our place growing up. Used to watch through the fence." He smiled slightly. "Never saw them excavate anything but dirt."

"I did that," Joan said, surprised again. "I used to drag my dad over to a dig at Bletchley." She hadn't thought about that in years.

They passed the pier, and the south bank came into view again—this stretch was just as altered. The last time Joan had been here, the Shard had stood alone: a single glass tower with only the chimney stack of the Tate Modern competing for the sky. Now another skyscraper rose between them: a spire with a golden top. More construction was in the works behind it. The new cluster made Joan think of skyscraper cities like Hong Kong and Shanghai. Would London eventually look like that?

They walked past the Millennium Bridge, elegant and spindly after the rivets and iron of Blackfriars. There, everyone on the path turned left, away from the river; the river walkway had ended.

Joan leaned against the embankment wall and craned her neck. The dock had to be just up ahead, but she couldn't see it. She thought about the Serpentine Inn. It had been part of a complex: a miniature village of shops, houses, a market—all hidden away behind walls and accessible only through nondescript black doors. "We're probably in the right spot already," she said, realizing. This whole area was a maze of buildings—a monster neighborhood could easily be hidden among them. They needed to start checking alleys and looking for plaques with—

Her eye caught on something beside her hand. On the stone cap of the embankment wall, there was a square black tile the size of her thumbnail, with an image that had been hand-painted before the tile had been fired. Joan bent to examine the picture, and then went still. It was a sea serpent wrapped around a sailing ship.

"What is that?" Nick said.

The tile was oriented with the ship's prow facing west. Joan turned in that direction and spotted another black tile—this time on the ground, grouted between bricks as if it had been there since the path had been laid. The new tile was oriented differently, the ship's prow pointing north, toward an alley.

Signposts.

"It's a trail?" Nick said. He'd already spotted a third tile—just a black dot from here—on a wall in the alley.

Joan looked up at him uneasily. In the twelve hours or so since the attack, he'd figured out how to recognize monsters by their clothes and hairstyles, and now he knew how to find a monster place.

The cold knowledge of that cleared her head; she hadn't realized how foggy with tiredness she'd been. She *couldn't* take Nick into a monster inn. It wasn't just the danger that he represented; *he* would be in danger, surrounded by people who could kill him with a touch.

"You should wait out here," she said. "I'll go in and fetch my gran."

Nick searched her face, and Joan felt the searing heat of his attention suddenly. "Why?" he murmured, almost to himself. "Because . . . humans aren't allowed inside?" He was too insightful at every turn. "All these things you've been telling me . . ." Joan could see him recalling her reluctance to explain. "Am I a risk to you? Could you be punished for telling me about this world?"

Joan's stomach churned. *Am I a risk to you?* Memories flashed: Nick, standing among the bodies of the monsters he'd killed. Joan kissing him and then unmaking him. "I'm a risk to *you*," she reminded him. "You were dragged into this because of me." His mouth compressed. He hadn't liked it when she said that earlier. It was true, though. "*You'd* be in danger in there," she explained. "You've already seen some of those powers. You've seen the people who use them."

Nick was silent for a long moment. "Do you think the attackers have given up on looking for us?"

Joan thought of the hard-faced men in the garden with Aaron. "No," she said.

"Then shouldn't we stay together?" Nick said. "We'll be safer if we can protect each other."

Joan hesitated. The truth was, she *didn't* want to leave him out here—what if attackers found him while he was alone? They'd already killed Margie. If she was with him and something happened, she could at least fight for him.

"How would anyone in there even know I'm human?" Nick asked.

That was a good question. If Gran had designated the Wyvern Inn as safe, then it wouldn't be a place that Olivers frequented. But still . . . "Some people have the power to differentiate humans from—" Joan checked herself before she said *monsters.* "From *not* humans. They need to be close to use their power, though. Close enough to see the color of your eyes." What else could she tell him? "They all wear a sigil. A mermaid." She had a flash of the dark tattoo on Aaron's flank, barely visible through his rain-soaked shirt. She swallowed. "Sometimes, it's hidden."

"It's a rune?"

"It's not magic," Joan clarified. "It's a family emblem."

Nick's eyes flared with understanding, and Joan knew he'd

put that together too. That different families had different powers. He was too smart, she thought again uneasily.

"So," Nick said slowly. "Don't get too close to anyone with a mermaid sigil. Or *no* sigil."

This wasn't him, Joan reminded herself. The other Nick had been forged and trained over years and years. His family had been killed over and over and over before he'd even begun to hate monsters.

"Don't worry," Nick said to her seriously now. "We'll take care of each other. We'll both be careful."

And how long would they even be at the inn? Just long enough to find Gran. Joan bit her lip. "All right," she said. "Let's stick together."

The tiles took them on a winding path. Eventually, they hit a dead end on a raised walkway. Joan looked around. There was nothing here but an office building. She leaned over the walkway's wall.

"That *is* the Queenhithe Dock," Nick confirmed, looking down too.

"It's smaller than I was picturing." Joan had imagined a proper dock full of boats. But this was just a square of brown water, cut into the land between buildings. It was silted up, its dirt base exposed by the low tide. It must have been out of commission for centuries.

"Could the inn be down there on the foreshore?" Joan wondered.

But the last tile on the wall pointed up, not down. What was it pointing at?

The office building continued for several levels. Joan went

over to the building's glass doors. In her experience, doors to monster places were plain black with a sea serpent symbol. But the only sign here was painted on the door: *Employees Only.*

Through the glass, Joan could see a big yellow-walled lobby with sleepy office workers in business suits carrying coffee cups and water bottles. Farther in, there was a flight of stairs and, around the corner, the edge of a reception desk.

"Should we go inside?" Nick seemed doubtful.

Joan was doubtful too. The workers had the air of people who wished they were still in bed. She would have bet the money in Corvin's wallet that they were all humans, starting their day at the office. "Maybe we missed a tile," she said.

Footsteps sounded. A security guard emerged from around the corner in the slow stroll of someone doing an everyday patrol. He scowled when he saw Joan and Nick. "This is private property. You need to move on."

"Sorry," Joan said. "We're a bit lost."

"Use your map app," the guard said dismissively. He turned to leave.

"We're looking for the Wyvern Inn," Nick said.

The guard stopped. Joan saw then what Nick had already noticed. The guard was in an ordinary dark security uniform, but his mousy-brown hair was slicked back, 1950s greaser style. The people in the office might be human, but this guy almost certainly wasn't.

The man looked them both up and down in reassessment. "You're not the usual clientele."

Joan wet her dry lips. She'd have felt relieved, but the reality hit her suddenly. This was the lion's den, and they were about to step into it. "My gran said to come here.".

"And who is your grandmother?"

"Dorothy Hunt."

The man's unwelcoming expression didn't change, but he stepped closer. His eyes were unusual: bright blue with dark flecks that made Joan think of cracks in ice. He wore a thin-chained necklace, silver and delicate and feminine. A silver charm sat at the hollow of his throat. Some kind of bird? An eagle?

The man peered at Joan, and she remembered with a jolt her own warning to Nick not to get close enough to see the color of anyone's eyes. "Who is your grandmother?" the man asked Joan. And it was strange that he was asking again, but Joan found she didn't mind. He had a beautiful voice—a sweet tenor, full of frankness and warmth. She had the impression that she was standing in front of the most honest man she'd ever met. She felt eager suddenly to return that honesty with her own.

"Dorothy Hunt," she said again. "And my other grandmother's human. She—"

"I don't need to know about the other one," the man said, and Joan closed her mouth. The silence felt comfortable, like she'd found a new close friend.

"Joan?" Nick said. He sounded weirdly concerned. He caught her arm. *"Joan!"*

The man shifted, and his pendant flashed sharply in a spike of sunshine. The little figurine had the head and wings of an eagle, but the body was something else. Something furred. It was a griffin.

Joan's head cleared slightly. "You're from the Griffith family," she blurted to the man. *Griffiths reveal*, the nursery chant went. The Griffiths could induce truth.

"Do you have a right to be in this inn?" the man asked. This time, Joan could *feel* him exerting his power on her. It wasn't like the cuff Corvin had used—a forced desire. Instead, Joan was warmly comfortable, as if she'd known and trusted this man all her life. *You can't trust him*, she told herself, but her own mental voice sounded hollow in contrast to the gut feeling of safety. Joan knew she could be honest with him. "I don't know if I have the right," she admitted.

"Give me your name. Do you have a sigil?"

Joan fumbled for her bracelet until the fox charm showed. "Joan Chang-Hunt. I'm half—"

"All right, then," the man said, cutting her off.

It was like being hit with cold water. Joan took a stumbling step back, bereft. The impression of meeting an old friend was gone; the man's eyes were a hard stranger's again.

And then reality truly hit her, and her heart was suddenly hammering. He *couldn't* do that to Nick—he'd expose Nick's humanity.

"Hey," she said quickly. "I'm the only one going in. I'm—" But it was too late. The man's attention was already turning to Nick.

"Give me your name," he ordered. Away from the influence of his power, his true tone was impatient and hostile. But to Joan's dismay, Nick's shoulders lowered, his face relaxing. "I'm Nick." Joan braced herself for Nick to add his surname. A beat went by. Another beat. Nick's mouth stayed closed.

Joan blinked. How had he resisted even that much? She hadn't been able to resist at all. She'd given the man more information than he'd asked for.

The man's eyes narrowed. "Tell me the rest," he said to Nick sharply.

"Nick doesn't have a family!" Joan blurted.

Nick's expression didn't change. He looked more relaxed than the man, who seemed taken aback. "He *what?*" the man said.

"I do have a family," Nick said, and Joan's heart sank. It had been a long shot anyway. But Nick was already adding easily: "They haven't seen me in years, though. Far as they're concerned, I'm dead to them."

Joan stared at him. He might have looked hazy, but his mind was *sharp*, even under the influence of the Griffith power.

She waited, tense, for the man's response. This surely wouldn't work if he asked Nick a more direct question: *Are you human?* But the Griffith was hunched—as if Nick had disclosed something he hadn't wanted to hear. "You never had a family power?" he asked. It didn't seem part of the standard questioning.

Nick shook his head, and the man drew back from him.

Joan had always known that family was a big deal in the monster world. But the man's reaction made her wonder if she really did understand it. His expression was one of sympathy and horror combined.

"Can he go in?" Joan said. The man hesitated. He still had more questions, apparently. On a hunch, Joan pressed: "Is he going to be allowed in? Even though he doesn't have a family name?" It worked. The man grimaced. "Just because he doesn't have a family power—" Joan started.

"Yeah, all right, all right," the man said quickly; he didn't want to hear any more. "Welcome to the Wyvern Inn." He was already backing up, wanting to return to a more comfortable task.

He couldn't go yet, though. "*Wait*," Joan said. "Where's the door?"

"What do you mean?" the man said. "You're in front of it."

"This office door?" Joan said, confused. But the man was already walking away.

Joan turned back to the glass doors. Inside, the office workers ambled up the staircase, sipping coffee and chatting sleepily. They looked less like monsters than ever.

"Maybe it's on another floor," Nick suggested. The haze in his voice was already gone.

Joan turned back to him fast. "Are you all right? I didn't know that would happen." She and Aaron hadn't been challenged at the Serpentine Inn; she'd assumed all inns were the same.

"I'm fine," Nick said. "What did you call it? The Griffith power?"

"He was from the Griffith family," Joan said, nodding. "I—I've never met any of them before."

"It wasn't as strong as the power in the courtyard," Nick said. "I think I could have pushed his mind out if I'd had breakfast." He smiled. Joan could tell he was mostly trying to reassure her.

Joan tried to smile back. It hit her again that *she* hadn't been able to make a dent in the Griffith power. Nick had resisted it, and his mind had stayed sharp. He'd been quick on his feet. He might not be the hero anymore, but maybe he still had some abilities. Maybe they were innate.

He stepped closer to her, and his dark hair fell across his brow. "It's going to be okay."

He was so big, his body so sheltering, that Joan still had that stupid feeling of safety when she was with him. She looked up at him. "I should be saying that to you."

"We can say it to each other." He held out his hand, and Joan reached for him instinctively, needing the physical contact; the confirmation that he was still alive. She hadn't expected him to be in danger before he'd even entered the inn.

"Ready?" she said, trying to sound more confident than she felt. He nodded.

Joan took a deep breath and pushed open the door.

She gasped as the interior revealed itself. Distantly, she heard Nick make a sound too. They both stared.

The inside of the building didn't match the view through the window. The lobby they'd seen was gone. All the office workers were gone.

Now, people sat at tables covered in white linens, chatting around towering tiers of sandwiches and scones and tiny cakes with sugared violets and roses. The diners wore crinoline and Victorian suits, flapper dresses, and eighties fluorescents. They were time travelers.

And above them all, hanging in midair, was a glass wyvern: a bipedal, winged creature with a dragon's head and two clawed feet.

This was the Wyvern Inn.

Joan was back in the world of monsters—with Nick.

NINE

"How is this possible?" Nick whispered. "We saw an office lobby from the outside."

"I don't know," Joan said. This was nothing like the yellow-walled room they'd seen through the windows. The Serpentine Inn had felt like an old-fashioned pub, but this had the atmosphere of a fancy café serving afternoon tea. Other than the glass wyvern, the decor was muted.

There were at least a hundred monsters in the room, eating at linen-covered tables, sipping tea and champagne. Hathaway animals wandered underfoot: a sleek ferret, a black cat, a foxlike dog.

Joan turned a slow circle. "I can't understand—" She stopped, staring at the windows.

She'd expected to see the south bank view they'd just left behind: the Globe Theatre, the Shard, the new construction around it. But all that was gone. And Joan understood now why the room was so sparsely decorated: the view was all the decoration needed.

The windows showed Londinium.

Joan stumbled to the nearest window—a vertical strip of glass that started at her knees. Southwark was unrecognizable. In her time, the river was tamed, the bank a straight walking path. But here, water spread into the land, making lacework inlets. In the distance, beyond the marshy ground, a columned temple stood among a scattering of terra-cotta-roofed houses.

And the Thames itself was *huge*—twice its normal width. To the left, a vast wooden bridge straddled the wide spread of the river. Figures moved across it: people and animal-pulled carts.

Nick joined Joan at the window. "Is that what I think it is?"

"Londinium." Joan could hear the awe in her own voice. "London in the Roman Empire. That's London's first bridge."

She'd done a walking tour once: *The remnants of the Romans.* There hadn't been much left—a bit of wall near the Tower, a section of an amphitheater in the Guildhall Art Gallery. It was hard to believe there'd once been all this.

Joan pressed closer to the glass. The river was so wide that there seemed to be no foreshore below—only brown water. A boat drifted past, rowed by a boy in an unbelted tunic. It was no bigger than Joan's bathtub at home and seemed to be made of something softly pliable. Maybe leather.

"If only Mr. Larch could see this," she whispered.

"Who?" Nick said, and Joan remembered with a jolt that Mr. Larch didn't teach at their school anymore.

"Just . . . someone I know. He'd love this." Mr. Larch had spoken about the first bridge as a marvel. *One of the great feats of ancient engineering,* he'd said.

Heels clicked behind them. A staff member came over, a girl of about nineteen, wearing a pale pink suit and hot-pink pumps. Her chestnut hair was wound into an elegant French twist that made her seem older than she was. *Edith Nowak,* her name tag read.

"I never get tired of this view." Edith had a pleasant voice, unexpectedly deep. "It's good to see people enjoying it."

Was no one else looking? Joan turned. They really weren't.

The other patrons were in conversation, eating and drinking. Apparently, this miraculous view was just a backdrop—no more interesting than their meal.

"It's beautiful," Nick said with so much feeling that Edith blinked. Joan saw the moment she registered Nick as attractive. Her eyes widened, mouth parting. Joan knew that expression—she'd caught it on herself in window reflections. She'd seen it on half the people at school.

"You've never seen a Portelli window before?" Edith asked.

Nick shook his head, and Joan braced herself. Would that be considered strange in a monster place? But Edith seemed delighted. "Well, this is a wonderful example of their work. As you know, the Portelli family power reveals other times. But they're also great glassworkers. Ordinary glass like that"—she pointed up to the hanging wyvern, diamond-bright above them—"and glass imbued with their power. Like *that*." She indicated the windows showing the ancient Thames.

Joan thought of the office lobby they'd seen from the outside. "So . . . when we saw all those office workers through the outside windows . . ."

"You were seeing a different time," Edith said, nodding. "Clever way to conceal a place, no?"

"Clever," Nick agreed. He added wistfully, "Can we go out there? I mean—" He breathed a laugh as he peered down. "We might have to swim out into it. I don't know."

Edith smiled toothily, seeming even more charmed. "It's only visual. You can't step through to the other side. And the people out there can't see *us*." She gazed out onto what would one day be Southwark. "I wish I could see it in reality as well." As if anticipating their question, she said, "I'm a Nowak." She held up her wrist, showing a bracelet with a clear hourglass charm containing grains of black sand. "I'll never get closer to Londinium than this."

Joan wasn't sure what that meant. Didn't the Nowaks travel in time like other monsters?

Before she could respond, though, Edith seemed to shake off her reverie. Her smile turned polite. "I understand you're Dorothy Hunt's granddaughter," she said to Joan. "We've not had the pleasure of your company before."

All Joan's wonder and curiosity at seeing Londinium gave way to profound relief. "You know my gran?"

"It has been some time since she was in residence," Edith said. "But we've sent a message to her. We'll fetch you when she arrives."

Joan closed her eyes for a moment, letting the words sink in. Gran was coming. She and Nick had survived the attack, they'd made it to London, and soon Gran would be here to help.

Edith offered Joan a small silver key. "The Hunts have a suite upstairs: second door on the left. And if you're hungry, there's a market on the floor above that. Food, currency, anything else you might need to fit into this time."

"*Thank you.*" They weren't out of danger—there were still monsters after them. But this was the safest Joan had felt since a monster had appeared at the bakery.

Edith gave the view one last look. "Enjoy your time at the Wyvern Inn," she said pleasantly. And then her heels were clicking against the floorboards again as she headed away.

Nick breathed out, deep and exhausted. Joan felt it too. "Why don't we clean up and eat while we wait for her," she suggested. They'd barely slept, and they were still in yesterday's clothes.

They made their way to the staircase at the back of the room—the same sweeping staircase from the office lobby. There, it had been plain white with yellow walls. Now, it was carpeted in tasteful dove gray with a wyvern pattern embroidered in gold.

As they ascended, Nick looked down over the banister at the figures below. "How many people with powers are there?" He sounded almost as awed as he'd been when he'd looked out onto Londinium.

"In the world? I . . . I don't know." Joan was surprised by the question. Did anyone know? "It would be hard to take a census of time travelers, I guess."

"They probably congregate in comfortable periods," Nick speculated.

He was just curious, Joan told herself. It only sounded like reconnaissance because she knew who he'd once been.

"Maybe they'd have home zones," he said. "If you traveled too far from your own time, language would become an issue. . . ."

"You'd want to avoid wars," Joan said slowly. "Plagues. Discrimination." How many monsters *were* there in London on any given day? What about in the rest of the world? Did they make up half a percent of the population? One percent? How many people were out there, preying on humans?

Nick looked at her, sharp and interested. His face was half in shadow, and out of nowhere Joan had a flash of her nightmare on the train—of him wielding a sword in the shadow of a high hedge wall.

For a moment, the boy with the sword and the Nick in front

of her seemed to merge. The image was so real that it almost felt like a premonition.

Joan thought again about how the people on the river walk had looked at him. Unease churned inside her. In the other timeline, by the age of eighteen, he'd trained and led warriors to slay monsters. In the right circumstances, could he be capable of that again?

"You'd want to stay near friends and family too," Nick said. "Time travelers who knew each other would probably cluster together."

Joan blinked. The warrior image vanished; he was an ordinary boy again—the boy who'd saved her life; who she'd brought to this dangerous place. "Makes sense," she managed.

Above them, the sounds of a market were rising: footsteps thumped, and vendors called in familiar rhythms.

But as Joan and Nick ascended the last steps to the landing, they found a hotel-like corridor. The market noises were coming from the floor above.

Joan suddenly needed a moment. "Why don't we start with the suite?" she said.

The second door on the left was a long way down the corridor. Joan saw why when she opened the door with the silver key. She'd been expecting a hotel room, but this was a small apartment—a living room with doors leading to a bedroom and a bathroom. It was simple but homey: a blue sofa, a wood-paneled kitchenette. The only Gran-like touch was a landscape painting above the sofa: an empty field under a stormy sky, a ruined building in the distance.

Joan doubted that anyone had looked much at that painting, though, because the view was Londinium again. From this higher angle, more of the river was visible, its single bridge spanning an immense width of water that no modern London bridge had ever had to accommodate.

"There are clean clothes in here," Nick called to Joan. He'd wandered into the bedroom.

Joan joined him, and Nick gestured at a huge walk-in wardrobe. It was full of clothes: utilitarian, formal, casual. "All kinds of sizes," Nick said, unfolding a soft white T-shirt.

"They must be from this time period." Joan couldn't see much difference between the cut of their own clothes and these ones, but she'd be glad to change into something clean.

She walked farther in and found a black jacket with an Elvis collar—flipped up, it would be high enough to cover the back of Nick's neck. She offered it to him, and to her relief, he took it.

"You want the first shower?" he asked. Joan shook her head. She wanted to take stock and think.

Joan sat on the sofa and laid out everything she'd stolen from Corvin on a glass coffee table: twenty pounds in old white banknotes, twenty-five pounds with that unfamiliar queen, and over three hundred in monster currency. Joan had spent all the contemporary money—she'd need to exchange some of this at the market to get more. She turned the wallet upside down and shook it; felt for secret pockets. Was that it?

No, that wasn't it. She reached into her shirt pocket and pulled out Corvin's chop, chain first.

The pendant was a burnt elm tree, withered branches

reaching up. On the underside, Joan made out reversed letters: *Corvinus Argent. Son of Valerian Argent.*

That was interesting. Corvin was the son of a family head, like Aaron. A prince of the Argents, probably equipped with a strong power.

The burnt elm sigil wasn't replicated on the underside. In its place was the winged lion of the Court. Corvin *had* been a Court Guard. Joan wasn't exactly surprised, but the hard proof made her feel sick.

A decorative half circle ran around the lion's left side. Joan held the chop up to the light, tilting it until the metal shadowed to reveal more detail. It wasn't a simple curved line but a thorned stem: a rose stem, without the flower. Joan had suspected that there was something different about Corvin's team. Was this the mark of a specialist group within the guards—one charged to hunt down people like her?

She folded her arms around herself. A specialist group . . .

Something had been nagging at her since they'd escaped from Nick's house. Corvin's words in the garden. *The intelligence was flawed,* he'd said. *That boy wasn't even supposed to be there.*

But how could the Court's intelligence have been flawed? Their historical records were perfect.

What else had Corvin said? *I think the rumors of unusual fluctuations are true.*

Joan closed her eyes. She was too tired to make sense of this. She didn't know enough to make sense of it. She needed Gran for that.

The bathroom door opened, and Nick stepped out in a puff of steam, hair damp and curling. He'd found dark gray trousers and a white shirt. Over it, he tugged on the black jacket Joan had given him. He came to join her. "Is this okay?" he said. He tugged at the shirt self-consciously. "Feels tight."

It was paint-tight. Joan could see every muscle. She forced her gaze up, feeling her cheeks heating as if she'd accidentally said it aloud. "Looks good," she managed. He looked *really* good. With his hair falling slightly over his forehead, he seemed more like a movie star than ever.

"Trying to figure it all out?" Nick said. Joan blinked at him, and he nodded at the pile of cash and the chop. He reached over to examine the monster banknotes. They were clear plastic with golden images: a winged lion, a crown, a striking serpent. With a thoughtful tilt of his head, he stacked them one by one until the overlaid parts of the notes formed a coat of arms: the serpent at the left, lion at the right, and the crown between them.

"There's royalty in this world?" Nick asked.

"There's a king." Joan had never seen this much of the coat of arms; she'd never had enough monster money. "People talk about him like he's all-powerful." She didn't know much more; didn't even know what he ruled over. *Our borders don't match what you'd think of as countries*, Aaron had once said. *They were drawn in a different time.*

"Like an ancient god-king . . . ," Nick said musingly.

It had only been Aaron, really, who'd talked about him that way. But then, the Hunts weren't the pious type; Joan couldn't imagine Gran revering anything. "They say he's never seen. I'm not even sure he's real."

She thought back, though, to the immense display of power at Whitehall. The palace had been wrenched from its time; a

Paleolithic moat had protected the Royal Archive. *I always heard that the King had power,* Ruth had said, *but seeing it . . .*

A chill crawled down Joan's back. *Someone* had created those marvels. *Someone* had that power.

Nick touched the winged lion on the crest, and then his gaze went to Joan's sleeved arm.

Joan didn't really want to look at the thing again, but she rolled up her shirtsleeve. Nick's eyes blazed with interest as the winged lion was revealed. It was more vibrant than a tattoo—pure gold with crisp edges. Joan ran a finger over it. It felt like her normal skin—as if it had always been part of her. The thought filled her with revulsion. It *wasn't* part of her. It had been put on her.

"It's a symbol of authority?" Nick said slowly. "Corvin called it a cuff. Like a handcuff? Were they trying to arrest you?" His forehead creased. "Because it seemed more like they were trying to kidnap you."

"I . . ." Joan frowned at that herself. "I don't know." She didn't know what they'd wanted. She'd assumed they'd have taken her to Aaron for identification and then executed her.

She registered curiosity mixed with something more danger-ous in Nick's expression. Protectiveness. Concern. It hit her that her tongue had been getting far too loose. She'd been trying to keep information restricted to things he'd already figured out; things that would keep him alive. Kings and authority systems didn't count. She stood quickly. "I should wash up."

If anything, the curiosity and concern in Nick's expression intensified. But he just said, "There are fresh towels and clothes in the bedroom cupboards."

Joan swore at herself as she stripped off her clothes. She kept telling him things she shouldn't. It wasn't just tiredness. Some bone-deep part of her felt she could trust him. And the more exhausted and raw she was, the more she felt it.

Joan pressed her forehead against the cold glass. She knew the reason. These were remnants of what the original Joan had felt for the original Nick in the *zhēnshí de lìshǐ*: the true timeline. That Joan had loved and trusted her Nick completely. So much that wisps of her feelings still remained. And some part of Joan was stupidly jealous of her—that long-lost Joan. What would it have been like to have such uncomplicated feelings for Nick? She wished—

She pushed away the thought and took a deep breath. She had to finish washing up.

Out of the shower, she couldn't find a hair dryer. She tied her wet hair into a ponytail and put on the clothes she'd found in the wardrobe: a long-sleeved black T-shirt, a green plaid dress, and a pair of black ankle boots. She had to tug the dress down, inch by inch. Nick was right. The cuts in this time were *tight*. When it was finally on, though, the dress was surprisingly comfortable.

Nick's eyes widened when she returned to the living room.

"I know," Joan said. The carpet was really thick. "I didn't even hear my own footsteps. Almost scared myself."

"No, that's not—" Nick seemed flustered for a moment. "Uh . . ." He stood up and gestured at the door. "Should we get some food?"

TEN

As they climbed the stairs, vendors' calls merged in rhythmic song: "Strawberries! Wild wood strawberries!" "Sweet cakes for your sweet!"

Joan's breath caught when they reached the top. The Wyvern Inn market was nothing like the rough-and-ready market at the Serpentine Inn. It was themed like a night garden. Murals of dark forests decorated the walls, and real flowering plants and artificial trees made warmly lit paths. The faint scent of jasmine wafted through the room. With the Portelli windows, this room could always be night.

The river-facing wall showed an ancient Thames at dusk. Joan could just make out the enormous width of it under the darkening sky. Without the lights of modern London, the south bank was barely visible.

Nick's eyes lifted to the ceiling, wide with wonder. Portelli glass showed a black night with bright, bright stars—thousands and thousands of glinting diamonds and the hazy rift of the Milky Way. "Can that really be a London sky?" he murmured.

They walked, looking for food, and found a stall selling cork-stopped cordials, the samples smelling of medicinal herbs. Then a cart with tiny iced cakes and wrapped sweets. Each cart and stall was half-hidden in the garden, so that coming upon them felt like a discovery.

Nick bought a curry with sweet potato and eggplant and bright red chilies, and Joan bought a baked potato. The vendor ladled what looked like a thick daal over the top and gave it to her in a cardboard box with a strange lightweight fork—it wasn't plastic, but it didn't feel like wood either. The daal was barely spiced, but it was piping hot and very filling, and Joan felt better from the first bite; she hadn't realized how hungry she'd been.

They ate and walked. Farther in, they passed stalls with handmade knives and golden coins thin as wafers. One vendor had only compact mirrors on his table, their golden cases intricately decorated with family sigils and enamel numbers. As Joan walked by, he lifted one of the compacts with a flourish of demonstration. She caught the number on the case as he flicked it open: *103*. To her surprise, the glass inside wasn't a mirror. The vendor tilted it to show a glimpse of blue sky, and then a glimpse of greenery.

"It's a tiny Portelli window," Nick realized. "A portable one. The number must be the year: AD 103." He looked at the other compacts with a little yearning. Joan wanted one too, but the price tags ranged from 1,000 to 5,000—depending on the year— and Joan didn't have that kind of money, in human or monster currency.

They kept walking. Joan was tense at first, bracing for someone to use the word *monster* or to talk about stealing human life, but the conversations around them were comfortingly mundane: the weather outside, which stall sold the best jewelry, gossip about other families. Joan slowly relaxed. Monsters didn't routinely talk about being monsters any more than humans talked about being human.

"Let's keep an eye out for my gran," she whispered to Nick.

"She's not Chinese—she's from the other side of the family. Bright green eyes and white hair—usually in a bun."

"What's she like?" Nick asked Joan curiously.

Joan was startled by her own emotional response; her feelings were hopelessly tangled. She'd have done anything for the Hunts—she'd have died for them. But at the same time, they were monsters who stole human life for their own amusement. Joan had barely begun to process how angry she'd been at them since learning that, how horrified. And at the same time, she loved them so much still. She couldn't explain any of that to Nick.

"She's . . . practical. No-nonsense. But loyal." Gran had died trying to protect Joan last time. Joan pushed away the memory of Gran's blood all over her hands. "She'll do everything she can to get us out of this." That, at least, Joan was sure of.

Joan finished the potato and spotted a bin at the feet of a vendor. "Okay if I throw out the box here?" she asked the man.

"Course, love," he said. He was thickly muscled with olive skin and a fuzz of close-cropped dark hair. In front of him, there were trays of bright fruit skewers threaded with fresh cherries and strawberries and pieces of candied apple. They reminded Joan a little of the candied hawthorn sticks Dad liked to get from the Chinese grocery.

"Could I get two cherry sticks?" she said impulsively. She kept her eyes down. She couldn't imagine an Oliver selling fruit sticks at a market, but you never knew. As the man reached for the cherry sticks, though, she saw a tattoo on his wrist: a pink-petaled flower. She didn't know that family sigil, but it wasn't a mermaid.

Joan risked looking up. "Seems busy," she ventured.

"Lot of new faces in town." With a neat twist, the man

wrapped the stick ends with paper napkins and passed the fruit to Joan with some coins. "Bounty hunters from all over."

Joan stiffened and felt Nick tense up beside her. "Bounty hunters?"

The man shrugged. "Nothing official, but there's a rumor going around about some dangerous fugitive on the loose. Everyone's in town trying their luck. All under the radar, of course." He misread her expression. "Don't worry, love. The fugitive's marked and mired. If a bounty hunter doesn't get her, the guards will."

If the situation had been less tense, Joan would have laughed at the idea that she was dangerous. She didn't even have a power anymore. She found a monster banknote—a twenty, not too big, and she hoped not too small—and put it down next to a stack of napkins. The market at the Serpentine Inn had been a place to buy information as well as food and goods. Maybe this market was the same. "Love a bit more of that gossip," she said.

There was a long pause, and the man's expression cooled. "Like I said, it's nothing official. Are you buying more food? That's all I sell."

Joan tried again. "Anyone around here who *does* like to gossip?"

"No," the vendor said shortly. He slid the note back to her. "Now, off you trot."

"Worth a try," Nick murmured as he and Joan walked away.

"I'd better keep that gold mark covered," Joan whispered back. She was glad of her long sleeves.

She offered Nick one of the skewers. He had to be wondering what she'd done to make all these people come after her. What criminal act. He only smiled at her, though. And, for the first time, Joan wondered if he was feeling the same bone-deep trust for her that she kept feeling for him.

"Cherries are my favorite," he said, almost like an admission. "Like those Bakewells you were going to give me." He bit a cherry off the stick, and red juice stained his bottom lip. He licked it off. "Almost feels like you know me."

A frozen second seemed to pass before Joan forced her own smile. "Funny, that." The Bakewells had been deliberate, but the cherries were a slipup. *Get it together*, she told herself. She couldn't make mistakes like that.

They passed a room just off the main market. The door was ajar, revealing a circle of people knitting together, backdropped by the Queenhithe Dock in the early morning. The view wasn't of the present day; the buildings were low, with thatched roofs.

"Tudor times." Nick looked wistful. "I wish those windows were doors. The places I'd go . . ." He turned to Joan, awe lingering, as if some of it was for her. "Have you been there? Have you been to Londinium?"

The places I'd go. For a second, Joan could imagine it clearly— the two of them traveling together, exploring London through time.

"I—I don't travel," she said. The desire was an ever-present hunger inside her, but time travel was fueled by human life. She knew how Nick would feel if he learned the truth of that. It wouldn't be awe.

Too late, she realized that she'd fed that hunger in herself with the too-vivid fantasy of traveling with him. She braced herself for the market sounds to mute; for the light to dim. Her senses had dulled like that almost every morning this week. But to her relief, the fade-out didn't start.

Joan pictured the golden winged lion hidden under her shirtsleeve. *They're both mired*, the military man had said back at Nick's house. *The girl's wearing a cuff.* Joan's desire to travel was still inside her, but with this cuff on, maybe that didn't matter. Maybe she was safe from fade-outs.

"You don't time-travel?" Nick seemed puzzled. "You can but you don't?"

"It isn't easy," Joan hedged. And to forestall questions about *that*, she added, "Why? Where would you go?"

"If I could go anywhere and come back?" Nick's eyes creased with a hint of sadness. He was thinking about his father—Joan could see it. About how much he missed him. "I—" He seemed to decide to say something lighter. "I'd go farther into the future, I think. I want to know what happens."

Joan bit her lip. Part of her wanted to acknowledge what he hadn't said. But she followed his cue to keep it light. "You wouldn't mind being spoiled?"

"Well, maybe I'd leave some of it a mystery." Nick smiled a little. "Why don't we travel together sometime? See what happens fifty years from now?"

Joan felt strangely tongue-tied at the half-joking offer. Even after a night without sleep, he was ridiculously attractive. Butterflies started in her stomach. She made herself answer in the same tone, though. "I'll go with you if you come with me to Londinium. I always wished I could visit. I always—" She stopped herself abruptly.

A trip to Londinium and back would cost eight thousand

years of human life between them.

"Deal," Nick said. His smile warmed, the trace of sadness gone. Joan felt butterflies in her stomach again. This time, though, the feeling was mixed with horror.

The monster world was full of wonders. But it was as terrible as it was beautiful. It was a world where you could look out of a window and see a Tudor city. But it was also a world where people would steal human life just to have a holiday in another era.

As Joan opened her mouth, someone nearby said: "—the operation in Milton Keynes." She jolted to a stop, exchanging a look with Nick.

They were outside a small, dark room, the Portelli windows set to night. Golden lamplight illuminated pairs and trios of people playing cards and chess and something with wooden tiles inlaid with gold. Between the tables, bronze statues stood like sentinels: a wyvern on its hind legs, a serpent with scales raised like hackles, a minotaur with bulging muscles and curled horns. Their heads were overly polished, as if the gamblers sometimes touched them for good luck.

Conversation bubbled, loud and occasionally rising to tipsy laughter. Joan had no idea who'd spoken. There must have been twenty people in the room.

The same voice sounded again: "—guards all over." And this time, Joan saw who'd spoken. A woman at the back of the room with glossy red hair. She was talking to a man. The two leaned close then and had a whispered conversation, too low for Joan to hear.

Joan exchanged another look with Nick. They really should go back downstairs and wait in the room for Gran to arrive. They needed to lie low. But she wanted to hear more. *Reckless and impatient*, Aaron would have said. He'd been a balancing influence on Joan. Nick, though, was sharp-eyed with interest.

They walked into the room together and settled by the window, pretending to admire the view. Cigar smoke hung in the air. Joan could taste it in the back of her throat, woody and floral.

Nearby, the red-haired woman and the man were playing the chess-like game that Joan remembered from the Serpentine. The woman moved an elephant piece diagonally. "Ready to cut your losses?"

"Still like my chances," the man said, voice deep and amused. He rolled an object between thumb and forefinger—one of the wafer-thin coins sold at the market. And that was strange. The cherry vendor had given Joan monster coins in change, but they'd all been silver and angle-edged. So what were these gold wafers? The man placed his wafer by the board and moved a ship piece. "Want to cut *your* losses?"

Joan needed them to return to the other conversation. She said to Nick: "What do you make of all that stuff in Milton Keynes?"

Nick didn't blink. His answer was as smooth as if they'd discussed it beforehand. "Seems like everyone's talking about it."

The woman added another gold wafer. She moved a pawn. Joan opened her mouth to try seeding the conversation again, and then the man said abruptly: "Has your family been hearing what we've been hearing?"

The woman's answer was cautious. "Depends. What have you been hearing?"

The man lowered his voice. "That the Court's been detecting huge fluctuations in the timeline."

Joan held her breath. Corvin Argent had talked about fluctuations too. What did that mean?

Beside Joan, Nick said, "Huh." There was something off-key in his voice. He was staring out the window.

Joan glanced over but couldn't see much of the view; it was darker than the dusk of the market. The only light out there was the glow and flicker of torch flame.

The woman lowered her voice too. "Can't be true, though, right?"

"Can't be true," the man agreed.

The smoky air seemed to stick in Joan's throat. Nick was still staring out the window, and it suddenly struck her as absurd and stupidly irresponsible that she'd brought him with her into a monster inn. What had she been *thinking*? All her justifications seemed thin now. She should have left him somewhere far away from her. Somewhere safe and human—a hotel. She should have left him there and never gone back. This world was dangerous. *Joan* was dangerous.

Nick whispered to Joan, "*Look.*" That strange note was still in his voice.

Look? Joan squinted, trying to see what Nick was seeing. She could just make out water below: the Queenhithe Dock at night, lit with torches. The reflection of flames moved in the murky water. Beyond were ramshackle wooden buildings—only a story high.

Wait . . . there was something *on* the water. Joan pressed closer. The modern dock had been silted up and unusable. Boats would have run aground if they'd tried to moor there. In the view through the window, though, the water seemed deeper, and there was something hidden in the dingy light. A long, thin boat, its bow curled at the tip like an animal's tail.

"All those *people*," Nick whispered.

Joan saw them then: figures running in the dark—some toward London city; some toward the river. Her understanding reframed. She'd misunderstood the scale. The flames around the dock weren't torchlight. All the buildings along the river were on fire. The people outside were running for their lives.

And that boat . . . Joan's breath caught. "That's a Viking ship," she said, recognizing it at last. "That's a Viking *invasion*."

Nick put a hand on the window, knuckles whitening.

"What about the other rumors?" the woman said. "About the fugitive. They're saying it's a girl with a forbidden power."

Joan turned back to them, heart thundering. The air was stifling; cigar smoke permeated, cloyingly sweet. She tried to take a breath and nearly choked on it.

"We're hearing that too." The man dropped another coin onto the pile. "I'll raise you five hundred," he added.

Five hundred what? Joan thought suddenly. She stared at the pile of coins. Why would coins have been for sale at the market? What *were* they if they weren't currency themselves?

What did monsters value? The man added another coin to the pile. It caught in the lamplight. And then Joan knew the truth. She knew exactly what they were gambling with. She just *knew*.

Those coins were full of human life. The man had just gambled five hundred years of human life. Cold horror seeped into Joan's bones.

Behind her, through the window, people were running for their lives among the flames, their deaths presented as entertainment for people who weren't even watching. And here in this room, people were playing with coins imbued with human life. At the end of the game, someone would scoop up all the coins, and then use that life to travel—for *what*? Tourism? To go to parties? To gamble more?

Joan reached behind her, needing the grounding of cold glass. She looked from table to table—at the piles of coins. How much human life was in this room right now—stolen away by monsters? How many humans had died earlier than they should have, their time ripped from them and embedded into these coins? In truth, this room was full of corpses.

"I know," Nick said, very softly. "This is *sickening*." And for a moment, Joan thought he *knew*. Then she realized he was still talking about the view. The Viking attack below.

It struck Joan that if any of these monsters knew Nick was human, they'd kill him right here—with just a touch to the back of his neck. They wouldn't feel any remorse. And his life wouldn't even be enough to fill up one coin. She turned to Nick to tell him they *had* to get out of here. But the words stuck in her throat.

A shard of light had caught her eye.

In the dark window, there was a small bright mark. Within the mark, Joan could see daylight and the twenty-first-century Queenhithe Dock, all silted up.

Joan's chest compressed painfully. She had a vivid sense memory of cold against her thumb. A moment ago, she'd pressed back against the window and brushed the glass right there. Now she placed her thumb to the glass again. It fit exactly. *She'd* made that mark.

With terrible certainty, she knew what had happened. She'd

manifested the power she'd last used on Nick. A power outside of the twelve families. A power she'd thought was gone.

Something forbidden. Something wrong.

In the other timeline, she'd reverted metal to ore, and now, it seemed, she'd reverted a portion of a Portelli window back to ordinary glass.

"Excuse me," a strange voice said now, making Joan jump. She turned fast, hiding the mark with her body. She registered pink silk. One of the staff members was standing in front of her: a kind-looking man with gray-speckled hair. Had he seen the glimmer of light behind her? Did he know what she'd just done?

The man tilted his head, as if Joan's expression was strange. "Your party has arrived." When Joan just stared at him, he added, clarifying: "Dorothy Hunt has arrived. You sent a runner for her. You can meet her in the River Room three doors up."

"Thank you," Joan managed. The man nodded in acknowledgment and strode away.

Gran was here. Joan felt weak with relief. Gran would get them out of this place. And Gran would know what to do about the window.

Joan went to move, and then realized she couldn't. Everyone in the room would see the shard of light. And people were already gossiping about a girl with a forbidden power. Someone would wonder, would make the connection.

Joan opened her mouth to call to the staff member—to ask if he could bring Gran to her—but he was already halfway across the room. If Joan called out to him, all the gamblers would look this way.

"Just stay right there," Nick murmured to her.

"What?" Joan blinked at him, confused, as he headed to a humidor.

A few of the gamblers turned toward the movement, but Nick only examined the cigars, a hand in his pocket. He moved a lamp aside, as if it was in his way. The gamblers went back to their games.

Nick had put the lamp in Joan's easy reach. She pulled it carefully toward herself and placed it in front of the window. It wasn't perfect—anyone standing at a sharp angle would see a shard of light—but to most of the room, the daylight would blend with the lamp's glow.

Nick returned to Joan's side. "Shall we?" He inclined his head toward the door.

Joan nodded. Her heart was beating so fast it hurt. Still, she tried to match his casual tone as they walked out. "Didn't want a cigar?" she said.

"Can't stand the smell," Nick said blandly. And then they were out of the room.

Joan could feel Nick's questions, but there was no time to talk. *The River Room three doors up*, the man had said.

Joan found the room and looked around frantically. It was at the corner of the building. The view outside showed the dock on one side and the river on the other. Around the room, people sat by the windows, eating tiered trays of sandwiches and scones.

There. Joan's heart lifted as she spotted Gran sitting on the river side. She was wearing her familiar green felt hat—the one that made her look like a 1920s flapper. The tightness in Joan's chest eased for the first time in what felt like weeks.

And then Gran glanced around the room idly.

Joan froze. For a long moment, she couldn't move. She could only stare.

Dorothy Hunt has arrived, the staff member had said. And he was right—Dorothy Hunt was here. But this wasn't Joan's gran. This woman was the wrong age. Under the brim of her hat, her skin was milky and smooth; her eyes were so green that Joan could see the color from across the room.

No, Joan thought.

Gran loved Joan. In the other timeline, she'd died for Joan. But her younger self hadn't cared about Joan at all—she hadn't known her yet. Joan had gone to the younger Dorothy for help, and Dorothy had informed on Joan to the Monster Court.

Now, to Joan's horror, the younger Dorothy's gaze started to turn toward her. Joan stumbled out of the room, pulling Nick with her.

"What's wrong?" Nick said as Joan withdrew into the safety of the market. "Wasn't she there?"

Joan shook her head. "My gran's not coming. She can't help us." Joan had assumed that Gran would fix everything—that she'd be able to protect Joan and Nick both. But that wasn't going to happen now. As long as the younger Dorothy was here, Joan's gran was inaccessible. The timeline didn't allow a person to occupy the same time at different ages.

Joan and Nick were on their own.

ELEVEN

"That's not my gran in there," Joan said thickly. She'd needed Gran's help. She'd been attacked in her own hometown; Margie had been *murdered*. Joan had needed one of Gran's rare hugs; to hear Gran's no-nonsense voice. Now she felt adrift.

"She won't help?" Nick said.

"She's . . . she's too young," Joan tried to explain. "She doesn't know me yet."

"She's still your grandmother, isn't she?"

She sold me out. She turned me over to the Court last time. Joan couldn't bring herself to say it. "She doesn't care about me yet," she managed. "We can't let her see us. We can't even go back to that suite. We can't trust her at all at this age." It hurt to say it.

Nick's head turned toward the River Room. Joan caught the edge of some emotion, a tightening jaw. "Hey, come on, then," he said. "Let's get out of here."

Joan took a deep breath. If Gran wasn't here, then she and Nick were truly on their own. She had to think practically. "We need to exchange some money." They'd spent all their contemporary cash on the train tickets. Would it be safe to connect their phones? Probably not. New burner phones, then. And they needed a safe place to lie low.

As Joan reached for Corvin's wallet, though, she registered a change in the atmosphere of the market. Nearby, a man leaned in to murmur something to his friend. Hissing whispers spread through the room, and the pitch of the market lifted to alarmed.

"What's happening?" Nick murmured.

Joan had seen the market at the Serpentine Inn turn like this, its mood shifting from cheerfulness to fear. Joan didn't need to hear the whispered words to know what was coming. She could feel it in the pit of her stomach; in the hairs rising at the back of her neck. "Court Guards," she whispered to Nick. Around them, people were mouthing the same thing. *Guards. Court Guards are here.*

Joan's mind raced. She'd just manifested a forbidden power, and there was evidence of it in the gambling room. Had someone seen it? Had someone called in the guards? Or was this just a routine raid? Court Guards had come to the Serpentine to confiscate illegal technologies on sale there. Joan hadn't seen anything illegal in this market, though—not by monster standards.

Raised voices sounded, and heavy footsteps. "They're in the foyer," Joan whispered. That meant the front entrance was cut off. There had to be another way out, though. This building must have a fire escape.

A click of heels sounded on the wooden floor. Edith Nowak, the staff member, strode toward them. "You need to go!" she said to Joan.

Joan stood her ground and shook her head. She wasn't about to walk downstairs, all docile, to guards who'd kill her and Nick both.

Edith looked impatient. "I'm a friend of your grandmother's," she said. "Not *her*," she added when Joan looked to the River Room, where the young Dorothy was still waiting. "*After* she grows a heart."

The commotion downstairs rose: heavy footsteps and loud commands. Nick glanced at Joan, but Joan didn't know what to do. A wrong call would get them killed. And Gran had never mentioned Edith's name.

Edith didn't seem to notice the exchange. "There's a man selling cherries over at—"

"We know the stall," Joan whispered.

"*Good.* Show him the mark they put on you. He'll get you out."

The winged-lion mark? Joan didn't like that idea at all. What if Edith was selling her out, like the younger Dorothy had?

"Go on," Edith urged. "I have to greet the guards."

Joan's gran—the older gran—had told the family that this place was a sanctuary. She must have trusted at least some of the people here. And if she trusted them, Joan surely could too.

Joan made a decision. "*Thank* you," she said. And then remembered to add, "I'll owe you a favor." It felt uncomfortable to say it, but monster culture was based around favors and debts.

To her surprise, Edith's face softened. "Don't worry about that." She glanced back toward the stairs—toward the incoming guards—and her expression twisted into a complicated mix of sadness and anger that made Joan wonder what *she'd* experienced at the hands of the Court. "*Go,*" Edith said. And then she was walking away herself, heading for the market's entrance.

Joan was grateful for the market's night-garden theme. The dusk lighting obscured faces, and the stalls were hidden from each other by night-blooming flowers and light-garlanded trees.

Some vendors were still calling out their wares: "Hot pudding pies!" and "Fine candles!" But when Joan and Nick reached the cherry seller, he was standing outside his stall, big arms folded, ready for the raid. His eyebrows drew together when he saw them. "I'm closed," he snapped. "Clearly."

Joan glanced around. The stall was more exposed than she'd remembered, open to the market's entrance. Big clomping footsteps said that guards were already on the stairs. She *really* hoped Edith was right about this guy.

"You hear me?" the man said impatiently. "Guards are about to—"

Joan backed as far as she could into the stall's alcove and tugged up her sleeve just enough to reveal the golden tip of the mark. The man's eyes jerked to hers in shock, and Joan felt Nick shift beside her, tensing.

"Fucking *hell*," the man breathed. He darted over to snatch Joan's sleeve down, although no one else could have seen. "I thought you were a *snitch*," he scolded, "trying to buy information."

"I wasn't!" Joan whispered.

"No shit," the man hissed. And then, almost in the same breath, "Get *down!*" Because the guards' heavy feet were pounding up the last stairs. He shoved Joan and Nick back behind his stall.

Joan ducked behind the red-striped tent, and Nick found a spot behind the heavy pot of a bay tree. They'd ended up in a gap between the market and the wall. From here, the room didn't look nearly as whimsical. Down the line of potted trees and tent backs, string lights trailed out to electric plugs. Half-unpacked crates and rubbish lay around. This was the part of the market that only sellers saw.

Joan peered around the edge of the tent. The entrance was too close for comfort. Court Guards were streaming into the room, intimidating in their blue livery, winged-lion pins glinting on their lapels. Joan peered closer. Their official pins didn't quite look like the usual pins; there was a curved line around the lion's right side. Joan pictured that thorned stem on Corvin's chop, and her next breath shook. Definitely not an ordinary raid. They *were* here for Joan and Nick.

Edith's clicking heels sounded. "I'm the innkeeper," she said, introducing herself briskly to the guards. "Can I help you?"

"You can turn on the lights," a familiar voice called.

Joan put a hand over her mouth, afraid she'd make a sound, as Aaron emerged from the stairs. His long stride exuded casual arrogance. Last night he'd been dressed as if on his way to a red-carpet event. Today he was in navy blue. Not the guards' livery but tailored Savile Row. His lapel bore no pin, but he was clearly in charge of the raid.

Even just standing at the entrance, he seemed to light up the room, so beautiful that he made the raid seem a little unreal. He surveyed everyone, one hand in his pocket, lord-like, and Joan's heart skipped a beat as his eyes reached the cherry stall and moved on.

"May I have your attention, please?" Aaron said loudly. "The Court is conducting a search of this premises. Guards will distribute descriptions of two fugitives."

"We cleaned up our act years ago," Edith said to Aaron. "This isn't a home for fugitives."

"Every inn is being searched," Aaron said. "No one is singling you out." He added mildly, "I believe I asked for some lights on in here."

"Why is a civilian leading this search?" Edith said. "Why are these guards under your command?"

"Why is an innkeeper asking so many questions?" Aaron countered. He didn't sound threatening exactly, but Edith blanched. In her pink uniform, among the guards, she looked like a bird, bright and a little fragile.

Joan swallowed. This was a small raid with a team of a dozen guards, but Aaron seemed more comfortable than she'd have expected in this minor position of power. It occurred to her—for the first time—that if he hadn't been disinherited, he would have led the formidable Oliver family one day.

What had Corvin said to him last night? *I'd have thought you'd seize this opportunity. From what I hear, you need the redemption in his eyes.*

Was Aaron hoping to get back into Edmund's good graces? If he captured fugitives for the Court, maybe he'd find favor with his father again.

Joan glanced over at Nick. Like everyone else, his dark eyes were fixed on Aaron.

Now the cherry seller backed up to the edge of the tent. "There's a wardrobe behind the stall," he murmured under his breath. "Inside, you'll find a lever on the floor. Up twice, then down, then up again. Go *now* before the guards circulate."

Joan didn't let herself hesitate, although she wished she could have asked for the man's name. He'd risked himself to help, and Edith had done the same. If she could repay this, she would.

The wallpaper was hand-painted to look like shadowed trees. Joan tried not to panic as she searched for any kind of handle; any kind of outline showing a cupboard. Beside her, Nick ran the flat of his hand over the wall, trying to feel for it.

A flicker behind them. Fluorescent lights snapped on. Joan blinked in the sudden brightness. For a split second, she was sure that they'd be seen; they were concealed behind the tent, but only from certain angles. The darkness had been their best protection.

But the light had illuminated the indentation of the door handle too. Joan grabbed for it, and she and Nick darted inside. She had a second to glimpse a tiny space full of coats before she got the door shut behind them, plunging them into darkness. She dropped to her knees, trying to feel for the lever, pushing aside shoes and something soft. A scarf?

"*Found it,*" Nick whispered beside her. A second later, a mechanism sounded—a barely audible whir—and the entire back wall of the wardrobe swung open like a door.

Ahead, there was a windowless brick passage, sparingly lit with naked bulbs. A rush of déjà vu hit Joan as she got to her feet. There'd been a hidden door like this at Whitehall Palace. Aaron had been with her that time. They'd saved each other's lives over and over by then. . . .

Now, behind them, the raid started in earnest, barely muted by Nick closing the secret door. Guards shouted orders and footsteps shuffled. Joan pictured Aaron examining each person in the room, one by one—looking for the half-human girl with a forbidden power and the human boy she'd run away with.

Joan couldn't drag her mind from him as she and Nick hurried through the passage. Behind them, the sounds faded. They climbed down a flight of concrete stairs and then another. The brickwork changed from yellowish to red and then brown, as if they were entering other buildings.

That filth. That was what Aaron would think of her if he

caught her now. Joan couldn't imagine him ever laying a hand on her, but he'd always had the Court mandate to kill her. The whole time he'd known her, he'd been disobeying the Court.

I won't remember what you mean to me.

"You okay?" Nick murmured. Joan blinked up at him. He'd been paying closer attention to her than she'd realized. When she nodded, he said, "That was Aaron? The boy from the garden?"

The weight in her chest felt like a physical thing—a lump of iron lodged in her heart. "Yes."

"You were more than just acquaintances, weren't you?" Nick said softly.

Joan drew a sharp breath, and something achingly gentle touched Nick's expression—so gentle that Joan swallowed. She could imagine what he was thinking—that she and Aaron had been something to each other, and that Aaron had sold her out. It hadn't been like that, though. Aaron was loyal to the core. He'd never have sold anyone out.

"The way you've seen him . . . He's not like this." Joan didn't know why she needed to say it, but she couldn't bear for Nick's image of Aaron to stand.

Skepticism started in Nick's face, but then they turned the next corner, and he shifted to alert. Ahead there was a short flight of stairs down, and a heavy door.

"End of the line," Joan whispered, tensing. What was on the other side of that door? Where had they ended up?

The staircase was stone, misshapen and weatherworn, as if it had once been outside. Even with the door shut, Joan could smell the marine brine of the river.

Nick gestured for Joan to open the door, positioning himself in case someone attacked. Joan took a breath and turned the handle, cracking the door just enough to show a slice of light. They were in a brick-walled alley. Joan went to push the door wider, and a shadow moved.

Before Joan could react, a voice spoke: "Joan? You need to come with me."

A figure appeared. For a moment, all Joan could see was a tall silhouette. And then her eyes adjusted to make out a handsome man in his mid-twenties with delicate Chinese features.

"Jamie?" she whispered. "Jamie Liu?" Beside her, she felt Nick relax; he'd been ready to attack, waiting for her cue. "What are you *doing* here?" she whispered to Jamie. She hadn't seen him since the summer. *I remember,* he'd told her. The Liu family power was perfect memory, but some of the Lius had a stronger ability than that—Jamie remembered fragments of the previous timeline. The one Joan had erased.

Joan marveled now at how healthy Jamie looked. He'd never revealed what had been done to him in the other timeline, but in the smuggled videos, he'd been gaunt, his fingers crooked and broken. He was still slim now, but he looked strong.

"Edith got word to me," Jamie whispered. "Tom's waiting with the boat." He stopped. "Is someone with you?"

Joan blinked, realizing that she'd halted in the doorway; that the door was still barely cracked. She stepped into the alley, and Nick followed her out.

"Who—" Jamie cut himself off. Shock and recognition spread across his face as he took in Nick's features, his muscled arms. His eyes flew to Joan's in disbelief. "Why is *he* here?"

TWELVE

Jamie was bone white. In the other timeline, he'd been the Royal Archive—witness and recorder to the aftermath of Nick's massacres. He, more than anyone, knew who Nick was and what he'd been capable of. *Dozens and dozens of massacres,* Jamie had said once.

"Why is he *with* you?" Jamie said shakily. "Joan, why would he be anywhere near you?"

Nick was clearly confused by Jamie's reaction. "We were attacked," he explained. "Me and Joan." To Joan he said, "I don't want to make trouble for you."

"It's okay," Joan assured him. She could hear the tremor in her own voice belying the words. "Let me talk to Jamie for a second, okay? I need to tell him what happened."

It was a long alley. To Joan's relief, Jamie let her draw him farther up it, toward the river and out of earshot. Without being asked, Nick retreated to the street end.

She could feel Nick's eyes on her as she whispered to Jamie: "Court Guards came for me, and he fought them off. He saved my life!" She willed Jamie to understand; for Nick not to wonder about Jamie's reaction. "And now the Court's after him too. We have to keep him safe!"

"You can't be serious," Jamie hissed. "We both know who he is!"

"He doesn't remember! You know he doesn't! He isn't the same person anymore!"

"*Isn't* he?" Jamie said fiercely.

Joan's chest tightened with that familiar ache. "*No.*"

Jamie's eyes darkened in sympathy and anger. "I know what he was to you, but, God, Joan! He's a wolf in sheep's clothing! How many of us did he kill? Hundreds? Thousands? And—" Jamie looked over at the door they'd just exited through. "You just came out of an inn," he said disbelievingly. "You took *him* into a monster inn. He'll be able to find it again!"

"He isn't a danger anymore," Joan said. "He's *in* danger. We barely escaped. We've been on the run since yesterday afternoon. If there's a safe place we can go—"

"You want me to take *him* to a safe house? On *my* boat?" Emotions flitted across Jamie's face: fear and anger.

The attackers had almost killed Nick yesterday. He'd stood still and helpless under the Argent power. "He can't protect himself," Joan whispered. *Please*, she willed. *Please understand.*

Jamie put a shaking hand to his mouth. What was he seeing in that perfect mind's eye? *Dozens and dozens of massacres.* Was he seeing the aftermath of them? The people Nick had killed?

"I'm sorry," Joan whispered to him. "I'm really sorry. You don't owe me anything, I know. I owe your family. But . . . he saved my life in the attack. He doesn't deserve any of this. And I can't just leave him here alone."

Movement at the other end of the alley. Nick was waving at them.

"The guards are coming," Joan whispered. "Jamie, if you can't help us, just tell me, and I'll take him somewhere else. But I can't leave him."

Jamie stared at Nick for a long moment. Long enough for Joan to think he'd decided to leave her and Nick in the alley. But his jaw tightened. He beckoned.

"Thank you," Joan said as Nick jogged toward them.

"Don't thank me," Jamie whispered to her. He watched Nick's approach, face grim. "This is against my better judgment."

Jamie's words echoed as Joan followed Nick's broad-shouldered figure and Jamie's slender one. She could feel Nick's questions building as Jamie took them on a roundabout route to avoid the guards.

They stopped near Southwark Bridge. There, an illegal pontoon bobbed under the high embankment wall. Lashed to it was a Dutch barge, rocking in the choppy water. Joan made out a two-headed hound painted along the side—the sigil of the Hathaways.

"We're climbing down?" Joan asked. There was an ancient river staircase against the wall, lethally steep. Iron bars had been installed to prevent people from accessing it. Had anyone been down there in the last hundred years?

"It's perfectly safe," Jamie said. It was curt but polite—Jamie was always polite—but tension simmered underneath it. Joan wished they hadn't met again like this. "The Hathaways use these river accesses all the time."

Jamie climbed over the barrier, and then held out his hand to help Joan too. She clambered over and grasped for the handrail fixed to the wall. The water side of the staircase was a sheer drop down.

Joan checked on Nick, but he didn't need help. He was already scaling the barrier with the surefooted agility of a cat.

They made their way down. Halfway, the stone became green with slippery high-tide lichen. There, even Jamie needed to grip the rail.

Joan found herself remembering the day she'd met Jamie. She'd gone to him seeking information—Jamie had been obsessed with the legends of the hero. At the time, he'd thought they were only stories.

Joan's throat tightened. In the alley outside the Wyvern Inn, Jamie had said, *Why is he* with *you? Why would he be anywhere near you?* But Joan hadn't sought Nick out. Jamie had to know that.

Jamie himself had told Joan about the *zhēnshí de lìshǐ*: the true timeline. *We believe that if people belonged together in the true time-line, then our timeline tries to repair itself by bringing them together. Over and over and over. Until the rift is healed.*

Lost in memory, Joan slipped on a wet step. A strong hand shot out and grasped her arm, steadying her. Joan blinked up. Nick had caught her so fast that she hadn't even had a moment of fear.

Thanks. Joan could only mouth it, her throat too tight to speak.

The timeline had brought them back together in Milton Keynes, but they were pieces of a damaged puzzle. Nick had killed Joan's family, and Joan had unmade him. It didn't matter that Nick had forgotten it all; *Joan* knew. They might have fit together once, but they didn't anymore. There was a rift between them that the timeline could never heal—even if it brought them together over and over again for the rest of their lives.

Joan took a deep breath and kept climbing down. But she felt the shadow of Nick's touch for the rest of the descent.

The pontoon wobbled under Joan's feet. Gaps between wooden planks showed choppy brown water. It wobbled again as Nick landed beside her with a thump.

Beside them, the barge seemed huge—a house on the water. It was lovingly maintained: freshly painted in forest green and burgundy, with a name in white lettering: *Tranquility*. The Hathaways' double-headed hound underlined the name.

Jamie leaned over to pat the boat's flank, absent and fond, like he might have stroked a passing cat. Then he started on the ropes. He shook his head when Joan reached over to help. "Faster if I do it."

On the boat, heavy footsteps sounded. A man emerged from the boat's interior, momentarily blurred by the wet plastic windows of the wheelhouse. He came into focus in the open doorway, a giant with a boxer's body and a battered face. *Tom.* Joan almost blurted his name aloud.

"There's two of them?" Tom grunted to Jamie.

"Long story." Jamie threw a rope, and Tom caught it easily.

For a moment, sharpness glinted on Tom's face like water catching the light, and then his expression slackened again. Tom was *smart*—Joan had made the mistake of underestimating him last time. Tom had encouraged it.

"I'm Tom," he said to them now.

"Joan. This is Nick."

"Thanks for the rescue," Nick said.

Tom's nod was part acknowledgment, part indication for them to go on inside.

Joan followed Nick onto the boat. The wheelhouse was a tent-like space. The lower half was waist-high wooden walls and soft seats that followed the curve of the boat. The upper half was green canvas with clear plastic windows, wet with river spray.

Tom opened a panel to hit some buttons. The engine kicked on with a loud hum that combined with the wash of water into a white-noise drone. At a gesture from Tom, Nick continued down a short flight of stairs into the boat's interior. Joan hesitated again. *I know you*, she wanted to say to Tom.

She knew him far better than she knew Jamie. In some ways, maybe she knew Tom better than Tom knew himself. She'd seen him in situations that this Tom had never been in—that Joan hoped he'd never be in. She knew what he was like laid bare with grief and desperation.

As she hesitated, Tom growled to her, "Joan, is it?" His voice was pitched lower than the engine, just for the two of them. When Joan nodded, Tom said, "I don't know you, but I know who you are."

"He told you?" Joan said, surprised. Over on the pontoon, Jamie had almost finished untying the second rope. His back was to them, dark head bent over the task. The last time Joan had spoken to him, Jamie had been keeping the other timeline from Tom. *Tom's happy in this timeline*, he'd explained to Joan.

Tom's jaw was a tight line. "He's always had nightmares, but they started getting worse a few years ago. He couldn't keep it from me."

Joan felt a strange surge of jealousy. And then guilt on top of that. It was *good* that Jamie had told Tom about the other time-line. It was *good* that Jamie had someone who loved him, who he could confide in.

"He told me what you did for us," Tom said. "You should know—you'll always have a bed and a meal among the Hathaways. Just say your name."

Joan felt even more guilty then. "You don't owe me, Tom. We helped each other." When she'd unmade Nick, she'd released Jamie from his terrible imprisonment. But she didn't deserve thanks for that. Without Tom and Jamie, her own family would still be dead.

Tom met her eyes, his intelligence unobscured for once. "Go on. Get down to safety," he said. "I have to stay up here and steer."

The boat's interior was wider and brighter than Joan had expected. A soft white love seat stretched along the wall, and there was a diner-style table for meals. The walls were white, with oak trim framing large round windows. Beyond, there was a galley, the cupboards the soft green of new grass. The whole place had a welcoming, homey feeling.

Nick stood in the living room, his back to Joan. Joan took in the lean muscles of his shoulders, his dark hair. He turned at the sound of her entrance, and her heart skipped a beat. Would she ever get used to being near him? To how much he looked like his other self?

"Hey." He looked uncharacteristically awkward. "Seems like your friend was only expecting you." He hesitated. "What did you say to get me on board?"

"Just the truth," Joan said. "That you were in danger. That I wouldn't leave without you."

Nick was silent for a long moment. "Am I making trouble for you? You said that humans aren't supposed to know about all this."

Joan's chest constricted. He looked more concerned about her than himself. "Don't worry about that. I told Jamie you were dragged into this. He knows that we have to keep you safe."

"Joan—"

"I'm not in trouble," Joan assured him. "Jamie and I know each other from way back. You don't have to worry about anything, okay?"

Footsteps sounded. Jamie joined Joan and Nick in the living area. He stopped on the last step and gripped the doorframe. The boat started with a gentle lurch. Through the big windows, the buildings of Queenhithe began to move. They were heading west.

"Did anyone follow us?" Nick asked Jamie.

"We'll know soon," Jamie said. "Can't easily hide a tail on the water." He gestured at the love seat. "Please. Sit. Things get a bit rocky this far up the Thames."

"Where are we going?" Joan asked.

"Somewhere safe," Jamie said. "We can talk when we get there."

Joan wanted to talk now. "Can I get word to my family there? Is it a safe house? Another monster inn?"

"Joan, you sound *exhausted*," Jamie said gently. "Why don't you just rest for a while? You said you'd both been running all night."

Joan opened her mouth to protest, and then registered that Nick had gone very still beside her. He lifted his gaze slowly to Joan's face. With a shot of horror, she realized that she'd said the word *monster* in front of him. *Another monster inn.*

Jamie continued, oblivious: "I'll get some blankets. The boat can be cold if you're not used to it."

Nick hadn't shifted his gaze from Joan. His eyes were piercing. Even in this timeline, he had an aura of charismatic goodness that made Joan think of old-fashioned heroes.

And she was a monster.

Jamie bustled in the galley, opening and closing cupboards. The engine droned. Water sloshed against the sides of the boat. Joan felt as if she'd pulled the pin on a grenade that she'd been holding for days. Her whole body felt tense.

"*Monsters,*" Nick murmured. Joan flinched, although his tone hadn't exactly been hostile. If anything, he seemed curious. "Is that what you call yourselves?"

Joan couldn't breathe. She couldn't even nod. She waited for him to ask the next question—the question she herself had taken sixteen years to ask. *Why do you call yourselves that?*

Jamie returned with two thick gray blankets. A familiar miniature bulldog waddled in with him, yawning.

"Frankie," Joan said shakily, and Frankie blinked at her with bleary eyes. She must have been asleep in the other room.

"Forgot you knew her," Jamie said. "Here." He passed them a blanket each. "I checked from the other deck. Couldn't see anyone following us."

Nick settled into the love seat. Joan hesitated and sat beside him. Frankie's paws scrabbled, and then her heavy weight hit

Joan's lap. She snuffled at Joan's face, and Joan put her arms around her. Nick's big hand appeared, stroking Frankie's soft head.

Jamie leaned against the wall opposite the love seat, posture stiff. Joan could feel his wary tension from here. "Are you hungry?" he asked.

"We just ate," Joan said.

"We're fine," Nick agreed. His big hand was still splayed over Frankie's head, and Frankie seemed to like the weight. She settled onto Joan's lap in a drowsy sprawl. "Your dog's lovely," Nick said.

"She's not usually so comfortable with strangers," Jamie said. His eyes had been on Frankie, but now his gaze lifted to Nick, as if compelled.

Jamie had been obsessed with the hero stories in the other timeline. He'd painted the myths; he'd become a scholar of them. His obsession had led to him being captured. Joan couldn't imagine what he was feeling now.

"I need to help Tom," Jamie said. And Joan wasn't sure if it was an excuse—if he wanted to get away from Nick. "Why don't you both sleep awhile," Jamie suggested. "You'll have some time. We'll be traveling around a bit until that raid's over."

Nick's thumb moved over Frankie's head as Jamie shuttered the windows, giving them some darkness, and then headed back up onto the deck. By the time Jamie was gone, Nick's eyes were closed and his breathing had lengthened and slowed. The movement of the boat was lulling, and Joan wondered if he might already be asleep. He'd told her he was an early riser. He'd likely been up far more than twenty-four hours now.

But as she watched him, his eyes opened again, and he tilted his head to face her. "Do you really call yourselves monsters?" It was the slow drawl of someone near sleep.

Joan imagined telling him the full truth. *Yes. Because that's what we are. We steal human life.* She imagined his reaction. He'd be scared. Horrified. He'd leave the moment the boat stopped. And the next time she saw him, maybe he'd be leading an army.

And now she imagined lying outright. *No, we don't call ourselves that. You misheard.* She dismissed the thought. He wouldn't buy it. For all she knew, someone else had said *monster* in front of him already, at the inn, and she'd missed it.

The silence was beginning to stretch too long. A few more moments, and he'd really get suspicious. "We *do* call ourselves that," Joan admitted. She tried to control her quickening breaths. Now what would he do?

Nick was silent for a long moment. "Why?" he asked sleepily.

Joan tried to make out his face in the dark. She couldn't see much but the outline of his big frame. This was the question she'd really been dreading. The question she herself hadn't asked until it was too late. Her family had always called themselves monsters. But she'd never asked why—not until Gran had told her: *He didn't do something to you. You did something to him.*

Aware again of the lengthening silence, Joan said haltingly, "You've seen how dangerous this world is. How dangerous the people are."

Nick was quiet again, taking that in. In the pause, Joan's heartbeat sounded very loud. She wondered if he could hear it. "I have," he said slowly. "But . . . why *monster*? There are bad people here, but there are good people too. Bad like Corvin, and good like you and Jamie and Tom. And you said Aaron wasn't a bad person really."

Joan's chest felt heavy with guilt. "Nick . . ."

"Is it a word that humans gave you all?" Nick asked.

"What do you mean?"

"Your people have powers," Nick whispered. "You'd seem dangerous to some humans. Maybe even monstrous. But . . ." He shook his head. "Back in that alley, Jamie was scared of *me*. Of being found out." With each word, he sounded sleepier.

He *had* picked up on Jamie's fear. Joan had a flash of the other version of him, the bodies of four monsters lying behind him.

"I think it's a word humans gave you because they were scared of your powers," Nick murmured. "Always about fear in the end."

THIRTEEN

Joan woke to the wash of water and the low drone of an engine. The porthole window framed a slow-moving view of brick buildings with white lattice windows. She'd fallen asleep in darkness, but Jamie must have opened the shutters. Now sharp sunshine glared off glassy water. The white sky had cleared to smears of cloud against blue.

Somewhere outside, raucous laughter rose; dogs barked; someone whistled a cheerful trill. They were nearing a mooring.

Nick breathed steadily beside Joan, still asleep, his head against the cushion, body slanted toward her. Joan felt the echo of his heavy warmth against her side. Had they been pressed together at some point?

Until now, Joan had been forcing her gaze away from him. Had been looking at him in glimpses. Now she let her eyes roam. His body was like a classic sculpture. A young Mars, she thought. The god of war. With his head tilted, the vulnerable underside of his jaw just showed. A sudden sense memory hit Joan—of her mouth *right there*, the prickle of stubble against her lips. Another memory followed fast: the rough pad of his thumb running over her own lower lip.

She sat up and squeezed her eyes shut. That had never happened. She'd never kissed him like that. He'd never touched her like that. It was just a fantasy of her tired mind. Or maybe a lost remnant of the original timeline.

Either way, this was just proof that she needed to be more vigilant about how she looked at him; how she thought about him.

Under her, the cushions shifted as Nick stirred. He breathed in sharply, tensing as he realized he was somewhere unfamiliar. For a second, he was a coiled spring.

"We're on the boat," Joan whispered. "We're safe."

She had expected him to tense more. The word *monster* stood between them now. But to her surprise, he relaxed at the sound of her voice, his shoulders loosening. "Joan," he said, voice gravelly. Her name came out lengthened and soft, like he was murmuring a prayer.

He opened his dark eyes, gaze seeking hers. Joan's stomach flipped over. Asleep, he'd been impossibly handsome, a classical statue. Awake, that football-captain, popular-boy charisma made his looks even more magnetic. For a second, she couldn't pull her eyes from him.

Outside, Tom called out something, and Jamie answered. The view rotated, showing a glassy marina lined with apartment buildings. And then they were drawing up alongside a narrowboat, much smaller than the barge. Like on *Tranquility*, a double-headed hound ran across the side, the painter's hand not as skilled as Jamie's.

"Where are we?" Nick said.

"I think we're with Tom's family—the Hathaways." Beyond that, Joan couldn't guess. The piled-up brick buildings said they were still in London, but the sun seemed too high in the sky for that. They must have slept hours, and it wouldn't have taken that long to get out of the city.

She stood, reaching for the wooden wall by the door for

balance. Her whole body ached. However long she'd slept, it hadn't been enough. Nick took her cue and got to his feet too, his long legs straightening. He stretched, T-shirt riding up to show defined muscles. Joan dragged her eyes to the porthole fast.

"Who's the artist?" Nick nodded at a jar of paintbrushes on the galley bench.

Joan hadn't noticed them. "They must be Jamie's. He grew up in his family's gallery."

"I like his work," Nick said. "I like that." He lifted his eyes to the wall above them.

Where the wall met the ceiling, there was a green feature panel. Joan had taken it in as solid color. But now she saw that it was a detailed illustration: a riverside scene. It ran like a ribbon around the boat, beginning with grazing fields here in the living area, and gradually becoming woodland in the galley, and then wildflowers in a glade. It was beautiful.

Joan followed the green line of fields and woodland. She'd wondered how Jamie could live on the water. He'd been wary of the rain when she'd last seen him—a vestige of his torture. Now, though, on the rocking houseboat, with the outside world visible through every window, Joan saw how far this really was from the stark, windowless cell he'd been kept in last time. Here, Jamie was always connected to the outdoors. Even with his eyes closed, he'd feel it.

"Can I ask you a question?" Nick said.

Joan took a breath. Some part of her had been bracing for it. She'd wanted to be standing for it. She'd said the word *monster* in front of him. He'd come to his own conclusion about it, but he'd been half-asleep at the time. Now, with a clearer mind, he must have been reassessing.

Joan readied herself. In her mind's eye, she saw one of Jamie's paintings. Jamie had been obsessed with the hero myths, and he'd depicted Nick standing outside a town house, poised to kill its occupants. *The hero knocks*, Aaron had said, as if it was a familiar subject of art in the monster world.

"You know . . . ," Nick said softly, "you get this look sometimes." Joan blinked up at him. She didn't know what he meant. "A hunted look," he said. "It's on your face right now. I don't want to be the cause of it."

Joan hadn't realized she was being so transparent. "What did you want to ask me?"

Nick searched her face. "You made that mark on the Portelli window, didn't you?"

Joan felt herself tense even more. That wasn't the question she'd been expecting. "Yes," she admitted. There was no point in lying about that. He'd seen her reaction to the mark. He'd helped her hide it.

Nick hesitated. "It was a power, right? Like the other powers we've seen?"

And suddenly this felt more dangerous than anything he could have asked about monsters. Could he hear her heartbeat? It seemed louder now than the water outside.

I used that power on you, she thought. *I unmade you like I unmade that glass.* The words she could never say echoed in her head. "Yes, it was a power."

"Is that why the Court is after you?" Nick asked. "The people in the gambling room were talking about a girl with a forbidden power. . . ."

Joan swallowed. She thought he'd missed that comment from the gamblers—he'd seemed consumed by the view of the Viking attack. But she should have known by now that he was always paying attention. Especially when it seemed like he wasn't.

"They've come after you before," he said. It wasn't a question. Joan nodded.

Nick's eyes darkened with something dangerous. "Why is it forbidden?" Joan imagined him comparing her power with the Argent and Griffith powers and finding it seemingly innocuous.

I unmade you with it, she thought again. *You used to be someone else.*

The truth was, though, she still knew almost nothing about her power. She didn't understand how it worked or where it had come from. She barely had control of it.

"I don't know," she said. But with a shiver, she remembered again the words she'd overheard in the other timeline. A guard had spoken of Joan in a whisper: *A half-human girl with a strange power. Something* wrong.

Nick was silent for a long moment. "Do your friends know about it?"

Joan bit her lip. "Jamie knows. And I think he told Tom. Other than that . . . only my gran. And now you. And . . . and I guess someone at the Court suspects it. My gran warned me never to tell anyone."

Nick's eyes flashed, the danger deepening. "I wonder how the Court found out."

The danger wasn't directed at her, Joan saw then, in slow realization, but at the people who'd come after her. Guilt gnawed at her. It *should* have been directed at her. She'd upturned his life. And if he knew how she'd last used that power . . .

"That look's still on your face . . . ," he murmured. His voice gentled. "I *promise*, Joan. You never need to be afraid of me. I won't tell anyone about that power. No one will learn about it from me."

Unease roiled in Joan as she ascended the short flight of stairs onto the deck. If Nick ever figured out what she'd done to him . . . who he'd been . . .

Was she endangering everyone here—Nick included—by keeping him with them? She'd told herself that it was safer to stick together while they were being hunted by the Court, but was that true? She had another flash of Jamie's painting—of the hero standing outside a monster house, ready to kill everyone inside. It seemed disturbingly prescient suddenly. Nick was in a monster house right now—this boat was Tom and Jamie's house.

She emerged to bright light and unimpeded sky. Someone had taken down the canvas walls, transforming the wheelhouse into an extended deck. Joan saw Tom first, working the steering, looking over his big shoulder as he backed up into the mooring space. And then Frankie, snoozing on the padded seat at the boat's nose; she'd found a sunbeam, and she lay with her white belly up, snoring, apparently unbothered by the shudders of the boat.

"Oh good, you're awake," Jamie called to Joan from a pontoon. He pulled at a guide rope. "We're here."

Joan shifted so that Nick could come up too. Where was *here*?

They were in a big marina full of boats—dozens of them: sailboats, speedboats, narrowboats, barges—bright in the afternoon sun. The closest boats were all Hathaway: barges and narrowboats with double-headed hounds on flags and in paint.

"This is Limehouse," Nick said, looking around. "We're not far from where we started."

"The Hathaways still call it the Regent's Canal Dock," Tom said, "but yeah. Had to play keep-away from the guards for hours. We were down in Putney for a while. Came back up here after the raid cleared. You two slept right through it. Even slept through the lock."

Joan shaded her eyes from the water's glare. The Hathaway sprawl was on the walkway too. Muscled figures sat on deck chairs, their animals snoozing and running around chasing seagulls.

Joan did a double take at a familiar figure at the edge of the Hathaway group; a familiar cloud of dark hair. Her heart slammed in her chest. "Ruth!" she shouted.

"*Careful*," Jamie said as he realized her intention. "I'm still tying up!"

But Joan couldn't wait. She jumped to the pontoon and ran. "Ruth!"

Ruth met Joan halfway up the pier, and Joan threw her arms around her, staggering, legs still wobbly from the boat. Ruth squeezed her back hard.

"You're here!" Ruth said hoarsely. "I couldn't believe it when I heard!" She bent her head, mouth muffled against Joan's shoulder. "What *happened*? You disappeared off the face of the earth! And then out of the blue, I get word from Edith Nowak that you'd shown up in this period at the *Wyvern Inn.*"

Joan was getting choked up already. "Long story."

Ruth pushed her back, scanning her, and Joan took the opportunity to look at Ruth too. She was in a black blazer and slim trousers—in the tight cut of this time. Her slash of red lipstick was more crimson than Joan was used to. Other than that, though, she seemed her ordinary self.

"What *happened*?" Ruth said again. "Gran thought you'd been taken by the Court!"

"A bunch of Court Guards came after me at work," Joan said. "They—They killed my friend Margie." She heard her voice shake. "And I guess I'm a fugitive now. They put a mark on my wrist."

Ruth pulled Joan back in at that, arms tight around her. "How did you get away? How did you find the Wyvern Inn? I heard you had a *human* with you." The word *human* was a whisper, like she was saying something scandalous. "That you took him into a monster inn."

"Nick was in the bakery when they attacked," Joan explained. "They tried to kill him too, but we escaped together. And the rest of it . . . It's a really long story." Too long for a rushed conversation on the pier, and she could hear the others approaching. She bunched her thumb and fingertips together in a hollow fist, and then flattened her hand. A Hunt hand signal: *later.*

Ruth's forehead creased. Joan could tell she wasn't satisfied, but she made the same signal in affirmation.

Joan turned to greet the others. "My cousin Ruth," she said, introducing her to them.

"Hi," Nick said amiably. "I'm Nick."

Ruth took him in—his square-jawed movie-star face, the muscles under his T-shirt. Her eyebrows went up. "Joan saved *you* from an attack?"

"He saved *me*," Joan said.

Ruth's guarded interest shifted to something far more serious at that. "He saved your life? Well, then our family owes him a debt."

Nick reddened slightly. "We saved each other."

Ruth gave him a long, thoughtful look. Then she turned to the others. "And you're the other rescuers?"

"Tom and Jamie," Tom said.

"And Frankie under Tom's arm." Jamie tilted his head. "And you're the infamous Ruth Hunt. Bane of the Liu houses." It was so straight-faced that Joan wasn't sure if he was joking.

It was Ruth's turn to flush, but Tom chuckled. "What did you do?" he asked Ruth. "Steal from them?"

"I would *never*—" Ruth started.

"A lot of times," Jamie said. "You know, you're technically banned from Liu houses. I don't know if we can take you to the safe house."

"Seriously?" Ruth said. Joan still couldn't tell if Jamie was joking either.

"I was banned from their houses for a while." Tom's tone was nostalgic. "Don't worry. They'll forgive you. They're all soft touches, the Lius." He glanced over at Jamie, and Jamie's straight-faced facade cracked into a twinkle.

Frankie wriggled in Tom's arms, and he bent to release her.

As soon as she was down, she shot along the pier to where the Hathaways were set up with their card tables. A black cat trotted up to greet her.

"Come on," Jamie said, starting to walk.

"Where are we going?" Joan said. "What's this safe house?"

"It's a place up ahead on shared Liu and Hathaway territory," Tom explained.

Joan took that in with puzzlement. "I thought Liu territory was up near Covent Garden."

"It is," Jamie said. He drew a lopsided shape in the air that Joan guessed was meant to show the territory. "The main Liu house used to be on Narrow Street. This is London's original Chinatown."

"Used to be *bustling* here," Tom said. "Big boats with cargo and passengers. Felt like the center of the world for a while."

It was pretty bustling now. Jamie led them around the marina, past half a dozen *Keep This Path Clear* signs. The Hathaways had ignored them; the walkway was full of deck chairs and card tables. Fresh fish and tomatoes and buttered bread sizzled and spat on portable grills. A white-haired man chopped parsley on a board. There were animals everywhere. Cheerful dogs jumped from deck to deck, nosing at snoozing cats. A sleek rat slept in a man's pocket, and a bright bird sat on the top of a Hathaway flag and trilled. There was even a large snake curled snugly around a boat's chimney.

Joan fell into step beside Ruth. Ahead, Tom and Jamie walked with Nick. Frankie bounced around Nick's ankles, and he bent to touch her soft head. "She's not a puppy," Tom said over the cheerful noise of the Hathaways—apparently answering a question from Nick. "She's a toy bulldog—an extinct nineteenth-century breed." Nick seemed fascinated.

They passed a woman standing on the roof of a narrowboat, mopping around a sleeping cat with mottled orange-and-black fur. She whistled a short phrase, high enough to cut through the cacophony on the walkway. The string of seven notes was full of sharps and oddly unmusical.

A few boats up, a big man with a heavy brown beard sat on his deck. He would have been intimidating, but as Joan watched, a cheerful-looking black dog trotted out from the interior and settled so that the man could lovingly brush its woolly fur. Without stopping his task, the man repeated the woman's unmelodic whistle.

And now the tune jumped across the walkway to a group of people chatting under an umbrella. They stopped their talking just long enough to echo the whistle in a mismatched chorus.

"It's a language," Ruth said before Joan could ask, "but not a complicated one. They'll just be saying that there are strangers coming in with Tom and Jamie."

"A language like the Hunt hand signals?" Joan asked. Did all families have a secret language?

"Yeah, but ours is better," Ruth said so seriously that Joan had to bite back a smile. Apparently, the rivalry between monster families extended into every corner of their lives.

Up ahead, the others had pulled out of earshot with their longer strides. Joan watched Frankie dart under a card table to investigate a morsel of dropped food. She darted back out again, a bit of buttered bread in her mouth.

"Hey . . . ," Joan said to Ruth tentatively. Part of her was afraid to ask, and part of her wanted to know desperately. "How's my dad?"

Ruth's eyes went soft. "He's okay. Gran told him some of the truth."

"She told him about monsters?" Joan said, shocked.

"Not all of it; just enough to explain what happened to you." Ruth took Joan's hand and squeezed. "He was trying so hard to find you himself—to start this big campaign in the media. She had to tell him to keep you both safe."

Joan took a shaky breath, near tears suddenly.

"I can tell him you're alive," Ruth said, "but you can't go see him; you can't talk to him. You're a fugitive—we can't risk it. We can't risk *him*."

Joan knew it, but she couldn't bear it. "How is he actually?"

"He's sad," Ruth said honestly, and Joan swallowed hard. "He's doing okay. He's still in the same house. He met someone last year—Elsa. She moved in with him last spring."

The thought was so strange—Dad with a woman Joan had never met. A woman named Elsa living in their house. It was hard to imagine Dad living six years of life when Joan had only seen him yesterday.

"She's nice," Ruth said. "She's a music teacher. She's teaching him to play the piano."

And that was hard to imagine too. "I want to talk to him," Joan whispered.

"Joan . . ."

"I know," Joan said. She closed her eyes for a moment. Ruth squeezed her hand again. "I know I can't. Thank you for keeping an eye on him. Thank you for keeping him safe."

"Don't be stupid," Ruth said. "He's our family like you are."

"What about the others?" Joan managed. "Is everyone okay?"

"They're not in this time."

"Just you here?" Joan said, surprised.

"We've been trying to find you," Ruth said simply. "Everyone's been chasing up different leads."

Joan's throat felt tight. She loved the Hunts so much, and they'd shown her how much they loved her back at every turn. They'd died trying to help her last time. She'd have died herself to bring them back.

"I'm so sorry I ghosted you all when I got home last summer," she whispered to Ruth. She'd left the Hunts' messages unanswered.

Ruth poked Joan's foot with hers—her most annoying habit from when they were little. She poked her again and then again, until Joan poked her back. "Stop it," she told Ruth, but she couldn't help but smile a little.

"I know why you didn't want to talk," Ruth said softly. "You found out we were monsters. You couldn't bear it."

"Ruth . . ."

"Don't look at me like that," Ruth said. "You don't even cheat at cards, and then you find out you're an actual monster. Course you didn't message me back. You didn't want it to be true." Her green eyes were just like Gran's—just like the photos of Mum. "You were so sick after you found out. Bertie kept saying that your body was rejecting the monster part of itself. You were sick for weeks. And then after that, you didn't want to talk about any of it."

Joan shook her head. She could see why Ruth would think that, but, in reality, Joan had burned herself out when she'd unmade Nick. That was what had made her sick.

Ruth was right about one thing, though. Joan hadn't wanted any of it to be true. She still didn't want it to be. Some part of her wished she'd never found out about this world; that she could somehow forget that she and the Hunts were monsters.

Jamie led them to a building that reminded Joan of a car repair shop. A roller door gaped wide, and inside there was a half-gutted boat with faded green paint. A muscled Hathaway woman was working on it, sleeves rolled up, wrench in hand. A black raven sat on her shoulder, watching interestedly.

"Hey, Sal," Jamie said, and she nodded, lifting the wrench in greeting.

It wasn't only a Hathaway place. Half-finished paintings lay propped against one wall, oils drying. A paint-spotted sheet was neatly folded under a bare easel. The place seemed part workshop, part studio. Part Hathaway, part Liu.

"Hathaways and Lius live here together?" Joan asked Jamie.

"We both have rooms here," Jamie said. "Although, to be honest, the Hathaways prefer their boats to beds on land. No one lives here permanently, though. It's . . ." He thought. "The Lius and Hathaways are allies, and this is one of the places where we meet. There's not really an equivalent in the human world." He lifted another roller door. "Just through here."

He showed them to a comfortable-looking break room that reminded Joan of the *Tranquility*'s interior—although larger. The kitchenette was galley-like, lining both walls here at the front. White sofas and soft single chairs were set up beyond it.

Filtered afternoon light spilled in from big round windows on the left-hand wall. Outside, wildflowers grew untamed in a garden that ended in thick ash trees and glimpses of what Joan thought at first was a road until she saw the slow movement of water and a moored narrowboat rocking gently. It was a canal.

In the galley, a slender Liu and a big Hathaway washed a heavy frying pan and stacked a dishwasher. Joan guessed that there'd just been a communal lunch; she could faintly smell fried fish and ginger.

Beyond, in the sitting area, about twenty people chatted and sketched and played on their phones—Lius with phoenix tattoos and Hathaways with cats and dogs on their laps.

It felt safe here. The atmosphere was relaxed—somewhere between the walled garden of the Liu compound and life on a boat.

Even as Joan thought that, though, the mood was punctured. One of the Lius caught sight of Nick and froze mid-conversation, shocked. And now the soft buzz of chatter slowed and stuttered as, one by one, more Lius noticed him.

Joan's stomach lurched. They knew who Nick was.

She should have guessed this would happen. Some of the Lius remembered previous timelines; of course they would have shared information about Nick with the rest of the family.

And the Hathaways were reacting now too—cued by the Lius. Big muscles bunched and jaws tightened. Heavy hands curled into protective fists.

In the silence, a boy of about eighteen got slowly to his feet. He had Chinese features and the same rugby-player heft as Tom. Joan wondered if one of his parents was a Hathaway. He was a Liu, though, in power—a tattoo of the Lius' multicolored phoenix was curled around one hulking arm.

Jamie lifted his hands slowly. "Liam, I can explain."

Liam said disbelievingly, "*Explain?* What's there to explain?" He pointed a shaky finger at Nick. "What's that *thing* doing here?"

"Don't call him that!" Joan blurted. "He's not a *thing*!" She felt really sick now. What had she been *thinking* bringing Nick here?

To Joan's alarm, Nick stepped forward to address Liam. "You're worried because I'm human," he said seriously in his deep rumble. Joan swallowed hard. He didn't know why they were actually concerned. "You don't have to be scared, I swear. I'll never tell anyone about this world. You don't need to worry about humans finding out from me."

"*Humans finding out?*" Liam repeated, incredulous.

Nick tilted his head. Had he understood the unspoken question in Liam's words: *You think that's what we're afraid of?* Or had he seen what Joan had seen: the Lius flinching and drawing back as Nick had spoken.

"You brought him to us?" Liam said to Jamie. His voice was shaking now. "To our *allies*? What the *hell*, Jamie?"

"Watch your tone," Tom growled, protective. He was frowning, though, with confusion. It seemed Jamie hadn't told him about

Nick yet. Tom didn't understand why the Lius were reacting like this to a human in their presence.

"Listen." Joan held up her hands. Was this about to turn violent? "*I* asked Jamie to bring him here, but that was clearly a mistake. I'm sorry. We're going to leave right now."

"No." It was a new voice. A woman stood, rising from the group. Whoever she was, she garnered respect from both the Hathaways and the Lius. The room hushed in an instant. "You can stay," she said to Joan.

She was around thirty years old, Joan estimated, tall and Black, with narrow eyes. Standing, she had the straight-backed posture of a ballerina.

It took a long, long moment for Joan to place her; she'd been younger when Joan had known her. Then recognition hit, along with a vivid memory of the bee-sting pain of a needle. Of waking in a cell. Joan's breath stopped. Her heart stopped.

"Astrid?"

What was Astrid doing here? She and Joan had been friends last time—until Astrid had revealed herself to be one of Nick's people. His right hand. When Joan had returned to Holland House, Astrid had captured her and thrown her into a cell.

Now, fear numbed Joan's hands, her feet. She stared between Astrid and Nick. They'd fought side by side last time. Were they in this together again? Had all this been a plan to infiltrate the monster world? Were they about to kill everyone in this room?

And suddenly this place didn't seem cozy; it seemed too small, too enclosed. An ideal location for a massacre.

But the gaze Nick returned remained guileless.

"You remembered me," Astrid said to Joan. "I wasn't sure you would."

And now confusion began to seep into Joan's fear. How could Astrid be here? Astrid was *human*. Joan had met her as a volunteer at Holland House, and—like Nick—Astrid had turned out to be a monster slayer.

"How do you know my cousin?" Jamie said to Joan slowly.

"Your *cousin*?" Joan felt her mouth drop open. At Holland House, Astrid had gone by Astrid Chen. Now, Joan felt out a new name. "Astrid Liu?"

"Yes, Joan," Astrid said with weighted patience, as if she'd expected Joan to have been quicker on the uptake. She addressed the others. "Find rooms for them. While you do that, Joan and I are going to talk."

Joan glanced back at Nick. He looked bewildered. He didn't know Astrid any more than he'd known Joan.

"How do you know my cousin?" Jamie whispered to Joan again. "She's an important person—a future head of family."

A head of family? Joan shook her head slightly, trying to take that in too. What was going *on* here? Why would a head of the Liu family have fought on Nick's side last time? It didn't make sense. Why did she want to talk to Joan now?

"It's all right, Joan," Astrid said. "No harm will come to any of you here. You have my word."

"Define harm," Joan said.

The corners of Astrid's eyes creased, although her mouth didn't move. Joan was reminded of the way Ying Liu smiled. Astrid raised her voice. "Clear the room, please."

The Lius took it as an order. They got to their feet, and the Hathaways followed suit, calling to their animals. Dogs and cats uncurled from sleep; birds fluttered to shoulders. Then people shuffled out—some heading to the boats; some to a door at the east end of the room.

Only Jamie and Tom hesitated.

"Shouldn't we stay together?" Ruth whispered.

Astrid's phrasing had been clear enough: *No harm will come to any of you here.* Monsters took promises like that seriously.

"It's okay," Joan said. She had to find out what was going on here. "Go and find those rooms. I'll come and look for you afterward."

"We'll be upstairs," Jamie said. "The Liu rooms are on the right."

Joan nodded. She made a quick sign for Ruth: pointing her thumb toward Nick and then crossing her forefinger over it. *Watch over him.* Promises or not, she didn't like the way the Lius had looked at him. And Nick didn't even know enough to be afraid of them.

Ruth nodded slightly to show she'd registered it. "I'm really going to need that long story soon, though," she murmured.

The room emptied. Joan stared at Astrid. She could see the Liu family resemblance now, in Astrid's straight-backed posture—Ying and Jamie had the same slight air of formality.

When everyone else was gone, Joan found her voice again. "You fought alongside Nick." She couldn't believe it. "You—" And then she was so angry suddenly that she could hardly speak. "You helped him kill my *family*." Her voice cracked with emotion. "You killed all those people! How *could* you when you're a monster? You're one of us!"

"One of who?" Astrid said. "I'm no more monster than you; and no more human. We just made different choices."

Joan stared at her. She was half-human like Joan? "But . . ."

"Come on," Astrid said. "I'll get you some tea, and I'll tell you exactly how much you fucked everything up."

FOURTEEN

Astrid went to the galley kitchen and opened a cupboard, revealing tins and cardboard boxes of tea, colorful as paints on a palette: red canisters with Chinese characters, fancy Fortnum blues, and big boxes of PG Tips and Yorkshire blend. Astrid selected a pale yellow tin. "You like ginger, right?" She spooned tea into a silver pot, and then filled the pot from a hot-water urn. Ginger and lemongrass scented the air in a slow diffusion.

Astrid had been a fencer in the other timeline. At Holland House, she'd taught tourists how to fight with foam swords. She still looked capable of fighting—she was lean and poised in her black trousers and black blazer. She opened another cupboard and took down a novelty ceramic jar—a red-and-white boat. It opened with a scrape. "Only orange creams left." Astrid wrinkled her nose. "What's even the point of them if no one eats them?"

Anger hit Joan again—it kept coming back. Why was Astrid fussing about biscuits and tea? "We hung out for *weeks* at Holland House!" They'd volunteered there together. They'd bonded over having Chinese fathers. They'd had inside jokes. Joan had told Astrid about her quirky London family. And all that time, Astrid had been plotting with Nick to kill that family.

"I remember," Astrid said. In the other timeline she'd always been animated—whether laughing or glowering or rolling her eyes, her expression had filled her whole face. Now, though, she seemed dialed down. Joan had no idea what she was feeling.

Joan took a few steps toward her. Her own emotions were all over the place. "Were you there that night?" She wanted to yell it—to have Astrid yell back. Joan's family had *died*. She needed an explanation. "*I* was. I was there when my gran died!" She could almost feel Gran's blood all over her again, weighing down her dress, smearing her hands, the butcher's shop smell of it thick in the air. She could hear her breath coming faster. "My cousin Bertie died. My aunt Ada. My uncle Gus."

"I'm sorry." Astrid met Joan's gaze, clear-eyed. "I'm sorry you went through that."

"You're *sorry*? You *killed* people! You helped him kill my family!"

"I *wasn't* there that night. I fought with him sometimes, but not that night."

Air hissed out from Joan's lungs, the wind punched out of her. "But you helped him. You were on his side last time."

"I helped him," Astrid agreed. "I fought with him." She anticipated Joan's next question. "The Lius don't know I was on his side."

"*Why?*" Joan couldn't understand it. "God, Astrid. How *could* you? He was *slaughtering* people!"

To her frustration, Astrid just poured tea into two little cups, one finger on the pot's lid. Steam rose, misting spots on the window. As she bent, her face shadowed, making her look younger—more like the Astrid Joan had once known. "How could I fight monsters—my own people?" Astrid said. "I don't know, Joan. How could you fight your own people?"

"I—" Joan stumbled at Astrid's phrasing. Joan hadn't fought against humans. She'd only fought Nick. "I didn't."

"So you haven't noticed the missing humans yet?"

It was Joan's turn to pause. The room seemed very quiet suddenly, the only sound the low machine hum of the fridge. "Missing?"

"People are missing from this timeline—people who were here last time."

"I don't know what you mean." But Mr. Larch's kind, round face had already flown into Joan's mind. He'd been missing from her school since the start of term. Margie hadn't even known who he was. *There's a Mr. Larch Reading Garden behind the library*, Margie had said. *Some teacher who died ten years ago. Is that what you mean?*

"Come on, Joan," Astrid said, with a little of her old impatience. "What do you think happened to them?"

Mr. Larch must have moved to another town over the summer break. He must have been teaching at another school. He had to be. "I . . ." *I don't know*, Joan wanted to say.

It wasn't just Mr. Larch, though. On her last days in London, Joan had noticed other faces absent in Gran's neighborhood: a girl who'd worked at the supermarket checkout; the panhandler outside the Tube station; the neighbor who'd always walked his poodle in the afternoon. She hadn't thought much of it at the time—people's routines changed. But now, she wondered . . . *What do you think happened to them?*

Joan shook her head, but her stomach spasmed painfully out of nowhere—like she was about to be sick. Like her body was starting to understand a truth too big for her mind to hold.

Astrid held up a cup. Joan hesitated. Astrid had drugged her last time. But she didn't get the feeling that any harm was intended now. Astrid was projecting something closer to a truce.

The cup was hot enough that Joan had to hold it by the rim. She blinked down at the chrysanthemum pattern. It was the kind of cheap blue-and-white cup you could get at any Chinese grocery—Dad had them at home.

"Where do you think they are?" Astrid's voice seemed gentler.

"I don't know."

"Yes, you do."

Joan shook her head again.

"Humans had a protector," Astrid said. "A hero. And you unmade him. You undid every action he'd ever done; would have ever done. Did you think there'd be no consequences?"

"I . . ." *I wasn't fighting against anyone except Nick*, Joan wanted to say. But where was Mr. Larch? Where were all the missing people? Joan's body spasmed again. It already knew. *Joan* knew. Deep down, she'd known the truth as soon as Margie had said, *Who's Mr. Larch?*

And suddenly Joan's hand was shaking too much to hold the cup. She put it on the counter, spilling tea on the dark wood.

Mr. Larch wasn't missing. He wasn't at another school. He was dead in this timeline. Monsters preyed on humans—they shortened human lives; sometimes they killed them outright. *You undid every action he'd ever done.* Joan had brought back every monster Nick had ever killed. How many humans had *they* killed?

"It's complicated for us, isn't it?" Astrid said. "We have human family on one side; monsters on the other. We're human and monster ourselves. If we fight *for* one side, that means fighting *against* the other. Our choices aren't clean or clear."

When Joan had unmade Nick, she'd thought she was making a choice between him and her family—her monster family. She hadn't been thinking about her human family, her friends, strangers. All the people he would have protected. She *should* have been thinking about them. Guilt washed over her. She couldn't justify it.

You fucked everything up, Astrid had said.

"You chose humans?" Joan whispered. "You went the other way?" She felt something on her face and touched her cheek. Her fingertips came away wet. Was she crying? How many people were dead in this timeline? How many people had Nick saved? It was too big—too terrible—to take in.

"No," Astrid said.

It took a second for Joan to hear it. "What?"

Astrid was looking out the window. Outside, the lawn was overgrown; pink and yellow daisies sprinkled the long grass all the way to the water. "No, I didn't choose humans *or* monsters," she said. The flatness was still there, but there was a thread of emotion underneath now. She *did* still feel things, Joan saw then. Astrid's flatness was a thin cover over something roiling and deep. "That wasn't why I fought with him."

You fucked everything up.

Dread started in Joan's chest, joining the thick feeling of guilt. Astrid was looking at that view like it was something precious and ephemeral. Like it was something that could be lost. Like there might be a fate worse than Nick's massacres of monsters;

than the loss of all those humans he'd saved.

Astrid sat down on a stool, her own cup clasped in her lap. The stools had been built for the giant Hathaways, but Astrid was tall enough that her long legs reached the floor.

"The Lius have perfect memory," Astrid said slowly. "And some of us have a stronger power than that. Some of us remember fragments of previous timelines. But there's a stronger version still. Only a handful of Lius have ever possessed it." Astrid didn't look proud of it; she looked as sick as Joan felt. Astrid took a shaky breath, and suddenly the emotion she'd been containing was all over her face. It was horror, Joan saw. Horror and fear. "We remember things that haven't happened yet," Astrid said. "And I've seen—" Her voice failed her. She tried again. "I've seen what's coming."

The hairs rose on the back of Joan's neck. "What do you mean?" Astrid seemed much older suddenly; resigned and weary. Her horror was weary too, and matter-of-fact. Joan had a vision of her as a soldier who'd fought hard and lost.

"I've seen the end," Astrid said simply. "The end of everything that matters. People will die. People on both sides—monsters and humans in uncountable numbers. *So* many more than he ever killed or saved. You want to know why I fought with him? It's because I saw how to stop it. *He* would have stopped it. He was already on the path." Her hands curled into fists. "But you stopped *him*."

"What are you talking about?" Joan whispered. "What's going to happen? *What's* coming?"

Astrid's gaze in return was strangely defeated, and Joan felt a wave of frustration.

"Well, *tell* me," Joan said. "Is it in the records? *What* would he have stopped? *When?*"

"What do you want me to say? That you need to step into his shoes and be the hero yourself? Or maybe we could work together. You and me. Stop the apocalypse together. Rally the troops."

"If you really believe something's going to happen . . . something *he* would have stopped—"

A blaze of emotion overcame Astrid, and for a second she was *here*—the Astrid that Joan remembered, full of life. "I *know* it! I've *seen* it! And I just—" Self-recrimination flashed over her face. "I knew we had to eliminate you. I told Nick that you were dangerous—even in that room, all by yourself. I told him we had to kill you, but he wouldn't let anyone touch you."

Joan swallowed. She hadn't known that Nick had protected her like that. And then her frustration was anger again. What did all this *mean*? *The end of everything that matters?* "You didn't tell *me* any of this!" she said hoarsely. "You didn't even tell me you were a monster! I would have—"

"You would have *what*?" Astrid said. "Made a different decision at the end?"

Joan paused at that. Deep down, she knew the truth. She would have done anything to save her family last time. It had been her single focus. Being warned about some nebulous terrible future wouldn't have stopped her. Being hit by a bus wouldn't have stopped her. She started to follow the rest of that train of thought. If she'd known about Mr. Larch and the other missing people . . . But that wasn't a question she could bear asking herself. She was afraid of her own answer. "My family was dead." Her chest felt so tight.

"They were dead," Astrid echoed. "And now the hero is dead in their place." Her mouth twisted. "I should have killed you myself." She saw Joan flinch. "Oh, don't worry. There's no point in any of that now."

Joan should have felt more afraid of her, she supposed. She didn't, though. Astrid seemed defeated. And that alone was unlike the competitive fencer she'd been in the other timeline. At Holland House, she'd demonstrated historical fighting styles for the tourists, and even in the exhibition matches—even when it hadn't mattered—she'd always fought to win. "Why do you keep *talking* like that?" Joan said.

"Like what?"

"Saying things like *there's no point.* Whatever you're afraid of, it hasn't even happened yet!"

"You sound like your grandmother." Astrid sounded tired. "She thought she could stop it without him too. But it's inevitable now."

Gran knew about this? Joan opened her mouth to ask, but Astrid was still talking.

"You ever seen two chess masters play?" Astrid said. "They never actually finish the game. Partway through, they both see the outcome. They stop playing, they shake hands, and they leave. What's the point in going through the motions when you know how the game will end?"

"Nothing's inevitable," Joan said. "I've changed the timeline before. My power—"

"Your *power*?" Another blaze of emotion from Astrid. "God, Joan, you really don't know anything, do you." She felt in her pocket and withdrew what looked like a simple business card: thick white paper with a blue bird printed in one corner. Someone had written on the card in pen: 5. 4. "You don't believe me yet," she said. "Not really. But you will soon enough. And when you do, you're going to want my help."

What *was* that card? Joan had seen numbers crossed out like that before—but where? The memory came to her. Aaron had given her a brooch with numbers scratched onto the back. It had been a travel token—an object with time embedded into it. "Wait!" Joan said, realizing Astrid's intention—she was going to travel in time. "You can't leave!"

Astrid had already turned. "When it starts, don't come and find me," she said. "I already fought this fight. I don't need to play the end game." She started to walk, vanishing mid-step, leaving Joan alone in the galley.

FIFTEEN

Joan gripped the counter, staring down at the teapot, its steam still curling. Could Astrid have been telling the truth? *Could* something terrible be coming?

In the mundane surroundings of the kitchen, the warning seemed surreal. And as for the rest of the conversation . . . Guilt sat in Joan's chest, heavy as lead. Mr. Larch should still have been alive; he *would* have been alive if not for her. How many other people were dead in this timeline because she'd wanted her family back?

Barely aware of moving, Joan found herself heading in the direction the others had gone. The next room was an empty sitting area—a gallery-like space with eclectic art: a cartoon sketch of a basset hound, a watercolor of a busy marina, an oil painting of the canal outside. The mix of art styles should have been chaotic, but the room felt pleasantly serene. And that was surreal too—to be in this tranquil space with such churning thoughts.

People are missing from this timeline. Where do you think they are?

It's complicated for us, isn't it? Our choices aren't clean or clear.

At the end of the room, there was a staircase. Joan stood at the foot of it, gripping the banister. She felt so sick. She'd undone Nick's massacres of monsters; and now humans were dead. If she could somehow reverse it, then monsters would be dead again in their place—her own family included. It was an equation where every solution was unbearable.

Astrid's words came back to her. *I didn't choose humans or monsters.*

Joan swallowed around the lump in her throat. Choosing her family over Nick had caused humans to die, but if Astrid was right, the consequences were only just starting. *People will die,* Astrid had said. *People on both sides.* So *many more than he ever killed or saved.*

Could Astrid be right? Could something terrible be coming—something Nick would have stopped? Would Joan be responsible for something worse than the human deaths she'd already caused?

Joan blinked down at her hand on the banister. *What do you want me to say? That you need to step into his shoes and be the hero yourself? There's no point in any of that now.* But if Nick could have stopped this thing, then surely someone else could stop it too. And Joan had changed the timeline before. . . .

Truth was, though, she'd only used her power once intentionally—on Nick. Every other time, it had come out without her volition. When Gran had died, Joan had accidentally transformed a gold necklace back to ore; when she'd been locked out at Whitehall Palace, she'd slammed her hand on the keyhole and it reverted in the same way.

Now, she shifted her grip so that she was touching the satiny varnish of the banister with just a fingertip. She wasn't even sure how it worked. All she knew was that it was a power of unmaking and that the Court considered it to be forbidden.

She took a deep breath and concentrated. Around her, the timeline felt like a slight resistance, like the gentle press of a breeze. Joan concentrated harder. There was a flicker of energy inside her that hadn't been there last night. Joan imagined the wood under her fingertip becoming supple and green, scabbing over with bark. *Unmake yourself,* she told it.

Nothing happened.

Revert, Joan told the wood. *Turn back the clock on yourself.*

"You just going to stand there?" someone said impatiently.

Joan startled, jerking her head up.

A boy of about eighteen stood above her, on the stairs. His hair was ash blond—almost gray toned—and it made a curtain around angular features and a soft mouth. Joan would have said that his eyes were his most striking feature—they reminded her of Gran's: bright green and hard as emerald—but then she saw his tattoo. The black lines were stark against his pale forearm: the withered branches of a burnt tree.

He was a member of the Argent family—like the man who'd ordered that Nick be still, as if Nick had been a dog.

The boy followed her gaze to the tattoo. "What's wrong?" he said. His eyes widened in a dramatic mimicry of horror. He was mocking her own expression, Joan realized. "Don't like Argents?" He bent so that he was looking right into Joan's eyes. "Are you afraid of me?" His expression shifted to unexpectedly sincere. "I think you are. I think you're so scared of me, you need to run from this room."

"What?" Joan blinked at him, confused now. She wasn't afraid of him. Disgusted by the Argent power, yes. Afraid, no.

The boy broke into a grin. "You know," he said, "I've always wondered if the Argent power would work on a half-human. Guess it only works on full ones."

"You tried to use your power on me?" Joan said. She hadn't felt a hint of compulsion, but the thought of being under this boy's control made her stomach roll. "That's *sick*," she said. "You shouldn't use that power on anyone!"

"Oh, okay," the boy said. He touched his forehead in a lazy salute. Then he pushed past her on the stairs and sauntered around the corner, out of sight.

Joan stared after him, shaken. Why was he even here? Wasn't this a Hathaway and Liu place?

And suddenly, she didn't want to be standing here alone, when the Argent boy could come back into the room. She had to get to the others. She turned to the stairs. As she did, a pale mark on the banister caught her eye. Was it a shard of sunlight? Joan placed her fingertip to the mark; it fit perfectly. She ran it back and forth—smooth varnish, then rough wood, then smooth varnish again.

Had she done that? Joan stared at the mark. Had she stripped away the varnish, leaving bare, untreated wood? As if in answer, she felt her power flicker inside her like a fanned flame. It was still faint, but it seemed a little stronger than before.

The floor above showed the bones of a warehouse conversion. On the ground floor, the walls had been plastered, but here, everything was exposed. Unpainted wooden beams ran crisscross along the ceiling and raw brick showed.

Joan walked along the wide corridor until she reached a door with a taped paper sign: *We're in here.* Inside, there was a small apartment with a homey living area. The mismatched sofas and hand-knitted throws reminded Joan of the main Liu house. She spotted Ruth and Nick on a balcony overlooking the canal. From this distance, their hair was the same near-black—Ruth's curly, Nick's straight.

A few months ago, Joan would have been terrified by the sight of them together; she'd have assumed that Nick was here to kill Ruth. And maybe Ruth would have gotten in a lucky shot and killed *him*.

"Hey, there you are!" Ruth called to Joan. She leaned over to push open the sliding door. "Come sit with us!"

Joan walked over. Outside, the building looked even more like a warehouse. Faded white paint on the outer wall hinted at old signage. The balcony itself was an add-on, its blue rails a bright modern contrast to the aged brown brick.

"Tom and Jamie aren't here?" Joan said as Ruth shuffled over so that she could take the seat between them.

"They're grabbing some food," Nick said. "Should be back soon."

"And you two . . . ," Joan said tentatively. "You've been all right together?" Ruth and Aaron had hated each other. And as for Ruth and Nick . . . They'd never actually met. Ruth had been stabbed by one of Nick's people—that was as close as they'd gotten.

Nick's mouth tugged up. "She knows everything about my life now." He didn't seem to mind that. "And she told me some stories about you growing up."

"What stories?" Joan said warily.

"Only the funny ones," Ruth said, waving a hand in a way that didn't reassure Joan at all. She sat up straighter. "I just remembered another one!" she said to Nick. "She tried to make a carrot night-light!"

"A what?" Nick said.

"Caught her trying to stick a carrot into a light socket one night. Because Gran told her carrots help you see in the dark!"

"I was *four*," Joan protested.

"That's practically scientific for a four-year-old," Nick assured her, but he bit at his own smile.

Joan opened her mouth, and then could only look between them. It was the kind of conversation she'd had a million times before—with friends, with family—but she'd never imagined Nick having an ordinary chat with any of the Hunts. Had the true timeline been like this, she wondered with a flare of yearning. Had both sides gotten along?

It struck Joan that she herself could never have been happy without the Hunts in her life. Had the original Joan lied to Nick about the truth of monsters too? No. Her remnant feelings were too pure; she'd trusted him completely. Joan supposed she must have lived in ignorant bliss. To have been happy like that, she must never have known what she was, and Nick must never have known either.

In the main room, a cheerful clatter indicated that Jamie and Tom were back. "Hiya!" Tom called. Under one arm, he held Frankie; under the other, the biggest parcel of fish and chips Joan had ever seen.

Jamie swerved to a cupboard at the corner of the room. He retrieved some plates. "Chopsticks or forks?" he called.

"Just fingers!" Ruth yelled back, and Jamie shot her a look.

Tom chuckled as he joined them on the balcony. "You're going to get yourself banned from the Liu houses again," he told Ruth. "Jamie's a stickler for cutlery." He placed the fish-and-chip bundle on the table, and Frankie on his lap. "We've got fried cod for those of us with taste. And grilled haddock for the rest." This was directed over his shoulder to Jamie, but his expression wasn't even teasing—it was full of adoration.

"Some of us want to eat fish, not batter," Jamie said, but his smile at Tom was just as adoring. He dropped a kiss on the top of Tom's head as he put down the plates and cutlery.

"I like it grilled," Joan said automatically, and knew without looking that Ruth was making a face in one of those family exchanges that was more ritual than argument. "Otherwise—"

"Otherwise, all the textures are the same," Ruth said, singsong. "Crunchy and more crunchy." In her normal voice, she added, "That's not even true. The chips are fluffy inside."

Nick grinned. He tore open the butcher's paper. Joan's heart skipped a beat at the smile, and then another beat when he passed her one of the grilled fillets. She could almost buy this fantasy, this shadow of the true timeline. But that timeline was long, long gone; it had been replaced with one where Nick was a monster slayer. And then Joan had made *this* timeline—where, apparently, a terrible event was imminent.

Joan didn't want to believe what Astrid had told her. But she couldn't stop thinking about Astrid's expression as she'd looked out at this view of the canal. Like it was something precious; something to remember.

Was something terrible coming? Would all this soon be gone?

Would Joan remember this moment as fleeting and precious too?

Something of Joan's feelings must have been on her face because she caught Nick looking at her with a slight frown.

"That woman downstairs . . . ," he said. "Who is she? Why did she want to talk to you?"

"Her name is Astrid," Jamie said. "She's a head of the Liu family."

Nick's expression didn't change. He really *didn't* remember Astrid; didn't know that he and Astrid had once been a team, standing against everyone else in this room.

"She . . ." Joan hesitated. She'd never been superstitious, but she almost felt like saying it aloud might make it true. "She wanted to warn me about something." A breeze drifted from the canal, ruffling her hair and smelling faintly of stagnant water. She looked at Tom and Jamie. "How much do you know about future events?"

"Future events?" Jamie seemed confused, and so did the others.

"What do you mean?" Ruth said. "Does she think you're going to be attacked again?"

"No, she—" Joan hesitated again. "She told me that something bad is going to happen." The superstitious feeling was growing stronger. "She made it sound like an apocalypse." Joan had hoped it would sound absurd out loud, but if anything, it felt more real, more concrete.

"What are you talking about?" Ruth said.

Nick sat up straighter, alert. "What do you mean? *What's* going to happen?"

"I don't know." Astrid hadn't given any details. Joan turned to Jamie again; all monster families kept records of events—past and future—and the Liu ones were the best. "Is it in the records?"

"You mean . . . is some cataclysmic event coming?" Jamie just seemed confused. He looked at Tom, who shrugged his own puzzlement. "No."

People will die. People on both sides—monsters and humans in uncountable numbers. Maybe it just wasn't true, Joan thought. Maybe Astrid had been messing with her. Except that she'd seen Astrid's horror; she'd seen her fear. And Joan knew that events could be hidden, even from monsters. Nick's massacres had been removed from all the family records. No one had seen *him* coming.

"Well . . . *is* it true?" Nick said, frowning. "We need to find out."

In profile, Nick reminded Joan again of a classical statue, of a hero of old. He'd pushed past confusion almost instantly. *You want to know why I fought with him?* He *would have stopped it.* Nick really had been a hero; he'd fought monsters and he'd saved humans. And if Astrid was right, he would have saved even more people than that.

"Can we talk to her?" Nick asked.

"She's left this time. She said the calamity was inevitable."

"Why would she say all that to you?" Ruth said. She was getting angry. "Why would she say that and leave?"

Joan swallowed. "It's complicated. It's . . . it's part of that long story I haven't told you yet." Before Ruth could ask, Joan made the *later* hand signal again.

Ruth blinked once. There was only one reason for Joan to use a Hunt signal. Ruth made a subtle signal of her own. With her hand by her side, she gestured quick signs—forefinger out:

trust; thumb pointing to Jamie and then Tom; fist clenched: *question mark.*

Joan put her own forefinger out. She trusted them. Ruth pointed subtly to Nick, and that was a much harder question to answer. Joan made the *later* gesture again. Ruth's eyes widened, and she gave Nick a more assessing look.

Aloud, Joan said, "Astrid said she has a strong version of the Liu power—that she can remember the future like she remembers the past."

"Astrid told you that?" Jamie said, looking troubled. "That's not her recorded power." He ran a hand over his mouth. "She *is* a head of family, though," he said, almost to himself. "They keep all kinds of secrets."

"But . . . *none* of this is in any records," Tom said. "And people travel to the future all the time. We'd know. *I've* traveled centuries into the future. No apocalypses—I promise."

Centuries into the future. The jolt of it hit Joan belatedly; Tom's casual tone had delayed her understanding of what he'd said. How far into the future had he gone? How much human life had it cost?

"We can't just ignore this, though," Nick said. "What if Astrid's right? We can't just let it happen."

Once again, Joan found herself looking at him, handsome and dark-eyed and grave. He didn't know anything, and already he wanted to step up and stop this. It was instinct for him.

And Tom's words had reminded her again of the truth too. This was a room full of monsters, of people who stole human life on a whim. Her stomach churned.

"Astrid mentioned my gran. She said Gran was looking for a way to prevent it."

"*Gran* knew?" Ruth repeated, surprised.

"Did she ever say anything?" Joan asked.

"About some apocalyptic event? *No.*" Ruth ran a hand through her thick curls, looking worried. "It's been nearly a year since I last saw her, though."

"A year?" Joan hadn't realized that Gran had been gone for so long.

"She never said anything before that," Ruth said. "I mean, if she'd known about it, she would have—" She cut herself off. "If she'd known about it . . . ," she said more slowly.

"What is it?" Joan said. Ruth's gaze had gone inward.

"It's probably nothing," Ruth said, but the way she said it made Joan tense. "I think she *was* preoccupied with something just before she left this time. I mean—" Ruth's eyes focused on Joan. "She was worried about *you*. But . . . I think she was worried about something else too."

Ice crawled down Joan's spine. Gran rarely worried about anything—or at least she rarely showed it.

Tom leaned forward. On his lap, Frankie made a querying *whuff*, and Tom stroked her head. "Preoccupied with what?" he said.

"I don't know," Ruth said. "She wouldn't tell me. But I got the feeling she was looking into something. Trying to figure something out."

Was there a way to find Gran now and ask her? She was shut out of this time, and Joan was mired here, but maybe they could communicate, at least. "Do you know what date she traveled to?"

Ruth ran her hand through her hair again. "I don't want you to worry, okay?" she said to Joan.

Another thread of ice. "Worry?"

"She's been off the radar since she left. No messages, no word of where she went." For a second, Ruth seemed about to say something else, but she didn't go on.

"You haven't heard from her at all?"

"You know what she's like," Ruth said.

Joan did know. All the Hunts went into hiding sometimes—Ruth included. A year without any word at all seemed a long time, though. And, on the face of it, Gran had been looking into something, and then she'd disappeared.

SIXTEEN

As soon as they started down the stairs, Joan knew something was wrong. A crowd had formed in the little gallery space—and if the atmosphere had been hostile when Nick had arrived, now there was a feeling of a boil-over.

"What's going on?" Joan said as she reached the foot of the stairs. There must have been thirty people crammed into the room, and they were all staring at Nick, some with arms folded, some clearly scared.

Liam Liu emerged from the clumped crowd. "Just stay calm," he told Joan. "No one's going to hurt him."

Calm? Joan's heart was already pounding. "What are you doing?" A creak on the stairs made her look up. There was a big man on the landing above, blocking the way back up. And, all around them, people had positioned themselves at the doors. "What *is* this?"

"We were promised sanctuary by a head of your family!" Ruth said to Liam, bewildered. "We had her word."

"You still have it," Liam said.

Joan didn't believe it—not with the way everyone was looking at Nick. In her own ears, her breathing sounded loud and ragged. "Jamie?"

"I didn't know anything about this." Jamie looked grim. To Liam, he said, "You had a meeting without Tom and me? That's not right, Liam."

"You and Tom are free to vote too," Liam said. He raised his chin defiantly. "I have to tell you, though, the vast majority has spoken. We've already come to a decision about what to do."

"A decision?" Joan said. What was he talking about? "You don't need to make a decision about anything!"

"You have sanctuary," Liam said, "but we can't tolerate his presence unchecked. We won't."

Joan's stomach churned. "Look," she said to Liam—to the rest of the room. She could ease this situation, she told herself. She had to. "I'm sorry. I shouldn't have brought him here. We'll just leave, okay? You won't need to worry about us. You never have to see us again."

"He can't just leave," Liam said. "He's seen this place. He's been to an inn."

"What are you talking about?" Joan stared at him. "You just said you couldn't tolerate him here! What do you mean he can't leave either?"

"Do you need me to make a promise?" Nick asked. He still sounded calm. Joan had a strange flash of him standing in front of the Olivers, sword in hand. He'd sounded calm then too. He addressed the whole room now. "You're afraid that I'll tell people about this world," he said to them. He didn't raise his voice, but his words rang out. "I swear I won't. You have nothing to fear from me."

"I'm sorry," Liam said. His own voice shook. "But that's not enough. We have to guarantee everyone's safety."

"Why do you keep *saying* that?" Joan said. "What do you mean?" Were they going to chain Nick up in a room somewhere?

Liam beckoned to a boy standing near the hearth. "Owen," he said. It was the boy with ash-blond hair who'd been rude to Joan on the stairs. The Argent boy who'd tried to use his power on her—just to see if he could.

"Wait, *what*?" Joan said. She felt for a second like she was going to be sick. "What are you *doing*? What are you going to do?"

"We won't harm him," Liam said. "We'll only compel him to make sure he won't harm *us*."

To Joan's dismay, Nick stepped toward the Argent boy. As he moved, there was a shuffle as Liam backed up. Joan caught frightened and hostile eyes in the crowd.

"What on *earth*?" Ruth muttered. She looked confused.

So did Nick. He tried again. "I won't harm any of you. I *wouldn't*."

"Then you won't even notice the compulsion," Liam said to him. Could Nick hear the fearful shake in his voice? "You won't even feel it."

Joan turned to Jamie, to Tom. "We *can't* control his mind!"

"I'm sorry," Jamie said. "I don't agree with this either."

This shouldn't have been an argument to agree or disagree with. They shouldn't have taken a vote. "It's wrong!" Joan said. "It's just wrong!"

"It's okay," Nick murmured to Joan. "If they're really this scared that I'll tell, I don't mind giving them a guarantee. If that's what they need."

"*No*," Joan said to him. All she could think about was Nick's horrible blank expression when Corvin Argent had compelled him. "They *don't* need this!" She turned to Ruth. "We can't let them do this!"

"We're not on Hunt territory," Ruth said apologetically. "I can't do anything about it."

"Why is this a problem?" Liam asked Joan, his voice still shaking. "This is a fair solution for all of us. He'll be able to walk among us, unharmed. And we'll have peace of mind."

"Why is this a problem?" Joan repeated incredulously. "Because you can't just *make* people do things! You can't insert yourself into people's minds! It's a violation!"

"Joan," Nick said. "It's okay." To Liam, he said, "I have no intention of harming any of you. If you need more than my word, then you can have it."

The boy by the hearth—Owen—began to walk over. Joan tried to get in front of Nick again, but strong hands tugged her away. One of the Hathaways. "Get *off* me!" she said.

"*Hey!*" Nick said. The first flare of anger he'd shown since he'd come back downstairs. He started toward the Hathaway.

Owen's voice rang out: "Be still." And just like in the courtyard, Nick froze. He was mid-step, his knee crooked uncomfortably. His eyes widened, and Owen said: "You're not afraid. You're calm."

"No!" Joan wrenched at the Hathaway holding her as Nick's breath released again, slow and even, like when he'd fallen asleep beside her in the boat. "This is dangerous!" Joan said desperately to the room. "What you're doing right now is making things dangerous! Don't you see that?" Didn't they understand? If Nick figured out the truth of monsters, he'd hate them for controlling his mind. Really hate them. *This* might put him onto the path of becoming the hero again. All their families would be in danger.

Owen came forward. After his unpleasantness in the corridor, Joan had expected him to gloat, but he looked very serious. "Look at me," he told Nick.

Nick lifted his head and met Owen's eyes. They were almost the same height. Nick seemed like a soldier standing before Owen: clean-cut and dark-haired. Owen's own hair brushed his shoulders.

"No!" Joan tried again to pull away from the Hathaway's grip, but he was too strong.

Owen said to Nick, casually: "You're fine with monsters. You don't want to hurt them. And you won't tell any humans about them."

Nick shook his head slightly, as if an insect had flown near him.

"Say it back to me," Owen said to Nick.

To Joan's horror, Nick answered, flat and obedient: "I'm fine with monsters. I don't want to hurt them. I won't tell any humans about them." Then, sounding more like himself: "Why would you think I even could harm you? You all have special powers. The most I can do is kick a football pretty far."

Owen shrugged. "It's done," he told the others.

"This is best for everyone," Liam told Joan.

Joan's heartbeat thundered in her chest. "Get off me," she told the Hathaway man holding her. She wrenched away, and the man finally released his grip. "Fuck you," Joan said to him thickly.

"Back at you," the man said without rancor.

Joan stumbled to Nick. She touched his shoulders, his arms,

as if there might be bruises. But it wasn't a visible wound. It was in his head.

"I'm fine," Nick said. He sounded just as he always did. His eyes were clear—he looked like himself. "I really am."

"I'm sorry," Joan said. "I'm sorry I let this happen."

"You don't have to apologize," Nick said. "I don't even mind. If that's the reassurance they need, I don't mind giving it."

This wasn't okay, though. It was so far from okay. Over her shoulder, Joan said to Ruth, "Look after him, please!" Ruth would have so many questions, she knew, but they'd have to wait. Right now, Joan had to find Owen.

He'd slipped out of the room. But Joan had been watching him. She raced to the east door. Clustered people avoided her eyes as she searched among them. Not here. She hurried to the next room.

Still no Owen, but Liam Liu was by the window, looking out onto the canal. This had been his decision. Well, he could bloody well undecide it.

Joan grabbed his arm. "Where's Owen?" she demanded. "He has to take that compulsion off Nick!"

"That's not going to happen," Liam said.

"Yes, it is!" Joan said. "We have to take it off him!" It wasn't too late. If they took it off now, it would be almost like it hadn't happened.

"Why would we?" Liam said.

Joan wanted to scream. "You can't manipulate humans just because you want to!" Why didn't he understand that? Maybe it was because no one could manipulate monsters; the Argent power didn't work on them. "You can't *do* this to people!"

"We're doing *you* a favor." Liam sounded frustrated. Bewildered. "We're harboring you, and we're allowing *him* to stay. This is the bare minimum we're asking—the only way we can tolerate his presence here. We're not harming him at all! We're not asking for much!"

"He's not even dangerous!" Joan said. "He doesn't even remember!"

"Well, some of us do!" The words burst furiously from Liam as if he'd been maintaining his temper with difficulty, and now he couldn't control it anymore. "*I* remember!" he said to Joan. "I remember him killing me!"

"*What?*" Joan stared at him, shocked.

"He came to the Liu gallery," Liam said. "He attacked the house. Him and his people. He killed my cousins. Uncles. Aunts. My sister Mabel." His voice shook. "I tried to save her. I tried to get her out the back door, but he caught us in the corridor." Liam drew in a hard breath as if he'd forgotten he needed to breathe. "He killed her in front of me. He broke her neck. I tried to fight him, but he pushed a knife into my chest, right here." Liam pressed his palm against his breastbone like he could still feel it; was still trying to stanch the blood. He focused back on Joan. "Don't tell me that you want him roaming among us unchecked. Not when so many of us remember our deaths at his hand."

"I . . . I didn't know." Joan remembered how the Lius had hushed when Nick had first walked into the room. She'd assumed their fear was theoretical—that they'd read about him in the Liu records. She hadn't imagined anyone here might remember the attacks. "I didn't know," she said again.

"Did you care to know? *Do* you care? Maybe you should be concerned about your own people." Liam's eyes burned. "Or *are* we your people? How do you think of yourself? Monster or human? Where does your allegiance lie?"

It was a strangely familiar question. Joan had said something like that to Astrid earlier. Sometimes she even talked about herself as *half.* Half-monster, half-human. Half-English, half-Chinese. As if she were made of construction blocks that had been put together and could be disassembled again. But that wasn't how she felt inside.

Jamie's voice sounded, startlingly close. "All right," he said. When had he come into the room? Joan hadn't even heard him.

"It's *not* all right." Liam sounded close to tears.

"I know," Jamie said gently. "I know it isn't."

Liam made a choked noise at the back of his throat. Joan stared after him, shaken, as he headed for the door.

How could Astrid have fought alongside Nick? How could she have made a choice like that? Joan couldn't imagine anything worse than what Liam had described of the Liu house massacre. Than the massacre of Joan's own family. But . . . She saw again the dull horror in Astrid's face. *I've seen the end. People will die.* So *many more than he ever killed or saved.*

How bad was the calamity that Astrid had seen? How could it be worse than all this?

"Joan," Jamie said. It took Joan a long moment to register her own name. "I might have found something."

Joan felt like she was about to burst into tears. "What?" she heard herself say. Liam's words were still echoing in her head. *He broke her neck. I tried to fight him. Where does your allegiance lie?*

"Ruth was right. Your grandmother was investigating something," Jamie said.

"Investigating what?" Joan's own voice sounded hoarse, as if she had been crying. *He killed so many of us.* She had a flash of herself running through Holland House, trying to escape Nick's people. She could feel Gran's blood on her hands again, the sharp-edged branches of the maze again.

"I don't know," Jamie said. "Your grandmother vanished a year ago. But before that, she *was* looking into something. We have records of her visiting a place near Covent Garden three times in the week before she disappeared."

"Is it near here?"

"Near enough," Jamie said. "I can take you. We'll need to be careful, though. There are still Court Guards on the streets."

"We'll be careful." Joan needed to get out of here. She needed to get Nick out of here. She needed to clear her head.

SEVENTEEN

Tom moored the boat by the Hungerford Bridge sometime before dusk. The Houses of Parliament loomed beyond the netting-like frame of the bridge.

Joan felt a jolt of disquiet as they disembarked. The events of the other timeline seemed to lurk, ghost-like. One street away, the gate to the Monster Court had opened. Just beyond that was St. James's Park and then Buckingham Palace, where Joan and Aaron had first arrived in 1993.

"Are you allowed to moor here?" Nick said doubtfully. "Isn't this a river bus stop?"

"Allowed?" Tom shrugged. "Don't know about that. But that symbol means something on the water." He nodded at the two-headed hound. "We could leave *Tranquility* here for a year, and no one would touch her."

They walked up the concrete pier, around a shuttered booth for river cruises. The roller door had a marketing photo of people laughing on a speedboat, the picture crimped by the lines of the door.

Joan found herself beside Nick. She searched his face for signs of the Argent power, but he looked like his ordinary self. "How are you feeling?" she asked him.

"I'm fine," he assured her. "I don't even think that guy used his power on me—I don't feel any different."

Cold wind gusted over the water, making Joan shiver. She found his lack of concern unsettling. "Nick—"

"Hey," he said. He caught her elbow gently. "I didn't want to hurt monsters before, and I still don't. I don't think it's affected me at all."

Joan swallowed, trying not to think about how warm his hand felt through the sleeve of her shirt. "Maybe it's already worn off," she said, hoping. "Corvin Argent's power didn't last long." And, according to Corvin's chop, his father was a head of family. His power must have been strong.

Ruth interjected from up ahead. "There must be a way to test it."

"You could try hitting one of us," Tom suggested over his shoulder. He had Frankie in his arms, and she was already starting to snooze. "Try hitting *me*."

Nick laughed. "Maybe later."

His equivocation made Joan's stomach squirm. She was pretty sure that the power *was* still working on him.

Farther up, Jamie didn't say anything. He'd argued against it, but Joan had the feeling he was relieved that Nick was leashed.

Jamie led them all up to Victoria Embankment—away from Whitehall. They passed the ancient stone obelisk of Cleopatra's Needle. Joan had always thought it a strange thing, an object out of its place and time. Covered in worn hieroglyphs, it was one of the few remnants of Heliopolis, a city that hadn't existed in a thousand years. How had it ended up here, planted beside the Thames?

Across the river, the new pyramid building of this time

caught the light. It was vast: a skyscraper with sides that glittered like diamonds. Together, Joan supposed, the pyramid and Needle kind of made sense: a modern building inspired by ancient Egypt standing opposite a real artifact, three and a half thousand years old.

"I always felt a bit sorry for it," Nick said. He'd followed her gaze to the Needle. "An orphan, far away from home, its original city destroyed."

Joan was surprised by how similar her thoughts had been to his. "Do you think they saw it coming? The people of Heliopolis? Do you think they ever imagined that, one day, the only remnant of their city would be objects like this?" She pictured Astrid again, looking out the window as if the world she knew would soon be gone. "I don't think *I* can imagine it," she admitted.

"We're going to figure this out," Nick said. "That's not going to happen to us." He gave her a crooked smile. "And if you think about it, Heliopolis isn't gone. Not for you. Not for anyone who can time-travel. Maybe we can visit it when all this is over."

Joan tried to smile back. *When all this is over.* What did that even look like? Would Nick ever be able to go home? Would Joan?

They turned from the river toward Covent Garden. The sun lowered as they walked past familiar and unfamiliar shops, toward the market.

"How did you two meet?" Ruth asked Joan and Nick curiously. "In the attack?"

"No, the day before," Nick said. "Joan dropped her phone in the field behind our school, and I found it."

From up ahead, Jamie met Joan's eyes.

I didn't want *to meet him again,* Joan imagined telling Jamie.

That would have been a lie, though. Being near this new Nick was unbearable, but the alternative had hurt even more. "Nick's really popular at school," she said to Ruth. "We're in different circles. So, yeah, we only met the other day."

Nick's eyes were soft as he looked at Joan, but his gaze was searching too, as if he'd heard something in her voice. "I'd seen you around, though," he said. "I was hoping we'd bump into each other."

Joan's heart fluttered out of nowhere, and heat flushed her cheeks. In her peripheral vision, she caught Ruth looking between them assessingly. She was wondering about that hand signal in the boathouse. Joan had indicated that she didn't fully trust Nick. But Ruth knew Joan better than almost anyone—she had to have seen Joan's blush too.

"What about you?" Nick said. "You two are cousins? You and Ruth?"

Joan opened her mouth to tell him, and then realized that she wasn't sure how she and Ruth were related. To Ruth, she said, "Your mum and my mum are cousins, right?" She knew that Gran wasn't Ruth's actual gran. "Are we second cousins?"

"Monsters would just say cousins," Ruth said.

Dad's side of the family was kind of the same. Everyone was a cousin or an aunty or an uncle. "Me and Ruth grew up together," Joan explained to Nick. "I stay with Mum's side of the family every summer."

They were in the theater district now. It must have been just after five o'clock. All around them, office workers walked briskly in the direction of the Tube while tourists milled about, peering at their phones.

"We usually—" Joan started to say. Then her voice stopped in her throat. They'd rounded the corner onto Bow Street, and ahead of them, the white columns of the opera house were tinted gold by the lowering sun. The sight was intensely familiar. *This has happened before*, she thought. *I've seen this exact view before.*

"What is it?" Tom said sharply. "Do you see a guard?"

"No guards." She reached for the feeling, but it was already fading. Clouds had drifted over the sun, dulling the portico. "I just had the strongest feeling of déjà vu."

Ruth squinted ahead. "Maybe you're remembering that time Gran took us to the opera."

"She did?"

"You've forgotten? That whole big weird show with all the horses?"

"You're probably thinking of *Pietro il Grande*," Jamie said absently. "Five shows in 1852."

"Oh, well, I guess it must have been me and Bertie, then," Ruth said. "Joan's never traveled like that."

Joan let the conversation wash over her as she followed the others up the street. The moment had felt a lot more like a memory than déjà vu. She looked over at the opera house again, picturing the sun's golden glow on the columns, trying to recapture the exact shade in her mind. The feeling didn't return, though, and it faded further as Jamie led them down another street and another, past shops with unfamiliar logos and advertisements for a buddy-cop TV show Joan had never heard of.

Jamie stopped, finally, outside a building with scaffolding all over it. It was a single-story structure, plonked in a street of shops selling pizza and coffee and clothes.

"*This* is the place Gran kept coming back to?" Joan didn't know what she'd been expecting, but it hadn't been a construction site in the most touristy part of Covent Garden.

"Maybe it wasn't under renovation a year ago," Nick said.

Joan stepped closer and cupped her hands against a window. The glass had a reflective coating, but she made out the vague shape of tables and chairs. "Looks like a café. Maybe Gran met someone here."

Jamie barely paused. "No," he said. "Our records have her coming here alone. This place has been under scaffolding for nearly two years."

Joan found herself doing a double take. "Well, that's . . . creepy that you know that."

"That's the Liu records for you," Tom said. "Creepy and useful."

"Where does the information even come from?" Joan asked.

Jamie shrugged. "Phone records, CCTV, social media posts, drone photos. Anything that's in any database eventually makes its way to us. And then—" He tapped the side of his head. "The storage is here."

"Like a hive mind," Nick said, looking intrigued.

"Maybe a hive memory," Jamie said.

"Hmm." Ruth slipped a soft black cloth from her pocket. "There goes the fantasy that we can ever avoid cameras."

"You're going to pick the lock?" Nick sounded faintly scandalized.

The door popped open. "Wrong tense," Ruth said. "I *have* picked the lock." She walked in. "Well," she said, "it's exactly as you'd expect."

Joan followed her, ducking under a low metal beam. Inside, the room was sunny with big windows along parallel walls. The space had been gutted, but the bones of a café were still here: a line of built-in booths ran beside the windows, and there was a counter at the front where the checkout would have been.

An unloved print hung on a wall behind the counter—a cartoonish map of London showing Buckingham Palace as a little castle and the zoo as a cluster of elephants and a giraffe. It was easy to imagine the place bustling with tourists, sun shining in on them from the windows. This had once been an American-style diner, Joan guessed.

Déjà vu rolled over her then—stronger than the moment at the opera house. It was accompanied by a rush of unease. *I know this place*, she thought. *I've been here before.*

"Maybe your grandmother did meet someone here," Nick said. "She could have traveled after she walked inside—to a time when it wasn't a construction site."

That made sense. Maybe there was a bathroom in here—Gran could have traveled without anyone seeing her. As Joan looked around, though, she was struck with a feeling that Gran *hadn't* come here to meet anyone. That she'd come here for something else.

"Look out," Jamie said. Joan followed his finger to two heavy security cameras at the ceiling corners. She felt another jolt of combined recognition and disquiet, as if this moment too had happened before.

"Don't worry," Tom said in a reassuring rumble. "Those cameras are old—like magnetic-tape old. Don't think they could be in working order." He looked around. "No sigils. No future technology. This isn't a monster place." Frankie wriggled in his arms, and he bent to let her down. She nosed at his shoes, pulling at the laces. "Frankie," he said mildly, and she shuffled over to sniff at Nick's trouser cuffs.

Ruth reappeared from a door behind the counter. "There's nothing in the kitchen," she said. "Nothing in the bathroom. What do you want to do?"

"Why did your grandmother come here?" Nick wondered.

Some instinct made Joan turn to him. He stood in a sunbeam. In the golden light, his dark hair was more brown than black. Beyond him, a window showed office workers on their way home. And then Joan *knew*.

She *had* been here before—in the previous timeline, when it had been a bustling café, serving all-day breakfasts to tourists. She pictured herself finding the sunniest booth. And then she pictured Nick sliding into the bench opposite hers.

"Joan?" Nick said now. "What is it?"

Joan blinked, barely seeing him.

Last time, he'd grabbed her wrists. *I can't let you touch me.*

And Joan had asked him the question that had been gnawing at her since the massacre. *Did you know they were my family before you had them killed?*

No.

Would you have killed them if you'd known?

He hadn't hesitated: *Yes.*

"Joan?" Nick said. He took a step toward her, and Joan startled, jerking back from him. His eyes widened.

It took Joan a long moment to collect herself. "Just give me a second." She could feel everyone looking at her now. She ran a hand over her face. She just needed to think for a second. Why had Gran come here? Why *here*?

Joan and Nick had sat at the last booth on the left. Joan found herself taking a few steps toward it. As she did, something on the floor caught her eye—white scratches on the dark wood. Drag marks from chairs? No . . . the configuration was too regular. . . . Joan peered down, and her heart skipped a beat. "Ruth!" she called.

"What?" Ruth came over, followed by the others. "What am I looking at?" she said. "These marks?" Then she recognized them like Joan had. *"Oh."*

"What is it?" Nick asked.

"It's a fox," Ruth said.

The Hunts had a way of rendering the family sigil, a fox drawn in three quick marks: a *V* for the head; then an upside-down semicircle for the body and legs; then a horizontal line striking through the whole thing, extending beyond the semicircle to create a tail.

"Gran *was* here," Joan said.

"Is it a message?" Tom asked.

"I've never seen it by itself," Joan said. The Hunt signature was usually accompanied by the person's initials and some instruction—a *get out* warning sign or a *safe here* sign.

"Maybe she was just saying she was here," Ruth said, puzzled.

Joan straightened slowly. The mark was about a third of the way into the room; Gran had placed it on a bare patch of floor, where the line of booths started. Joan pictured Gran standing here. What had she been doing? What had she been thinking? Ruth had said she was worried in the week she'd come here.

Joan took another step. As she did, her arm struck something invisible. She gasped.

"What is it?" Ruth asked. She reached out herself, and her hand stopped abruptly in midair. "What the hell is that?"

The object seemed flat—or perhaps slightly curved—with no temperature. Joan pushed at it tentatively, and it pushed back, feeling more like magnetic repulsion than a physical object.

Nick ran his palm across the air like he was stroking the flank of a horse. "Feels like a wall of some kind. A barrier."

"A barrier?" Jamie reached up and recoiled as he found the object too. He reached again, and this time there was a hint of awe in his expression. "I think . . . I think this is an Ali seal."

"An Ali *seal*?" Ruth said wonderingly. She seemed as surprised as Jamie, and maybe a little scared.

"Why would someone put a seal in here?" Tom murmured. He stretched to his full height; the barrier continued as far as he could reach. Joan imagined it going all the way up to the ceiling.

"What's an Ali seal?" Joan asked.

Frankie had discovered the barrier now too. She batted it

with a paw, her squashed head tilted in doggy puzzlement. She barked at it warningly.

"The Ali family has the ability to lock away places and times so that no one can access them," Tom explained.

"These seals are *rare*," Jamie said.

The hairs rose on the back of Joan's neck. She peered into the sealed-off area; it looked just like the rest of the café. Was it just a coincidence that she and Nick had been here? And why had Gran visited this place three times? Why had she left a mark where the seal started? "There has to be a way to get in there."

"You mean *break that seal?*" Ruth said, as if Joan had suggested they fly to the moon.

"Can't an Ali do it?" Nick said.

"That's not . . ." Ruth shook her head. "It's not just that seals are rare. The Ali *power* is rare—most Alis can't even wield it." To the others, she said, "I think they get an exemption at the panels, right? They don't have to demonstrate a power to be confirmed as an Ali?"

"Not quite," Tom said. "My little sister manifested as an Ali. She does have some kind of power." He scrubbed a hand over his mouth, considering. "Best I can say is that Laila has an affinity with the timeline. It likes her."

"Likes her?" Ruth said.

"You know how the timeline is," Tom said. "We push it, and it pushes back. But it doesn't seem to mind the Ali family as much. I can always sense the timeline flowing differently when Laila's nearby. Like . . . it's happier. I guess the panel can sense that too."

Joan was surprised by the mention of Tom's sister, and curious too. She'd wondered what happened when monster siblings manifested different powers. Had Tom and his sister been split into different households as children? Were they close, or did they barely see each other?

"That's interesting," Nick said.

There was a tiny pause among the others, and then Tom said amiably, "I always thought so."

As they'd walked here, the five of them had been chatting, apparently comfortably, but now Joan realized that there'd been a subtle gap between Nick and the rest of them this whole time. It didn't matter that he was bound by the Argent power; they were all wary of him—even Ruth, who didn't know *why* he'd been bound.

Ruth broke the silence. "Could your sister help?" she asked Tom. "Does she know any powerful Alis?"

"We're not bringing my sister into this," Tom said easily, but there was a clear note of warning there too.

"Listen . . . ," Jamie said to all of them. "This seal can only have been put here by the Court. Any Ali powerful enough to do this would have been scooped up by the Court as soon as their power manifested—voluntarily or not." He folded his arms, and Joan knew he was remembering being taken himself by the Court to be the Royal Archive.

Tom saw it too. He put a hand on Jamie's back. "Let's get back to the boat," he said. "We're not going to figure out anything here."

They should return, Joan knew. Gran had clearly come here for whatever was beyond that barrier, but there was no way to know what was in there, and no way to break the barrier. This was a dead end.

But at the same time . . . Joan was missing something, she was sure of it. She stared at the scratched fox mark. Then she frowned and crouched down. There were more scratches beside the fox, but they seemed cut off at a distinct line.

"What are you doing?" Ruth said.

Joan ran a finger down the line. On the side of her finger, she could feel the barrier: tepid compressed air. "Part of this mark is *in* there," she said. "It's *inside* the seal."

"You mean this was sealed off after Gran came here?" Ruth said.

That was possible. "Or," Joan said slowly, "Gran found a way to open it. Right here."

Ruth's laugh was a hard puff. "Gran can do a lot of things, but there's no way she could recruit an Ali with that kind of power."

Joan knelt up, pressing a hand to the barrier. "I've felt something like this before," she murmured. *That* was what she'd missed. It wasn't just the space that was familiar. The seal itself was familiar too.

"What do you mean?" Ruth said.

An invisible barrier, slightly curved . . . Where had Joan encountered that? The realization hit her. "There was a seal like this at the Monster Court." It had surrounded Jamie's prison cell, locking him off from the world.

"At the Court?" Ruth looked bewildered, and so did Tom behind her. *You were both there with me,* Joan thought. They didn't remember.

"What do you know about the Monster Court?" Ruth said. "Do you mean you were *at* the Court? No one can get to the Court!"

"I'll tell you," Joan promised. There was so much to tell Ruth. "I just—" She scrambled up, looking around. She needed something like the rolled rug they'd used last time—something that could be turned into a loop. She spotted the touristy picture behind the counter and unhooked it from the wall. It was nearly as big as she was. She dragged it back to the others.

As they stared at her, Joan shoved out the glass, the print, and the cardboard backing. Then she pushed the empty frame into Ruth's hands.

"What are you *doing*?" Ruth said.

"Gran broke this seal with the Hunt power, and so can you— you just need this frame."

Ruth blurted out another laugh. "What are you talking about?"

"The Hunt power allows you to push an object into a moment in time, right?"

"Well . . . ," Ruth said. "Yeah, I suppose that's how it works, but—"

"When you do it, there's a short period where you hold the object in two times at once. You can do that using this frame."

"What are you *talking* about?" Ruth said again.

"Just try," Joan said. "Just push the frame through that barrier and hold some of it *here* and some *inside* the seal. You'll make a bridge. It'll be a portal we can walk through. That's what Gran must have done."

"Joan, there's *no* way the Hunt power can break an Ali seal," Ruth said. "Most *Alis* couldn't break this seal. In a thousand of them, maybe one could."

"Humor me," Joan said. "If it doesn't work, we'll go back to the boat."

"Then we're going back to the boat," Ruth said. She leaned the frame against the barrier. It sat there, seemingly propped up by nothing. "See?"

"You need to hold on to it," Joan explained. She went over and gripped the other side to show her. "Imagine you're using the Hunt power to hide the frame right where the barrier is. Put it partly *inside* the barrier. Just do the Hunt power like you normally would. But when it's partway gone, don't let go."

Ruth stared at her, but she took hold of the frame properly. "We are going to have a *long* talk after this." She closed her eyes, though, concentrating. Then she pushed the frame against the barrier. It wobbled at its base, and Joan steadied it. Just like in the other timeline, Ruth said, "I really don't think the Hunt power can do this. I don't think *I* can—" And then her eyes flew open.

Joan heard her own gasp at the same time as Tom's. The others had identical looks of shock—except for Nick, who leaned in with curious interest.

Inside the frame, the sun shone weakly, from a different angle.

Ruth had made a portal—an opening in the seal.

EIGHTEEN

Joan peered through the frame. The sealed-off portion of the room looked just as it had from the outside: the same booths alongside the same big windows. The only difference was the direction of the sun. Inside the seal, soft light shone through the eastern windows. Outside the seal, the sun was on the other side of the room.

Gran's sigil was clearly visible on the floorboards now, the fox with another symbol: three lines forking in different directions from a single point. It looked like a bird's claw. Gran's initials, D.H., were next to it.

"What does that symbol mean?" Joan asked Ruth.

Ruth wrinkled her nose. "Isn't that the *opportunity* symbol? Why would she put that *here*?"

Who was the message *for*, then, Joan wondered. The Hunts were thieves, and the *opportunity* symbol was used to indicate a potential target location. Joan lifted her gaze back to the seal's opening. "What do you think's inside?" Despite the *opportunity* symbol, all she could feel was trepidation.

"No, I have another question," Ruth said to Joan. "How the hell did you know the Hunt power could break an Ali seal? You don't even have the Hunt power anymore. You haven't had it since we were kids."

Ruth looked just like Gran sometimes: curly hair and sharp green eyes. "It's such a long story," Joan whispered to her.

Ruth searched her face. "What *happened* to you after that attack?"

Joan's chest felt heavy with all the things she couldn't say—not with Nick here. "That's not when it happened."

More questions were in Ruth's eyes, but Jamie interjected. "If we're going in, we should go in," he said. "If there's a seal in here, the Court might be monitoring this place." To Ruth, he said, "Think you can hold that gate open for a few minutes?"

"Yeah," Ruth said. "I mean . . ." She dipped her head so that Joan could only see her dark hair. Her shoulders went up and down in a deep breath as if she were assessing how long she could hold a heavy weight.

"Hey," Joan said, feeling uncertain then. *The Hunt power isn't supposed to open gates like this,* Ruth had said in the other timeline. She'd been sick with exhaustion after she'd opened the portals. "You okay?"

Ruth lifted her head again. Joan could already see the strain around her eyes. "I can do it."

"Ruth—"

"I'm fine. I can do it," Ruth said. She jerked her chin at the frame. "Go on. I want to know what's in there too."

"We'll be in and out," Joan promised Ruth. "You won't have to hold it long."

"Okay," Ruth said. "Good to know." The strain was in her voice now too.

Joan didn't know why she was feeling so reluctant suddenly. Last time Ruth had opened portals, they'd had to cross a Paleolithic winter; they'd had to cross the void itself. This was nothing in comparison. This was just one step.

Joan faced the frame head-on. Then she made herself take that step.

As her foot breached the frame, nausea rolled over her—like seasickness on a boat just starting to rock in bad weather. That was new—she hadn't felt sick last time, when she'd crossed through the Paleolithic moat. She took a deep breath and then another one.

It was morning here, and colder than it had been outside the seal. The sun shone weakly through streaks of cloud.

Other than the pale light, the place looked the same as it had from the outside: a stripped-back diner under renovation. Bare booths lined the walls, one for each window. To the east, the view was the back alley: black-windowed modern flats. To the west, the main street was unnervingly empty of people. A second ago, it had been packed with hurrying commuters and window-shopping tourists.

Joan turned and had the bizarre view of Ruth holding an empty frame in the middle of the room. From this side, the barrier was invisible, but the point where the sun changed directions was a distinct line. As Nick stepped across, the others craned their necks, trying to get a view through the frame. The Ali barrier was a one-way view, Joan realized. She could see Ruth, Jamie, and Tom outside the seal, but it seemed they could only see *her* through the frame's eye.

"Well, that's disorienting," Nick said, staring at the main street. "Are these Portelli windows, or did we travel in time?"

"I'm not sure," Joan said. "This place feels . . . cut off from the world." *The Ali family has the ability to lock away places and times so that no one can access them*, Tom had said. The last time Joan had had this feeling, she'd been at the Monster Court—a place detached from time entirely. "Feels like we're in the middle of *nothing*," she said.

A groan behind them. Tom had followed Nick through. Now he clapped a hand over his mouth, as if he'd smelled something foul, his freckles stark against his blanching face. "Oh, what is *that?*" he mumbled.

"What's what?" Nick said.

Joan still felt nauseated too. Nick, though, didn't seem affected at all.

"There's something in here," Tom said. "Something *wrong.*"

"What do you mean?" Nick said.

Jamie's reaction was even stronger than Tom's. He gasped as he breached the frame, bending double to retch. Tom moved fast—Joan was always surprised how quickly that giant body could move. Within a second, he had an arm around Jamie's slim waist. Frankie trotted over and barked at Jamie questioningly, looking as concerned in her squashed-face way as Tom. Like Nick, though, Frankie herself didn't seem ill.

"Everyone okay?" Ruth sounded worried.

"We're okay!" Joan assured her. "How're you doing with that portal?"

Ruth's long pause made Joan uneasy, but she said, "Fine. I can manage it."

Tom helped Jamie straighten up, one big hand splayed protectively across Jamie's back. "Let's get you out of here," he murmured to Jamie. "Just a few steps." He started to guide Jamie back to Ruth, but Jamie stopped him.

"No, I want to see," Jamie managed. There was a sheen of sweat on his forehead. "I want to know what's in here."

"I'll figure it out," Tom said. "Just let me get you out of here."

"*Tom*," Jamie said. It was just one word, but Tom pushed out a breath as if Jamie had offered a full rebuttal. "I'm safe," Jamie whispered. He covered Tom's hand where it was still pressed to Jamie's chest. "I'm here with you." This seemed to be part of an argument they'd had before.

Joan saw a flash of something raw on Tom's face, an echo of how he'd looked last time, when Jamie had told him to stop searching for him; to search for the hero instead. Joan looked away, feeling now—as she had then—that she was eavesdropping on something private.

Tom had said there was something in here. . . . Joan closed her eyes. She had a vague sense of an off-key note at the very edge of her hearing. No, not a sound. A *feeling*. Something dissonant.

"*Joan?*" A warm hand on her shoulder. "Joan?" It was Nick's voice—sounding, oddly, as worried as Tom had. "You don't look well."

"We should *all* leave," Tom said shakily. He scooped Frankie up. "We shouldn't have come in here. We shouldn't have broken that seal. Someone made it for a reason."

"If you say so," Nick said. "But . . . it just seems like an empty café. Just tables and chairs."

Joan tried to sense the source of the dissonance. She turned, letting the feeling guide her. She found herself looking right at the booth where she'd sat with Nick.

She walked toward it, distantly aware of the others calling to her as she retraced her own steps from the other timeline. It *looked* like there was nothing here. Everything had been stripped out of the room except for the bolted-down tables and booth chairs.

And then Joan rounded the back of the last booth, and she *saw* it.

It was a gaping wound in the world, its edges jagged and ruined. A hole. It hovered, half sunk into the table. Joan recoiled, stumbling back.

The thing had the visceral horror of a flesh wound; it went against the laws of nature. Joan knew just looking at it that it shouldn't exist. And she knew, too, that *this* was what Gran had been investigating. This was what had been sealed off from the world.

Footsteps behind her and then a retching sound. Tom had a hand over his mouth again, and as Joan turned, his chest heaved in another retch. Behind him, Jamie's knees collapsed.

"Jamie," Tom gasped, reaching to help him. Jamie was sipping breaths, short and sharp. Fingers shaking and barely able to focus, Tom managed to undo the top button of Jamie's green cardigan and loosen his collar, his big fingers very gentle.

A warm hand on Joan's shoulder. "Joan?" It was Nick. "You don't look well." He looked as worried as Tom—but still not sick himself. He looked over at the wound in the world. "What *is* that thing?"

"I don't know," Joan managed.

Tom glanced over at it, and then away again fast, as if he

couldn't bear the sight. "It feels like *nothing.* The absence of anything. I think it's the void beyond the timeline. A . . . a tear in the fabric of the world. It's like a tear in the timeline itself."

Joan couldn't suppress her own shudder as she remembered standing at the gate of the Monster Court. She'd encountered the void there—a horrifying nothingness that had surrounded the whole Court. Now she took a deep breath and made herself *look.*

It *was* a hole of some kind, ragged-edged with a dark space within. The void.

Jamie murmured something. He was breathing a little better, but he was deathly pale.

"I know," Tom said. He lifted his head to Joan and Nick to explain. "Holes in the timeline only exist in stories about the end of days. This shouldn't exist. It's an *anathema.*"

"It's like the timeline's in pain," Jamie managed.

Joan could feel it too. The timeline sometimes seemed like a great beast, and right now, Joan could sense it writhing and wounded.

Nick walked to the side where Joan had sat, his easy movements a contrast to how affected the others were.

"Frankie, *stay!*" Tom said sharply when Frankie went to follow him.

Joan forced herself to inch closer to the thing. Her body didn't want to do it; the urge to run away was a desperate twinge at the back of her neck. But she needed to understand why Gran had been investigating this, and why the thing was *here*—where Joan and Nick had once been.

"You okay?" Nick murmured.

Joan nodded. She was as close to the thing now as she could get without actually sitting in the booth. She made herself look at it directly and then flinched back.

The hole wasn't empty; there was something shadowy inside it. And somehow that horrified Joan more than the void itself.

She clenched her hands into fists, trying to force herself to look more closely; trying not to grab Nick's hand, trying not to gather up the others and run back out of the seal.

As she looked, the shadows seemed to coalesce into something solid. A table. The same table that was *outside* the hole. Joan frowned, confused. They looked the same. They had the same wood grain.

No, they weren't quite the same. The table *inside* the tear had marks on it—they looked like handprints. Like someone had gripped the table's edge.

Joan was struck with a vivid memory then of Nick pulling a knife.

I told you. I won't kill you here, he'd said.

And Joan had said to him: *You should. I'm going to come after you. I'm going to kill* you.

As Nick had gotten up to leave, she'd clutched the table to control herself—her family had been just two days dead. She'd put her hands right where those marks were now.

She leaned closer. The varnish had been stripped, leaving raw streaks of untreated wood. Light against dark. She drew a sharp breath. She'd seen something like this before. She'd *done* this before. She'd used her power to remove varnish from the wooden banister at the boathouse.

Had she made these marks too? Had her power manifested

here when she'd gripped the table?

But . . . how could she be seeing this? Those marks would have been made in a whole other timeline.

It's like a tear in the timeline, Tom had said. Were they looking at the previous timeline?

Feeling weirdly compelled, Joan reached to fit her fingers over those marks.

"Don't!" she heard Jamie say behind her.

But Joan couldn't stop. To her horror, her hand suddenly felt detached from the command of her mind. Her fingers crossed the barrier, and the terrible dissonance seemed to intensify, unbearably loud. Except that it wasn't a sound; it was a discordance in the whole world.

There was a feeling under Joan's hand like tissue paper being torn. *Stop!* Joan thought. There was a pause then—in the noise; the feeling—long enough for Joan to take a breath, to hope that the dissonance *had* stopped. But as she released the breath, there was a feeling of pressure, and then the jagged wound in the booth seemed to explode.

It was violent. Joan flew off her feet, and her head hit the floor with a hard *thunk*. Her vision blurred. People were speaking, but Joan couldn't make out the voices. She opened her eyes. Was there something different about the ceiling? It seemed to be drooping down, wires hanging. The dissonant feeling had thankfully stopped, but everything seemed fuzzy. Joan shook her head, trying to clear it. But that only made nausea throb through her. She groaned.

"Joan!" Nick's voice.

Joan tried to focus on him. He was on his knees beside her.

"Did you fall?" she asked him. Was everyone all right?

He frowned, and Joan blinked, confused. "You're the one who's hurt," he said softly. He touched the back of her head very gently. Joan didn't know what he was looking for. She started to push herself up and was prevented by Nick's firm grip on her shoulder.

"Don't get up yet," he murmured. "You hit your head."

Joan squeezed her eyes closed and opened them. She felt dizzy.

"You all okay?" Nick asked the others.

"Me and Jamie are," Tom said.

"What *happened*?" Ruth craned her neck through the frame but didn't seem able to see them from her angle. "I heard a crash!" She seemed unaffected by the blast; she'd been protected by the seal, Joan guessed, relieved.

"Not sure!" Nick called back. "But we're all right!"

What *had* just happened? Joan had had an irresistible urge to touch those marks, and then the dissonant feeling had intensified, and then . . .

A gasp from Jamie. "The tear's *gone*."

"*What?*" Joan said. She reached for the edge of the table to pull herself up.

Nick put a steadying arm around her waist. Joan swallowed, trying not to lean into him like she wanted to. His presence alone made the whole situation feel weirdly safe. It wasn't, though, she knew. Something very strange was happening here.

"It's gone," Jamie said again. "I don't even feel sick anymore."

Joan stared. The jagged hole really was gone.

Tom made a soft sound as if about to speak. Joan turned to him and found him staring too, wide-eyed. But he wasn't looking at the space where the tear had been; he was looking at the window.

Joan followed his gaze.

Outside, the main street was unrecognizable: dilapidated and worn. A second ago, there'd been cafés, clothing shops, a perfumery—windows beautifully dressed to tempt tourists. Now, all the shops were gone. They'd been replaced with buildings that struck Joan as not quite Victorian. Not quite any style she knew. She wasn't even sure what was off about them. Maybe they were too tall. Maybe the brick was too dark.

"I don't understand," she heard herself say. Farther down the street, one of the buildings puffed thick smoke from its chimneys, graying the sky and giving the impression of an impending storm.

"Did we travel in time?" Nick asked.

Had they? A strange object caught Joan's eye. A gleaming bronze statue stood opposite: the only shining thing on the whole street. It depicted a woman crowned with flowers. Fresh roses lay like offerings at her feet. Two words were carved into the plinth there: *Semper Regina.*

Unease seeped into Joan like a chill.

"I don't recognize the architecture," Jamie said slowly. "Or what the people are wearing. This is no era I know."

Joan had thought that the street was a ghost town, but now she saw what Jamie had. There were people on the other side of the road—walking quickly, pressed tight to the walls, like they were hurrying to avoid rain. Their clothes blended with the black brick and gray shadows of the buildings; the style was unfamiliar: wool paired with a lightweight material that Joan didn't recognize.

"What *is* this?" Joan said. "If we didn't travel in time . . ."

Movement at the edge of the window. A slim blond man had rounded the corner at a run. He glanced over his shoulder, eyes darting; his chest heaved with desperate breaths. His clothes were filthy, and his hair clung to his face, soaked with sweat. Joan could almost smell the fear on him.

"Why's he so scared?" Nick said slowly.

The words were still in his mouth as a van turned into the street. It was as black as a hearse, a pale light blinking on its roof. The police? No. There was a coat of arms on the door in gold: a rose, the fanned feathers of a peacock, and—Joan's heart started to pound—a winged lion. The sigil of the Monster Court. Right out in the open. What was going *on*?

A man with raven-black hair and patrician features exited the van, the slam of his door inaudible through the café window. He wore tailored black and a gold pin of the Monster Court. His polished perfection was a strange contrast with the dilapidated street.

The guard glanced toward the café. Joan flinched back, but his eyes grazed past; apparently, he couldn't see them through the window. He adjusted his cuffs and, with an air of casual entitlement, he beckoned to the blond man.

The blond man had stopped running, Joan saw then. His posture was utter defeat. Now, hesitantly and reluctantly, he walked toward the guard.

"What *is* this?" Joan whispered. The scene was all wrong. On the other side of the street, people were still going about their business as if nothing unusual was happening, as if the van with the Monster Court sigil was a common sight.

No, that wasn't quite true. Here and there, people snatched glances; they weren't uninterested, Joan realized. They were *afraid* to show interest. And that made her heart beat faster too.

The guard said something to the blond man; he was cautioning the man, Joan guessed. Arresting him. The blond man stood there, chest heaving, eyes glassy. He whispered back, and Joan read the words on his lips: *I'm loyal. I'm loyal.*

Joan waited for the guard to pull out handcuffs, but instead he stepped closer, cupping the blond man's neck almost possessively. *You're nothing*, he said.

"No!" Joan heard herself say as she realized the guard's intent. "*No!*"

"What's wrong?" Nick asked.

And then the blond man crumpled to the ground.

Joan heard herself make a horrified sound. She had a clear view of the guard's emotionless face. He might as well have swatted a fly. She could hear her own breaths coming out in harsh gasps. Across the street, no one was sneaking glances anymore. They'd all turned away.

"What . . . ," Nick said numbly. "We—We need to go out there and help that guy. We need to call an ambulance!"

He didn't know the blond man was dead. He didn't know that the guard had just stolen all his life from him—in front of dozens of witnesses. A monster had just killed a human in broad daylight as if he'd had the right.

Did we travel in time? Nick had said. Joan couldn't catch her breath. *Had* they?

The guard glanced up at the gray smoke clouding the sky. Then he wrenched open the back of the van.

And— Joan gasped. There were more bodies inside. She took in the details in disconnected flashes: a woman's shoe with a broken strap, foot still in it; a boy in some kind of uniform; a middle-aged man with a mustache.

Joan shoved back from the booth in horror, half falling into Nick behind her. And then the world seemed to shudder. In the time it took Joan to blink, the worn Victorian-like buildings were gone. The guard was gone. The van full of corpses was gone.

Everything was as it had been when they'd arrived—even the misshapen, jagged hole was back. There was nothing inside it now but the void.

"Did you see that?" Nick said disbelievingly. "What *was* that?"

Joan couldn't stop shaking. She hadn't felt like this since Ruth had told her that her family was dead. Since she'd seen the bodies of Nick's victims lying in the garden.

What was that? If she were to guess, it had looked like a London where monsters lived openly among humans; where a monster could kill a human in broad daylight; where onlookers didn't dare protest.

"Was that the future Astrid saw?" she whispered.

"But it was wrong." Jamie sounded numb. "That's not the future; there's never a time like that."

"But what *was* it?" Nick said. "What did he *do* to that man? I don't understand! I think he *killed* him! I think he killed all those people in the van!"

"We need to get out of here," Tom said firmly. "We can figure things out on the boat. We shouldn't have stayed so long. This place has to be monitored."

Joan squeezed her eyes shut, trying to pull herself together, trying to unsee the inside of that van. She opened her mouth to call to Ruth, and then stopped as she saw Ruth's face. Ruth was as shaken and pale as Joan felt.

Ruth put a finger to her lips. *Shh*, she mouthed. *Guards.*

For a long moment, Joan couldn't process what she meant. *Guards?*

Still silent, Ruth jerked her chin in the direction of the windows—on her side of the seal. There was a crash then. Someone called, *"Got that scaffolding off!"* Keys jangled.

Joan had a second to think, *They'll see Ruth first.* And then Nick was sprinting past Joan, faster than she could have believed. As the lock clicked and the café door opened, Nick was through the frame. He shoved Ruth back into the sealed part of the café and then knocked the frame aside. It was still falling as the first guard entered. It hit the floor with a loud clatter, making the guard start back in surprise.

"No!" Joan shouted. *"Nick!"* She sprinted to him unthinkingly, and her shoulder hit the invisible barrier. She rebounded, gasping. "Nick!"

There were three guards in the room now; they looked around, and Joan knew they were seeing nothing but an empty café and Nick. The view through the seal only went one way.

"Nick!" Joan shouted again.

"They can't hear you." Ruth's voice shook. "When I was out there, *I* could hardly hear you, even with the portal open."

Two of the guards snatched Nick's arms, wrenching his hands behind his back. The difference in strength was almost laughable. Nick's muscles rolled in his confined arms. The guards looked like children restraining a bull.

"Nick!" Joan said. She slammed at the barrier with both hands. Maybe Nick could fight them off. He was untrained in this timeline, but he was still strong. He'd knocked Corvin Argent out in the courtyard.

But Nick was just standing there placidly. It took Joan a long moment to remember that he couldn't fight. *You're fine with monsters*, Owen Argent had told him. *You don't want to hurt them*. Nick couldn't defend himself.

Joan was suddenly close to tears. Were these guards going to kill Nick in front of her? "Ruth, you have to open another portal!" she blurted. "He can't fight with the Argent power on him! We have to help him!" She looked around. She needed to find another frame. A rug. *Anything* that could form a large enough loop to act as a conduit.

"Joan . . ." Ruth shook her head, and Joan focused properly on her face. Ruth's eyes were sunken and dull. Joan had a flash of her like this in the other timeline—burned out from making gates at the Monster Court. "I don't have anything left," Ruth whispered.

Joan's own breath came out in a sob. *You don't understand what he means to me*, she wanted to tell Ruth. *I'd die if anything happened to him.* But Ruth looked utterly spent.

Desperate, Joan flattened her hands against the barrier, willing her power to work. *Dissolve*, she told the seal. *Be unmade.* Nothing happened. She heard herself make a frustrated sound, and she pushed at the barrier hard with both hands, putting all her weight into it. Her power always came out when she didn't want it to. Why couldn't it come out *now*, when she needed it most?

One of the guards—a spiky-haired man—came out of the kitchen. "There's no one else here. Guess those weird fluctuations are still at play."

"Those fluctuations are just rumors," another guard said.

"*Right*," the spiky-haired guard said, drawing out the word into a drawl. "It's the intelligence that's wrong, hmm?" He surveyed the room. Joan felt a jolt as his gaze swept over her, unseeing. His eyes lingered for a second on the fallen picture frame, and then moved on. He lifted a thin phone to his ear. "We found the boy. He's here alone, just outside the seal."

Who had he spoken to? All three guards were just standing there, Joan realized. What were they waiting for?

The spiky-haired guard glanced at the front door, and Joan amended her own question. *Who* were they waiting for? Her heart stuttered.

As if in answer, the handle flicked down. Nick lifted his head. And Aaron Oliver walked through the door.

NINETEEN

The guards' manhandling had untucked Nick's shirt and rumpled his hair. Aaron was a pristine contrast: crisp suit and perfect golden hair. He walked over to inspect Nick, a hand in his pocket.

Joan, Aaron, and Nick had been in a room together just once before in the previous timeline. Nick had been restrained then too. He'd seemed powerless at the time, but by the end of that night, he'd slaughtered Aaron's whole family and Joan's.

Aaron and Nick faced each other now. Nick was only a little taller than Aaron, but his muscular build made Aaron seem slender. Joan had thought they'd be a mismatched pair, but they highlighted each other's looks: Aaron, fair and otherworldly; Nick, dark-haired and classical.

Aaron's gaze lingered on Nick's face. "He's human," he said after a pause.

"We already knew that," one of the guards said. "He was susceptible to the Argent power."

"Well, I'm confirming it as requested," Aaron said dryly. "Anything else I don't have to be here for?" The man's jaw tightened, but Aaron ignored him; his gaze was still on Nick. Joan thought of the way people's heads always lifted as they passed Nick, looking to him in the way a compass pointed north. She didn't know why she'd assumed Aaron would be immune to him.

Nick didn't seem immune to Aaron either. His gaze scoured

Aaron up and down. Aaron had his full attention; the restraining guards might as well have been absent.

"Where's the girl?" Aaron asked.

Nick's chin lifted defiantly.

"Was she here?" Aaron pressed. "We have reports that you came here as part of a group."

"Why did you come *here*?" the spiky-haired guard asked. "Did you know there was a seal here?"

When Nick still didn't answer, Aaron shrugged with exaggerated nonchalance. "You can talk now, or you can be made to talk later." He held out an elegant hand to the guards. "Give me a cuff."

"No," Joan breathed. Where was Aaron going to take him? She'd been afraid they'd kill Nick right here, but this prospect was somehow almost as frightening. What were they going to do to him? Were they going to interrogate him? Hurt him? If they moved him in time, how would she ever find him?

A familiar gold cylinder was placed into Aaron's hand. He flicked it open with a lazy jerk of his wrist.

"No!" Joan slammed her power at the seal again and again. She could feel the flame of power inside her, straining against the barrier. It *was* manifesting, but she wasn't strong enough to break the Ali seal. She visualized the flame leaping higher and higher. She visualized the seal dissolving under her hands. But still, nothing happened.

Aaron stepped into Nick's space and went to take his arm. Before he could react—before Joan could—Nick's hand shot out. He planted his palm in the center of Aaron's chest as if to shove him back. Joan gasped, terrified for Aaron suddenly.

But Nick didn't push; he stood there, hand splayed, his dark eyes full of intent. For a beat, Joan couldn't make sense of the frozen tableau, and then she remembered again—Nick couldn't fight.

Aaron's expression flickered from fear to confusion, and then to something Joan couldn't quite read. His breath hitched as the restraining guards grabbed Nick's arms again.

"Jamie?" Tom said suddenly.

Joan was aware then that Tom had been saying Jamie's name over and over, and that Jamie had been absolutely silent in response. She turned, and the hairs rose on the back of her neck.

Jamie stood beside her, eyes wide. He was staring—not at Nick or Aaron, but at the closest guard. At his winged-lion pin.

"Jamie?" Tom said again. "What's wrong?"

The word *wrong* seemed to echo in the small space. And something *was* wrong. Jamie was trembling—more afraid than when he'd seen the jagged hole in the air; more even than when he'd seen Nick outside the Wyvern Inn.

Jamie opened his mouth, but no sound came out. He tried again, and this time he managed to speak. "I know that sigil. A rose stem without the flower."

The thorned stem? Joan had seen it at the Wyvern Inn— etched on Corvin Argent's chop; as a curve on the guards' pins. She'd assumed it had signified a special class of guard.

Outside the seal, Aaron's voice rose. "Let's go, then. She'll want to question him herself."

She?

Out of nowhere, Joan's heart stuttered. "Where have you seen that sigil before?" she asked Jamie slowly.

Jamie turned to her. His eyes were black with fear.

Cold washed over Joan. She had a flash of the bronze statue on that strange London street. *Semper Regina*, the plaque had said. *Always Queen*. The face on that statue had been familiar. . . . Joan was already shaking her head when recognition finally dawned.

Last time, a mysterious woman had stepped into Nick's ordinary world and altered his personal history. Joan had seen some of the recordings. Nick's family had been murdered to make him hate monsters—not just once, but over and over until his origin story was exactly as the woman had wished it to be.

"*It's her sigil*," Jamie whispered. "The woman who captured me. The woman who turned him into the hero."

"But we haven't seen any sign of her in this timeline," Joan said stupidly. The woman *couldn't* be back. If she was . . . *No*. Joan turned around and slammed at the barrier with both hands. "Nick! *Nick!*" But Nick couldn't hear her. He couldn't fight. They'd compelled him not to harm monsters. And he didn't *know*. Joan hadn't told him the truth when she'd had the chance.

A guard pushed up the sleeve of Nick's jacket, baring his wrist. Aaron laid the cuff onto Nick's arm. Nick didn't flinch as the metal fizzled and hissed and buried itself into his skin to form a winged-lion tattoo that matched Joan's own.

"He's anchored to me," Aaron said. He gripped Nick's forearm, his fine-boned hand covering the tattoo.

Nick's eyes swept over the café, apparently casual. As his gaze passed the sealed area, he smiled—slightly—as if trying to reassure Joan and the others.

Aaron took a step, pulling Nick with him.

"No!" Joan screamed. She shoved at the barrier, willing it to unmake itself, but it remained stubbornly intact. "No!"

Then, between one blink and another, Aaron and Nick were gone.

TWENTY

—◦—

Joan stared numbly at the empty space where Nick and Aaron had been. Where the guards had been. "We have to go after them," she managed. But she had no idea where they'd gone. They could have been anywhere in the past; anywhere in the future. She shook her head. "She *can't* be back," she whispered. The woman from the other timeline *couldn't* have Nick again. Aaron *couldn't* be working with her this time. Joan didn't want to believe it.

"Who are you talking about?" Ruth said. Exhausted as she was, her green eyes glinted razor-sharp. She wanted answers, and she wasn't going to wait any longer for them. "Who's *she*?"

"Someone I thought was gone," Joan managed. "Someone I thought . . ." She couldn't finish the sentence.

Joan had only ever seen the woman once—in a recording of Nick's creation—a cold, cruel beauty with golden hair and a long, swan-like neck.

And the woman's power over the timeline should have been impossible: she'd stopped and restarted events, erasing and honing Nick's personal history over and over until she'd brutally conditioned him to loathe and kill monsters. *Again*, she had said. *Again. Again.* Ordering that Nick's family be killed again—in a different order this time. That Nick be tortured again. And at the end, she'd told Nick, *You're perfect*, her approving tone at odds with her icy expression.

Then Nick had gone on to kill Joan's family.

I know how much you hate me, Nick had said to Joan at the end. Joan had shaken her head. She'd hated him. She'd loved him. She'd wanted to be with him more than anything.

I love you, he'd said. *I always have.*

They'd kissed and, just for a moment, Joan had let herself *feel* it. And then Joan had unleashed her forbidden power on him. She'd unraveled his life, and at the end of it, her family was back, and the Nick she'd loved had been gone. She and Nick were broken puzzle pieces now. They'd fit together once, but they didn't anymore.

"She wore that sigil in the other timeline," Jamie said. "I see it in my dreams." He was nauseated again, Joan could see: arms folded around his waist, fingers tucked in. The same woman had captured him when he'd come too close to learning the truth behind Nick's creation. Jamie had never told Joan what the woman had done to him, but he'd been transformed by it.

Tom's hand flexed on Jamie's shoulder. His heavy jaw was tight. "We *have* to find out who she is," he said. "She's clearly high up in the Court."

"That doesn't tell us much," Jamie said gently. "A lot of important people are high up in the Court. Powerful courtiers . . . certain heads of family . . . people with unusually strong powers . . ."

"What are you all talking about?" Ruth said. "Other timeline?" The words came out slowly, as if they were a huge effort. Joan and the others all turned to her and realized at the same moment how exhausted she really was. "There's only one timeline—the King's timeline. *This* timeline."

Joan put an arm around her. "Hey," she said. She guided Ruth a few steps back to the nearest booth seat. She put a hand on Ruth's forehead; her skin was ice-cold.

"What's going on?" Ruth said. "And don't put me off this time."

Joan had never wanted her family to know the horrors of the other timeline. Sometimes it felt like it was always with Joan now. The sounds Gran had made before she'd died. Ruth with a knife in her gut, screaming at Joan to *run*. All the people in the garden, the mess of their limbs, the blood. And the way Joan had felt, the way she still felt—how lost she'd been in the overwhelming grief of losing her family.

She crouched in front of Ruth's seat and took her hand, trying to find the words. "You asked how I knew so much about monsters. How I knew you could open that portal . . ." She took a deep breath. "There was another timeline before this one—a timeline where something went really wrong. Where . . ." She faltered. "Where our family was killed. Gran. Aunt Ada. Uncle Gus. Bertie."

"What are you talking about?" Ruth whispered.

Joan saw Gran's blood all over her hands again, all over her dress. All over Ruth's clothes. She'd never wanted Ruth to know. She'd never wanted any of the Hunts to know. Her breath hitched. "Ruth . . . they all *died*."

"What are you *talking* about?" Ruth said again. She didn't sound angry exactly—she was too exhausted for that. "Why would you *say* that?"

From behind Joan, Jamie spoke. "She's telling the truth.

There *was* another timeline. Some of the Lius remember."

"A timeline when we all died?" Ruth said.

"Not us," Joan whispered back. "Not you and me. But the rest of our family . . ."

"No," Ruth said. She was starting to take it in now. Her forehead creased. She didn't want to believe it, Joan could see. But she knew Joan too well—she knew that Joan would never make up something like this. "*How?*"

"A human boy was trained to kill monsters," Joan said. She swallowed hard. "He came after all the monsters of London."

Ruth's confusion cleared slightly. "There are *myths* about a human hero—Gran used to tell us the stories. Remember? But those are myths, Joan. The hero's like King Arthur. He isn't real. I don't know who told you all this, but it isn't true."

"I was *there*," Joan said softly. "He was real." There was a lump in her throat again. She couldn't believe Nick was gone—would he be the hero again the next time Joan saw him? Would he hate her? Would he try to kill her?

"The human hero from the myths killed our family?" Ruth said. She tried to smile—inviting Joan to say it wasn't true. When Joan didn't, Ruth stared at her. "He killed our family?"

"Not just our family," Joan said. "The Olivers, The Lius. Every monster family in London."

What had the woman's plan been the first time? Joan had never understood why a monster would create a monster slayer. She had a flash again then of the *Semper Regina* statue in that terrible London. Had *that* been the woman's goal? Would she have used Nick to facilitate it?

But Astrid had said Nick would have stopped it. *He was already on the path.* That didn't make sense. Unless . . . Joan bit her lip. Would Nick have figured out what had been done to him—and who had done it? Had Joan taken out the hero of the story and given the villain free rein?

"But I still don't understand," Ruth said to Joan. "What does this woman have to do with all this?"

"You need to tell her about *him*," Jamie said to Joan softly.

It was so hard to talk about the other Nick. Joan pressed her nails into her palms. They felt rough. She opened her hands again. Her nails were torn. When had that happened? Had she clawed that hard at the barrier? "I knew the hero," she told Ruth. "He and I met before I learned what he was; before he learned what I was. I had feelings for him."

Ruth trained her gaze on Joan. "You had feelings for the guy who killed our family?"

It sounded even worse when Ruth said it like that, but Joan nodded. "I found out later that he and I were together in the *zhēn-shí de lìshǐ*. The true timeline."

Emotions flittered over Ruth's face. Joan could almost read each thought. *But the true timeline is also just a myth.* Then understanding dawned. "Some people believe that those who belonged together in the true timeline are soul mates. That the timeline will always try to bring them back together."

Joan nodded. "When I got home after the summer, in *this* timeline, there was a new guy at my school."

"You met him again?" Ruth breathed.

"He didn't remember me. He didn't remember the other

timeline. And then he was caught up in that attack." Joan's voice cracked.

Ruth's eyes widened. Her gaze flicked to where Nick had last been, and then back to Joan. "Oh, *Joan*," she whispered.

Joan hadn't even said the worst of it. "There's more. I . . . God, Ruth, I *hated* him after what he did. I wanted to kill him. I would have. But . . . it wasn't like I thought. You know how the stories go: *Once upon a time, there was a boy who was born to kill monsters. A hero.* But that wasn't right. That was never his destiny. A monster *made* him into the hero."

"What do you mean?"

"I don't know why she did it," Joan said. But she found herself thinking again of that statue. *Semper Regina.*

"You keep saying *she*," Ruth said. "*Who*—" Then her gaze turned again to the empty space on the other side of the seal.

"That thorned stem is *her* sigil," Jamie said. "She's back. And she has him again."

Ruth's eyes widened with understanding.

"We *have* to get out of here!" Joan said shakily. "We have to get Nick away from her!"

And Aaron . . . Was Aaron working with her? Did she have Aaron too? Joan had to get them *both* away from her.

"I know there's more to all of this," Ruth said. At Joan's questioning look, she arched her eyebrows. "Why isn't he the hero in *this* timeline, for one thing. How are our families alive again?" She shook her head as Joan opened her mouth. "Let's get out of here first." Ruth looked toward the back of the room—where the tear in the timeline was still submerged in the table. "That *thing* back there is making me want to throw up."

Tom came up with the idea of tying their jackets and sweaters together in a loop for Ruth to use as the portal frame. Then he dragged two chairs from the back of the room and set them some ways apart. He slung the tied-together clothes over the backrests, creating an open hoop they could all step through.

"You're up," he told Ruth. He looked dubious. Joan was too. Ruth was exhausted, head drooping and shockingly pale.

Tom flicked a worried look at Jamie, who was flagging too, although he was trying not to show it. He'd tucked himself in the farthest corner from the tear, and most of his weight was on the wall.

Ruth caught the look. "Help me up."

Joan and Tom helped her stand, and then shuffled with her to the makeshift frame. Ruth gripped the cloth hoop and squeezed her eyes shut.

Jamie came over too, with some apparent effort. "How will we know if you open a portal? When you opened it from the other side, the view through the frame changed."

Joan pointed at the floor. Outside, the room was darkening, but here in the seal, it was still early morning. The edge of the seal was demarcated by a ruler-straight line where the light changed. "That line of light will break when the seal opens," she said.

She pulled out her phone for good measure. She flicked on the flashlight and aimed it through the eye of the hoop and onto the floorboards beyond. The light didn't penetrate past the barrier. As soon as the floor lit up, though, they'd know for sure.

She saw idly that Gran's etched marks were still on the floor. She'd almost forgotten they were there: the *opportunity* symbol.

Why would Gran have used that symbol *here*? Joan couldn't imagine what she'd been thinking.

She shrugged off the thought, focusing back on Ruth; on the line of darkness.

Minutes went by. Nothing happened except that Ruth got paler and paler.

"You opened it in flashes last time," Joan said, worried. "You didn't try to keep it open continuously."

"You're going to tell me *exactly* what happened after this," Ruth said hoarsely.

Joan was relieved to hear her voice; it was the first thing Ruth had said in a while. "You got us out of the Monster Court."

Ruth's eyebrows went up disbelievingly, but Joan was relieved by that too. The exchange seemed to have reinvigorated her slightly.

"Tom got us in," Joan said. "He was looking for Jamie." Tom grunted, seeming curious. "You told us how to fake being on the guest list," Joan said to him. She had a flash of Aaron watching her worriedly; she'd had to talk her way past the guard at the entrance. Her heart constricted. Aaron had known he'd be an enemy to her in this timeline, but it was like Joan still couldn't process that. Some part of her couldn't believe it.

"*There!*" Tom said. There was a patch of light suddenly on the other side of the seal.

"Go!" Ruth said. "I won't be able to hold it!"

Tom didn't waste time speaking. He pushed Jamie through and scooped up Frankie to jump through too. On the other side, he bent over and took the deep, gulping breath of someone who'd emerged from water. "Come through!" he called back. "You'll feel better too!"

Jamie blew out a breath. "Almost forgot what it was like *not* to feel nauseated."

"Go on!" Ruth said to Joan.

"We're going through together now," Joan told her.

"I don't think that's going to work," Ruth whispered shakily.

It had to. No way was Joan leaving Ruth in here. "It worked last time. You ready?"

"No," Ruth said. But she allowed Joan to take her free hand.

Joan took a deep breath, focusing on the hoop in front of them. She gripped Ruth's hand tighter. "One," she said. "Two—"

"What if I can't—" Ruth started.

Joan ducked through the clunky construction they'd made, dragging Ruth with her. Ruth stumbled through.

As they reached the other side, Ruth exhaled hard. Joan felt it too—the sudden lack of nausea was an intense relief.

"The Hunt power is *not* made for that," Ruth gasped.

"That was *amazing*," Joan told her. Ruth rolled her eyes, but her mouth twitched up.

Joan glanced back. There was no sign of the barrier. No sign of the jackets and sweaters or the chairs they'd used to support them. And where it had been daytime on that side of the café, now the whole room was dark, lit only by the streetlights outside.

Tom followed her gaze. "That *thing* is still in there. The seal doesn't feel like enough."

"What *was* it?" Jamie said. "What did we see in there?"

The pause afterward was telling; that jagged wound in the

world—and the vision they'd seen—had been so unnatural that no one really wanted to delve deeper. Joan had so many questions, though. Why had it been *there*—in the place where she'd once used her power? Why had Gran been investigating this? Why had she left an *opportunity* symbol on the floor?

"From my angle, it looked like the whole room changed inside the seal," Ruth said. "Floor, ceiling, view through the windows . . ."

Joan wished she could unsee that view. It was still there in her head, like the afterimage of a flash of light: worse now that the immediate shock was over. The corpses in the van, limbs tangled. The blond man slumped on the pavement like rubbish.

I've seen what's coming, Astrid had said.

Even now, even with the seal closed, the horror of that terrible London lingered like the scent of black smoke. "Is this what Astrid was talking about? What she was warning about?"

"I don't know," Jamie said.

"That police van with the Court motif," Tom murmured. "It was out in the open. In broad daylight for humans to see."

"But there's no future like that in the records," Jamie said. "Monsters *never* live openly among humans. There's never a time where monsters rule."

Where monsters rule . . . Joan hadn't put it into words like that, but she saw again the bodies in the van. The terrified onlookers. She shuddered. "Did you see the statue on the other side of the street?"

Jamie barely blinked as he retrieved the view with his perfect memory. "The *Semper Regina* statue?" Then his eyes widened. "That was *her.*"

Joan took a deep breath and tried to control her exhale. She didn't know what was going on here, but only one thing really mattered right now. "We have to get Nick back from her."

"We don't know where he is," Ruth said. She held up an exhausted hand before Joan could argue. "I'm in. I'm just saying we don't have a place to start."

Jamie bent absently to soothe Frankie, who was pawing again at the edge of the seal. "We have to figure it out," he said. "Because you're right, Joan. She was planning something last time. She made him into the hero for a reason. She can't be allowed to do it again." Tom made a protesting sound, and Jamie's expression shifted to stubborn determination. "I can't run from this," he told Tom. "We always knew she might be back someday."

Joan knew what he meant. Some part of her had been waiting for the woman's return too; had been braced for this moment ever since she'd woken up in this new timeline.

"Jamie—" Tom started.

"Something is really wrong here, Tom," Jamie said to him softly. "Whatever's sealed off in there . . . it shouldn't exist."

Tom looked raw in the way he only ever did around Jamie. "I'm *there* when you have those nightmares," he whispered. "I'm there when you wake up. I can't let anything like that happen to you in this timeline. Just—" His voice cracked. "Let *me* face this. Stay home with Frankie."

Jamie took Tom's hand. A nonverbal conversation seemed to pass between them. Jamie apparently won the argument because Tom dropped his head. Jamie held on, running his thumb over Tom's ring until Tom looked up at him again, his face so full of love and fear that Joan hurt for him.

"I wish I could remember more details about her," Jamie whispered. "I wish I could remember something actually helpful. But . . . she could have taken him anywhere. I can't think of any clear leads."

A car drove past, flaring light into the room. They all turned nervously to the windows. The view outside was mundane now: coffee and clothes and perfume shops, all lit up. No guards in sight.

There *was* one obvious lead. The thought filled Joan with dread and a strange kind of yearning ache. "We know who took Nick," she said.

"We know she's associated with the Court," Tom said, "but—"

"I don't mean her," Joan said. She saw again Aaron's fine-boned hand on Nick's wrist. *"Aaron Oliver* captured Nick. To find Nick, to figure out what's going on here, we have to go after Aaron."

TWENTY-ONE

Joan was braced for guards as they slipped from the café. Maybe even for Nick to reappear with a knife—transformed back into a monster slayer. But Covent Garden was its ordinary evening self, brightly lit and crammed with people: tourists and theatergoers meeting up for drinks; workers rushing home.

Jamie consulted the records in his mind as they walked back to the boat. "There'll be a masquerade party at the Oliver estate on Sunday. Aaron will be there."

The Oliver estate. A kind of reckless urge washed over Joan. She wanted to go there now—without even a plan. She just wanted to get this done.

She took a deep breath. *Think*, she told herself. A house full of Olivers was dangerous. The true Oliver power was rare, but in a gathering of Olivers, it seemed likely that at least some of the guests would have it. *Aaron* had it. He—and some of his family— would be able to identify Joan's forbidden power just by looking at her. They'd know that Ruth was from an enemy family.

But there was a clear solution to *that*, at least. It was a masquerade . . . Joan and Ruth could veil their eyes with masks.

"Their actual house?" Ruth sounded somewhere between intrigued and nervous. Joan was relieved to see how much better she looked. The color was already back in her cheeks, and she was walking under her own steam again.

"Well, *outside* the house," Jamie said. "It's to be held in their famous gardens."

They passed the arches of the market, lit up like Christmas. Music pounded from somewhere nearby, heavy with drums. Aaron would have hated everything about this scene, Joan thought with a pang, from the loud music to the shuffling pace of the crowd.

She could hardly believe she was heading toward him now. She'd spent months telling herself she'd never see him again. And when she *had* finally seen him, she'd had to run from him.

"What do we know about Aaron?" Tom asked. He bent to pick up Frankie, tucking her under one arm.

Jamie ran a hand through his dark hair, thinking. "He has a reputation—the Nightingales loathe him."

"The Nightingales?" Joan said. What did the Nightingales have against him?

"His own *family* hates him," Ruth said. "He was supposed to be the next head of family, but his father removed him from the line of succession." She lifted her eyebrows. "Hated by the Nightingales *and* the Olivers . . ."

"Two formidable families," Tom murmured. "What did he *do*?"

Joan had wondered about Aaron's disinheritance too. She'd wanted to ask him about it last time, but it had clearly been a tender subject for him.

"Whatever happened, both families kept it from public record," Jamie said. "Everything about the disinheritance is scrubbed."

"Imagine doing something so bad that even the *Olivers* draw the line," Ruth said.

Jamie shrugged, and to Joan's surprise he walked on in

silence, as if he had nothing more to say.

"That's all you know about him?" Joan said to Jamie. Didn't he remember that Aaron had been on their side?

Jamie thought. "I suppose everyone knows he's the child of Edmund's second marriage. And his mother was executed by the Court." He saw Joan's expression and tilted his head. "What else is there to know?"

Joan felt another pang. The Liu power only gave Jamie fragments of the previous timeline. He *didn't* remember. "Aaron was with *us* last time. He helped us stop Nick."

For a moment, all their expressions were the same. Blank—as if Joan had said something so nonsensical that they couldn't process it. Then Ruth's mouth pursed in incredulity. "We're talking about *Aaron Oliver*," she said, like Joan had gotten him confused with someone else.

"I escaped the massacre with him," Joan said. "He and I fled together, and you found us later." Her heart constricted when Ruth just kept staring at her. She'd never get used to having memories that no one else did. "I saved his life, and he saved mine. You saved his. He saved yours. . . ."

"No." Ruth's voice was certain. Apparently, she could believe that she'd broken into the Monster Court, but not that she and Aaron Oliver had saved each other's lives.

"*Yes*," Joan said. "He helped us. We got really close. By the end of it, I trusted him completely."

Disbelief flickered across Ruth's face, and then something more protective. "How much time did you actually spend with him, Joan?"

Joan had to think for a second. "A—A few days." It felt weird to quantify it like that. It had seemed so much longer.

"Oh my God," Ruth said. She lifted her eyes to the dark sky. "You did *not* know him." As Joan opened her mouth, Ruth went on fast, "I'm not saying you didn't meet him. I believe you, okay? I'm saying that Aaron Oliver has a reputation. If you trusted him, he was hiding his true self from you."

Joan shook her head. "He *wasn't*." Aaron had had his secrets, but Joan had known him. Aaron had taken them all to his mother's safe house. He'd risked himself to protect them all.

"Let's talk about this later," Ruth said.

They turned onto a quieter street. The night was cooling. Joan didn't want to talk about it later. She supposed she shouldn't have been surprised by the pushback. The Olivers and the Hunts were enemies. And the three of them—Aaron, Joan, and Ruth—had met under such different circumstances last time.

"We'll need a plan," she said. They needed to find out where Aaron had taken Nick. But how? He wasn't likely to give up the information easily.

"Aren't we just going to kidnap him?" Ruth said. "Force him to talk?"

"What?" Joan was startled by the idea of violence against him. "*No.*"

"Joan—"

"We can't," Jamie said to Ruth before Joan could protest again. "He's not the most beloved of the Olivers, but he's still Edmund's son. We can't actually kidnap him from Oliver territory."

Joan took a relieved breath. They did still need the information, though. She remembered the Griffith security guard outside the Wyvern Inn. He'd gotten information out of Joan with ease. "Can we pay a Griffith to come with us? To induce truth from him?" Subtly, so Aaron wouldn't know it had happened.

"Not many Griffiths would risk antagonizing Edmund Oliver in his own house," Ruth said, but she looked thoughtful.

"George Griffith might do it," Tom said to Jamie.

"George won't make a move like that against Edmund Oliver," Jamie said. "Not on Oliver territory."

"He might take some persuading, but his father's a Nightingale," Tom said. "It's like you said—they *hate* Aaron Oliver. I've heard them talking about him."

Joan felt uneasy at that phrasing. She chewed her lip. "What about getting into the party?"

"In and out will be easy enough," Ruth said. "We'll just need the right clothes."

"And masks," Joan said. *You have to stay far away from me. From me and from my family*, Aaron had told her on their last day together. She suppressed a shiver. She'd promised him she would, and now here she was planning to walk into his own home.

Sunday evening was crisp and very clear. A crescent moon hung in the sky. Tom pulled *Tranquility* into a Richmond mooring. Dense weeping willows obscured the platform, their heavy branches brushing the water. This wasn't the Oliver mooring—Tom had been worried that someone would spot the double-headed hound—but it was close enough that Joan could see fancy pleasure boats lined up farther along the river.

Above them, helicopters whirred as even more people arrived.

"Masks on," Joan said. She didn't want to risk being spotted by the wrong guest.

Ruth had volunteered to find clothes and masks for all of them, and she'd done an impressive job. Everything fit perfectly, even Tom's dinner suit, which actually looked tailored to his huge frame.

Joan's dress had a semitransparent black skirt. The low-backed bodice was threaded with gold beading and gold embroidered flowers. The skirt glinted in the moonlight, which surprised her; the tiny crystals of sparkle hadn't been visible during the day. Her mask was gold too: a delicate filigree headpiece that covered the top half of her face, evoking a fire-like tiara. Underneath it, she wore a strip of black lace to obscure her eyes. Long black gloves concealed the fugitive mark on her wrist.

Ruth had found herself a slinky dress in champagne silk. Her mask was an oversize gold and royal-blue piece inspired by a butterfly. The wings were fine as lace, rising above her head, Valkyrie-like. Mirrored blue glass mimicked butterfly markings, and they'd been strategically placed to hide Ruth's eyes.

Tom and Jamie matched. Their dinner suits were dark, dark green—almost the color of the shadowed leaves around them. Their masks were leather: single sycamore leaves in burnished autumn brown, with only their mouths showing.

Now Tom peered into *Tranquility*'s wheelhouse. Frankie gave him a squashed-face blink and yawned. "You're not coming?" he asked her, surprised. "There'll be food." Frankie yawned again and turned in a circle to go back to sleep.

"Fair enough," Ruth muttered. "I wouldn't want to hang about with the Olivers either."

They made their way up the gentle slope of the bank. As they crested the rise, Joan felt her mouth drop open. *"That's* the Oliver house?" *That* was where Aaron had grown up?

The principal building shone from the hill: a four-story manor house with castle-like turrets and glowing windows. Beyond it, a domed conservatory shone, bright as a light box; and beyond *that* there was a vast formal garden. Joan stared. She'd had some idea of Aaron's background—she'd pictured him sleeping in posh school dorms and lounging about in country houses. But this . . .

"Bit over the top, isn't it?" Ruth murmured.

"It's a palace," Joan said wonderingly. The Olivers had owned Holland House in the other timeline, but this was even grander than that. No wonder Aaron had seemed so at home among the priceless paintings and sculptures of Whitehall Palace, and so out of place at the rough-and-ready rooms they'd found on the run.

Tom turned back to the grassy bank. "Where's George?" he murmured. They'd arranged to meet George Griffith among the willows at the edge of the river.

"He's not late," Jamie whispered back. "It's not quite ten yet."

But an hour passed, and George remained absent. The moon rose and the temperature dropped. Joan shuffled closer to Ruth for warmth. Every few minutes, a slick black car rolled up the long driveway, and guests emerged in sparkling gowns and dinner suits, masks glinting in the moonlight. They followed a lamplit path around the house, guided by liveried footmen.

"We're going to miss our window," Ruth said. "If we arrive too late, our entrance will be memorable. And we really don't want to be memorable."

"Let's give him a few more minutes," Joan said.

Half an hour after that, Tom's phone lit up with a message. He read it grim-faced.

Joan's heart sank. "George is a no-show?"

"Got a better offer apparently."

"Seriously?" Ruth said. "This is why I don't work with Griffiths."

Joan's stomach squirmed. They'd really needed a Griffith for this—someone who could induce truth.

"What do we do?" Jamie said.

They were already here, dressed for the part, eyes shielded. They had to take this opportunity. "Let's just go in and figure it out," Joan said. Ruth was right. They were about to miss their window to get in.

They'd need to get Aaron on his own. And then . . . There had to be a way to get Nick's whereabouts from Aaron *without* the Griffith power.

The path around the house led to a garden walled with a high hedge and an open iron gate. Two stone figures held the hinges. At first glance, they looked like angels, but as Joan got closer, she saw that they were Oliver mermaids with scaled tails. On the other side of the gate, a path led into the grounds. Even from here, the scent of sweet evergreen trees and flowers was intoxicating.

A red-liveried footman stood at the entrance. "Please follow the lit path," he said with a nod.

The path wound around thickets of trees that opened here and there to lush lawn. Joan could imagine having picnics here. She wondered if Aaron ever had. "I was worried they'd ask for invitations," she whispered to Ruth as they walked.

"Doubt there even *are* invitations," Ruth murmured back. "No enemy of the Olivers would show up to an Oliver party." She nudged Joan with her elbow. "Except idiots like us, I guess."

"What do we have against them?" Joan knew that the Hunts and the Olivers had been enemies for millennia, but she'd never heard a reason why.

"They're slimy, sneering snakes who pretend they're loyal to the Court," Ruth said. "But they're only loyal to themselves."

"The origins of the alliances and enmities are all forgotten," Jamie said. "There are only myths about them now."

"Who's allied with who?" Joan asked.

"You don't know the rhyme?" Tom said. He chanted softly into the night: *"The phoenix and the hound. The mermaid and the starling. Dragon makes vows with the desert and undying. Griffins' faith is found with the white horse, never yielding. Nightingale is bound with the elm tree, always shielding."*

Jamie elaborated. "Lius are allied with Hathaways. Olivers with Mtawalis. Portellis with Alis and Nowaks. Griffiths with Patels. Nightingales with Argents."

"The Hunts don't have allies?" Joan asked. She vaguely remembered Aaron taunting Ruth about that last time.

"Who needs allies?" Ruth shrugged. "It's all just boring meetings and politics and compromising with each other."

"Yeah. Can't stand those meetings where we compromise with each other," Tom said so mildly that Joan almost missed the grin he shot at Jamie. Jamie shook his head slightly, but his neck reddened in the darkness, and he bit at his own smile.

"The enmities shift around more, depending on the time period," Jamie said to Joan. "The only real lasting ones are the Olivers and Hunts. Nowaks and Nightingales. Griffiths and Argents."

Tom craned his neck ahead. They could all hear the party now, in the distance: raised laughter and sweet stringed music. Bright light glinted through the leaves. "What would actually happen if a Hunt got caught in an Oliver house?" he mused.

Ruth grimaced. "Best not get caught." She'd gone with blue lipstick tonight, to match her butterfly mask, and her mouth was a clear downturned arch.

Joan had had the Hunt power as a child—the ability to hide objects in thin air. It had faded, though, and a new power of unmaking had emerged in its place—a power that Gran had warned Joan never to reveal to anyone, not even Ruth. A power that had turned out to be forbidden.

Until Nick had asked about it on the boat, Joan had only spoken about it with Aaron.

I'm not a Hunt, am I? she'd said to Aaron. They'd been in the corridor of his mother's safe house. The sun had been setting, throwing golden light over his beautiful face. It was a question she hadn't even been able to ask herself. Because for monsters, power was family and family was power, and Joan didn't have the Hunt power anymore.

In a human sense, they're your family, Aaron had said. *You love them and they love you.*

But in a monster sense, they weren't, and Aaron had known it from the night they'd met—from the moment he'd been close enough to see the color of her eyes.

Rare among Olivers, he had the true Oliver power—he could do more than differentiate monsters from humans; he could differentiate family from family. And on the day his own power had been ratified, he'd been given a special instruction by the Court. He'd been told to kill anyone with a power like Joan's.

He should have killed her the night they'd met—as his father had tried to do. Failing that, he should have turned her in to the Court. Instead, he'd kept her safe from the other Olivers and from the Court itself. He'd protected her.

What am I? Joan had asked Aaron. Why did she have a power outside of the twelve families?

I don't know, he'd said. He'd looked at her with an intensity that had stolen Joan's breath. *All I know is that if you undo the massacre, you can't ever meet me. You can't ever trust me. I won't remember what you mean to me.*

Joan touched her mask now, checking that it was tight on her face. Ahead of them, the trees were finally clearing, revealing the great conservatory and the gardens—and the Oliver masquerade.

"Wow," Ruth said grudgingly.

"It's stunning," Jamie said.

The bright light they'd glimpsed through the leaves was the glowing dome of the conservatory, connected to the house via a gilded glass passage. The gardens before it were classically formal: strolling paths crafted from low hedges. It was all fairy-lit, with ghost-white splashes of late-blooming dahlias.

But it was the masquerade itself that had Joan's attention. The Olivers were as beautiful, and as dangerous, as she'd remembered.

Her gaze jumped from one guest to another. Over there, a woman in a wedding-like dress with a long train; when she turned, her mask was a skull in the same shade of white. And over there, a man with raven hair and an imposing brass mask, elaborate with filigree and with no eye slots. And here, a woman whose golden mask rose above her head in a radiant corona; her dress was crafted from gilded feathers. Footmen wove among them, bearing trays of champagne.

They made their way down the lawn. Ruth took a visible deep breath as they reached the entrance of the formal garden: an elaborate sculpted hedge that formed an arch overhead. "We're really doing this?" she whispered. "We're really walking into the lion's den?" She sounded nervous now that they were here. Not even Gran would have dared enter an Oliver occasion uninvited.

Joan was scared too. The last time she'd been in a place full of Olivers, Edmund had entertained himself by having her fight for her life. She'd had a knife, and his brother Lucien had had a sword. Joan touched her side unthinkingly. The fight hadn't happened in this timeline, but she still half expected to find a scar where the stab wound had been. If Nick hadn't stopped the fight, she'd have died that night.

As they entered the garden, Joan looked around for Aaron's familiar silhouette. The space was disturbingly mazelike; the hedge walls ranged from waist to neck high.

"Let's hope he's not wearing one of these huge masks," Tom murmured as they passed a man in a horned helmet that covered his eyes and hair.

Joan wasn't worried about overlooking Aaron. Mask or not,

she'd know him as soon as she saw him. "We need to get him alone and persuade him to talk," she said.

"We could get him drunk," Ruth whispered back. "Bet he's a talkative drunk."

Joan almost smiled at the thought. He probably was. She doubted that he'd touch a drink offered by a stranger, though.

And how did she know that? As she'd said to Ruth, she'd only known him for a few days. But . . . it was like she'd seen right inside him last time; like he'd let her see. He'd opened himself up like a gift.

They reached the circular clearing at the center of the garden. A dozen people were dancing, Regency style, in neat steps, dresses swirling. A stringed quartet sat to one side, the players in bright bird-inspired masks. The music was staccato, in a minor key, and it made the old-fashioned dance steps seem eerie.

As Joan watched, the raven-haired man from earlier joined the dance. He bent his head slightly to greet his dance partner, vulture-like, and Joan's breath caught. Behind the eyeless filigree mask, she made out the long gloomy shape of Lucien Oliver's face.

As the music played on, Joan saw it all again—the beginning of the massacre. Lucien's sword coming toward her in a blur; the sharp slap as Nick caught the blow; Lucien's last punched breath as Nick shoved the sword into his heart. Lucien hadn't even known that he'd been killed by a figure from the myths.

"You know him?" Ruth whispered. She'd seen Joan looking.

Joan shook her head. She forced herself to keep walking. "Let's go up to the conservatory." It was higher on the hill, and they'd have a better view of the garden from above.

A reflecting pool lay in front of the conservatory, a rippling mirror of the glowing dome before them. Up close, the building was vast: a two-story glass structure with iron bones.

Tom led the way in, followed by Jamie and then Joan and Ruth. The space was as humid as a butterfly house, and it smelled sweetly of earth and leaves. Guests strolled down paths lined with leafy ferns and, above, on a mezzanine level, forced chrysanthemums and birds-of-paradise bloomed.

It was hard to focus on the beauty, though. Joan spotted Victor Oliver, in an ox-shaped mask, the familiar mermaid tattoo on his wrist. He'd castigated Aaron for slumming with a Hunt, and he'd died in the South Garden of Holland House. And there was Marie Oliver, dark-haired and beautiful, her face mostly visible in a silver-feathered mask that only covered her mouth. Joan had last seen her lying dead in a colonnade.

She stared at the people before her, in their elegant clothes and masks, drinking and chatting and laughing. How many more of them would she recognize from the massacre if they took off their masks?

"What is it?" Ruth whispered to Joan.

Joan swallowed hard. "I've seen some of these people dead," she admitted. And now they were alive again. Joan had brought them back to life. Ruth squeezed Joan's gloved hand tighter. "Ruth—" Joan started. And then she heard a familiar cruel voice from the mezzanine above.

"—tired of the authority of humans. The masquerade."

A chill seemed to permeate the whole room. Joan couldn't suppress her shudder as she looked up to find Edmund

Oliver—Aaron's father and the head of the Oliver family. He wore a charcoal suit and waistcoat and a half mask in bone-white porcelain that seemed to emphasize his high cheekbones. He stood on the mezzanine, gripping the gilded banister, surveying his guests with cold regard.

Joan reached for her own mask again for reassurance. Edmund had a special hatred of humans. *Half-human, half-monster,* he'd said to her once. *If your mother were an Oliver, you'd have been voided in the womb. But the Hunts have such tolerance for abominations.* Her skin crawled at the memory.

Most monsters took human life in small increments—a few days from this person; a few days from that one. But Joan suspected that Edmund took all he could; that he killed people outright. And Joan had brought him back to life too.

Did you think there'd be no consequences? Astrid had said.

"That's why I prefer the early centuries," the man beside Edmund answered. He was gray-haired and stooped, with a plain black mask. "There's a certain agreeable leeway in the unrecorded shadows of history."

Edmund grunted in response.

"What do you think?" the gray-haired man asked.

It took Joan a second to realize that he wasn't speaking to Edmund, but to a figure on Edmund's other side. Joan drew a sharp breath. It was Aaron.

"Aaron doesn't have thoughts," Edmund said dismissively.

Aaron didn't react. His angelic face was half-concealed by a delicate golden mask that skirted the bridge of his nose and covered his eyes. His blond hair was unmistakable—as rich as the mask. He usually wore gray, but he was all in black tonight: suit, waistcoat, and shirt. There was no hint of emotion in his posture, but to Joan's eyes he looked like he was in a bubble, alone.

Joan had one of those flashes of overlaid memory; the first time she'd seen Aaron, he'd been standing alone in a window recess at Holland House.

Ruth followed Joan's gaze. "I'll grant him one thing," she murmured. "He always looks good." It was as grudging as when she'd admired the Oliver gardens.

"He does," Tom said absently, and then to Joan's surprise, he reddened.

Jamie bit back a smile. "I think we can all appreciate the aesthetic." He turned to Joan. "Don't you think?"

Joan felt herself starting to redden just like Tom. To her relief, Ruth interrupted the moment. "I count five on the security team," she whispered.

The security team? Joan saw then that some of the people on the mezzanine weren't normal guests. They had plainer suits and were maskless. They formed a knot around Edmund and Aaron, and Joan felt a flash of despair. She hadn't realized how inaccessible Aaron would be.

Aaron doesn't have thoughts, Edmund had said. It was clear that his father had him on a short leash. Even if George Griffith had been here, it would have been near impossible to force Court secrets from Aaron without Edmund or those minders clocking it. And without George . . .

Ruth said it first, whispering, "I don't like this. I don't like being on Oliver grounds. I don't like being this close to Edmund Oliver."

"Our plan with George already fell through," Tom said. "We should cut our losses and go back to the boat."

But Aaron was still their best chance of getting to Nick. "We need that information," Joan whispered. She turned to Jamie. "Are there any Liu records of Aaron going out on his own?"

"He's remarkably good at avoiding cameras," Jamie said. "He doesn't appear in the Liu records casually. And when he's at events like this, he always has minders."

Joan bit her lip at that. Aaron hadn't had minders when she'd known him—but then, they'd mostly been on the run. And every time she'd seen him recently, he'd been with Court Guards.

"Should we go back?" Ruth asked.

"Wait," Joan said. "Wait." She needed to think. "Could he have told someone else where he took Nick?"

"His father, maybe," Ruth said.

"Someone easier to question?"

"He was doing a job for the Court, so he would have to log it in the Oliver records," Jamie said. "My guess is that he added the information to the Oliver records and didn't tell anyone else."

Joan glanced around. They'd been talking in whispers, and their voices had been drowned out by the general chatter of the party around them. But to be even safer, she beckoned the others to the rounded glass wall of the conservatory, where a rushing fountain sounded. "You've done research on the house, right?" she whispered to Ruth. "Do the Olivers keep their records *here*?"

Ruth seemed puzzled by the question. "Yes, of course. This is their main house."

"Can we get to them?"

Tom's mouth opened as if she'd suggested breaking into a

church. "You want to break into the Oliver records room?"

"You want to *look at their family records*?" Ruth was as scandalized as Tom. Joan had seen her break into houses without any compunction, but she looked truly shocked by the thought. "Read other people's records?"

"Is it possible?" Joan said.

"I mean, yeah," Ruth said. "But . . ." She looked between them all. "Family records are *sacred*."

"Once they're logged, no one can touch them but the family archivist," Tom said. He glanced again at Aaron, who was still in the knot of people with Edmund. "They wouldn't be expecting a breach, though. . . ."

"The archivist is at the party," Jamie murmured. "Edelie Oliver." He nodded at a woman on the side of the room. She wore a black silky gown and a Gothic crow-like mask. Her long red hair spilled down her back, a bright contrast to the black. "She looks occupied to me."

Ruth mistook Joan's expression. "Did you meet her last time too?"

"No," Joan said. She'd seen her lying dead in the South Garden at Holland House, her beautiful red hair splayed in leaves and dirt. Joan took a breath, and suddenly all she could smell was crushed hydrangeas. She tried to concentrate on the rich tropical scent of the conservatory.

"I'd only need a minute in the room," Jamie said. He didn't seem as scandalized as the others. "Less, depending on the format of their records."

Joan could still smell hydrangeas. She forced herself to speak.

"What do you think?" she asked Ruth.

"It's in the old servants' wing," Ruth said. "Near the kitchens." They all paused at that, turning to the stream of service workers with trays of champagne and hors d'oeuvres.

"The kitchen will be full of people," Joan said.

"So will the main route from it," Ruth agreed. "But we could bypass that." She paused, and Joan knew she was picturing the house plan. "From the back stairs, we can get to the storage corridor and the records room."

"Me and Tom as lookouts, then," Joan said. "You'd pick the lock. Jamie would do his thing. . . ."

Ruth blew out a breath. "Are we really doing this?"

"Well, they wouldn't be expecting it," Tom said.

"And we wouldn't be messing with their records," Joan said. "Just *looking*."

A glass passage connected the conservatory to the house. Joan had thought that they'd need to sneak through it, but other people were moving in and out; the fringes of the party extended beyond the conservatory.

Joan found herself holding her breath as she reached the end of the passage and entered the house itself. Her first impression was that it was intimidating and had been designed to give that impression. They'd entered a long gallery with paintings of Olivers along the walls in gilded frames. Joan spotted one of Edmund with a hunting rifle and a dead deer; the painting beside him was of a blonde woman wearing a silver tiara. Were these all Oliver heads of family? Hand-painted glass cabinets broke up the line of paintings, and there were treasures inside: jeweled ornaments and tiny porcelains.

"Wouldn't mind fifteen minutes in here with a sack," Ruth murmured.

Jamie's eyebrows drew together in disapproval. "We're not thieves. Not tonight, at least. Keep moving."

Ruth sighed, but together they slipped out of the gallery. Ruth led them through a series of passages that became progressively less grand: marble floors shifted to parquetry and then ordinary floorboards and gray carpet. The sounds of the house changed too: from the faint buzz of party conversation to the clatter of kitchen work.

Joan had been tensed for alarms to go off; for someone to catch them. But at the next corridor, Ruth gestured for Joan to shut the door behind her.

Ruth turned the lights on, and they all blinked. "This is it," she said. "The storage corridor at the back of the house." It was wide with whitewashed walls, and so far from the rest of the house that the silence was complete. "It's L-shaped with exits at each end," Ruth whispered. "Two storage rooms off each arm."

They checked the rooms quickly: one was full of linens and old clothes, neatly folded; the second had old kitchenware; the third room, oddly, wasn't a storage room but a small bedroom—a servant's room. The fourth was locked.

"That's *it*?" Joan said. "Just here with the linen closet? I thought monster records were sacred."

"They are," Ruth said. "But even the Olivers are practical about it. And no one would ever actually break into an archive."

"Except us, apparently," Tom said wryly.

"All right." Joan pointed. "I'll keep watch up this end."

"I'll watch the other end," Tom said. He headed around the corner of the *L* and out of sight.

Joan took her place and listened at the door. It was so quiet that she was reminded of the Monster Court, the palace frozen in time. She could see Ruth and Jamie from this angle. Ruth took two pins from her hair and had the door open within seconds. *Crap lock*, she mouthed to Joan as she and Jamie slipped inside.

Joan tried not to fidget while she waited. She strained, listening for footsteps or telltale creaks. She folded her arms and shifted, trying to warm up without making any noise. The corridor was freezing, even on a warm night. The little bedroom opposite must have been ice-cold to sleep in.

Whose bedroom *was* it? In houses like this, servants' quarters were usually in the attic. And there wouldn't have been one bedroom alone. Joan peered inside, trying to puzzle it out. A thin-mattressed bed stood against the wall; the iron frame reminded her of school camps. In the corner, there was a small wardrobe; a latticed window showed a dismal view of a dirty brick wall and a bit of sky. Joan was struck by how mean and punitive the space was. This was a mansion with views of the most beautiful gardens in the country. And yet a worker had been put in *here*.

Whoever it was, they'd made the best of it. There was a beautiful floor lamp beside the bed: the glass was a deep-sea shade of blue. And the room was ruthlessly tidy: there wasn't a speck of dust on the floor; not a crease on the white sheets of the bed. The only small sign of disarray was a book on the pillow—*The*

Canterbury Tales—and a half-written letter with old-fashioned handwriting. A pen lay beside the letter.

Joan stared. She knew that handwriting. . . .

She took a step closer, putting her on the cusp of the room—still close enough to the end of the corridor to hear footsteps. There was a mermaid on the letterhead and a typeset name in elegant cursive: *Aaron Oliver.*

It took her a long moment to understand.

This was Aaron's bedroom.

But why would he be sleeping *here*, in this cold place, cut off from the luxury of the rest of the house? Joan had pictured him sleeping in a four-poster bed, amid damask silk and velvet. She'd pictured him with a suite of his own upstairs. But his family had hidden him away here, in this freezing room in the servants' wing.

She fought the impulse to step across the threshold. She had a terrible urge to read that letter; to open that wardrobe. Tears pricked in her eyes. She wasn't even sure why, except that she missed him more than she'd ever imagined she would. And she'd never get closer to him than this again, she knew. And she hated that he was in this house, with people who seemed to despise him.

She made herself take a step back. As she moved, a latch in the corridor sounded. She jumped. *Aaron*, she thought automatically. But no. Ruth and Jamie reemerged from the records room.

Ruth waved at Joan, looking triumphant, and Jamie jogged over to get Tom.

"You have it?" Joan whispered.

Ruth nodded. "Date and address!"

They took the same route back out, walking fast. *Date and address.* Joan glanced down at her gloved arm. She was still mired. If Nick had been taken to another time, Joan wouldn't be able to go after him. Was there a way to remove the cuff?

As she glanced up again, she realized there was someone right in front of her—not Ruth, but someone taller—entering the conservatory as she was exiting. They collided, and Joan stumbled back, narrowly avoiding a server with a tray of champagne glasses. She had the vague impression of something falling near her feet.

"I'm terribly sorry," a familiar voice said.

Joan's breath stopped.

Aaron had been beautiful from afar, but this close he was devastating. The golden mask was a perfect mold around his eyes, and he and Joan were a matched set—Joan in a gold-and-black dress, and Aaron in the gold mask, black dinner suit, and black shirt. They could have come here together. His eyes were as striking as she'd remembered: the gray of the sky before a storm.

Those eyes lingered on her as Aaron slowly took the mask from his face.

Joan's hand flew to her own face. To her horror, her fingers met bare skin. Her golden mask and the black gauze hiding her eyes lay on the ground. They'd fallen in the collision.

If you undo the massacre, you can't ever meet me. You can't ever trust me. Never let me close enough to see the color of your eyes.

For a moment, everything seemed suspended: Aaron's face was tight with shock; Joan was frozen.

"Aaron," Joan heard herself say pleadingly.

The sound of her voice broke the spell. Aaron's expression twisted into a loathing Joan had never seen from him.

"Aaron, *please*," Joan said. *You know me*, she thought. But he didn't. It didn't matter that they'd saved each other's lives. It didn't matter that the last time he'd seen her, he'd taken her to his mother's safe house. He'd told her that she'd meant something to him. He didn't *remember*.

"Security!" Aaron shouted. "To me!"

And then everything was happening at once—a blur of bodies in black suits. A man's heavy hand caught Joan's shoulder. And then her arms were being pulled back. She could hear Aaron's voice, heavy with hatred and sounding more like his father than himself: "Take her! She's an enemy of the Court!"

TWENTY-TWO

At Aaron's gesture, Joan was dragged from the conservatory to the edge of the reflecting pool, where the formal hedge work started. Joan caught a flash of Ruth's horrified face on a path ahead, Tom and Jamie on either side of her. *Go*, Joan signaled. Ruth shook her head, and Joan signaled again. *Go.*

Tom murmured into Ruth's ear, and to Joan's relief, he and Jamie bundled Ruth out of sight. Joan could only hope that no one had seen the four of them together. That the others would make it back to the boat.

Joan turned to Aaron. Alone among the guests, he and Joan were unmasked. As always, he was immaculate—not a golden hair out of place. This close, Joan could see the details of his suit: a delicate brocade of black on black. He still held his mask in one hand.

Joan was aware of her own disheveled contrast. Her hair had loosened from its half-braided style in the struggle, and threads hung from her dress where beads had come off.

"What did she do?" one of the security team said. There were three of them, Joan saw now—all in black suits.

Aaron ignored the question. His eyes were fixed on Joan's. And he might not know her anymore, but Joan knew him. She could read his expression, his body language. She knew exactly what he was remembering. He'd manifested the true Oliver power at the age of nine. As soon as he had, he'd been taken to view a man in an iron-barred cage. Aaron had told Joan about it, the horror of it still lingering with him after all those years: *They shocked him with a cattle prod until he looked into my eyes. They told me that if I saw anyone like him again, I was to kill them. Or inform the Court if I couldn't do it myself. I never saw anyone like him again. Until I saw you in the maze. Until I was close enough to see your eyes.*

"Just let me go," Joan begged Aaron now. "I know you don't want this." The Court had commanded him to kill people like her, but Aaron wouldn't want to be responsible for someone's execution. And he could still release her. He could just say there'd been a mistake. No one had really noticed this yet. "Aaron—"

Aaron's mouth twisted like when he'd called her *that filth* in Nick's front garden. "Stop saying my name," he said, and Joan swallowed around the lump in her throat. Was she going to be able to hold it together? "I know my duty," he said, hard. His hand came up to touch his side. Under that pristine suit, there was a tattoo of a mermaid—Joan had glimpsed the outline once, under his wet shirt. Was the Oliver motto there too? *Fidelis ad mortem*—loyal unto death. He lifted his head to the minders behind Joan. "Fetch my father."

"No, *please!*" Joan said. But one of the black-suited men broke away, jogging down the path to find Edmund. Joan took a deep breath, trying to get her emotions under control. Edmund had tried to kill Joan last time. Nick had saved her, but Nick wasn't here now. Nick wasn't even himself anymore.

"What did she do?" one of the team said again. "Did you catch her stealing something?"

"Stealing?" Aaron said with mild incredulity—as if catching a thief would have been far beneath him. "Give me her right wrist."

Joan fought it, but one of the guards caught her elbow. Aaron tugged her glove, working at the fingertips and then sliding down the base until the first hint of gold showed on her arm.

One of the black-suited men gasped. "She's a fugitive?"

And *now* they were drawing a crowd. Olivers were gathering in clusters nearby, staring at her and whispering. *"Fugitive,"* Joan heard. *"An enemy of the Court."* Their masks ranged from exquisite to lavishly grotesque: a scaled snake head with tiny shining diamonds; Lucien, with that eyeless filigree.

Joan tried to back up, but the grip on her was too tight. "Aaron, *please!*"

"Stop saying my *name!*" he snapped. "Stop saying my name as if you know me!" Joan flinched, and Aaron's eyes widened as if taken aback by his own outburst. He ran a shaky hand through his blond hair.

A heavy weight settled in Joan's chest, as painful as if it were pressed against her heart. *This isn't the first time we've met,* she wanted to say. *We knew each other in another lifetime.* But he wouldn't believe her, she knew. Her throat felt tight: the hurt of Aaron's disgust combining with the humiliation of the Olivers staring at her.

"What on earth is this fuss about?"

Joan flinched again at Edmund's voice. The crowd parted for him, and he strode over to Joan and Aaron.

Joan had forgotten how imposingly tall he was. He'd discarded his own mask, leaving his handsome face bare. His blond hair was paler than Aaron's. In his youth, he might have been as beautiful as his son, but age and the set of his face had turned those familiar features austere. "You had me fetched?" he said to Aaron. He made it sound dangerous.

"I found a fugitive on our grounds."

If Edmund was surprised or impressed by his son's capture of Joan, he didn't show it.

"Look at her eyes," Aaron said.

A flicker of interest then. Edmund peered down at Joan. His own eyes were the gray of flint. With his white-blond hair and black suit, he might have stepped out of a monochrome photograph. The moment stretched, and Joan's breath shallowed in fear. Something very much like this had happened before. Edmund had examined her just like this before he'd ordered her to be killed.

Joan had a flash of *her* Aaron again, brushing her cheek in the golden light of sunset. He'd been desperate for her to stay away from him. This was the exact scenario he'd feared. He'd known it would be like this.

"It's been a long time since I saw one of your kind," Edmund said. Joan shivered, and he smiled slightly. He'd enjoyed her fear last time too. He put his mouth to her ear. "You know what most delights me?" he murmured. "You don't even know what you are. None of you do. You all die without knowing."

Slowly, so that Joan could see it, he pushed back his jacket and slid a shining knife from a sheath.

"*No,*" Joan whispered, and his smile widened. She bit at the inside of her mouth. He *wanted* her to cry and beg before he killed her. He wanted to see her in pain. It was hard to believe *this* was Aaron's father. Aaron was nothing like him.

Edmund lifted the knife, letting the silver blade glint in the moonlight. The hilt was beautiful: shaped like a mermaid with a blue-and-green enamel tail. And Joan was properly shaking now. This was really happening—a continuation of the night in the Gilt Room when Edmund had ordered Lucien to kill her. This was what *would* have happened if Nick hadn't been there. And Edmund was right. She didn't know what she was.

To her horror, it got worse then. Edmund flipped the knife around and offered it hilt-first to Aaron.

No, Joan thought. *Not by Aaron's hand.* She couldn't stop shaking. She turned as best she could to Aaron. If she was going to die, she'd die with him in her eyes, and not Edmund's cruel face. Aaron had cared about her once, even if he'd never know it in this timeline.

Aaron stared down at the blade in his hand. He was deathly pale. "They want her alive." It came out so softly that for a second Joan wasn't sure she'd heard him right.

"What?" Edmund sounded impatient.

Joan didn't dare breathe. Was Aaron pushing back against his father? He'd tried to last time, but when Edmund had ordered him from the room, he'd gone. He'd left Joan to die.

"The instruction was to bring her to the Court Guards for questioning," Aaron said.

"The *instruction* has always been to kill abominations on sight." Edmund's gaze was scouring. "I wonder sometimes if you're even my blood. No son of mine would be so weak as to ask Court Guards to do his duty for him."

Aaron's eyes darted over Edmund's shoulder to the watching Olivers. His cheeks flushed. "I *am* your blood," he said tightly to

Edmund. "I have your name. I have your power."

Edmund surveyed Aaron from his looming height, drawing out the moment until Aaron blinked and looked away. "And isn't it wasted on you," he said scathingly. He shook his head when Aaron offered the knife back to him. "Keep it. Perhaps you'll find your spine on the way to the guardhouse."

Aaron stood there, the flush still high on his cheeks as the Olivers filtered back to the party. Joan's breath was still coming fast. She'd been braced for the agony of the knife; she could hardly believe she was still alive.

"Why did you—" she started.

Aaron cut her off, his beautiful face cold. "You'll be interrogated and then executed. As it should be." He retrieved a small golden disk from his pocket and pointed the thing at Joan's tattooed wrist. "You're anchored to me," he said. To the security men, he ordered, "Have someone bring a car around."

Aaron led her around the corner of the house. As soon as they were out of sight of the party, Joan bolted in the direction of the road.

"Stop!" Aaron called after her.

To Joan's shock, her body jolted to stillness. She jerked her head to Aaron, openmouthed. He was a full twenty paces behind her; he hadn't touched her. The security team had melted away as they'd walked, and Joan had thought—hoped—she'd have a chance to run. "How did you *do* that?" she said.

"Come back here!" Aaron said.

Joan's legs started toward him without her volition. Her heart pounded. "How are you *doing* this?" It wasn't the Argent power—she didn't *want* to obey. It was more like Aaron had bound her with invisible rope and was moving her around like a marionette.

"You're anchored to me through that cuff," Aaron said, as if surprised she didn't know. "Did you really think you could run?"

"But . . . it didn't work like that before," Joan said. She was horrified. Corvin Argent had used the words *anchored* and *cuffed*, and *he* hadn't been able to move Joan around.

"Well, I don't know why," Aaron said. "It should have. But I suppose it malfunctioned when you traveled with Corvin." He tilted his head. "When did you land?" he said curiously. "We were never able to work it out."

Joan shook her head. Why was he asking that? She and Nick had landed in the same time and place as Corvin. She still didn't understand why the Court hadn't been waiting when they'd landed.

"A question for the guardhouse, I suppose," Aaron said.

A shiny black Jaguar waited in the parking area, a gray-capped driver inside.

"Get in, please," Aaron told Joan. The flush was gone, and his face was very pale in the moonlight. Beside the driveway, the side of the house loomed, huge and intimidating, the pale stone wall fortress-like.

Joan balked. If she got in that car, her options would become very limited. She pressed her fingertips to the golden mark again, as surreptitiously as she could. *Unmake*, she told it. *Unmake*. Nothing happened; the tattoo remained unbroken gold.

"Oh, just get in," Aaron said. "I don't *like* using that cuff." And that seemed oddly true. The Argents had appeared to enjoy their power, but Aaron had been stiffly reluctant every time he'd pulled Joan along with him.

"You don't have to do this," Joan said pleadingly. "It's not too late to just let me go."

Aaron opened the car door and gestured without speaking. Joan's body twitched into motion. She ground her teeth as her limbs maneuvered themselves into the seat. How could she reach him? Was he even accessible? They'd met each other last time under such different circumstances—both of their families killed, corralled together on the run, saving each other's lives.

Aaron slid in beside her. "Get on the A4 and travel east," he told the driver. "I'll tell you when to turn."

The vast size of the Oliver estate became even more evident by car. The grounds around them shifted from lawn to trees to a field before they reached the road. As the driver turned into Richmond proper, Joan found herself watching Aaron. Just like with Nick, some stupid part of her still saw him as *her* Aaron.

At the same time, fear was unfurling in her as the reality of the situation hit. How long would this car ride be? If she couldn't break the cuff, Aaron was going to force her into the guards' custody—and then what? "You said they wanted to question me?"

There was a slight pause before Aaron answered. "They'll want to know who's been harboring you, for one thing."

Joan's mouth went dry. "No one's been harboring me." She could hear how unconvincing that sounded. At least she'd left her Hunt bracelet on the boat. . . .

"You can fight the Griffith interrogation as much as you like," Aaron said. "But you'll lose to the guards in the end." This had an odd note, as if he was speaking from experience.

"You can't want to hand me over to them," Joan whispered.

Aaron had fallen into shadow again. His voice was hard. "I don't know why you keep saying that."

Because I know you, Joan thought. *I know how horrified you were when you were given this mandate by the Court.*

But then headlights lit the car, and Joan saw the naked loathing on Aaron's face. *That filth,* he'd said. And that was how he was looking at her now, like he despised her; like he *wanted* her dead. "After you answer their questions, the guards will execute you," Aaron said. "And I'm going to stay and watch."

Joan's heart felt as heavy as lead. "You're going to *watch?*" she whispered disbelievingly. Edmund enjoyed seeing people scared and in pain, but Aaron wasn't like that. "You're going to watch them kill me?"

Even though he'd been the one to say it, Joan's question seemed to surprise Aaron into a real reaction; sick horror flitted across his face.

"You don't even know why they want me dead," Joan whispered. "You were told to look out for people like me, but you don't know why." *Joan* didn't even know why.

"I know why," Aaron said. He'd regained his equilibrium. "I'm doing it because people like you shouldn't exist. You should never have been born."

Edmund's words in Aaron's voice. Joan's chest felt so tight, she could hardly breathe.

"Maybe it's tempting to think that you know me," he said, and his gray eyes were serious. "I'm rather well-known. But you have no idea how much joy I'll take in your execution." On some level, he meant it—Joan could see it. Some part of him really was anticipating her death.

And just like that, Joan was near tears. She'd known that he'd meant a lot to her—she'd thought about him every day—but she hadn't realized how much until this moment. Until he'd shown her that he didn't feel it himself anymore. By the time the driver pulled into a parking space, it was taking everything Joan had to keep her eyes dry.

She felt a tug on her elbow. Aaron had gotten out of the car and was beckoning Joan to join him.

"Don't make me drag you out," he said.

Joan slid along the seat until she could climb out onto the pavement on Aaron's side. She took another step and was tugged back so sharply that she nearly fell.

"I shortened the leash," Aaron said coolly. "In case you were tempted to run again."

Keep it together, Joan told herself harshly. *If you don't, you're going to die.* She needed to escape this. She needed to *think*.

She forced herself to look around. Where was the guard-house? They were standing in front of a fenced park. She couldn't see much of it in the dark. The other side of the street looked big and commercial—cafés and clothes shops and a supermarket, all closed for the night.

Déjà vu hit Joan then—as strong as the feeling in the café, and even more unnerving. The shops themselves weren't familiar, but the configuration of the park and shops was.

"This is Holland House," she said slowly. Or it had been—the house itself had been in ruins for decades. The hairs on the back of her neck rose. "What are we doing *here*?"

"It's the local guardhouse," Aaron said, seeming bemused by her reaction.

"But . . . the house is in ruins," Joan said. It was too much of a coincidence—too strange—that Aaron had brought her *here*. Their families had been killed here; Joan had saved Aaron's life here; she'd met him and Nick here.

The timeline manipulated situations sometimes—like when it had brought Joan and Nick back together at Joan's school. Could it have brought Joan back here for a reason too? Joan sought the turning-gears feeling of the timeline manipulating events. And she couldn't feel that exactly, but around them, the air seemed to stir.

It wasn't a physical breeze, but a ripple of the timeline. Joan could feel it like an alerted animal. As if their presence here was somehow worthy of its attention.

Aaron frowned slightly; he'd felt it too and couldn't make sense of it. He answered Joan's question, though. "The guard-house isn't in this century."

That was all the warning Joan had.

The pang of yearning hit her out of nowhere. Before she could blink, the sky snapped from black to white. Her eyes watered at the sudden brightness. She squinted, trying to adjust her eyes. The air was hot and summery, and it smelled heavy, like smoke and animal dung. The sounds had changed too—the background grind of car engines had vanished, replaced by a cacophony of horses' hooves and market cries.

As Joan's vision cleared, she stared down Kensington High Street.

Horses and carriages streamed in chaotic paths down the

road as far as she could see. Ahead of her, a man ran to catch a horse-drawn omnibus, already packed with other people. He was dressed in a gray suit and a bowler hat, and he put a hand up to steady the hat as he ran. A hand-painted ad on the bus read: *Cadbury's cocoa. Absolutely pure therefore best.*

A woman cycled by, her long skirt bunched. She stared openmouthed at Joan as she passed, and Joan was abruptly aware of her own out-of-place clothes: the gold-and-black party dress from the masquerade. The woman herself was in a blousy shirt and tailored jacket.

When *was* this?

Joan took in the horses and buggies and bicycles and shops with homemade signs. More advertisements—for ice machines, Lipton Tea, Huntley & Palmers biscuits.

She turned back to the park. The gilded wrought-iron gate was still in its place, but the grounds had expanded, swallowing up the Design Museum to the west and the whole row of buildings beyond it.

A footstep sounded, making Joan jump. A man appeared at the Holland Park gate. He wore the formal uniform of a Court Guard: navy serge with gold buttons, a braided cap.

He surveyed Joan and Aaron through the iron bars, taking in their twenty-first-century clothes and the golden lion on Joan's arm.

"She's a fugitive," Aaron said. "Marked for execution."

The guard nodded, as if receiving condemned prisoners was an everyday occurrence. "Bring her in."

TWENTY-THREE

Aaron's grip on Joan was still tight as they stepped through the open gate. The path ahead was gloomy under the white sky. Through the trees, Joan glimpsed vast grounds—far bigger than the current park. More like the one she'd known when she'd worked here. Chimney smoke curled up into the sky—the first sign of the house. Joan stared. She'd never actually seen the house chimneys in working order.

She caught Aaron's head tilt as he peered through the leaves. "Does it look familiar?" she asked him tentatively.

Aaron started to frown automatically, and then he just looked puzzled. "Well, of course. I've been to the guardhouse before."

Not because of that, Joan thought. *Because this was your childhood home.* That wasn't true in this timeline, though. A lot of things weren't true in this timeline. . . . Her chest felt heavy again. *That filth*, he'd called her. Where had that word come from? He'd never spoken about her like that. He'd never looked at her like he'd hated her.

She'd never thought it could hurt this much when he did.

You were more than just acquaintances, weren't you? Nick had said to Joan at Queenhithe.

Joan still felt bonded to Aaron beyond the actual time they'd spent together. They'd escaped a massacre together. He'd taught her about the monster world.

For the first time, though, Joan wondered if there'd been

anything more between them than that. Was that why this hurt so much? Had she felt more for him than just friendship?

No, she told herself.

And then: *I don't know.*

She blinked. She hadn't expected to answer her own question like that.

She forced herself to be honest now. She'd been attracted to him last time. She still was. Probably most people who encountered Aaron wanted him, at least a little. But she'd actually liked *him* too.

Had he felt the same about her? It didn't seem possible; someone like Aaron could have anyone he wanted. And yet . . . There'd been a moment at the end when he'd touched her face. When it had seemed as if he'd been about to kiss her. And she'd felt . . . She swallowed. She'd felt something for him in return.

And what about now? How did she feel now?

A gust of wind rippled through the leaves, ruffling Aaron's hair, harsh enough to make Joan's eyes sting.

She released the thought. It didn't really matter how she felt about Aaron, did it? Any more than it mattered how she felt about Nick. They were both gone.

Joan looked back over her shoulder. A sliver of Kensington High Street was still visible. A horse-drawn hackney rolled past, driven by a man in a tweed suit.

"What year is this?" she asked Aaron. How far away from home was she now?

"The guardhouse is here from 1889 until 1904," he said, sounding as cold as ever. "They wanted you brought to 1891."

Joan took that in. Even if she *could* escape from these grounds, she'd be stuck here, mired by the cuff. And she'd stand out in these clothes. She had a flash of the woman on the bike staring at her, with the kind of goggling shock someone might have at seeing a stray zoo animal.

When Joan was in Aaron's company, most people looked at him, but Joan's clothes had clearly been so outlandish that—

Wait . . . Joan replayed it in her mind's eye—the woman hadn't just been looking at Joan's clothes; she'd been staring at her face too.

Joan almost groaned aloud. How big was the Chinese population here? If she managed to get out of this place, she wasn't going to escape the guards with a change of clothes. She was a Chinese girl in Victorian London. She'd be memorable wherever she went.

"Come on," Aaron said.

Ahead of them, the house appeared in pieces: the fairy-tale roofline, the gingerbread edges, the glint of glass. And then the path opened up onto the lawn, revealing the full scope of it.

Holland House was as beautiful as Joan had remembered—a grand Jacobean manor in red brick and white trim. Despite the horror of the situation, Joan drank in the sight of it: the turrets, the colonnades. This was fifty years before the Blitz; before the west wing would fall; before fire would consume the elegant library, the Map Room, the Gilt Room. . . .

And at the same time, it wasn't quite as she'd remembered. She'd only ever known it as a museum—a re-creation with ropes barring access to rooms, with fireplaces sealed up. This was the real house, alive.

Aaron frowned slightly. "It's strange. I feel like . . ."

Did he remember something? "You feel what?" Joan said. Like he'd been here before?

The guard had been silent except to guide them down the path. Now he spoke. "Holland House," he said. "Beautiful, isn't it? King William III once considered making it his palace. He chose Kensington instead."

Aaron's face cleared. "Yes, very nice," he said briskly. He started walking again. Joan stared after him until the cuff jerked her forward. Had a memory of the previous timeline almost been triggered in him? Was that possible?

She followed Aaron and the guard across the lawn, poking the grass with her shoe as she walked. The curators had consulted old paintings when they'd made the house into a museum, but it seemed that the painters had rendered the lawn as more lush than it had really been. The actual grass was pale and patchy, and muddy in places from rain.

They reached the stone steps of the porch, and the guard pushed open the door. Joan looked down automatically at that first familiar tile. *Cave Canem*, it said. *Beware the Dog.*

The entrance hall wasn't quite as Joan had known it either. The tile pattern was the same: wreathed fleurs-de-lis in blue and gold. But the pylons with their marble busts had been removed, along with the chairs and the grandfather clock. Even bare, the room was beautiful, though, with wooden paneling, intricately carved. Arched openings framed the next room—the inner hall—with its tapestries and frescoed ceiling of cupids and clouds.

"Put her in there." The guard nodded at the smoking room at the end of the entrance hall.

Joan walked in and only realized that Aaron and the guard weren't following when the door closed behind her.

A rustle of silk made her turn.

She froze.

Joan had only ever seen the woman once—in a recording of Nick's first kill: a cold beauty with golden hair. She sat now at the smoking desk of Holland House, as if at a throne, her hair cascading down her shoulders. In the recording, she'd had a regal authority. In person, that quality was far stronger, reminiscent of a force of nature; of a ruler unafraid to shed her subjects' blood in war.

"Hello, Joan," the woman said.

TWENTY-FOUR

She was a fairy-tale princess come to life—around twenty-one years old, Joan guessed. Her blue dress was medieval—long-sleeved silk, with a straight cut. Her eyes were blue too, like an afternoon sky.

For a long moment, Joan couldn't believe her own eyes. She couldn't believe the woman was *here*. And then the moment passed, and her heart was drumming painfully in her chest.

This woman had ruined Joan's life; had forged Nick from an ordinary boy into the slayer who'd killed Joan's family. She'd been behind the deaths of all their families. *All* of them. Joan's, Aaron's, and Nick's. She'd taken Jamie captive and put him in a cold, dark cell. She'd torn Joan and Nick apart, turning them from soul mates into enemies.

Again, she'd said in the recordings. *Again*. She'd tortured Nick and murdered his family, rewinding time to do it over and over. The timeline shouldn't have allowed it, but it had bent to the woman's will.

Nick had resisted his new destiny at first. He hadn't wanted to be a killer.

With respect, must we use this boy? the woman's assistant had said. *How many times have we killed his parents? He's always so* virtuous *afterward.*

This is the boy, the woman had replied. *Not in spite of his virtuousness, but because of it. When we break him, that quality will turn into righteous fury.*

It had taken two thousand iterations before Nick had killed a monster without remorse. And at the end of it, the woman had given Nick a cold, approving smile. *You're perfect*, she'd said.

"Why?" Joan said now. She wanted answers to so many questions, but that was the one that came out of her mouth first. Why had the woman forged Nick into the hero? Why had she wanted all those people dead? Why had she torn Joan and Nick apart? "Who *are* you?" Joan said.

Something complicated passed over the woman's face— pain and anger and sadness combined—before her expression smoothed. "The amnesia of new timelines is quite a thing, isn't it," she said. Her voice was as Joan had remembered from the recordings too: measured and deep. "Honestly, I'm a little disappointed, Joan. I didn't expect you to arrive in a cuff. Maybe you're losing your touch."

Joan stared at her. The woman's tone had been intimate— although mockingly so. *The amnesia of new timelines.* Did she know Joan somehow?

Something else from her wording had snagged too, but Joan had another flash of those recordings: of Nick's face when he'd found his family dead on the kitchen floor.

And suddenly, Joan just didn't care that this woman knew her name. She didn't care how this woman knew her. "Where's *Nick?*" she said. The woman had him, and nothing else mattered. "Is he *here*? What have you done to him?"

"Nick," the woman repeated softly. Her tone was mocking

again, but Joan had the impression of something complicated and seething underneath it. "It's always about Nick with you, isn't it? And that blond boy."

"What?" Was she talking about Aaron?

"God, you really don't remember, do you?" the woman said. "You don't remember me."

What was Joan supposed to say to that? She *didn't* remember. It was disconcerting that the woman seemed to know *her*. Joan was more used to being on the other side of the memory divide. "Well, *tell* me, then," she gritted out. "Who *are* you? Why did you want all those people dead? My *family* dead?"

For a second, Joan thought she saw a spark of cold rage in the woman's blue eyes. But then the woman's mouth curved up. "Honestly? Him killing your family was just a bonus."

Joan felt something snap inside her. She started furiously toward the woman, and the woman raised a hand almost lazily. Joan's body stopped, manipulated again by that stupid cuff.

"Oh, I *like* that cuff," the woman said. "I like seeing you cowed."

Joan clenched her fists. She wasn't cowed. The woman's smirk deepened as if she'd heard the thought.

"Did it mess you up?" the woman said. "When I turned that virtuous boy into a killer?" She drawled the word *virtuous*, as if Nick's decency was something to be mocked. "Did you hate him for killing your family? I bet you hate him still—a little bit. Even now that you've made him weak and innocent again."

Joan wished she could get close enough to throw a punch. She hated the way the woman was talking to her—like there was something personal between them. Joan searched her face, trying to trigger any kind of memory in herself. Nothing came—not a feeling, not a sense of déjà vu. "Why *did* you make him into a killer?" Joan demanded.

The woman smiled. "It *did* mess you up."

Joan ground her teeth. *She was planning something last time*, Jamie had said. "Did I ruin *your* plans by unmaking him?" Joan asked. "Did you need him for something?"

A flicker of irritation. "You inconvenienced me, but I'm resourceful." And then—as if she'd abruptly tired of the conversation—the woman stood. She beckoned to Joan with one finger, pale nail polish gleaming. Then she strode imperiously from the room in an elegant sweep of silk.

To Joan's frustration, she was forced to scramble after her. At the same time, her mind was racing. *Did it mess you up?* The woman had wanted to hurt Joan, but she'd given away something too. *Him killing your family was just a bonus.* And: *You inconvenienced me.* Jamie had been right—the woman *had* been planning something. She'd wanted to use Nick for something.

The woman led Joan into the inner hall. It was the house hub, and guards streamed in and out of the breakfast room and the white parlor to get to the west and east wings of the house. Aaron stood near the staircase, his posture stiff.

As the woman and Joan entered, the busy guards stopped and stood at attention. By the staircase, Aaron put a hand to his chest and folded into a perfect bow.

"The Lady Eleanor of the *Curia Monstrorum!*" a guard announced.

Joan stepped back, shaken. The *Curia Monstrorum*—the

members of the Monster Court—were the King's arms and executioners: the enforcers of his law. And if Joan's situation here had seemed bad before, it was dire now. The *Curia Monstrorum* had power beyond any equivalent in the human world.

"Rise," the woman said to Aaron. She'd always carried herself with authority, and she looked regal now, as if that golden head should have borne a crown.

Aaron straightened, his gray eyes fixed on her in awe.

Joan stared too. She should have guessed Eleanor's position— how else could she have commanded guards? Who else could have locked up Jamie in the Monster Court? Could have amended the family records to hide Nick's massacres . . .

At the same time, it seemed even more strange that Eleanor could have ever known Joan—in any timeline. This was a woman who ruled the monster world, beneath only the King himself.

"You may approach," Eleanor told Aaron, and Aaron walked over from the stairs, head ducked shyly. He stopped a few paces away.

"I understand you found the fugitives," Eleanor said. "The boy *and* the girl."

"Yes, my lady," Aaron whispered.

"You have done very well," Eleanor told him. "You have pleased the Court. You have pleased *me*."

Aaron flushed pink all the way to the collar of his black shirt, drinking in Eleanor's approval like an under-watered flower.

Joan pressed her nails into the palms of her hands. Eleanor's smile somehow made her look colder. It was the same smile she'd given Nick when she'd told him he was perfect. Joan couldn't bear the thought of Eleanor hurting Aaron like she'd hurt Nick.

Aaron was more vulnerable than he seemed—loyal to the core. And Joan hadn't realized until this moment how desperate he was for approval from an authority figure. Had he ever received it from his cruel father? *I wonder sometimes if you're even my blood,* Edmund had told Aaron in front of the entire Oliver family. *No son of mine would be so weak.*

"Why are you doing all this?" Joan said, wanting to draw Eleanor's attention from Aaron.

A jolt of the leash from Aaron—Joan felt it in every joint. Not painful exactly, but humiliating enough to be irritating. "Watch your tone, or hold your tongue!" he said, voice low. "You stand before a member of the *Curia Monstrorum.* The Lady Eleanor herself."

Cruel amusement flashed over Eleanor's face—quicksilver, like a brief ripple in a still lake—it seemed oddly directed at Aaron as much as Joan.

Why was Eleanor doing this to them? Why had she split lovers into a monster and monster slayer? Why had she mentioned Aaron earlier—*that blond boy?*

For a second, under Eleanor's cool gaze, Joan felt as if she were standing high above, looking down at them all, tangled up in something complicated and big: Joan, Nick, Aaron, Eleanor . . .

Joan opened her mouth to ask again where Nick was, and her throat spasmed without sound. She tried again, but the only noise from her mouth was air. She turned to Aaron. *Watch your tone, or hold your tongue,* he'd said. Had he silenced her with that cuff? Joan opened her mouth again. *Aaron, let me speak! I need to talk!*

But Aaron wasn't even looking at her anymore—his attention had turned reverently back to Eleanor.

Eleanor smirked at Joan and gestured to Aaron with a curl of her fingers. "Follow me."

Aaron started after Eleanor, and the leash made Joan stumble along with him. *Aaron,* she tried to say. To her frustration, she couldn't make a sound.

Eleanor led them up the principal staircase, past the familiar tapestries and chocolate-curl wall carvings. Where was she taking them?

Watch your tone, or hold your tongue. Joan took a deep breath, trying to gather herself. Maybe she'd be able to speak if she *watched her tone.* "Aaron," she managed. It worked. She was able to speak as long as she sounded calm. She took another breath, trying to keep the fear from her voice. "Something's going on here. Something bad." She reached for him, but the cuff tugged her hand back down. Joan ground her teeth. *Stop moving me around,* she tried to say. Aaron didn't even look back—didn't even know she was trying to speak, and somehow that was even more humiliating than if he'd watched her mouthing the words. "You can't trust Eleanor," she managed.

Eleanor threw an amused look over her shoulder, and Aaron flushed red, as if Joan was showing him up.

"Quiet," he hissed. *"You're* the one who can't be trusted! *You're* the enemy of the Court!"

As they reached the entresol above, Joan's legs went shaky. Up here was the Gilt Room where the Olivers had died, and—

"Open it." Eleanor gestured at the library door. A square had been cut out of the wood, and someone had installed iron bars.

Aaron lifted a heavy wooden latch from the door. Joan's first impression was a dizzying familiarity. The room had been stripped of books, but she knew this long gallery space as well as her own home. She'd met Nick here. She'd kissed him here.

"Joan!"

Joan turned fast. *"Nick!"*

She scrambled to get to him and only realized that her leash had been cut when she fell to her knees in front of him. He was chained by the wrist to a heavy ring embedded into the wall. He was still in the black T-shirt from the Wyvern Inn, although his jacket was gone, leaving his neck vulnerable and his muscled arms bare.

"Are you okay?" Joan said hoarsely. "Are you all right?"

"Hey," Nick murmured. He knelt up as best as he could, and Joan swallowed hard, relief hitting her whole body, all at once. He was here. He was *alive.*

The door slammed behind them. Joan turned just as the heavy latch fell, locking her and Nick in. She pushed back up and ran to the door. *"Aaron—"* she started, but Eleanor stood outside the door alone now, watching through the door's barred window.

"I dismissed the blond boy," Eleanor said. Her eyes bored into Joan. "He's a pretty one, isn't he? Maybe I'll keep him." There was a challenging note in her voice, as if she wanted Joan to react.

"Leave him *alone*," Joan blurted, and then wished she hadn't. Eleanor had already messed with Aaron downstairs. If she thought Joan cared about Aaron's welfare, maybe she'd hurt him too. She swallowed. "Why are you *doing* all this?"

"All this?" Eleanor said.

"I know you're planning something!" Joan said. "I *know!*" Joan thought again of the statue of Eleanor as queen. The terrible vision through the window had to be part of it. Joan took a guess. "I saw the world you want to make."

"You saw *what?*" Eleanor's eyes widened. The hairs rose on the back of Joan's neck. Eleanor hadn't exactly confirmed it, but her expression had changed from mocking to raw, as if she'd momentarily dropped a veil. "We caught Nick outside an Ali seal," Eleanor said slowly. "You broke the seal? You saw something in that tear in the timeline?"

Joan drew a breath. Tom had guessed right when he'd said that the jagged wound in the world had been a tear in the timeline itself.

"What did you see?" Eleanor demanded.

Joan had a vivid memory of unbearable dissonance; of something tearing—viscerally—like tissue paper under her fingers. And then that terrible world had appeared. The terrified man, and the monster who'd killed him. The onlookers too afraid to protest. . . .

"I saw a police van with Court livery. I saw a Court Guard step out of it."

Eleanor gripped the bars, pressing closer, her expression full of yearning—as if Joan had just given her something precious. She lowered her voice, soft enough that it was just for Joan; soft enough that Nick, still chained to the back wall, wouldn't hear. "You saw a world where monsters reign. A better world."

"Better?" Joan had a flash of the bodies in the van, and her stomach lurched. "I saw hell!" she whispered. She could hear the horror of it in her own voice.

I've seen the end of everything that matters, Astrid had said.

The yearning melted from Eleanor's face—replaced by the complicated expression from earlier. What *was* it? Not cruelty, but pain. And an old, old anger. "You saw the world as it *should* be. As it *will* be when I've remade it."

Joan searched her face and found only conviction. "You didn't see what I saw." If Eleanor had . . . "Go and look at the tear for yourself! Go and look at that world!" Maybe Eleanor would understand then. Monsters stole human life, but only a few days from each person. Most of them didn't go around killing people. "There were human bodies piled in a van! Fifteen of them! Twenty!" Not even monsters would want to live in a world like that.

"It's already in motion," Eleanor said. And now the pain and anger were in her voice too. "That timeline is coming."

Joan found herself glancing back at Nick. He was chained to the back wall—too far away to hear this whispered conversation. But he was watching, his gaze steady. He *would have stopped it*, Astrid had said. *He was already on the path. But you stopped* him.

Joan clenched her fists. "No." She turned back to Eleanor. "I'm going to stop *you*." It came out solemn as a vow. She didn't know how she'd do it—she was locked in a cell, a mark of execution on her arm. And Eleanor had authority in this world beyond anyone but the King. But Joan knew one thing: she herself had removed the hero from the world. That meant *she* was responsible for fixing this.

Eleanor's knuckles whitened where she was gripping the bars.

"You never understood. You still don't. *You* were always the one who had to be stopped, Joan."

Joan blinked at her, confused. "What?"

Eleanor just shook her head. She released the bars. "I'll be back when I'm ready for you." Then she turned, and Joan heard her footsteps fading as she made her way through the entresol and back down into the house.

TWENTY-FIVE

Nick was chained in place by one wrist. They'd put him just under a picture window that looked out onto the Dutch Garden. Joan knelt on the parquetry floor in front of him.

"Joan." He wrapped his free arm around her, and Joan pressed her forehead to his shoulder. His free hand came up to thumb a tear track from her face. When had she started crying? "We're going to get out of here," he said seriously. "We'll figure it out."

Joan touched his tethered wrist. Under the manacle, his skin was chafed raw. The cuff was attached to a cruelly short chain that ended in a metal loop embedded halfway up the stone wall of the fireplace, like a ship's mooring ring. Its position meant that Nick had to sit awkwardly with his hand raised above him. And if he got to his feet, he'd have to uncomfortably stoop. "How long have they made you sit like that?" Joan said. There was new chafing over old.

"Don't worry about it." Nick pulled her closer, mouth pressed to the top of her head. His voice seemed to rumble through her whole body. "I'm okay." His voice darkened. "How did they capture you? Did they hurt *you*?"

Joan shook her head against his shoulder. "Let me get that chain off you," she managed.

She looked around. The Holland House library was a long gallery that spanned the full width of the house. In its prime, its shelves had been full of leather-bound books, its walls crammed with oil paintings. But Eleanor had stripped the space bare, leaving the shelves and walls eerily empty. The only remaining decoration was the evening-blue ceiling with its constellation of silver stars, and the red wallpaper of rich Cordova leather.

Joan couldn't see anything that would help with picking a lock. She had a couple of pins in her hair, though. She always did now—ever since Nick had chained her up in this same house.

She pushed away the memory of her own shackled leg and cuffed hands, and she took his wrist to study the keyhole. Nick's pulse jumped under her touch.

Joan was aware suddenly that she'd just been pressed right up against him, his mouth against her head like a kiss. They were still close enough that the air between them felt warm. His T-shirt was so thin that he could have been bare-chested. Joan could see every muscle.

"How . . . how long have you been here?" she asked again.

"A few weeks," Nick said.

Weeks? Joan said, horrified. Eleanor had had him for weeks? What had she done to him in that time?

"They brought me here in a horse and carriage. This is the past, isn't it?"

"It's 1891," Joan said, and Nick made a soft sound like when he'd looked out onto London's new landmarks. *Weeks*, Joan thought again. "Did she do anything to you? Hurt you?"

"She?" Nick seemed puzzled. "You mean the woman you just spoke to? I've barely seen her."

Joan took a deep breath, trying to feel relieved. She had too many questions, though. Why had Eleanor taken Nick again? Why had she made him into the hero in the first place? Why had she put Joan and Nick in here together?

"Where'd you learn to pick a lock?" Nick said.

Joan looked up at him, and his eyes crinkled—he was trying to distract her from being scared. Joan tried to smile back. She focused again on the lock. It was a little large for bobby pins. "My gran taught me," she said. "She used to make a game of it with me and Ruth and our other cousin Bertie."

"Racing against each other to pick locks?"

Joan found herself smiling a little for real. "Nah. Bertie doesn't like games that people can lose. Gran used to put chocolates in locked boxes. If we could break the lock, we could keep the prize."

"My brother Robbie's a bit like Bertie," Nick said. "Ruth reminds me of Alice."

Joan blinked up at him. It felt strange to be talking about her family with him—in this house where they'd died. Where Gran had bled out in Joan's arms. This Nick didn't remember that, though.

Joan touched his arm—careful to stay away from the raw redness of his wrist. "You miss them," she whispered, and Nick nodded.

"All of them. My mum, my sister Mary . . . I used to walk the little ones to school." His forehead creased. "God, they haven't been born yet here. My grandparents haven't been born yet."

Joan knew how he was feeling. The first time she'd traveled, she'd felt unmoored. She'd arrived in 1993—a time before her own birth, before Dad had immigrated to England. She hadn't known anyone but Aaron. "I'm so sorry I haven't been able to get you home."

Nick lifted his eyes to hers. "The blonde woman . . . ," he said. "The one you spoke to. I heard her name—Eleanor."

It creeped Joan out that Nick didn't remember her. Eleanor had molded him into the hero last time. "She's an authority figure in the monster world," Joan explained. "Just below the King himself. I think she's trying to change the timeline—to that vision we saw through the café window?"

Nick's jaw tightened. "The van with the corpses." *You saw the world as it* should *be,* Eleanor had said. *As it* will *be.* Joan clenched her fists. No, it *wouldn't* be.

"Eleanor wants to make that world a reality. She wants to change the timeline."

Nick's gaze was very clear. "It's not going to happen. We're going to stop her." He sounded so certain that Joan could almost believe him. A flicker of sickness crossed that clear gaze, and Joan knew he was seeing them again. The dead people. "I don't understand why she's doing this," he said. "We saw a murder in broad daylight. All those people in the van. Who would want to create a world like that?"

Joan dropped her head. To answer that question, she would have to tell Nick the truth of what monsters were. And if she did that, she'd lose him. Again. When Gran had told Joan the truth, Joan had run from the family house. It had seemed too horrifying to believe.

Joan had already lost Aaron in this timeline—she'd been confronted with the truth of that tonight. Her heart felt half-broken in ways she didn't want to think about yet. If she lost Nick too, she'd finish the job on her heart. She wouldn't be able to bear it. One loss too many.

Joan opened her mouth to speak, and then felt tears at the back of her throat. It took her a second to understand why. It was because some part of her had already decided. Had maybe decided in that conversation with Astrid.

He *would have stopped it. But you stopped* him. *Did you think there'd be no consequences?*

Astrid had fought alongside Nick because she'd believed he'd save the world. Joan could believe it too. Eleanor might have turned him into the hero for her own purposes, but he'd been a true hero.

The woman who made him . . . she believes no one can stop her, Jamie had told her once. *But she's wrong. She thinks she made the hero perfectly. She didn't. She made a mistake with him.*

Eleanor's real mistake had been underestimating Nick. He had a core of goodness, and someone like Eleanor could never have understood that. Nick would have figured out his own origin story; he'd have turned against her and righted the world. He'd already wanted peace between monsters and humans by the end.

And Joan had unmade him.

"Joan?" Nick said.

Joan lifted her head to look at him. She was going to lose him, but it wasn't about her. He deserved to know the truth; it had been wrong to keep it from him. She took a deep breath. "It wasn't just a man killing a man," she said. "That's not what we saw through the window."

Nick held her gaze, steady. "What did we see, then?" His eyes were as intelligent as ever. If Joan gave him time, that piece of information alone would be enough for him to figure it out already, she knew. But she had to say it.

Her hands shook in her lap. She pressed them between her knees, trying to stop the shaking. Her mouth felt dry. "There's something I haven't told you," she said. "Something I *should* have told you." She hesitated, and then forced the words out: "Monsters steal human life. It's the cost of time travel."

Nick's expression didn't change. He searched her face. "What?" he said.

Joan's whole body felt tense. "The world we saw—the world with the dead humans . . . It was a world where monsters rule. *That's* the world Eleanor wants to create."

"Well, we can't let that happen," he said. It sounded a little flat, and his expression still hadn't changed. "We can't let her do that."

Joan stared at him. When she tried to speak again, her voice failed. He was in shock, she realized. He'd react fully in a second. Nick wasn't the type to raise his voice, but she'd seen him in the state Eleanor had called *righteous fury*. This was the person who'd led massacres of monsters. A figure of myth and terror among monsters.

"What's Eleanor's plan?" Nick asked.

"I . . . I don't know," Joan said.

Why wasn't Nick telling her that he hated her? Her muscles were starting to ache with the tension of being halfway to fight or flight.

"*Nick,*" she whispered. "Did you hear what I said? Monsters—"

"Monsters steal life from humans," Nick said. "It's the cost of time travel." He added, almost as an afterthought, "That's very wrong." His tone was still oddly flat, though. He tilted his head. There was a little more expression in his face, but only curiosity in his tone. "The man we saw . . . the *monster* . . . He touched the other man's neck. Is that how monsters steal life? Do the humans always die?"

Joan stared at him again. "I . . . No, they . . . Monsters usually take a day or two of time from individual people. They don't tend to kill people outright like what we saw, but . . ." And suddenly the tension was too much. She felt her mouth crumple. "Why are you being so calm? I told you that monsters steal life from humans! They prey on humans! They're out there living among humans, and humans don't even know!"

Nick grimaced slightly. "I heard what you said." He looked more closely at her, and his face creased with concern. Concern for *her*? "You're shaking," he said. "Were you afraid of how I'd react?"

This was wrong. This was *wrong*. Why was he talking like that? "You're almost acting like . . ." She stopped. *Like you're fine with it*, she'd been about to say.

Owen had told Nick back at the safe house: *You're fine with monsters. You don't want to hurt monsters.*

The terrible understanding dawned. "You're still under the compulsion of the Argent power," she breathed. "You're not yourself."

"How did you think I would react?" Nick said. He looked even more concerned suddenly—by far his most intense emotion since she'd told him the truth. "Were you afraid to tell me? You don't have to worry—nothing bad will happen, even if this power wears off. I'd never hurt you."

It hadn't occurred to Joan that the power might just wear off, but now she realized that was likely. This was just a reprieve. When it *did* wear off, Nick would react properly. Joan squeezed her eyes shut for a second. It didn't feel like a reprieve. It felt like drawing out something terrible.

"Joan . . ." Nick touched her back, warm and reassuring, and Joan choked with the guilt of it.

"You shouldn't," she said thickly. *He* shouldn't be comforting *her.* His touch withdrew fast.

He looked stricken. "I'm sorry. I shouldn't have presumed."

Joan's heart clenched. "That's not . . . I *want* you to—" She stopped herself, but not fast enough. Nick's eyes widened as he took in what she hadn't said.

Joan's heart thudded. She hadn't meant to say that. She hadn't even known that she'd felt like that about this new Nick.

Did she feel like that?

No, she told herself. *No, no, no.* He just looked like the boy she'd loved. The boy she'd killed. And, God, this was so messed up. *She* was so messed up.

He looked at her searchingly, eyes darkening, and Joan's breath hitched. She'd seen that look before—just before he'd kissed her the first time. She couldn't always read this new Nick, but she could read that.

"Sometimes . . . ," Nick said tentatively, as if he was feeling out the words. "Sometimes . . . I feel like I've known you forever. I know we've just met, but it feels like I've known you my whole life."

Of all the cruel tricks that the timeline played, this was the cruelest—the way that emotions lingered from lifetime to lifetime. Joan and Nick had belonged together in the true timeline, and some resonance of that remained. *If you're feeling anything for me, it isn't real,* Joan wanted to say. *It's just something that someone else once felt.* "You're going to hate me so much soon," Joan whispered. *That* would be real.

"I won't hate you," Nick said to her, frowning. "I could never hate you. It's the *opposite.* I—"

"Don't," Joan pleaded. *"Don't."* He couldn't finish that sentence. He was saying all the things that she wished he'd really say, and she couldn't bear how much he'd regret it when the Argent power wore off. "Nick, when that power leaves you, you'll despise me. You'll—" Her breath shuddered, and she clenched her teeth, trying to get herself back under control. But a sob came, and another. When he understood, she'd lose him for good. Again. Always, always, always. Whatever they'd had in the true timeline was never coming back.

Nick didn't move toward her, but he looked devastated, like it hurt him to see her hurting.

His wrist was still chained uncomfortably above him. Joan wanted to work on the lock again, but when she went to twist the bobby pin, she found her hands were shaking too much.

"Whatever you think is going to happen . . . ," Nick said softly. "Whatever's making you cry . . . You don't have to worry. When this power is off, we'll *talk*. I'll listen to you, and you'll listen to me."

Every word he said only confirmed that he wasn't himself. "Even with that power on you, some part of you hates what I told you," Joan whispered. She said it again: "About how monsters steal human life." And *there* it was—that small grimace. Some part of him *could* feel it. Or maybe some part of him was fighting the compulsion.

"I'm not as far under as you think," Nick said. "I know it's wrong." But he said the last bit without emotion, like he was talking about something abstract.

"I think you're further under than you know," Joan whispered.

She'd instigated this, she reminded herself. Whether the Band-Aid came off slowly or quickly, it had to come off. He'd deserved to know what monsters were.

Nick shifted to face her as much as he could. "*Why* do monsters travel in time?" he asked. "Why do it at all if the cost is human life?"

Joan blinked. It wasn't the first question she'd have asked. It wasn't a question she'd even thought about. She'd always yearned for other times—even before she'd known what she was.

"It's like an urge," she admitted. "I can feel it all the time. I always want to travel."

Nick took that in. "And *do* you? Do you travel in time? Do *you* steal human life?"

For some reason, Joan hadn't expected him to ask that question either. She felt off-balance. She was struck again by his physical presence. The size of his shoulders, his arms. Even without his

abilities—even leashed by the Argent power—he seemed dangerous: a predatory animal in a fragile cage. When he broke free . . .

"You *don't*," Nick said slowly. "You told me that at the Wyvern
Inn. You said that you didn't travel. I couldn't understand it at the
time. I didn't understand the cost."

"I don't— I mean . . ." Joan could hear how guilty she sounded.
The strange thing was, she'd never traveled of her own volition
in this timeline. In the previous one, though, she'd stolen so much
life trying to bring back her family. She felt sick at the memory of
it. "I *have*," she whispered. "I've done it before."

"But not anymore." Nick sounded certain.

"I have," Joan said. "Never again, though." *Never.*

"And your family?" Nick said. "Ruth?"

Joan couldn't bring herself to nod.

"It's wrong," Nick said, serious.

"I know," Joan said.

"How can you stand it?" Nick whispered. "How can you stand
what they're doing—your own family?"

"I don't know," Joan blurted. "Maybe I can't stand it." She
blinked at her own admission. She hadn't meant to say that. She'd
never said it aloud.

Nick released a heavy breath, and Joan was struck by a sudden intense memory of them both sitting against the far wall of
this room on the night they'd kissed. The house had been empty
and silent around them, and Nick had tilted up her face with one
big hand . . .

"That must be difficult," Nick said. And Joan was off-balance
again. She'd expected him to say something harsher. "It would be

difficult for me," Nick said. "If they were my family, and I loved them."

"What would you do?" Joan whispered.

"If I found out my own family were stealing human life?" Nick's mouth curled down. He might have found the scenario difficult, but he couldn't fight his natural disgust. Another hint of how he'd react if his mind were free. "Well . . . if I'd found out that a member of my family had murdered someone, I'd turn them in to the police." He ducked his head, thinking. "But I suppose there's no way to turn in a monster. You wouldn't be believed. So . . . I think I'd try to convince them first. To try to get them to understand why it's so wrong."

Turn them in to the police? Talk to them? Try to get them to understand? Was this Owen Argent's power talking? Or was this how Nick really thought?

Joan remembered those videos of him being tortured. He'd fought so hard against being turned into a monster slayer. His inclination had been toward empathy for so long. Even after his family had been murdered, he'd assumed their killer was unwell rather than a real monster. It had taken nearly two thousand attempts for Eleanor to turn him into someone who could kill monsters with thoughtless ease.

Would he still think like this after the Argent power was removed?

No. Monsters had controlled his mind. How could he ever forgive that? How could he ever forgive Joan for allowing it to happen?

"Eleanor . . . ," Nick said, and Joan blinked up at him. "You said that she wants to create that world we saw?" He frowned—a real frown.

"She *can't*," Joan said. "That world *cannot* exist. I have to stop her." What *was* Eleanor's plan, Joan wondered again desperately. How was she going to create that timeline? Joan had changed the timeline in a small way through Nick—she'd unmade him, turning him back from the hero into an ordinary person. She'd created a timeline without the hero. But what could possibly create the world they'd seen through the café window?

"*We* have to stop her," Nick said to Joan. When Joan looked up, his expression was set with determination. "We have to get out of here."

Joan swallowed hard. He was right. They had to figure out what to do. "We need to—"

She stopped as Nick held up a hand, head cocked. She heard it then too. Footsteps outside the door. The latch lifted, and the door opened.

Joan scrambled to her feet. Nick knelt up beside her, still pinned by the manacle. Joan swore at herself. She should have gotten that off him while she'd had the chance.

A guard entered the room. He was an older man with thin gray hair and a puckered scar across his cheek.

"Almost had you in Milton Keynes," he growled at Joan. There was a slight slur to his words, as if the knife wound had gone through his tongue too.

Milton Keynes? Joan looked at the man again. He was tall and thin, with catlike eyes. Recognition came slowly. The last time Joan had seen him, he'd been thirty or forty years younger.

"*Corvin Argent*," she said. The man who'd killed Margie.

"It's been a long time for me." Corvin's mouth twisted, pulling at the scar. "You took my wallet and my chop."

Was he serious? He was still angry that she'd stolen from him? "You killed my *friend*!" She wished he'd come closer. Elderly man or not, she'd get a kick in and more. "Why are you even here? Are you going to interrogate us?"

"Do I look like a Griffith?" Corvin said, sounding contemptuous. "I'm here for the boy."

Joan stepped in front of Nick.

"Oh, *relax*," Corvin said. "You just said that there's an Argent power on him. Well, Eleanor wants it off him. I'm here to remove it."

TWENTY-SIX

"You were listening to us?" Joan said to Corvin. Was there surveillance equipment in here? She looked down the long gallery of the library, lit by skylights and picture windows. Were there cameras in here? What else had Eleanor and her people overheard?

Corvin was still standing in the doorway. "Move away from the boy," he told Joan.

Joan shook her head. She was still in front of Nick, half blocking him from Corvin's view, as if she could somehow protect him.

"Joan," Nick murmured. "It's okay."

It *wasn't* okay.

"Don't you *want* the Argent power off him?" Corvin said. "Sounded like you did. Don't tell me you've chickened out after telling him the truth."

Joan flushed. So they'd overheard all of it, then.

Eleanor wants it off him.

Why? Why would Eleanor want that? Was she trying to turn Nick into the hero again? Joan glanced back. Nick was watching Corvin narrowly. And Joan *hated* that he was on his knees, on the bare wooden floor of the library. She hated that he was shackled by a chain—and by the Argent power.

Joan forced herself to step aside, and Nick flicked her a reassuring smile. Joan tried to smile back, but she couldn't hold it. "We'll be okay," Nick murmured to her. "You and me. You'll see."

Joan knew that wasn't true. This would be the last time Nick smiled at her. The last moment he trusted her. When Corvin was done, *they'd* be done.

"Frankly," Corvin said to Joan, "I doubt that power's still active. The boy's been in here three weeks." He stalked over to Nick and gazed down at him. "Huh," he said, sounding surprised. "Well," he said to Nick, "it *is* still on you. I can see it in your eyes. What were you told to do?"

Nick's expression glazed slightly. "I'm fine with monsters," he said obediently. "I don't want to hurt monsters."

"Crude," Corvin said. "Well, your former compulsions are undone. You're free of the Argent power." He sounded almost bored.

We'll be okay, Nick had said. *You and me.* Joan waited now for horror to bloom on his face as he took in the truth. She waited for his dark eyes to fill with betrayal and anger. But his expression didn't change.

"Nick?" Joan whispered. And then she saw that Corvin was frowning. "The power's still active!" she said to Corvin.

"So I gather," Corvin told her irritably. To Nick, he said, "You're free of the Argent power! There are no restrictions on how you feel or act toward monsters!" Corvin waited expectantly, and then with slow-building bewilderment and frustration. "Who put this compulsion on you?" he demanded.

"Someone stronger than you?" Nick suggested.

Corvin's jaw tightened. "I very much doubt that." He glared down at Nick. "I'll have to try something else, I think." He turned as if to leave, and then seemed to change his mind. Before Joan could stop him—before Nick could even flinch—Corvin closed the gap between them and kicked hard at Nick's upturned face.

Nick's head cracked back against the hearth's stone wall, and he gasped in pain and shock. Blood smeared his mouth.

Joan threw herself at Corvin, furious. Corvin shoved her with both hands, and Joan fell backward. She started to scramble up. "Stay down!" Corvin told her, and Joan clenched her teeth in frustration as the cuff activated with a familiar jolt around her joints, trapping her on her knees. She'd landed right beside Nick, in front of the fireplace, but she couldn't help him. She couldn't move.

She still had her voice, though. *"Don't!"* she screamed as Corvin slammed his foot into Nick's chest. Nick grunted in pain.

"Hurt me back!" Corvin ordered Nick. "Fight back!" Joan could practically feel his power now—like the warmth of a fire. He seemed to be throwing everything he had at Nick.

"I . . ." Nick flinched back. "I can't."

Joan struggled, but she could barely move. *"Stop!"* she begged Corvin.

Corvin growled at Nick. "Hit me!" he ordered. "Hurt me! I just hurt *you*! Hurt me back!" When Nick didn't move, Corvin turned to Joan. "Who the hell put this power on him? It shouldn't have lasted three weeks! It shouldn't be resisting *me*."

Had Owen been that strong? Joan hadn't sensed anything like the heat of Corvin's power from him. Corvin threw a punch, connecting with Nick's jaw. Nick made a short sound, guttural and pained.

"You're just beating up someone who can't touch you!" Joan screamed at Corvin.

Corvin punched Nick in the face again. *"Hit* me!" Another punch. *"Hit* me! Just—" Corvin drew his hand back, and he was *really* going to hurt Nick this time—Joan could see it. But instead of throwing the punch at Nick, Corvin changed his aim and swung hard at Joan.

Joan cringed back, but Nick moved faster than she could take in, hand shooting out to catch Corvin's fist.

For a long moment, the library felt strangely silent—the last sound the impact of Corvin's fist against Nick's palm. Joan could hear her own gasping breaths. Pinned with the cuff, she'd only been able to flinch. Now she replayed the moment in her mind—Corvin changing his aim, and Nick intercepting the punch.

Nick had reacted *fast*—as fast as the hero would have.

"Nick?" Joan whispered. She could hear how tentative she sounded. She met his eyes, and they were *his* eyes. Her Nick's—serious and dangerous.

"Let me go!" Corvin said. Joan was beginning to recognize the intense note in his voice as the Argent note—the way Argents spoke when they used their power.

Nick seemed to recognize it too. But he didn't let Corvin's hand go. Instead, his face hardened, and his knuckles whitened around Corvin's fist.

"Stop!" Corvin said. *"Stop!"* His voice turned panicked, losing the Argent note. "You're going to break my hand!"

Nick released Corvin's fist in a deliberate gesture, almost careless. "Try to touch her again, and I won't just break your hand."

Corvin clambered to his feet, his hand cradled to his chest.

Had he known who Nick had once been? Maybe not. His face was a shocked mask as he stumbled back.

Corvin banged on the door with his good hand: three quick pounds. It opened, and he scrambled out. Joan heard the lock click and the heavy latch fall.

There was a long silence. Joan shifted experimentally. Relief hit her. She could move again. She eased herself to her feet and backed up from Nick, trying not to spook him. She was overly aware that she was locked in here with him. That she couldn't escape as easily as Corvin had.

Nick's eyes were fixed on her searchingly, as if trying to make sense of her expression. He was still chained, but he reached for her with his free hand. "Are you all right?" he said.

For a moment, Joan wasn't sure how to answer the question. "He didn't hit *me*."

Nick's eyes weren't quite the hero's anymore. That dangerous expression was already fading to confusion.

"You're bleeding," Joan whispered. "Are *you* okay?"

Nick's hand rose to touch his bottom lip. His fingers came away smeared with blood. He frowned and wiped the blood away with the back of his hand. "The Argent power's gone," he said. "I felt it break."

"And . . ." Joan's mouth was so dry. "How do you feel about monsters now?"

Nick's expression turned inward as he considered her question. "How do I feel?" he said.

In the window behind him, every cloud was perfectly still. Joan felt just as still as she waited for his reaction.

And there it was. Nick's face filled with understanding, with horror. He lifted his gaze to Joan's. "Monsters steal human life," he said. "Monsters prey on humans."

Joan's heart felt like a drum. She stepped back.

Nick's dark eyes were nearly black. "If people found out the truth . . . ," he said, very low.

By people, he meant *humans*. What *would* happen, Joan wondered, if they found out? Would there be a war? Who would win? In any given time period, there were surely more humans than monsters. But monsters had access to technologies from the future. And if all the monsters of history converged during the period of the battle . . .

Joan remembered then something that Aaron had told her: the Monster Court placed monsters high up in human circles. He'd been talking about the police at the time. But who else in authority were monsters?

Nick answered his own question. "Humans would fight," he said, and Joan couldn't prevent her shiver. *He'd* fought last time.

Nick went to stand and was halted by the chain. He blinked down at it, head tilted. Joan had the impression that he was calculating angles. Then he put his foot against the fireplace's stone wall and wound the chain around one arm. He wrenched at it, heavy muscles straining. He yanked it once, twice, and it broke away, stone crumbling around it.

Joan gasped. She'd known that Nick had abilities in the other timeline—he'd killed Edmund by throwing a sword with perfect accuracy. But she'd never seen the extent of what he could do.

Nick straightened, his body moving easily despite the beating.

He focused on Joan again. "Why do you look so scared?" he said slowly.

Images flashed through Joan's head—Nick slicing into Lucien Oliver's body; Nick throwing a sword into Edmund Oliver's chest. Nick telling Joan: *If you ever steal time from a human again, I will kill you myself.*

And now the Argent power was gone. He knew what monsters really were. What Joan was.

Nick took a step toward her, and Joan couldn't stop herself from stumbling back. Nick's eyes widened. He stopped in his tracks, looking sick. "Are you scared of *me*?" he said. There was still blood on his mouth from where he'd been struck. Joan was horribly reminded of his torture in that chair. "You think I'd hurt *you*?"

"Do you . . ." Joan hesitated. *Do you have any new memories along with those new abilities?* "Do you feel like yourself?"

"Nothing's changed for me," Nick said softly. "I told you we'd just talk, and we will."

Joan had meant it as a different question: *Are you him? Do you remember?* But she had her answer. This *wasn't* him. The other Nick wasn't anywhere anymore. She'd felt it from the moment she'd woken up in this new world—in the hollow absence inside her. The boy in front of her was still the new Nick, untrained and untortured.

Except . . . he'd caught Corvin's punch. He'd torn a chain from the wall. He hadn't just broken through the Argent power; he'd broken through to something else too. "Nick . . ."

"I'm *myself*," Nick said now. "The Argent power's gone.

Joan . . . you said I'd hate you when the Argent power came off. I *don't*. I . . ." He looked vulnerable suddenly. Uncertain. "All the things I said are still true."

I could never hate you. It's the opposite.

He couldn't have meant that. Joan shook her head.

"I want to be with you."

Joan felt like her heart was being crushed in her chest. All of this was so wrong. He *had* to hate her. She'd hidden the truth—that monsters stole human life. "I'm a monster," she said to him. "I'm a *monster.*"

"I know," he said softly. His hand twitched toward her and then back, as if it were killing him not to touch her. But she'd told him not to, and he'd never go against an instruction like that. "You told me that," Nick reminded her. "You also told me that you don't steal human life. You told me that you love your family even though you can't stand what they do."

Guilt sat heavily in the pit of her stomach. "I can't . . . I don't understand."

"Don't understand what?" he said gently.

"Why you're still talking to me. Why . . ."

"I never want to stop talking to you," Nick said. "Joan . . ." He took a step toward her, and his shoes crunched. He blinked down. Shattered stone lay at his feet. He hadn't broken the chain itself; he'd pulled the anchoring ring from the fireplace wall, and bits of wall had come with it. "What . . ." He stared at the chain wound around his arm, tracking it to the ring. "I did that," he said, but with a lifted note at the end as if he wasn't sure of it.

Joan saw questions rise up in him. He was silent for a long

moment. Then he said, as if feeling out the thought: "When we first met Jamie . . . he was afraid of me. Like you were afraid when I caught that punch. And then we got to the boathouse, and half that room was terrified. Of *me*. I couldn't make sense of it. All those people with all those powers, and they were afraid of *me*." He looked down again at the end of the chain, lying loose on the ground. For a second *Nick* looked scared—and lost. "Why were they afraid of me?"

"Nick . . ."

He waited, listening. His expression was the same one he'd had outside his house—like Joan was a lifeboat in an ocean.

"There was another timeline before this one," she said.

"Another timeline?" Nick's forehead creased.

"The Lius remember it, and so do I."

"The *Lius* were afraid of me," Nick said, realizing. "Only the Lius. They knew something about me . . ." Joan could see the wheels turning in his head. "What did they remember?" His gaze focused on Joan. "What *am* I?" His posture was stoic. He seemed braced for something terrible.

"You're not a *what*," Joan said.

"All right, then. *Who* am I? Who *was* I . . . ?" He stumbled over the words. "Who was I in that other timeline? Who was I that people are still afraid of me? That *you're* afraid of me?"

Joan couldn't help but react to that; her breath caught in her throat. He noticed it. Of course he did. It cut through her—the way he was looking at her. Joan was reminded as always of old comic-book heroes who protected the vulnerable and punished those who hurt them. She remembered the relief she'd felt when he'd rescued her from the Olivers that very first time.

"You were a hero," Joan said. "Not just a hero. You were a legend. Like King Arthur."

Nick went to laugh, but the uncertain amusement died on his face when he saw that Joan wasn't laughing with him. "You can't be serious," he said.

"My grandmother used to tell me bedtime stories about you," Joan said.

"People aren't afraid of heroes."

It wasn't funny, but Joan heard her breath come out hard.

For a moment, he looked confused, and then understanding put a shadow in his eyes. "*Monsters* are."

"You were a *hero*," Joan said, needing him to understand. "You were more than just a hero. You were *the* hero. People told stories about you. Made art depicting you."

"That doesn't seem like me."

Joan had never asked that other Nick how he'd felt about it. Maybe he'd found the thought just as strange and alienating. There'd been so many myths about him—adventures, tragedies, horror stories—they obviously weren't all true.

"I'm not anything like that," Nick said.

Joan had spent all this time thinking of how different he was from her Nick, but now—with him looking down at her, serious and dark-eyed and handsome—she was struck by their similarities. And struck again by the realization that she'd met him here in this house—in this room. He'd walked through that door into the library, head bent over a book, and when he'd looked up at her, Joan's heart had turned over.

"When I got caught by the attackers at the bakery, you came back to help me," she said. "You could have escaped, but you came back. Your first instinct is to take care of people. You didn't know why the Lius were scared, but you wanted to make them feel safe. There's something that's just *good* inside you."

This Nick *was* different—he seemed more complex, more difficult to read. But both Nicks shared the same core of goodness. In the other timeline, Nick's torturer had told Eleanor: *Must we use this boy? He's always so* virtuous. It had taken them two thousand attempts to break him. They never really had.

Nick's gaze roved over Joan's face. "That's how you see me?" he whispered.

Joan nodded. There was no way to actually explain to him how she saw him. He was a bright light in the darkness. Every version of him.

"Before . . . ," Nick said, and now he sounded tentative. "You said you *wanted* . . ." His voice felt like a low rumble in Joan's bones. "What did you want?"

"I . . ." Joan's voice faltered. She couldn't say it even to herself. She *shouldn't*.

"I can tell you what I want," Nick said steadily. "I want to be where you are. In any way you let me."

Joan couldn't take her eyes from him. She'd expected to lose him today; she could feel the phantom ache of it now. She hadn't realized how important this Nick was becoming to her until she'd had to face the prospect of that loss.

"I want . . ." Joan's breath shuddered out. *What do you want?* She'd hardly let herself want anything since she'd woken up in this new timeline. Wanting was dangerous and it hurt. Yearning for other times led to fading out of this time as her body tried to jump. Wanting meant watching Nick from afar, knowing she couldn't ever be with him.

Except he'd just told her she could be with him.

And she felt . . . Joan took a sharp breath. This wasn't Nick. It wasn't *him*. But . . . she let herself admit the truth. She'd been falling hard for this Nick too. Every iteration of him was the same at his core.

"I want you," she admitted. He seemed to light up from the inside at her words. Her heart clenched. "I don't want to hurt you," she whispered.

"I don't want to hurt you either," he whispered back. His eyes were as clear as a new day. "So we won't," he said.

Could it be that simple?

"Can I?" he said. He held out his hand. "Please?"

It only took three steps to move to him. Nick's hand came up to cup her face, one big thumb sweeping over her cheekbone. Joan's breath caught. Another sweep across her cheekbone, and Nick's eyes darkened. "God, you're beautiful," he said. "I thought that the first time I saw you. You're *so* beautiful." *He* was beautiful. He was a work of art. A painting. His dark hair was just curling at the ends, framing his handsome face. "I really want to kiss you," he whispered.

Joan was already crying as she lifted her face. She could feel his confusion as he wiped away her tears. She'd missed him *so* much. And this wasn't him. But it *was*. This was him as he could have been.

Nick bent and kissed her and it felt like everything she'd missed and wanted. She kissed him back desperately.

"So sweet," a cold voice said from the doorway. "So touching to see new love blossoming."

Joan jerked back from the kiss, turning fast.

The library door was open. Eleanor swept into the room, along with a handful of courtiers and guards—and *Aaron*, Joan saw with dismay. He didn't look at Joan as he followed Eleanor in.

"Such a sweet first kiss," Eleanor said to Joan.

Joan flushed. What did Eleanor *want*? Why was she taunting them? It was clear that she knew it *hadn't* been their first kiss. "What do you want with us?" Joan said.

Eleanor turned to Nick. "I heard what she said to you. She almost sounded sincere, didn't she? Like she hasn't been lying to you this whole time."

"I *wasn't* lying," Joan blurted, confused. Eleanor's mouth lifted in a cruel, amused smile. "I mean . . . ," Joan said to Nick, faltering. She'd only *just* told him the truth.

Nick dropped his hold on Joan's waist and took her hand, reassuring and comforting. *It's okay*, his touch said. *We're okay*. He turned to Eleanor and said coolly, "Answer her question. What *do* you want with us? Why are you keeping us here?"

Eleanor looked at their clasped hands and smiled wider. "The timeline is such a romantic old fool, isn't it? It was always going to bring you two back together." Nick looked confused, and Eleanor laughed. "Oh, she hasn't told you that part of it? Well . . . I bet there's a *lot* she hasn't told you."

"You'd be surprised," Nick said softly.

"Would I?" Eleanor's eyes dropped to the broken chain. Her expression brightened. "Now, look at that. All we had to do was threaten *her.*"

"You . . ." Joan stared.

Did Eleanor think she could make Nick into the hero again? If so, she was going to fail. Joan had already told him the truth of monsters. He'd been horrified, but he hadn't turned into a killer. He'd suggested talking to Joan's family. He'd wanted to persuade, not fight.

"Well, now that we're all here," Eleanor said, "the show can start."

"Show?" Joan said slowly. A feeling of foreboding rose in her then. "What show?"

"The show that's always here." Eleanor nodded at one of the guards—a man with a pink flower tattoo like the cherry seller who'd saved Joan and Nick at the Wyvern Inn. The man walked over to a space just south of the picture window—a few feet from Joan and Nick. Then he reached into the air with a pulling motion, like he was opening a curtain. There was a discordant sound. No, not a sound. A *feeling.* Joan was hit with a shock of nausea. The man was an Ali, she realized belatedly. He'd just opened a seal.

Around the room, the guards groaned in horror. Aaron stumbled back, and then he bent over double, retching. Nick grabbed Joan's hand and drew her back.

Joan stared. The opened seal had revealed a tear in the timeline—like the one in the café. Joan and Nick must have been just a few paces from it the entire time they'd been here. The tear stood beyond the fireplace, and its jagged edges rent the air—Joan was reminded sickeningly of a torn shroud. Inside were the shadows of the void. . . .

One of the guards whispered something and made a quick gesture, fingers rising and falling. Joan didn't recognize the motion, but she guessed it was some traditional warding against evil.

"Poor old timeline," Eleanor said to Joan. "It's more fragile than you'd think."

"Why is this here?" Joan whispered. She'd been in this room a hundred times, had cleaned every inch of it when she'd volunteered at the museum. There'd never been an Ali seal here before. There'd never been a hole in the timeline.

"Look closer," Eleanor said.

"At what?" Joan said. But as she spoke, the shadows inside the tear seemed to shift and coalesce into shapes.

"What *is* that?" Nick said.

There was something familiar about the scene that was forming inside the tear. It was this library in the evening. And there were figures within it. Joan squinted, trying to make them out.

"Give it a second," Eleanor said.

And then the image sharpened and brightened, and Joan gasped.

The figures inside the tear were Joan herself from the previous timeline—and Nick. *Her* Nick. The Nick she'd unmade and lost. Joan heard herself make an agonized sound of grief. She'd dreamed of him, but that didn't come close to seeing him again. God, she'd missed him so much. She'd missed him like part of herself had been lost.

He wasn't flat like a screen image; he was three-dimensional and real, as if he were really here, as if Joan could have taken a few steps and touched him.

"They can't see you," Eleanor said. "The timeline can still protect itself that much."

The new Nick took a step toward the vision, still gripping Joan's hand tight. "What is *that*?"

"It's the previous timeline," Joan said shakily.

"That's him?" Nick said uncertainly. "The hero? And . . . *you*?" He turned to Joan.

Joan didn't know what to say. Now that the two Nicks were in the same room, she could truly see their similarities. They radiated the same earnest goodness. They both looked at her in the same way. Like they couldn't believe she was here with them. There were differences too, though. The new Nick didn't have the same shadows in his eyes, and the old Nick had an exhausted edge to him that Joan hadn't remembered.

"The timeline was always going to bring you two together," Eleanor said to Joan. "I knew if I brought one of you here, the other would follow. And then you'd both get to see this."

"To see *what*?" Joan said. "To see . . ." She stared at the scene inside the opened seal. And understanding slowly dawned about what exactly Eleanor was about to show them; why she'd brought Joan and Nick to the guardhouse. Joan looked over at the new Nick's still-trusting face, and her stomach lurched. "*No*," she said to Eleanor. "Close that seal back up! *Please!*"

"Joan?" Nick said, confused.

"Hush," Eleanor said. "This is my favorite part of the show."

Through the tear in the timeline, Joan watched Nick pull her into his arms, his face full of love and wonder and relief.

I've loved you since the moment I saw you, Joan said in that other timeline.

I love you, the other Nick said. *I always have.*

Joan heard her breath shudder out, and beside her Nick turned his gaze to her. His expression was so raw that Joan was almost undone by it. He was remembering their own kiss, she knew. The way she'd reacted to it.

In the other timeline, Joan kissed him. She'd been crying then, and she was crying now again. Her past and present selves both knew what was coming next.

Joan? It was the Nick from the previous timeline. He pulled back, face filling with shock and agony. Joan flinched now, as if she were the one in pain.

"Joan?" Nick said now. "What's going on?"

In the vision, Nick spasmed as if he'd been jolted with electricity. The ceiling rattled, and Nick started to scream. Joan knew that sound like it was from her own throat. She'd heard it over and over in her dreams.

Joan, he cried out. *Please.*

Joan could see herself mouthing, *I'm sorry. I'm sorry. I'm sorry.*

"I'm sorry," she whispered now. She didn't even know who she was saying it to—Nick then or Nick now.

Nick stared at her now as if he'd never seen her before. The betrayal had already started in his expression. "What did you do?" he said. "What did you *do*?"

"She unmade the hero," Eleanor said. But her gaze was

directed at Joan, triumphant and furious, as if she knew exactly what Joan was losing, and she only wished she could hurt her more. "She unraveled the hero's life, and she replaced him with an ordinary boy. I suppose you could say she killed him."

Nick reeled back, tearing his hand from Joan's grip and staring at her in horror.

Humans had a protector, Astrid had said. *A hero. And you unmade him. Did you think there'd be no consequences?*

Eleanor lifted a pendant from under her collar. Joan had a moment to see that it was a coin on a chain. A travel token. And then Eleanor was gone. She'd vanished. She wasn't even going to watch the aftermath of all this.

Nick was still staring at Joan as if he'd never seen her before. "You killed the hero?"

"I—" Joan saw Mr. Larch again in her mind's eye—kind, loud Mr. Larch, her history teacher from last year . . . He was dead. So many people were dead, just like Astrid had said. Joan had unmade the hero and everything that the hero had done. Joan saved her family and doomed every human that Nick had ever saved.

Nick's eyes burned into Joan's.

"Nick—" Joan was interrupted by the sound of shattering glass. The window exploded inward, and a cloud of white smoke billowed into the room.

Joan choked. Through the smoke, a guard crumpled. There were heavy thumps—the bars on the window falling. And then Joan couldn't see anything but thick white fog. Someone grabbed her hand. She yanked away from the grip.

"It's *me*." Tom's voice, close to her ear. Something covered

Joan's face. An old-fashioned gas mask. Joan wrenched it off. *"Nick,"* she said to Tom, and choked again on the smoke. Beside her, Nick slumped. The smoke was laced with something soporific, Joan realized. Her vision darkened. *"Nick,"* she tried to say again. Nick *knows.*

Tom settled the mask back onto her face. "We have him," he said gently. "We have you both."

TWENTY-SEVEN

Joan slipped in and out of consciousness. She jerked awake when a gust of wind hit her face. She was lying on her back on something soft. A blanket, maybe? It was dark, but there was enough moonlight to make out Nick beside her. He was unconscious, shadowed bruises blooming on his cheekbones. From the sound of hooves and the jolting movements around them, they seemed to be in a horse-drawn trailer of some kind.

"Nick," Joan mumbled.

"It's all right." Ruth's voice. "Don't worry. Nick's safe. You're both safe."

"No," Joan mumbled. She started to sink back into the darkness again. *He knows,* she tried to say. *He knows what we are. He broke a chain with his bare hands.* But she couldn't get her mouth to work.

The next time Joan woke up, Nick was awake too. He wasn't beside her anymore. He was sitting on a rattling bench, facing her. They were in a different vehicle, Joan realized—one a little more comfortable. A carriage.

The side windows showed low brick buildings and a dark sky. There was no view of the driver from in here.

Joan struggled to sit up. She was sore all over from sitting in cramped positions and from being jolted around on the bench.

Nick's expression didn't change as he watched her efforts; his gaze was hard. The bruises on his face had darkened. He must have been in pain too, but he wasn't showing it. He lounged back in his seat, as if the ride were completely comfortable.

Joan was almost afraid to ask the question. "Where are the others?"

"Why are you saying it like that?" In the dull light, Nick's bruises made him look dangerous. Someone who'd been in a fight and would fight again. "You think I did something to them?"

A thread of fear ran through her. How long had she been unconscious? Her heart pounded painfully. She flashed on an image of washing Gran's blood from under her fingernails. "Did you?" she blurted.

"They're in another carriage," Nick ground out. *"Alive,"* he added, in answer to whatever look was on Joan's face. "We changed vehicles and split up to avoid detection."

Joan's chest still felt tight. "And when we meet up with them again?"

Nick gave her a long look. Joan felt as if he were seeing right inside her. "He must have been really something if you're afraid that a single human could hurt all those monsters with all those powers."

He had no idea. Legends had been built around him. He'd been a bedtime story to frighten monster children.

"I thought . . ." Nick's jaw worked for a moment. "When you told me what monsters were . . . When I understood what they were . . . I thought that at least I still understood *you*. But I didn't understand anything, did I? You said that we needed to protect humans. But someone was protecting humans already. And you killed him."

You'd killed my family, Joan wanted to say. But there was no excuse for what she'd done. He was right. He'd protected humans, and she'd removed that protection.

In her mind's eye, Joan saw him catch Corvin's fist. Catch the hilt of Lucien's sword.

Nick seemed to know what she was thinking about. "When that man tried to hit you." There was a flare in his eyes for a moment. "When he tried to hit you, I knew how to stop him. I think I could have broken his arm. I knew where the bone was weakest. I knew how much pressure it would have taken to make it snap."

"Nick . . ."

"I know how to get out of this carriage," Nick said. "I know to wait for an acceleration—to make it harder to chase me. I know where to kick the door and how hard. I know how to jump to prevent injury."

"You're not a prisoner." Joan heard her own voice crack. "If you want to leave, you can leave."

"I suppose if I don't, you'll ask an Argent to make me forget all of it," Nick said. "Forget what I saw. Forget what you told me."

That thought hadn't even occurred to Joan, and she was horrified by how tempting the idea was. For just a moment, she let herself imagine Nick's face slackening until the betrayal eased from it. As though she could click *undo, undo* until he was the version of himself who'd kissed her in the library again.

And then her stomach dropped as if she was going to be sick. "*No.* I wouldn't do that."

"Why not?" he said. "You've done it before."

He didn't even know the extent of how he'd been manipulated. Eleanor had unmade and remade him before Joan had. Monsters had meddled with his life more than he knew.

The carriage turned. Between buildings water shone, black as oil. Where were they? Nick turned to watch their progress. "Truth is," he said, "I'm not sure the Argent power would work on me again. I can feel how I'd break it. I know how."

He shifted his weight, and Joan flinched. He turned back to her, registering the movement. "You're so afraid of me," he said. "I didn't understand it before. Why would *you*—a monster—be afraid of me? But you knew what you'd done. You knew from the moment you met me." He frowned, remembering. "You touched my neck the first time we met. Did you steal time from me?"

"*No,*" Joan blurted. She couldn't believe he'd think that of her, but then . . . Joan had also asked that of Ruth when she'd first learned the truth. *Did you ever steal life from my dad?* she'd said to Ruth. *From me?*

"You were testing me," Nick said, realizing. "You were checking to see if I was still *him.*"

"You weren't," Joan whispered.

"No," Nick said flatly. "I'm not him. I don't remember anything he did."

Joan's heart tugged at the aching loss of him again. "What are you going to do when this carriage stops?" It occurred to her, with horror, that he might just be waiting to get back to the others. Was he going to kill them all? Joan had a flash of Ruth, of all of them, lying dead. She wouldn't have time to warn them.

Nick's eyes narrowed, as if he'd guessed what she was thinking. "Something terrible is coming," he said. "We both saw it—in that tear in the timeline. That world can't exist."

Joan barely dared hope. "You're going to help me stop it?" Astrid had said he'd have stopped it last time. *Could* he stop it now that he had some of his abilities back, if not his memories?

"We're going to work together," Nick said. "We're on the same side until we stop her. But after that . . ." Moonlight played across his face, making the shadows around his eyes darken. "After that, our paths will diverge."

Joan swallowed hard. The carriage turned, suspension rattling over uneven ground.

"You said you loved him," Nick said. He wasn't quite looking at her, and that blank note was in his voice again. "In that previous timeline, you told him you loved him before you killed him. Was that true? Was any of it true? Did you ever care about him?"

He didn't need to say the rest. *Did you ever care about* me?

Joan's eyes felt hot with unshed tears. *I still do,* she wanted to say. *I don't think I'll ever stop.* "Would it change anything if I did?"

The shadows flickered over Nick's face again. "I suppose not."

They were silent for the rest of the drive.

Eventually, the carriage drew to a stop. The windows showed only darkness and fog, but Joan had the impression of a busy street outside, of early-morning workers. The air smelled of herbal medicines and fish and brine. She guessed they were near some docks, although she couldn't have said if they were north or south of the river.

Footsteps came around the carriage, and the door opened, revealing Tom's ruddy face. Tom had changed clothes; he was in a rumpled dockworker's shirt with heavy trousers and a low cap. Behind him, there was a nondescript brick building with a heavy black door. "We're here," Tom said.

Joan tensed herself for Nick to make a move. But he just jumped out and thanked Tom with apparent sincerity.

"Go get those injuries checked out," Tom told Nick. "There's a doctor waiting for you."

Nick walked on toward the building, hands in his pockets, without looking back. When he reached the door, he pulled it open without hesitation. Joan felt a shiver of unease, watching him enter.

"He'll be all right," Tom said to Joan, following her gaze. "We checked him out earlier too. Those bruises are superficial."

"Tom . . ." Joan needed to tell him that Nick was dangerous. That he'd broken the Argent power.

But if she said that, what would Tom do? What would happen to Nick? Would they try to lock him up? Kill him? Nick would fight . . . Joan saw in her mind's eye a massacre like the one at Holland House.

No, not yet, she decided. Nick had promised to be on their side for now. He'd keep his word. He always had before.

But afterward . . . After they'd stopped Eleanor . . .

Well, the boathouse would need to be cleared out, for one thing. And the Wyvern Inn. Joan had been so stupid to take him to monster places.

"Joan?" Tom said, and Joan realized that she'd been staring at nothing. "You should get checked out too."

"I'm fine," Joan said. She wasn't hurt. "I need to talk to you."

"Jamie and Ruth are grabbing something to eat. Go find them, and I'll join you. We can talk then."

"Tom—"

"Eat," Tom said. "You'll need it. I think it'll be a long session with the prisoner."

"The prisoner?" Joan said.

"We captured Aaron Oliver when we freed you." Tom's heavy jaw tightened. "He's been working with *her*. We're going to interrogate him until he tells us everything he knows."

TWENTY-EIGHT

The sky showed a hint of pink, and Joan felt a disoriented lurch. Was it sunset or dawn? *Dawn,* she reminded herself. They'd been in the carriage at night, and now morning was coming.

She ran a hand over her face. She couldn't untangle her emotions. She'd kissed Nick, and then Eleanor had torn them apart. Again. No . . . Joan couldn't blame Eleanor this time. *Joan* had done something unforgivable, and Nick had found out. *That* was the plain truth. The question was, would he keep his promise? Would he remain on their side until Eleanor was stopped?

Early as it was, the street sounded like a fish market. *"Eels!"* a woman called out as she walked by, a heavy bucket on her head. She adjusted her thick shawl. *"Eels! Eels! Live eels!"* The bucket shook with the fury of its contents. Farther up, another woman shouted: *"Fish! Fish! Sweet as cream!"*

The carriage had brought them to a narrow cobbled street. In Kensington, the air had smelled of horse manure and bitter smoke. Here, near the docks, that distinctive stink was joined by wafts of rotting fish and sewage, and the faint scent of something more pleasant and familiar. Something Joan couldn't quite place. . . .

She looked around. The shop opposite displayed dried roots and herbs in glass jars. Chinese characters were daubed on the window. "That's Chinese medicine," she said, surprised. She recognized the faint scent then as incense—joss sticks.

Amid the cacophony, she caught a few familiar words: *Hǎo de.*
Hǎo de. Okay. Okay. Through the gloom, she made out two men
carrying wooden planks on their shoulders. They had Chinese
faces and queue braids. Joan felt her mouth drop open. This really
was the nineteenth century. And some part of her—the monster
part that loved history—just wanted to keep walking, to explore.

"This is the outer edge of Chinatown," Tom said. "Where the
early sailors settled." He nodded to the west. "The Regent's Canal
Dock is that way."

"We're back in Limehouse?" Joan took in the black door in
front of them. "This is the boathouse," she realized. The street
was narrower in this time, and the roller door of the future was
a wooden door here. The building itself was still the same clay-
brown brick, though. Still the same height.

Joan took a deep breath as she reached for the door handle.
Nick had gone in barely a minute ahead of her, but she was hit by
a sudden fear of what she might find inside.

To her relief, though, there was no sign of violence when she
opened the door—and no sign of Nick. A ginger cat lay stretched
out just inside the doorway. Joan bent to pat it as she walked in.
From a mezzanine above, someone whistled a trill—the Hathaways' private language.

The interior layout was very different in this period. In the
twenty-first century, the boathouse would be a series of rooms.
Here, there was a single large space with a mezzanine balcony
that wrapped around the walls. Arched brick alcoves ran under
the mezzanine. Some held dark stacks of what might have been
dried fish; others, wooden beer barrels and filled burlap sacks.

Joan could just make out mosaic artwork on the second-floor walls: phoenixes and hounds.

At the far end of the room, several wooden tables held whole steamed fish and pots of rice and fresh bread on boards. Joan spotted Ruth and Jamie—and Frankie on Jamie's lap—among the people quietly eating.

"Joan!" Ruth stood up as Joan reached her, and dragged her into a hug. "Oh my God! I was so worried! When that Oliver boy caught you . . ." She squeezed harder. "I could have killed him!"

Joan hugged Ruth back. "Can't believe you broke into a guardhouse."

"You'd have done the same any day." Ruth pushed Joan back gently. "You sort of *did* do the same in that other timeline." She stuttered the words *other timeline* as if she still hadn't quite gotten her head around the idea.

"I . . ." Joan paused as she took in Ruth's clothes. "What are you *wearing*?" Jamie had on a lightweight shirt and trousers—he looked like the Chinese men outside. Ruth was in a black vinyl catsuit.

"It's a rescue outfit," Ruth said with dignity.

"Seriously?" Joan bit back a smile in spite of herself.

"It was an integral part of the plan."

"You don't like late Victorian clothes?"

Ruth wrinkled her nose. "All those blousy blouses and buttons. Anyway . . . I'm not the only one—notice Jamie hasn't shaved his head to fit in here?"

"I have a wig for outside," Jamie said peaceably.

Joan pulled Ruth into another hug. At the back of her mind,

though, she found herself doing the math—to get here, Jamie, Ruth, and Tom had to have taken hundreds of years of human life between them. And Joan's feelings were a confused mess of gratitude at being rescued and horror at the cost. And love. Joan loved Ruth so much. She loved her family so much. She couldn't reconcile it.

Did Astrid ever feel like this, she wondered. Like she was being torn apart?

"Here." Jamie put some fish into a small porcelain bowl. "Bread or rice?"

"Rice," Joan said. But she knelt by Jamie's chair. "I need to tell you something." Jamie's smile faded. Joan's tone must have hinted at what she was going to say. "You were right," she whispered. "She's *back*."

Jamie put the bowl down as if afraid he'd drop it. "You saw her?"

"I spoke to her. Her name is Eleanor."

"Eleanor?" Ruth looked blank, but Jamie was suddenly gripping the table's edge, knuckles bone-white.

"You're *sure* her name was Eleanor?" Jamie whispered, and Joan nodded. Jamie breathed something that might have been a prayer or a curse.

"Who's Eleanor?" Ruth looked between them.

"Ruth," Jamie said, almost gently.

Ruth's blankness lingered for a moment longer, and then her eyes widened slowly. "No." She turned to Joan, shock filling her face. "Eleanor of the *Curia Monstrorum*?" she whispered. "The most feared and ruthless member of the Monster Court?"

"The most feared?" Joan said. From Ruth's and Jamie's reactions, she was starting to understand that Eleanor was even more dangerous and formidable than she'd realized.

It hit her that Ruth and the others had barely missed Eleanor—Eleanor had left the library just moments before they'd arrived. As if she'd known the rescue was coming. A thread of uncertainty ran through Joan at the thought. She tried to shrug it off. The important thing was, they'd all escaped.

"She told me she's going to create a new timeline," Joan said. "The one we saw, where monsters rule."

Jamie closed his eyes and took a deep breath. "We need to get everyone together," he said. "Tom should hear this." As Joan went to stand, he stopped her. "Eat something, though," he said. "We might not get another chance for a while."

The last thing Joan wanted was to eat. Her stomach was churning from her conversation with Nick; from the way he'd looked at her when he'd realized she'd chosen monsters over the hero. "Did you see Nick come in?" she said.

"He's fine," Jamie said reassuringly. "The doctor's checking him out. But he seemed fine."

"Jamie—" Joan started.

She was interrupted by commotion from the door—raised voices and heavy boots. She turned fast, half anticipating guards. Or—worse—Nick. Had he changed his mind? Had he started an attack?

But it wasn't Nick. Tom was marching a blindfolded boy into the room. The boy's hands were cuffed behind his back. His blond hair glowed even in the dim light.

Joan's heart clenched.

Aaron.

She pushed herself to her feet. As she did, a man with white-blond hair rose from a nearby table. He was dressed for the 1890s—although not for the docks—in a slim frock coat and an embroidered silk vest. He made his way over to the front door, smoothing down his coat with a finicky elegance that reminded Joan of Aaron.

Tom pulled Aaron out of the man's way, clearing the door for him. But to Joan's shock, that elegant man didn't reach for the door. Instead, he grabbed Aaron's neck and shoved him into the wall. Aaron's head thudded back with a sickening thump.

Joan pushed away from the table, scrambling to get to them.

"What's this fucking traitor doing here?" the man said. He shoved Aaron again. "You know I could kill you?" he said to him. "It would be so easy. I'd just have to touch your neck." He slid his hand from Aaron's throat to the back of his neck.

"Hey!" Joan reached them, using her momentum to push the man away. He stumbled back, hands slipping away from Aaron. "What are you *doing*?" Joan demanded.

"Joan," Tom murmured. "Best stay out of this."

"What?" Joan said incredulously. Who *was* this guy? He'd just threatened to kill Aaron. He'd had his hands on Aaron's *neck*.

Aaron's shoulders were rising and falling in quick, panicked breaths. His head turned from side to side as he tried to make out what was going on around the edges of his blindfold. His blond hair was in disarray and his jacket was rumpled. Joan's heart twisted. The last time she'd seen him that scared, one of Nick's men had had a knife raised against him.

Joan rounded on the man who'd grabbed him. He was about thirty years old, paler than Aaron. His frock coat wasn't quite right for the era, Joan saw now. On the pocket, there was silver embroidery: the silhouette of a caged bird. Joan suppressed a shiver. *Nightingales take*, the children's chant went. All monsters could steal life from humans, but the Nightingales could steal life from monsters too. They were the most feared of the families.

The Nightingales hate Aaron, Tom had said back in Covent Garden.

"Sebastien," Tom said to the Nightingale. The pronunciation was French. "We need him. We need to question him."

Sebastien seemed to calm slightly. "Do you need help with that? Aaron never could handle pain. If you need someone to inflict it, any Nightingale will volunteer."

Joan didn't know what the Nightingales had against Aaron, and she didn't care. "That's *not* how we're doing it."

"No . . . I suppose a Griffith would be more efficient," Sebastien said with regret.

Aaron was still breathing fast. Joan wanted to tell him everything was going to be okay. She'd make *sure* it was okay. She'd never let anything happen to him. But if she tried to reassure him, he'd push her away. He'd never believe that he had someone on his side here.

She saw with a start then that they had an audience. People were watching them—people on the mezzanine, people on the warehouse floor, Ruth and Jamie. "Come on," Joan said to Tom. "Let's get him out of here. We don't need to make a spectacle of him." She took Aaron's arm. "He hasn't actually done anything wrong, okay?" she added to Sebastien, to the people watching. Aaron had come after Joan, but it had been at the order of a member of the *Curia Monstrorum*. He couldn't have said no, even if he'd wanted to.

"Hasn't done anything wrong?" Sebastien said, eyebrows rising. "Is that what you think?"

"Get out of the way!" Joan said. When Sebastien didn't move, she added, frustrated, *"I'm* the one he captured! And yeah, that's what I think!"

"He has such a pretty face," Sebastien said. "Makes you want to like him, I know. But we Nightingales know the ugly truth behind that face. We know what he is."

Aaron lifted his head in his best attempt at his usual haughty posture. "No need to make it a cliffhanger, Bastien." Under Joan's hand, his arm felt very stiff, like he was trying to hold himself together.

Sebastien gazed down at Aaron's blindfolded face. "I never thought I'd stand this close to you again," he whispered. "How does it feel to be powerless? Like *she* was at the execution?"

Who was he talking about? Whoever it was, Aaron knew. Around the blindfold, his pale skin had gone milk white.

"I saw you turn away just before the ax came down," Sebastien said. "You couldn't bear to see what you'd done. Well, *I* saw. She was crying. She was terrified. She looked at *you* in her final moments, and you didn't even look back!"

The answer hit Joan like a shock of cold water. "You're talking about his *mother,"* she said. Marguerite Nightingale had been executed, she knew. "That's . . ." Joan didn't have the words. "That's *cruel*," she said. Whatever the Nightingales had against Aaron, it was just wrong to throw his mother's execution in his face.

"Cruel?" Sebastien said. He drew out the word as if examining it. "*Cruel* is informing on your own mother to the Court. *Cruel* is setting her up to be executed. *Cruel* is the executioner dragging her by the hair to the block. Humiliating her in her last moments."

"What?" Joan whispered.

"I know what you are," Sebastien said to Joan softly. He glanced around, and then lowered his voice even more. "She was protecting someone like *you*. That's why she was executed. Because she helped someone with your power. And Aaron turned her in for it."

"What?" Joan said again. She was shaken that Sebastien knew of her power. And more than that, she couldn't take in what he'd said. Aaron's mother had harbored someone with a forbidden power like Joan's? Aaron had turned his own mother in to the Court? "No," she said stupidly. Aaron would never have done that.

Right?

Sebastien didn't seem to hear her. His attention had returned to Aaron. "I know you're an Oliver," he said to Aaron. "I know you don't care about any family but your own. But she *loved* you. And you betrayed her. You called the guards on her!" His eyes shone. He was near tears, Joan saw then. "Marguerite Nightingale was the best of us, and you gave her up to the Court!"

Joan shook her head. She didn't want to believe it was true. She wondered suddenly how Sebastien had known Marguerite.

Could he be a cousin of Aaron's? An uncle? They had the same high cheekbones, the same porcelain-fine skin.

"You should see how all these people are looking at you right now," Sebastien whispered to Aaron. "You should see the disgust on their faces. How they despise you. Because that's what you are. You're despicable." Joan glanced around. People *were* watching with expressions of revulsion.

Under the blindfold, Aaron's face had been very pale, but now an ugly red flush appeared. His chin was still up, defiant. Joan stared at him. *Cruel is informing on your own mother.* Around the room, people were whispering about it.

Aaron Oliver, Joan heard. *Turned in his own mother. Disinherited by the Olivers too.*

"Keep *that* in mind when you talk to him," Sebastien said to Joan. He blinked and a tear fell. It seemed to bring him back to himself. He scrubbed at his face. "And don't free him afterward," he said roughly. "Or he'll inform on all of us." He stalked away before Joan could answer.

Aaron's head had been tilted slightly in Sebastien's direction, listening to Sebastien's footsteps fade. But now, as if he sensed Joan looking at him, he turned back to her. "Well?" he said tightly. "Do you have questions for me? Or shall we just keep standing here—apparently with people gawking?" He hadn't denied anything Sebastien had said, Joan realized slowly. Did that mean it was all true? That he *had* turned his mother in to be executed?

"Come on," Tom said softly. "We've prepared a room at the back of the boathouse. It has a door we can lock."

As they started to walk, something made Joan look up. Nick

was heading toward them. He found Joan's eyes, and Joan's breath caught at his expression.

"Can I meet you there?" Joan said. She released Aaron's arm reluctantly. "Don't start questioning him before I get there, okay? I just need to check on Nick."

Nick had changed his clothes; he was dressed for the era now in a brown flatcap, worker's shirt, and waistcoat. He was always hand-some, but there was an edge to his looks today: the bruise across his cheek made him look like the fighter he'd once been.

"What did the doctor say?" Joan asked.

Nick's eyebrows went up in slight irony. But he answered, "Bruised ribs. Nothing broken."

"That sounds painful."

Nick's eyes sparked with hurt before the cold overtook him again—as if he wanted to believe she cared but didn't. Joan folded her arms around herself. He was right here in front of her, but he'd never felt so far away.

"Why don't you ask me what you really want to know?" he said.

Joan pictured the carpet of flowers at Holland House, dark blood staining them. "*Do* we have a truce right now?"

"I gave you my word," Nick said. It was low, the dangerous rumble of a lion. "Even if I hadn't, I know what's right. We can't allow Eleanor to create a world where monsters rule. Until we stop her, we're on the same side."

Joan should have been relieved, but her chest was painfully tight. *After that, our paths will diverge,* he'd said.

"They captured Aaron when they rescued us?" Nick said.

Joan nodded.

"You knew him in the other timeline, didn't you? That's why you were so upset when he came after you in this one." Nick sounded so cold. "You care about him, and he doesn't remember you anymore."

It took Joan a moment to get the word out. "Yes."

His mouth twisted wryly. "That sounds painful."

Joan swallowed hard. She really couldn't bear to cry in front of him right now. She clenched her hands into fists until her nails bit into the flesh. "We need to go and question him," she said.

Nick was right. Eleanor had to be stopped. That had to come before anything else.

TWENTY-NINE

Joan was very aware of Nick at her back as she led him to the rear of the warehouse. Tom was waiting for them outside one of the arched brick alcoves. The ones on either side were crowded with neatly stacked burlap sacks. Only the alcove behind him had doors.

"We've brought in George Griffith to question him," Tom said. "He was nearby in 1890—didn't mind popping over."

Joan felt Nick shift his weight. *Nearby in 1890.* He knew now what that meant—a man had stolen a year of human life to travel here to 1891.

Joan couldn't meet Nick's eyes. She *had* to tell the others that Nick knew. That he was free. But how? She was so afraid of what they'd do. Of what Nick would do if they attacked him or tried to control him again. . . .

What if Joan said the wrong thing, at the wrong time, and got people killed?

She registered, belatedly, the name George Griffith. "Isn't he the guy who stood us up at the masquerade?"

"Turns out he just needed a bit more persuasion." Tom rubbed his thumb over his fingertips in a *paid him* gesture. "Come on." He opened the heavy wooden doors.

It was a proper room—not just an alcove—with a small cot on one side and a table with a jug of water and some bread on the other. The sparsity oddly reminded Joan of Aaron's actual bedroom—the one she'd seen at the Oliver mansion.

Weak light filtered through a tiny iron-latticed window; it was still barely dawn. The walls were raw brick, and the ceiling was a low crisscross of rough-cut wood. This was the underside of the mezzanine balcony, but Joan wouldn't have known it. The thick brick walls made the room feel like a private space, far away from anything.

Aaron stood with his back against the wall, as far as he could get from the door. The others sat on the cot—including a stranger Joan assumed was George Griffith.

"Oh good, more warm bodies," Aaron said as Tom closed the door behind him. The room *was* stuffy—they'd landed in a summer month. Someone had removed Aaron's blindfold and restraints, and he looked more flustered than Joan had ever seen him, his golden hair curling in the humidity and his beautiful face flushed. Aaron's gaze lingered on Joan for a moment, and then moved to Nick. "And look . . . ," he said. "You brought a human to a monster house. Apparently, the King's Laws mean nothing here."

Nick moved to the table and poured water into a small wooden cup. Aaron tried to back up as Nick approached, but there was nowhere to go.

"Not in the mood to be drugged," Aaron told him.

Nick tilted his head, maybe at the phrasing. "Is it drugged?" he asked the others.

"No," Tom said.

"Do you need me to drink some of it?" Nick asked Aaron.

Aaron paused, as if considering it, and then shook his head. When Nick offered the cup, he took it warily. His gaze stayed on Nick's face as Nick stepped back; Aaron didn't seem to know what to make of him. Joan knew that he didn't spend much time with humans.

"So . . ." George Griffith stood slowly. He was around thirty years old, with red-tinged hair in a bowl cut that made Joan think of the early Beatles. He wore a heavy silver griffin pendant the size of Joan's palm. "What do we want to know?"

They needed to know how Eleanor was planning to change the timeline. They needed to know how to stop her. And there were things Joan just *wanted* to know: why Eleanor had turned Nick into a monster slayer; what Eleanor had against Joan.

"Who asked you to search for me?" Joan said to Aaron.

Aaron gave her a long look, apparently weighing what to say.

"Answer her," George said, his tone so casual that Joan wasn't even sure if he'd used his power.

Aaron shrugged. "The Court informed my father that there were fugitives on the loose. He was asked to nominate an Oliver to assist with the search."

"Why did he choose *you*?" Ruth said from the cot. Aaron's only response was to glare at her.

Edmund had nominated Aaron because he had the true Oliver power, but Aaron wouldn't talk about that unless he was forced. It was an Oliver secret.

"Do you know who you're up against?" Aaron said. He was still in his masquerade clothes; his black jacket lay neatly folded on the windowsill. He'd rather have hung it, Joan knew. "The Lady Eleanor herself has been after these fugitives." He gestured at Joan and Nick.

None of the others reacted—Jamie must have spoken to them already.

"They're paying me quite a lot," George said to Aaron.

Aaron's face fell. He'd clearly hoped that Eleanor's name would frighten someone into freeing him. And he was usually better at masking his emotions. He was scared.

"No one will hurt you," Joan promised him. "We just need information."

Aaron's eyebrows arched incredulously. He beckoned to her. Joan blinked, confused, and Aaron's mouth lifted slightly. "Guess that cuff isn't working anymore."

"We cut your anchor to it," Tom growled. "Smashed that little anchoring device."

"And took my travel tokens," Aaron said. "Yes, I know." He folded his arms.

"Were you working directly with Eleanor?" Joan asked.

Aaron gave her a look of mild contempt. "I'm not going to betray the Court by telling you anything about her."

"Answer the question," George said, and this time Joan felt the push of his power, like the heat of a lamp.

Aaron shook his head, but the movement was a little jerky, as if it had taken some effort to ignore George's request.

"*Eleanor's* the one betraying the Court," Joan said, trying to appeal to Aaron's loyalty. "She wants to change the timeline."

"Stop speaking of her like that," Aaron said tightly. "The timeline can't be changed. And Eleanor would never move against the King."

"Do you honestly believe that?" George said to Aaron. The question had the full backing of his power. Joan could almost feel it pressing on Aaron, and Aaron's shoulders relaxed. Joan remembered how the Griffith power had felt herself—like she'd been in the presence of an old friend.

"Course I believe it," Aaron said almost dreamily. "The Lady Eleanor wouldn't turn against the King. The timeline can't be changed." And then, almost at once, his eyes focused. He scowled.

He really did believe what he'd said. Joan released a breath, torn between disappointment and relief. If he didn't know Eleanor's plans, he wouldn't be able to help them much. But it also meant that he wasn't complicit. Joan had been so afraid that he was working with Eleanor directly to create that world; that he'd wanted that world to exist.

Jamie shot Joan a look. *He doesn't know anything*, his expression said.

Joan bit her lip. "Eleanor left the library just before we were rescued. Do you know where she went? Did she talk about a place? A person? A plan?"

"Where is she now?" George said quietly.

"I—" Aaron grimaced. Joan's stomach turned over as he fought the Griffith power. "I— I'm loyal to the Court."

"Olivers are only loyal to Olivers," Ruth muttered from the cot.

"What would you know?" Aaron managed. "Hunts aren't loyal to anything!"

"Where did Eleanor go?" George said.

"I—" Aaron stopped. "I—" His pressed his lips together. He took a shaky breath, clearly struggling not to answer. Sweat beaded on his brow. "Hah. Hmm. I've had the Griffith power used on me before," he gritted out. "Last time it felt stronger." He bared his teeth at George. "What are you—ten steps removed from a head of your family?"

George's eyes flashed with anger. "Watch your tongue! My father is a Nightingale, just like your mother was. You talk about loyalty to the Court, but we both know there's not a loyal bone inside you."

Aaron's head lifted. "I think the problem is that I *can* watch my tongue. Your power just isn't strong enough to break me." He looked defiant. "Do you have a brother? An older sister? Maybe they can have a go at me."

George's eyes blazed. "Where's Eleanor? Think aloud!"

"*Wait*," Joan said as Aaron's eyes softened. That was too intrusive to ask of anyone.

"I—I—" Aaron put a hand flat against the wall for support. His breath was coming faster than normal.

"I said *think aloud*!" George said.

"I think I'm going to die here!" Aaron blurted. He sounded real and vulnerable suddenly, all the bravado gone. "I don't think anyone's coming to help me! I don't think even my own father would—"

"*Stop!*" Joan said, and she had the impression of movement from Nick—as if he'd been about to stop it too. Her heart was in her throat.

Aaron's eyes focused on Joan, his mouth snapping shut like she'd broken the spell. Then he looked sick.

"I know we'll have to sift through his stream of consciousness," George said to Joan, "but—"

"We're not doing it like that!" Joan told him.

"Joan," Tom said, "if you can't stomach this—"

"We can't force him to say everything on his mind!" Joan said. "It's violating! It's—" She looked around at them all. Tom and Nick were looming by the door like prison guards. Ruth and Jamie were still on the cot, Frankie quiet on Jamie's lap. Ruth and Tom both looked grim, as if they'd have been fine for George to continue with the interrogation. Jamie looked troubled, though— and Nick . . . Joan had thought for a second that he'd been ready to stop George too, but his face had gone blank and unreadable.

Joan turned back to Aaron. His expression had smoothed again. She could still picture that sick look on his face, though. And he was still as far as he could get from them, pressed against the brick wall, the cell-like window above him. *I think I'm going to die here.*

Joan couldn't bear it. "I want to talk to Aaron alone."

"Is that a good idea?" Nick said behind her. "Talking to him alone?" Joan blinked at him. Nick had almost sounded protective, but that didn't make sense after what had happened last night. Protective of their alliance, maybe.

"It's *not* a good idea," Ruth said.

"No, *this* is not a good idea," Joan said, and George scowled, as if she'd insulted him directly. She supposed she *was* insulting his power.

"We should restrain him if you want to be alone with him," Nick said, and Joan blinked at him again.

Joan looked at Aaron. His hands were in fists, white knuckled. He was taller than her, but he'd always fought with words. She shook her head. "No restraints." She couldn't stomach it.

Jamie stood up from the cot and drew Joan to the door. "Joan," he murmured. He glanced at Aaron and dropped to a whisper just for her. "This is a new timeline, and he's a new person. He doesn't *know* you anymore. *This* Aaron has been working with the Court to hunt you down and *kill* you."

"He doesn't know me, but I know *him*," Joan whispered back.

In this timeline, Nick was different. His whole life had changed. He hadn't been brutally forged into the hero as a child; he'd lived an ordinary life. This Aaron, though, was almost identical to the Aaron who Joan had known. He'd lived the exact same life for seventeen years. The point of divergence hadn't come until the massacre at Holland House.

Inside, he had to be the same Aaron, with the same unswerving sense of loyalty, the same secretly soft heart. He *had* to be.

Joan answered Jamie's dubious expression. "Just give me an hour with him."

Jamie sighed. "If you need to play it out, you can. But you have to know, you're just hurting yourself. He isn't the person you knew."

"If I don't have anything in an hour, we can bring back George Griffith," Joan said. "Just let me talk to him. Please."

Jamie looked troubled, but he backed up. "Come on," he said to the others. "Sometimes you need to play it all out to understand that things have changed." This was said so wearily that Joan wondered if he might be correct.

"We'll be right outside the door," Tom said. This was directed at Aaron, who offered a half shrug.

And just like that, Joan and Aaron were alone.

Joan turned to face him. Aaron had relaxed slightly now that he wasn't outnumbered. He'd been pressed back against the wall, but now he looked more like he was leaning against it.

"Aren't you scared?" he said.

"Of you?"

"I can see you're half-human," Aaron said. "Aren't you afraid that I'll steal your life and use it to escape?"

Joan had been afraid every time she'd stepped into a monster space. She'd been afraid of Nick sometimes. She'd never been afraid of Aaron, though. "You wouldn't do that."

Even in here, flushed and with his hair awry, he was stupidly beautiful. And *he* was still the one who looked afraid. For all his casual posture, his gray eyes were wide and glazed. *I think I'm going to die in here*, he'd said.

"You *won't* die in here," Joan said to him. "I swear it."

"Don't bother making promises you won't keep," Aaron said. "Sebastien Nightingale gave away the end game. I'm not getting out of here."

"On my life," Joan said. "After we've talked, you can go anywhere you want."

Aaron shoved his hands into his pockets. "You know, I think this would work better if the Griffith played good cop. I'd believe it more from him than a Court traitor." He tilted his head. "Do your friends even know what you are? About that power of yours?"

Joan heard herself take a sharp breath, and Aaron heard it too. He looked satisfied. His arrow had hit its target. Joan remembered again the guard's words: *Something forbidden. Something wrong.* "*You* don't know what I am," Joan said. That was what

Aaron had told her last time. "The true Oliver power doesn't tell you that. And . . . I don't know either. I don't know what this power is, or where it came from."

His eyes narrowed. For a second, Joan was sure he was going to ask what she knew of the true Oliver power. But he just said, "What do you *want*?"

"We need your help," Joan said. "Eleanor's working against the King. She's trying to create a new timeline, and I've seen it. If she succeeds, people will die." *In uncountable numbers,* Astrid had said.

"I told you. That's not possible," Aaron said.

"What's not possible? Another timeline?"

"All of it!"

"You *saw* another timeline tonight," Joan said. "You saw that tear appear in the library. It showed the previous timeline inside it!" Her throat tightened as she saw it again in her mind's eye, the way she'd looked at Nick; the way he'd looked at her. The sound he'd made as she'd started to unravel his life.

"You lie like a Hunt," Aaron said, but with a touch of uncertainty. It occurred to Joan then that Aaron might not have had a clear view of the scene in the library. As soon as the seal had opened, Aaron had bent over double, retching. The tear in the timeline had made him sick. "I don't know what I saw," he said even more uncertainly.

"I'm not lying to you," Joan whispered. "Aaron . . . there was another timeline before this one."

"If you start preaching to me about the true timeline—"

"I'm not talking about the *zhēnshí de lìshǐ*. I'm talking about a timeline where something went wrong. A timeline where the human hero was real."

Aaron paused then, long enough that Joan knew he'd seen or heard something at the guardhouse about Nick being the hero. Still, he said, "The human hero is a fairy tale."

Joan shook her head. "There was another timeline before ours. He was *real* in that one." She knew how ridiculous the idea would sound to Aaron, though. She was telling him that a fairy tale was real. "In that timeline, he killed our families. Yours and mine. And then you and I worked together to stop him. To bring our families back to life. And we *did*. They're alive again in this timeline."

Aaron's expression had been getting more and more skeptical as Joan went on, and now he barked a laugh. "This is so farfetched that I don't even understand the game!"

"Aaron, it's the truth! We knew each other before this."

"I'd rather have this interrogation with the Griffith. At least he seemed sane."

Joan opened her mouth to snap back at him, but the urge twisted into a nostalgic ache. She'd even missed this—the way he always pushed back at her. "We *were* friends," she said. "And the hero didn't just exist. Eleanor took a boy and *made* him into the hero. She *made* him into a monster slayer."

"Hell, bring the *Nightingale* in," Aaron said. "I'd rather be tortured than listen to you tell me that we were *friends*. I'd rather Sebastien Nightingale drained my life."

That should have stung. But Aaron's voice had cracked as he'd said *Nightingale*, and Joan's heart stuttered at the fear and misery underneath his stiff mask.

"The Nightingales really hate you," Joan said, and she regretted it when Aaron's expression closed again.

"They don't like people who betray Nightingales," Aaron said. "And my mother was a Nightingale."

Joan searched his face. His jaw was stiff. He'd barely spoken about his mother when she'd known him, but she'd had the impression of deep emotion from him every time he had.

"Sebastien said you turned her over to the Court."

"I don't need the recap. It was barely fifteen minutes ago," Aaron said tightly. "You know why she was executed, right? Because she was helping someone like *you*."

"Yes," Joan whispered. "That's why you told me you wanted to watch *my* execution. Because your mother died for someone like me." And it hurt to say that out loud—to acknowledge that Aaron hated her in this timeline. But at the same time, she saw Aaron's cold expression slip again; he looked sick. Joan swallowed. "I don't care what Sebastien said. I know you didn't betray your mother to the Court. You'd never have done that to someone you loved."

Another crack in Aaron's expression. "You're not even asking me questions anymore," he said. "You're just saying things. What's the point of this?"

Joan couldn't make sense of it. "Why are you letting the Nightingales hate you for something you didn't do?"

Aaron's fists clenched. "Stop pretending you know me. This mind-fuck isn't working on me."

"I know you would have protected her," Joan said.

"You don't know anything about me!"

"You protected *me* last time. When the Court came after me, you took me to a safe house."

"What?" Aaron said. He'd taken a breath to snap at her, but now he was just staring. "What safe house?" He seemed to gather himself. "I don't know what you're talking about."

"It was in Southwark. A one-bedroom house with a little kitchen, a sitting room. Your mother had stayed there."

Aaron looked shaken for a moment. "I would *never*—" He stopped. His fists clenched and opened, and the shock slowly faded. When he spoke again, his voice was cold. "A few minutes ago, you used the term *true Oliver power*. Where did you hear that?"

Joan hesitated, thrown by the change of subject. "From you," she said. "You told me about it."

"That's a *lie*," Aaron blurted. "That's—" He worked his jaw. "Go on, then," he said challengingly, full of disbelief. "Tell me the circumstances. Tell me *exactly* what I said."

Joan remembered his soft footsteps in the hallway as she was leaving the safe house. *Let me come with you*, he'd said. "I'd figured out where the hero was," she told him. "I knew I had to go after him alone. But . . . you intercepted me before I could go. You wanted to come with me."

Aaron looked both skeptical and pleased, as if he'd caught Joan in a clear lie. "You make me sound so noble."

He *had* been. "You don't think you'd fight a monster slayer?"

"You really *don't* know me," Aaron whispered.

"Maybe you're braver than you think."

"I've never been susceptible to false flattery," Aaron said. "And I can't help but notice that you still haven't told me how you know the term *true Oliver power.*"

He really didn't believe it. He didn't see himself that way. Joan thought back to that night with an ache. She'd *missed* him. "We'd been looking for a way to change the timeline," she said. "To bring our families back from the dead."

"It's not possible to change the timeline," Aaron said again.

"That's what you thought last time," Joan agreed. "But by the end, I guess you'd changed your mind, because you told me that if I managed to undo the massacre, I could never meet you. I could never trust you. You said . . ." *I won't remember what you mean to me.* Joan heard her own voice crack. "You—you said you'd hate me in this new timeline."

Aaron's expression was hard. "Well, your fictional me was right about that."

Joan's heart hurt like someone was squeezing a fist around it. He'd warned her that he'd hate her, but she hadn't understood how it would feel. She forced herself to keep talking. "You told me about the trial that monsters undertake as children—the trial of family power. You took yours when you were just nine years old."

"I was precocious," Aaron said, but he frowned a little. As if answering a question he'd raised himself, he said, "It's common enough knowledge that I manifested my power early."

"And more strongly," Joan said. "Ordinary Olivers can differentiate humans from monsters. But you demonstrated the *true* Oliver power—the rare ability to differentiate family from family."

A flicker in Aaron's expression. Joan knew it was because she'd correctly described the power. The Olivers kept that aspect of their power a secret.

"After you demonstrated that power, you were taken to

another room," Joan said, and Aaron's chin jerked up. She really had his attention now. "They showed you a man in a cage with iron bars. They used a cattle prod on him until he looked at you. And they told you to arrest or kill anyone who had eyes like his."

"You must have heard that from someone else," Aaron whispered. "I'd never tell anyone that."

"You told me that you never saw anyone like him again until you met me." She remembered how he'd pushed her hair from her face as if he'd been about to kiss her. "You gave me a brooch just before I left," she said. "You'd found it in a cupboard at the safe house. A brown bird in a cage."

"*What?*" Aaron sounded truly shocked now, and Joan's focus shifted from the images in her head to him. He was staring at her as if he were seeing her for the first time. As if he'd forgotten that he was a prisoner here.

"It had belonged to your mother," Joan said. "It had time imbued in it—fifty years. You told me that it wouldn't feel as bad to travel that way."

"Why would you feel bad?" Aaron said—it was a real question, not a challenge. He answered himself softly: "Because you're half-human, and you'd barely traveled. It would have been easier for you to travel with a token."

"It *was*," Joan admitted. "It was still human time. It was still wrong, but . . ." It had been just as bad morally, but it hadn't felt as bad—and what did that say about her?

"Why would I give you my mother's brooch?" Aaron murmured, almost to himself. He hadn't taken his eyes from her.

"Because of the time imbued in it," Joan explained again. Aaron didn't reply. He just stared at her.

"Why do the Nightingales think that you informed on her?" Joan whispered. "I know you didn't."

"Why do you keep saying that?" Aaron said. He sounded wary, but there was a new vulnerable note in his voice as well.

"You just wouldn't. You wouldn't do that. If anyone had informed on her, it would have been—" She cut herself off as the truth finally clicked. "Your father," she said slowly. In response, Aaron made a soft sound. *"Oh,"* Joan said as the rest of it fell into place. The last piece of the puzzle. "You have the true Oliver power," she said. "Your power is so strong that it was confirmed when you were just nine years old. You should have been the next head of family. But your father removed you from the line of succession." *If I could have stripped you of your name too, I would have,* Edmund had said. "He disinherited you because you tried to *protect* your mother from the Court. Because you *didn't* inform on her."

Aaron seemed about to say something, but no words came out. The mask had slipped completely. He looked raw.

Joan felt like her heart was breaking for him. "Why did you never tell the Nightingales? Why did you never *tell* them that you tried to protect her?" But Joan knew the answer as soon as she asked. *"Fidelis ad mortem,"* she said. That was the Oliver motto. *Loyal unto death.* "You'd never turn against an Oliver," she realized. "Not even him. *Especially* not him."

Hated by the Nightingales and the Olivers, Ruth had said. People talked about him behind his back. They despised him. Joan felt her eyes well at the unfairness. "It's not right," she said.

Aaron's own eyes seemed to shine wetly for just a moment, and then he looked away.

"It doesn't have to be like this," Joan said. "Let me tell Sebastien Nightingale that—"

"*No,*" Aaron said roughly. Joan braced herself for a return to hostility, but when he met her eyes again, he'd blinked away the shine. He looked calmer. "Your name is Joan, right?"

Joan was still caught in the shock of realization. "I . . ." And then she heard what he'd said. It cut with the same knife jab as when Nick had asked for her name.

Aaron's eyes flickered over her face; he'd caught the emotion. His voice gentled. "It's Joan?"

Joan nodded.

"Okay, Joan," he said.

"Okay, what?"

"Okay, I believe you."

Joan's throat felt thick with tears suddenly. She hadn't expected him to say that. Not so quickly. If she was honest, she'd never expected him to say anything like that ever again. He'd felt as irrevocably lost to her as Nick had been. "You believe we knew each other?" she said.

"I believe everything you said."

It felt like relief from pain. Joan felt her shoulders drop. She could hardly take it in. He'd told her last time: *You can't ever meet me. You can't ever trust me.* She'd never let herself imagine the reality of him looking at her again, clear-eyed and without hatred.

"I—" Joan tried to smile, but she couldn't force one. She felt more like crying.

"What is it?" Aaron whispered. "What were you going to say?"

"I missed you," Joan managed. "In this timeline." It came out with so much emotion that Aaron looked surprised. *"Sorry,"* Joan said. "I know you don't remember me. We just . . . We went through things together that no one else did. And I missed you. A *lot.*"

Aaron was silent long enough that Joan could feel herself reddening. It was too much to tell him—that she'd missed him when he'd barely met her.

"You're right. I don't know you," he said finally. Joan tried not to feel the blunt ache of it. He didn't remember her, and that was just the truth. "I do know, though," Aaron said, his gray eyes serious, "that if I gave you that brooch, I must have—" He hesitated. "I must have trusted you very much."

Joan blinked. She had the impression that he'd been about to say something else before the hesitation.

There was a well of emotion inside her that she couldn't think about right now. It struck her anew that his own father had betrayed him. That his mother's family had cast him aside for something he hadn't done.

Aaron pushed a hand through his hair. "You really think Eleanor is working against the King?"

Joan nodded. She didn't trust her voice.

"We need to talk properly, then," Aaron said. "Because you're right. I think I can help."

THIRTY

Joan opened the door and found the others standing just outside. Behind them, the warehouse had brightened. The sun had risen, and daylight streamed in through the lattice windows, illuminating the mosaic artwork wrapped along the mezzanine walls.

"You want George back?" Tom said.

Joan shook her head. "I convinced Aaron myself." She looked over her shoulder. Aaron had ventured a few steps toward the door. After a moment of hesitation, he followed Joan out.

"Really?" Tom said, eyebrows going up. "That was a quick turnaround."

"It's as she said." Aaron was back to haughty, a hand in his pocket. "She convinced me." In that magical way of his, he'd smoothed his hair and clothes to perfection. "She knew things about me that . . . Well, I believe her."

Tom looked deeply suspicious, and Ruth more so. Even Jamie looked doubtful. Joan's heart sank a little. But she couldn't have had that conversation with Aaron in front of anyone else. It wouldn't have been fair to him to make public the private things he'd only shared with her.

Nick was leaning against the wall by the open mouth of the door. His posture was apparently casual, but Joan had the feeling that he'd positioned himself strategically. He could have pushed into the room if needed. She swallowed. *Had* he been protecting her? His eyes were on Aaron, his expression unreadable.

George Griffith had vanished; Joan had insulted the man's family power, she supposed. Apparently, he hadn't stuck around to be insulted more.

Now, Ruth stepped closer to get a better look at Aaron's face. "She *convinced* you?" Her tone was heavy with skepticism. "Convinced you of what exactly?"

Aaron lifted his chin. "That I knew her once. That she knew me."

"That we were close," Joan said to Ruth. "That we once trusted each other." Ruth looked even more skeptical at that. "We *all* worked together last time," Joan said, looking around at them: Ruth, Tom, Jamie. She hesitated when she reached Nick, still standing against the wall.

Nick's dark eyes met hers, and his mouth lifted wryly. They'd all worked together against *him*, and he knew that now. Joan swallowed. How long would it be before they truly were on opposite sides again?

Joan looked over his shoulder. There were more people around now: Hathaways and Lius dressed as Victorian sailors. They strolled in and out of the building—through the front door, and through a second one that had opened nearby, on the western side. It led directly onto the canal. Beyond the open door, a horse clip-clopped along the bank, tugging a laden barge. It was led by a man in a soft hat and suit that read to Joan as smart enough for a wedding but were probably considered workers' clothes in this period.

Nick addressed Aaron. "I take it you have information?"

Aaron straightened, as if at Nick's serious tone. Or maybe because Nick had cut to the point. It wasn't only Aaron, though.

Joan suppressed a shiver as she saw how they'd all unconsciously canted toward Nick as soon as he'd spoken. Joan was reminded again of a king of old.

And what was going to happen after they all stopped Eleanor? What would Nick do when their *paths diverged*, as he'd put it? Last time, he'd had followers; maybe this time, he'd raise an army against monsters.

Joan shook off the thought. They had to actually stop Eleanor first.

She turned to Aaron too. "You said you knew something that could help," she prompted.

Aaron dipped his head in acknowledgment. "Eleanor never spoke of her plans," he said. "But the senior guards and courtiers talked. I overheard things."

"What kinds of things?"

"There were guards searching for you two," Aaron said, nodding at Joan and Nick. "But there were rumors of another group. Guards with different orders."

The way he said it gave Joan a chill. "Different orders?" And at the same time, she wondered again: *Why?* Why had Eleanor wanted Joan and Nick? Why had she made Nick into the hero? And Eleanor had held Nick for the last three weeks at Holland House. What had she done to him in that time?

Did I ruin your plans by unmaking him? Joan had asked Eleanor.

You inconvenienced me, but I'm resourceful, Eleanor had replied.

What had she meant by that?

Joan flicked a look at Nick now. His gaze was on the wider room—he was watching the Hathaways and the Lius, almost sizing them up. Joan would have bet anything he'd counted the number of people here and clocked all the doors and windows.

"What orders did the other guards have?" Jamie asked. He looked troubled.

"I don't know," Aaron said. "All of this was just rumor."

"Who *is* Eleanor?" Joan murmured, half to herself. "I mean, I know she's a member of the *Curia Monstrorum*, but who actually is she? She looked like she was in her early twenties. How did she get so much power so young?" And how had she known Joan in the original timeline?

"I don't think anyone knows," Aaron said. "Members of the *Curia Monstrorum* have to revoke all ties to their family when they join the Court." He hesitated. "She seemed like a Nightingale, though." This was directed at Joan, and she understood what he meant—he'd been close enough to see Eleanor's eyes. To see that she'd had the Nightingale power.

"I suppose that makes sense," Jamie said. "We know that Conrad was once a Nightingale, and people say that he and Eleanor are siblings."

"I can't help but notice," Ruth interrupted, "that nothing Aaron's said has been useful. Lots of rumors and *I don't know*s."

"Ruth," Joan said.

Ruth's jaw was tight. "Joan, whatever he told you in that room, he only said it so you'd let him out! Don't you get that? He won't give us anything useful. And first chance he has, he'll be out of here, informing on us all!"

"He won't," Joan said.

"He informed on his own mother!"

"He didn't!" Joan said. "He would never betray anyone like

that!" She turned to Aaron and was surprised to find his eyes on her, with an expression she'd only seen on him in the other timeline. Like he couldn't make sense of her, like she was a puzzle to solve.

"We should bring back the Griffith," Ruth said. "Olivers always lie."

Aaron's gaze hardened as his eyes flicked back to Ruth. "Bring in anyone you want," he snapped. "Olivers aren't liars! *Hunts* are!"

"Don't talk about my family!"

"Stop it!" Joan said, frustrated. They'd bickered like this last time too.

"Joan, we *cannot* trust him," Ruth said. "He's an Oliver! He's the worst of the Olivers! The enmity between our families—"

"—goes back a thousand years!" Joan said, frustrated. "I know! We've had this conversation before!" She wished they'd just let that old enmity go. "Next thing he'll say is that the Hunts are thieves. And *you'll* say the Olivers are snaky schemers. And *he'll* say no family is allied with the Hunts because we're just that unlovable. And *you'll* say that you don't understand what the Mtawalis see in his family. And around and around and around. And we need to *stop*! We need to focus on the real enemy here!"

She paused to catch her breath. Ruth and Aaron both looked rattled, as if they really had been about to recycle all their same arguments from last time. But Ruth was staring at her too; Joan could only have recalled that argument if something very like this conversation had happened before. If Ruth and Joan really had known Aaron before.

"Listen," Joan said. "Something really bad is coming. That hole in the world showed it to us. Eleanor told me she had a plan in motion to make it happen." She asked Aaron, "Did you hear *anything* else about that other group of guards? About what their orders were?"

Aaron shook his head, a little apologetic.

"Convenient," Ruth said, but all the sharpness was gone. She ducked her head, looking more thoughtful. "You never heard any other rumors going around?" she asked Aaron.

Aaron's mouth twisted, as if his instinct was to bite back at her. But instead of snapping, he frowned slightly. He was thinking about it. "I *did* hear something else," he said slowly.

"You did?" Joan said, straightening.

"I heard that the Alis had been contacted like the Olivers were," Aaron said. "They were ordered to send adjuncts to assist the guards, but . . ." His frown deepened. "I never saw an Ali searching for fugitives."

"They were with the other group of guards?" Tom said.

"Possibly," Aaron said. He was still frowning.

"Why would Eleanor need members of the Ali family?" Ruth said.

"To seal things up," Joan said. That was the Ali power.

"Or unseal them," Nick said, his voice so low that Joan felt it in her bones. She blinked up at him. It was the first thing he'd said in a while. He stood with his back to the wall. He could have belonged to this era, dressed in his white shirt and dark trousers, except that he'd rolled up his shirtsleeves as if prepared to fight.

Joan felt a tug of unease—and not just about Nick. *To seal things up or unseal them.*

Joan had been avoiding thinking about the Ali seals and what had been hidden behind them. The truth was, though, that there had been two tears in the timeline in the exact places where she'd used her power—in the café at Covent Garden and the library of Holland House.

For some reason, Tom's words popped into her head. As he'd crossed the threshold of the seal, he'd sensed the tear in the timeline. *There's something in here. Something* wrong.

Those words were too familiar. *Something forbidden,* a guard had said of Joan's power. *Something* wrong.

The room was warm, but Joan found herself folding her arms. For the first time, she made herself face the question that had been at the back of her mind since she'd seen those jagged wounds in the world, hidden behind the Ali seals.

Had *she* torn those holes in the timeline when she'd used her power?

And if she had . . . what did *that* mean?

"Eleanor wants to create a new timeline where monsters rule," Nick said. "How would she do that?"

Joan herself had changed the timeline in a relatively small way by unmaking Nick—erasing everything he'd done as the hero. But the world they'd glimpsed through that tear in the timeline had been a very different London: the governance had changed, the people had been cowed and fearful, even the architecture had seemed strange. "How *would* she do it?" she asked. How had the King done it when he'd erased the true timeline? They'd never figured that out.

Jamie ran a hand through his smooth black hair, barely ruffling it. Then he inclined his head. "Follow me."

He led them to the open door on the western side of the building. Outside, the canal was littered with straw and leaves and splintered wood, the water so stagnant that the detritus barely moved.

Jamie ushered them onto a platform outside the door—it was designed to allow Hathaway boats to pull up, Joan guessed. It was just big enough for the six of them—plus Frankie, who sniffed with interest at the water.

"Oh, this is vile," Aaron said, looking across the canal. There was a paved path on the other side and, beyond it, ramshackle houses—almost huts—their wooden fences missing pickets and half-collapsed. To Tom and Jamie, he said, "Why on earth would you have a house in the slums?"

"We have houses where our territories are," Tom said mildly. "We like it here."

"Good lord," Aaron said. His hands were in his pockets, as if he wanted to limit the amount of his bare skin exposed to the air here.

"Don't even *think* of jumping in," Ruth warned him.

Aaron's eyes flicked with horror to the murky water. "Why would I?"

"To escape. To run back to your family and inform on us all."

Aaron turned his horrified look on Ruth. "Much as I'd love to be rid of your company, I don't desire it enough to catch hepatitis."

Joan felt uneasy. Would the others let Aaron leave later, or was she going to have to help him escape? Beside her, Nick shifted his weight. His gaze was on the other side of the canal, but she could tell he was listening. It struck her suddenly that she might not get any warning before Nick left. When the time came, he'd probably just go.

As if he'd heard her thoughts, Nick's dark eyes turned to her.

For a second, Joan felt the echo of his hands cupping her face; his soft lips against hers; and her chest hurt so much that she couldn't breathe.

Aaron and Ruth were still arguing. "I've changed my mind!" Aaron said. "I'd prefer that canal to you!"

"Just—" Joan held her hand up. She couldn't bear them bickering right now. "Stop. Please stop."

In her peripheral vision, she saw Aaron turn to her like he'd heard a strange note in her voice. His attention shifted from Joan to Nick and back as if he'd picked up on the tension between them. No one else seemed aware of it.

Joan took a deep breath. The air smelled of unmoving canal water, but it was crisply cool enough to sharpen her mind. She suspected that was why Jamie had brought them all out here—to give them space to think.

If anything, though, the small platform had brought them all closer together. Joan was almost touching Nick on one side, Aaron on the other. She squeezed her eyes shut for a moment, trying to focus. "How *would* Eleanor change the timeline?" she asked again. "How would she create that world we saw?"

"There are lots of theories about how to change the timeline," Tom said. He glanced at Joan in acknowledgment. She'd done it by unmaking Nick.

"To make the timeline we saw, Eleanor would have to change something significant," Jamie said. "I would say a significant historical event."

"What event?" Ruth said.

Jamie spread his hands. "I don't know. To change the timeline on the scale that Eleanor wants to . . ." He shook his head.

"Only the King has ever done that."

"How did the King do it?" Joan wondered. How had he erased the original timeline? "What significant thing did *he* change?" She chewed her lip, thinking. They'd seen a statue of Eleanor. *Semper Regina.* Always Queen. So they knew something of Eleanor's final goal, at least.

Aaron shifted his weight beside Joan. "We're thinking about this all wrong," he said suddenly. Joan blinked at him. His hands were still in his pockets, lord-like, and for a moment Joan almost knew something important. About Eleanor, about herself. About why Eleanor had turned Nick into a slayer. Why she'd said, *It's always about Nick with you, isn't it? And that blond boy.*

And then Aaron said, "The timeline doesn't allow change," and the feeling vanished like a popped bubble, leaving Joan reaching for it. "None of this should be possible."

What had that feeling been? What had Joan almost known? Now that the moment had passed, she wondered if her mind had been playing tricks on her. When had she last slept? She closed her eyes for a moment, and a wave of tiredness hit her. She'd been unconscious for a few hours last night, she guessed, but she didn't exactly feel rested. She forced her eyes open.

"What do you mean the timeline doesn't allow it?" Nick said. To Joan, he said slowly: "You told me there was a force in the world—one that stops events from being changed. . . ."

They'd had that conversation on the train from Bedford. He'd trusted her so much more back then. "The timeline pushes back against us," she said to him now.

"The timeline abhors change," Aaron explained to Nick. With some distaste, he bent to pick up a stone from underfoot and tossed it into the canal. Water rippled around the drop. "When we time-travel, we're like stones thrown into a river. We create cascades of changes—like ripples—wherever we go."

"I know the metaphor," Nick said softly.

"Keep watching," Aaron said.

In the canal, the ripples flattened until all signs of the stone were gone.

"The timeline always returns to its previous state," Aaron said. "It smooths away our changes."

"It's a law of nature," Ruth agreed.

Joan stared down at the near-still water where the stone had been, and a chill seeped into her. No force had stopped her when she'd unmade Nick. She'd thrown a stone, and the ripples had kept rippling without end, in unnatural perpetual motion.

And what happened when you defied nature itself?

Joan saw again the holes in the world, their edges as ragged as torn shrouds, and the black void within them. Pieces of the timeline destroyed in the exact places where she'd used her power . . . Could that really have been a coincidence?

You should never have been born, Edmund had said to her once, his pale eyes cold. *An abomination.*

A sound made her jump. On the other side of the river, a man in a flatcap walked by, pushing a wooden wheelbarrow laden with straw. He did a double take as he spotted Joan's group—they must have seemed a strange crew: two Chinese people, two girls, a giant, a tiny bulldog.

Joan was very aware suddenly of her masquerade dress with its semitransparent skirt. The gold lion tattoo was still stark on her bare arm. "Should we go back inside?" she murmured to the others. "Get some period-appropriate clothes?" Ruth was still in a catsuit too.

Jamie shrugged, unconcerned. "As long as we're not out on the street, people will mind their own business."

"Limehouse is a 'den of iniquity' in this period," Tom explained, making air quotes. "Great thing about that is it's much less uptight than the posh parts of London."

Aaron scowled halfheartedly, apparently taking mild insult at *posh parts of London*.

Joan felt a tingle then at the back of her neck. She lifted her eyes and found with a jolt that Nick's attention wasn't on the man across the river—as everyone else's was. He was looking at *Joan*. And there were questions all over his face, along with something more dangerous. *If it shouldn't have been possible to change the timeline, then how did you do it? How did you kill me?*

I don't know, Joan wanted to say. She still knew almost nothing about her own power. *You don't even know what you are,* Edmund had said to her. *You all die without knowing.* This time, Joan couldn't suppress the shiver.

"Look . . ." Jamie ran a hand over his face. "The timeline's resistance aside . . . we don't have enough information. All we know is that Eleanor will try to change *something* significant on the timeline. As I said, it's likely to be a significant historical event. If we're going to find her, if we're going to stop her, we'll need to know more than that."

Nick shifted. His eyes were on the canal now, where Aaron had thrown the stone. "An event?" he said, so mildly that Joan almost missed it.

"What?" Ruth said to him.

Nick was still looking at the canal. "Jamie thinks that Eleanor is targeting a historical event. But what if her target is something else? What if she's going to try to change a person?"

"A person?" Ruth sounded confused. "How would changing a person change the timeline?"

Nick didn't look at Joan, but suddenly her heart was thumping in her chest. She saw again the scene in the library. *I've loved you since the moment I saw you*, she'd said to him. She'd kissed him, and then she'd used her power on him while he'd begged her to stop. Joan had unmade him.

She unraveled the hero's life, Eleanor had told Nick, *and she replaced him with an ordinary boy.*

Maybe Nick was remembering the scene too, because raw hurt flickered over his face. Then his walls went up again, and his expression was blank.

"How would you change a person at all?" Ruth said.

Joan tensed for Nick to tell Ruth what had happened. A beat went by. Another beat. It took Joan a moment to understand why he was still silent. He'd made her a promise on the boat when she'd told him about her forbidden power. *I won't tell anyone*, he'd said. *No one will learn about it from me.* Even now—even knowing that she'd betrayed him—he wouldn't tell. It wasn't in his nature.

Joan swallowed. Ruth didn't know about Joan's power at all. And Aaron only knew that it was forbidden. He'd seen something of Eleanor's show at Holland House, but how much had he understood of it?

Gran had told Joan once: *You can trust no one with the knowledge of it.*

Gran had been wrong to say that, though. You had to trust

people sometimes, and Joan could trust Ruth. She could trust Aaron.

Joan took a deep breath. "At Covent Garden," she said to Ruth, "you asked me how the timeline was changed. . . ."

"Joan," Tom said warningly. He flicked a meaningful glance at Nick.

Joan hadn't actually intended to talk about Nick's role in it. Nick wasn't supposed to know that monsters preyed on humans. He wasn't supposed to know that he'd once slayed monsters. "I wasn't going to—" Joan started to say to Tom.

But Tom was suddenly searching her face, and Nick's. His eyes widened. He'd clocked the truth in Nick's expression. "You told him?" Tom said to Joan. It wasn't a question. There was an undertone of danger in his voice, and then Joan's heart was really pounding.

Nick's weight shifted beside Joan. His shoulders tensed.

"You did. You told him," Tom said to Joan. This time it was flat and sure, and the danger was right out in the open.

Joan's stomach dropped at the way Tom was holding himself, his hands in hard fists. She hadn't expected him to grasp Nick's new knowledge just like that. Just by looking at his expression. She should have, though. Tom was *smart*.

Whose side are you on? Tom didn't ask the question, but it stood between them, as clearly as when Liam Liu had said it.

Was this tentative alliance about to end before it had even started? Had Joan already put a rift between herself and the others? "Tom—"

But Nick spoke first. "Joan didn't tell me how the timeline was changed," he told Tom. "*Eleanor* did."

Joan hesitated. She supposed, technically, that was the truth. Joan had told Nick most of it, but Eleanor had given him the final piece.

"Eleanor told me that I used to be a monster slayer," Nick added.

Aaron drew a sharp breath. Joan had the impression the information wasn't completely new to him. He must have heard something about it at the guardhouse. Or maybe he'd put some of it together from what he'd seen during Eleanor's show. This was a confirmation for him, though, and he stared at Nick now with fear and fascination.

Nick added to Tom, "Does it matter that I know about monsters?" His brown eyes were guileless. "You leashed me, remember? You put the Argent power on me." And that still wasn't a lie, exactly. But it was another misdirection. Nick wasn't under that power anymore.

Tom's eyes narrowed as if he sensed something wrong in Nick's manner but couldn't quite put a finger on it. "Maybe we should re-up that compulsion just to make sure."

"If you like," Nick said, and Tom relaxed slightly.

Joan tried to steady her breaths. *Everyone* was watching Nick warily now. But Nick had chosen his words carefully. Maybe it was as important to him as it was to Joan that they protect their fragile alliance for now.

Nick didn't look at Joan, but Joan could almost see the wheels turning in his head—would *she* tell the others that he was free?

Joan's stomach was still churning. *She* didn't want to break this truce either. They needed each other to stop Eleanor.

"*Someone* needs to explain," Ruth said.

Nick leaned against the wall. He'd chosen a shirt with a high collar, Joan saw for the first time. One that protected his neck. Had anyone else noticed that?

Joan wet her dry lips. Tom's reaction had brought home the reality of what she'd done by telling Nick the truth. *Eleanor told me*, he'd said to Tom. But the truth was that *Joan* had told him about what monsters really were. *Joan* had told him that he'd once been a figure of legend, a hero.

At the time, it had seemed the right thing to do. She'd been thinking about the pain monsters had caused Nick. The consequences of her unmaking him—the humans she'd doomed.

And what Astrid had said: He *would have stopped it.*

But now—standing here among people who'd protected her, who'd risked themselves for her, who cared about her, who she cared about—it all seemed far more complicated. *Where does your allegiance lie?*

"Joan?" Ruth said, bringing her back into the moment.

Joan took another deep breath. "*I* changed the timeline," she said to Ruth.

Ruth looked blank. "You changed it?" she echoed.

Joan glanced at Tom. He'd relaxed only slightly. Nick was still watchful.

"I manifested a power," Joan said. Ruth's forehead creased. Joan understood her confusion; Ruth had grown up thinking that Joan couldn't even time-travel.

"*What* power?" Ruth said.

Even now, every instinct screamed at Joan not to talk about it. *You can trust no one*, Gran had said. *You're in very grave danger, graver than you know.* "It's like I can revert things back to their previous state. Unmake them."

"But . . . I don't understand," Ruth said. "How did you change the timeline?"

Joan forced herself to say it. The worst thing she'd ever done. "I used that power on Nick." She could feel Nick's eyes on her, but she couldn't bear to return his gaze.

Ruth made a soft sound as she took that in.

"There's something *I* don't understand," Nick said to Joan, casually, as if he hadn't noticed anyone else's reaction, as if Joan's words hadn't made him feel anything at all. "Why didn't the timeline stop you? The timeline shouldn't have allowed it, right?"

Silence followed while they all processed what he'd said. In the pause, the canal washed against the platform in soft sloshes. Inside the building, faint chatter and laughter sounded from the Lius and the Hathaways.

Aaron answered first, the words tentative. "The timeline should have stopped you, Joan," he agreed. "Didn't it try to resist you?"

Joan still had nightmares about that moment. It was hard now to deliberately put herself back into the memory.

How *had* she unmade Nick? She'd kissed him, and then she'd poured her power into him. He'd begged her to stop. And then . . . And then, she'd woken up, sick and depleted, in her bedroom at Gran's house, in this new timeline.

And that was it. That was all she remembered. "It was like the timeline just let me do it," she said to Aaron. "I can't explain it." As she said it, she felt a curl of unease. Why *hadn't* it stopped her? It really should have.

"Do you think that Eleanor could change the timeline like that too?" Ruth said.

"I don't know," Joan said, feeling that unease again.

"Well . . ." Aaron looked troubled. "Eleanor's a Nightingale. So, if that's the plan, she'll need someone else to do it."

"An ally with the same power as Joan's?" Ruth suggested.

"More likely a prisoner." Aaron's mouth flattened. "The few people who manifest that power are marked for death by the Court. But . . . it's possible Eleanor kept one of them alive, for herself."

Joan shuddered, remembering Aaron's account of the man in the cage. *Was* Eleanor keeping someone like Joan prisoner? She felt Aaron turn toward her; he'd registered the tremble. His expression was still tight, but to her surprise, he smoothed his face into something more reassuring when he caught her eye.

"Marked for death?" Ruth hissed out. She'd gone pale and pinched with worry. Joan wanted to talk to her about it—about how scary this had all been—but this wasn't the time.

"Well . . . however Eleanor does it," Tom said, "the way I see it, she has two problems to solve. She has to figure out *what* to change. And she has to figure out how to get around the resistance of the timeline."

"Eleanor talked like her plans were already underway," Joan said. *You saw the world as it* should *be. As it* will *be when I've remade it.* As a member of the *Curia Monstrorum*, Eleanor wielded almost infinite power. She controlled Court Guards; she could have people executed at her whim. Joan felt sick. "How are we going to stop her? We don't know where she is. We don't know what she's going to change—what event or person." She avoided looking at Nick. "*I* wonder," she said, feeling out the idea as she spoke, "if we should just go to the Court."

There was silence after she said it.

Aaron spoke first. "To what end?"

"To turn Eleanor in." It seemed so obvious suddenly that Joan wasn't sure why she hadn't thought of it before. But the others didn't seem to think so. Aaron and Ruth for once were in accord, both frowning. Jamie and Tom exchanged unsettled looks.

"Who would we tell?" Jamie asked.

"*Any* other member of the Court," Joan said. Was it such a terrible idea? It made sense to her. The Court was full of powerful people; they ruled the monster world beneath only the King. Eleanor was just one member. "She's working against the King, right? She's trying to change the timeline—isn't that blasphemy? Isn't that treason?"

"Joan." Ruth was clearly trying to sound reasonable, but she looked appalled. "The Court is full of vipers."

"Involving the rest of the Court is too much of a risk," Tom agreed. "We don't know how far Eleanor's influence goes. What if this is a coup? What if she's turned other members of the Court against the King? We wouldn't know who to trust."

Joan looked out onto the unmoving canal water. The view that Astrid had seen as precious and ephemeral. "We can't let this happen," she said. "We can't let her create that world."

"You're right. We can't." It was Nick, sounding steady, and Joan took a deep breath. The other Nick would have stopped this. He wasn't here anymore, but *this* Nick was. Joan was. Jamie, Tom, Aaron, and Ruth were. "We need to figure out who or what Eleanor is targeting," Nick said. "Who or what she wants to change.

Once we know that, we'll know where to find her."

"How do we figure that out?" Joan asked.

"We should talk to the Lius," Tom said. Tension was still tightening his voice. "They're the scholars of the timeline."

"Most of the scholarship isn't officially recorded," Jamie said thoughtfully. "We'd need to speak to one of the scholars directly."

"Would anyone be willing to talk to us?" Joan asked him. At the same time, she thought: *Astrid.* She wished she could speak to Astrid again—Astrid had known this was coming. But Astrid had been very clear: *When it starts, don't come and find me. I already fought this fight.*

"My father will," Jamie said, surprising her. "He's in residence in this time."

"Ying?" Joan said. She'd met Ying last time. He'd helped her, but not for free. She still owed the Lius a favor because of it.

"You know my father?" Jamie said, sounding surprised too.

"He helped me once," Joan said, and Jamie tilted his head in curiosity. Would Ying have a way to get a message to the Court, she wondered suddenly. He was a head of family. He'd have access to official channels. Maybe he'd know who in the Court could be trusted against Eleanor.

"The main Liu house is on Narrow Street," Jamie said. "Heart of Chinatown."

A breeze ran over the canal, cool through the fine mesh of Joan's skirt. She looked down at what she was wearing. "I'd better find some nineteenth-century clothes," she said.

THIRTY-ONE

Joan walked out into 1891 in a pale blue skirt and a white shirt with sleeves so voluminous that she could easily have tucked Frankie inside them. Ruth had reluctantly changed out of the catsuit into a tailored dress and a tweed jacket. Aaron was in a beige suit with a waistcoat that cinched in tight at the waist, highlighting his lean silhouette.

Jamie had donned a braided wig and black hat that made him look like the Chinese sailors Joan had seen that morning. He scratched under the hat. "The wig itches," he confided to Joan.

Now that the sun had risen, Joan had a better grasp of their surroundings. The boathouse was on a muddy street lined with buildings on both sides. The end of the road disappeared around a curve, but this stretch had a Chinese medicine shop; a shop that said *coffee house*, but oddly seemed to be serving steak puddings and mutton chops; and a dingy pawnbroker, its soot-blackened window showing secondhand shirts and coats. The street seemed rougher than it had in the early morning. Two men scuffled outside the pawnbroker, ignored by the sailors and dockworkers walking past.

Ruth's eyes landed on everyone with suspicion. Before they'd left, all the experienced time travelers had automatically removed rings and watches and monster chops, secreting them into hidden pockets inside their clothes. Joan and Nick had followed suit.

"Pickpockets everywhere in this era," Ruth had explained to Joan. "With far quicker fingers than mine."

Joan knew she should have been watching for thieves like Ruth was, but she was mesmerized by everything around her. Nick too had dropped his guard and was staring at their surroundings in fascination.

The fish and eel sellers from earlier had been replaced with louder, more showy costermongers than the predawn crowd: women in ostrich-feathered hats and bright shawls, men with silk kerchiefs tied around their necks. They stood on opposite sides of the road, their calls competing with each other and with the distant hiss and roar of steam trains.

"Peas pudding hot! Peas pudding hot, hot, hot!" a man shouted. A short line of sailors waited patiently for him to scoop yellow mash from a pot onto cabbage-leaf cups.

"Sweet oysters!" a woman shouted at the same time. "Sweet, sweet oysters!"

All the way up the street, trails of discarded cabbage and shells showed the paths of their customers. Frankie was in bliss. She sniffed at the mud with interest, at a putrid oyster, an eel tail.

Ahead, quick movement drew Joan's eyes. A little girl ran down the street, neatly dodging the scuffling men outside the pawnbroker. She bent to scoop up something from the gutter, tucked it into her smeared apron, and ran on.

"What's she doing?" Joan said curiously, watching the girl bend to pick something up again.

"You *really* don't want to know," Aaron said. He had his hands in his pockets, and his mouth was a downturned grimace of disgust. "What I wouldn't give for tea at the Savoy," he said, almost to himself.

This wasn't Aaron's kind of place—there was rubbish everywhere. Fish scrapings rotted in the gutters; horse manure gathered flies. Joan lifted her skirt so that it wouldn't trail in something rotting and black. And it didn't smell good, but Joan didn't mind that. She wanted to try all the food from the carts; she wanted to wander down to the docks.

Nick caught Joan's gaze, and the wonder in his expression vanished, leaving him guarded again. Joan's heart felt like lead suddenly. Over the last few months, she'd become used to the punched-gut yearning of seeing him from afar, knowing she'd lost him. But this new divide was so much worse.

"People are staring," Ruth murmured.

Joan looked around. Ruth was right. Everyone from the coster-mongers to sailors to children.

"We should have coordinated our clothes," Aaron hissed.

"*You're* the one who doesn't match! Dressed like a lord in Limehouse," Ruth muttered to him.

"*I* look good!" Aaron snapped. "You should all have matched to *me!*"

"Come on," Jamie said. "Let's keep moving."

Joan had thought the buildings around the boathouse were in disrepair, but farther in, the streets grew cramped and dark, and there were more broken windows than intact ones. Dark smoke drifted from chimneys and hung in the air like black mist. Joan was reminded, uncomfortably, of the dilapidated buildings of Eleanor's world.

They reached a back-alley pub as a group of gray-clothed workers tumbled out. Joan felt pinprick stares on the back of her neck as she passed them.

Aaron fell into step beside her. He grimaced as a rat skittered across their path. There'd been top hats in the Liu dressing rooms, but Aaron had selected a gray felt and silk hat. *Looks like you're in a gangster movie*, Joan had said when Aaron had put it on. Aaron had arched an eyebrow, amused. *It's a Homburg*, he'd said. *They were invented in this period. They had a renaissance in the 1970s.*

Aaron's golden hair shone beneath it now. He looked ridiculously out of place here, and it wasn't just his fine clothes. His ethereal beauty was a contrast to the tired and lined faces of the working people around them.

Joan opened her mouth, and then realized that she didn't know how to talk to him anymore. She could have said anything to his old self, but this Aaron had barely met her.

"You're new to traveling," he said quietly to her, and Joan was surprised that he'd initiated something. He usually held back and waited.

Joan felt a strange twist of nostalgia then. This had been one of their first conversations. *You're new to this*, he'd said last time. *You've barely traveled.*

"You can tell just by looking at me?" Joan said. "Is it part of the Oliver power?"

"It's not that," he said. "Or not *only* that. It's the way you look at everything here like it's new. Like you're not jaded by it all."

Joan couldn't imagine ever being jaded by time travel. "I always wondered," she said tentatively, "how much *you'd* traveled."

Sometimes Aaron had seemed to have manners from another age.

His gray eyes flickered at *always wondered,* and Joan felt another twist—this time, sadder. *Always* implied a longer relationship than he remembered. He answered, though: "I moved around a lot growing up. We spent a couple of years in the nineteenth century. A year in the eighteenth century, a year in the seventeenth . . ." He anticipated her next question. "I suppose I think of the twenty-first century as home. I've spent the most time there. I . . ." He hesitated.

"What is it?" Joan said as the pause stretched.

"Just . . ." He gave her the penetrating look he'd given her when she'd told him what the true Oliver power was. "I don't usually like to talk about myself."

That had been true last time too. He'd been like the other Nick in that way. Joan hadn't understood why Nick had been so closed off until she'd seen the recordings of him being tortured, his family murdered.

Aaron, though . . . Some part of her had instinctively understood that Aaron's reticence had been self-protective.

They'd fallen some way behind the others. As if sensing her observation, Nick glanced over his shoulder at her. Aaron tilted his head, seeming to register again the tension between Joan and Nick—the only one of them who had. And there was more in his expression again too—an awareness of Nick as a figure of nightmarish legend.

In her peripheral vision, Joan saw Nick turn away again.

Joan bit her lip. "Can I ask you something?" she said to Aaron.

Aaron put his hands in his pockets. "Of course."

"At the masquerade party, your father said something to me."

Aaron visibly braced himself, perhaps remembering that Edmund had given him a knife and told him to kill Joan on the spot.

Joan didn't want to think about that part of it. She rushed on: "He said to me . . ." She quoted Edmund: "*You don't even know what you are. You all die without knowing.* What did he mean?"

Aaron seemed puzzled by the question. "He wanted to intimidate you. Scare you."

"Yes, but . . ." There were a million ways he could have frightened her. He'd used such specific words. *You don't even know what you are.* Joan glanced ahead again; the others were still out of earshot. "After your Oliver power was confirmed, they took you to see that man in the cage. They told you to kill anyone with a power like his. With *my* power."

"They didn't tell me why," Aaron said, answering the question she'd really wanted to ask. "But the Court does all kinds of things without explanation." He searched her face, and his expression gentled. "You mustn't listen to my father. He has an ability to sense the cracks in people. To know how to hurt them."

Maybe Aaron was right. Maybe Edmund hadn't meant anything by it.

But the question of *why* echoed as they followed the others onto the next street—a small stretch of flats with an eating house at the intersection. Gray clouds had rolled in, darkening it all. Joan felt the prickling sense of eyes on them again. She looked around. Faces stared through the window of the eating house, from windows above.

A bucket of slop splashed down into the gutter, brown muck smearing the pavement by Joan's feet. She stumbled back and saw a woman peering down, her lined face hostile.

The others were still a little way ahead. Joan sped up to catch up with them, and so did Aaron. She frowned, thinking. Was the hostility being directed toward Aaron in his too-posh clothes? No, she realized slowly. The hairs rose on the back of her neck . . . All the eyes had been on *her*.

She replayed the stares of the gray-clothed workers from the pub. Some of them had been looking at Jamie, but most of them had been looking at her then too. Was it because she was a girl? Early Chinese immigration had mostly been male, she knew. Or could people tell that she was mixed race? She wondered suddenly if mixed marriages were even legal in this time. She had a vague memory that they'd been banned in some countries in this period. Not in the UK, though, right?

They turned the corner. A man in a blue sailor's uniform overtook them, mumbling something that Joan didn't catch. In a flash, Aaron had grabbed the man's shoulder, perilously close to his neck. An inch more, and he could have killed him if he'd wished.

"Aaron?" Joan said. They'd caught up to the others, and now they all stopped. Joan had never known Aaron to threaten violence before. Not that the man understood that his life was at risk. She glanced at Nick, afraid that he might hurt Aaron in response—he knew what a monster's hand to the neck meant now. But to her surprise, Nick had a dangerous expression too. He stared down the sailor.

"You should not speak so to a lady," Aaron told the man softly. "You should not speak so to anyone." Joan felt her mouth drop open. She'd heard the man mutter something but had no idea what he'd said. Aaron's grip tightened, and even though Aaron was slighter than him, the man paled as if some primal instinct had told him that he was in the hands of a predator, something inhuman. "Your next word had better be the right one," Aaron said, his cool tone uncannily like his father's. The man mumbled something again. It must have been an apology, because Aaron released him with a shove and watched him hurry away.

Joan turned to Aaron again. His beautiful face was ice-cold. "What did he say?" she asked him.

Aaron's jaw clenched. "Nothing repeatable." To Jamie and Tom, he said, "How much more of this ghastly place must we be forced to traverse?"

"We're almost there," Jamie said.

The sun reemerged as they reached Narrow Street, a long road of eclectic buildings. Well-maintained brown brick terraces stood alongside ramshackle wooden structures with drooping balconies and peeling paint.

"Well, the name is accurate," Aaron said.

It was—the street was as narrow as an alleyway but crammed full of people: South and East Asian people, Black people, white people. Joan heard half a dozen languages within a minute. If everyone had been wearing different clothes, this could have been modern London.

"The Thames used to run farther inland," Tom said. "This

whole street was once a medieval wall to hold the river back."
He gestured at a gap between buildings, and Joan glimpsed the
Thames—as packed with boats as the street was with people. "All
these buildings face the river on the other side."

As they walked, loud hammering and sawing sounded. Joan
pictured workshops for making rope and repairing sails for the
boatyards. The buildings seemed to be a mix of housing and
manufacturing and shops. They passed a ship-biscuits baker, a
mast-maker, and shop after shop with Chinese characters painted
on windows and walls—a grocer, a restaurant, another Chinese
medicine shop.

Jamie stopped, finally, about halfway up the street, in front
of a tea shop, the window display showing wooden tea chests and
samples of tea leaves on tiny plates. The man at the counter was
Chinese, dressed in a beautiful three-piece suit, his waistcoat
embroidered with a phoenix design. He looked up as Jamie pushed
open the door.

Jamie said something to him in Mandarin. Joan caught *wǒ
bàba*—my dad.

The man gestured at a door in the back wall, its edges almost
hidden by wooden paneling. If he hadn't pointed it out, Joan
doubted she'd have seen it.

"He's in," Jamie said.

The door opened into a large courtyard space that reminded
Joan of the square complex behind the Liu gallery in 1993. A covered corridor ran around the edges of the courtyard. To the right
and the left, there were doors leading to more buildings in the
complex. Some of the other shops on the street must have been a

facade for the Liu house, Joan realized. Directly opposite, a carved wooden frame provided a picturesque view of the Thames. The courtyard itself had been made garden-like with potted plants and trees.

Ying Liu stood with his back to them in the center of the courtyard. He was painting the river scene of boats and water with plain black ink. Joan felt a wave of déjà vu. In the other time-line, Ying had talked to her and Aaron in a courtyard like this, among easels and paintings.

The atmosphere here was so serene that Joan almost wished they hadn't interrupted it. At the sound of their entrance, though, Ying put the brush into a glass of water and wiped his hands on a cloth. He turned, apparently unsurprised to see them, although for a moment his gaze tripped up on Nick.

"Hi, Dad," Jamie said. "We need to talk."

Ying was older than when Joan had last seen him—he'd been in his forties then, and Joan guessed he was around sixty now. Age had peppered his hair and deepened the sad lines of his face into knife-like cuts. Otherwise, he looked much the same: handsome and grave.

Ying dropped his head slightly now, as if under a heavy weight. "I know why you're here," he said. "You've spoken to Astrid. You want to stop what's coming."

THIRTY-TWO

Ying brought over a low table and some wooden chairs that had been stacked under the covered walkway. Jamie ducked back into the tea shop and emerged with a tray: a bronze teapot, a stand, and ceramic cups. The pot was charmingly bird-shaped—the Liu phoenix. Steam drifted from its beak, and its tail swirled up to form a handle.

Jamie set the pot onto a small stand and lit a candle within it to keep the tea warm. The black metal had cutouts of creatures that came alive with the flickering candle. Phoenixes too—made of fire.

There weren't enough chairs, so Joan and Aaron sat on the bench overlooking the Thames. There was a steep drop below. This side of the building stood in the river, brown murk swirling around its wooden-stilt legs. Next door, a ladder ran from the balcony to the water—for boat travel and deliveries, Joan guessed.

The river was a highway of tarp-covered barges carrying goods in boxes and bales, rowboats with passengers, little barges with rusty-red sails, and steamships with cylindrical chimneys that belched black smoke. In the distance, one huge ship with billowing sails retreated from sight.

Aaron followed Joan's gaze. "It's the end of the Age of Sail," he observed. "There'll be fewer and fewer sailing ships as the decade progresses, although the barges will last a little longer."

He nodded at the red-sailed boats.

On the other side of the river, the docks were crowded with ships and people and costermongers. Weird to think that in 150 years, this whole stretch would be terraced housing. Joan craned her neck, trying to see farther west. "Can you believe that Tower Bridge is still being built in this time?" she murmured to Aaron as the others pulled their chairs over and sat. "And the Crystal Palace is still standing." She'd always wanted to see it.

"You should go back a few decades," Aaron said. "If you want to see the Crystal Palace at its height."

Joan automatically gripped her knee to feel the rough fabric of her skirt, grounding herself in sensory detail. Aaron had taught her how to prevent fade-outs. Except . . . she didn't need to do that anymore, she remembered. She was still mired by the tattoo.

With a heavy patter and a thump, Frankie joined them on the bench to sniff at the river air. Joan stroked her soft head and floppy bulldog ears; she felt a wave of melancholy suddenly. Maybe it was the thought of that retreating ship from a vanishing age. Or maybe the possibility that all this might soon be swallowed up by another timeline. . . .

Frankie climbed over Joan to nose at Aaron. Aaron smiled slightly as he focused on her. Then he blinked, as if he hadn't anticipated his own tender response.

And it was strange. . . . Frankie hadn't shown any hostility toward Aaron. Everyone else had. Could Frankie remember something of the other timeline? Did she remember Aaron as a friend?

Across from them, Ying took his seat. Jamie poured tea, and

Ying opened a tin so extravagantly decorated that it could have housed jewels.

"Opera wafers," Ruth said reverently, reaching for a thin finger biscuit.

Ying's eyes creased into an almost smile. "I also miss them in later periods," he said. "Please." He gestured for the rest of them to take a teacup and some biscuits too.

Joan's stomach growled. When had she last eaten? She wasn't sure. She took a wafer and bit into it—it was light with a rich chocolate filling. The tea was good too: pale green and delicately floral.

"So," Ying said. He leaned forward in his chair, hands steepled. His clothes seemed slightly anachronistic—closer to the 1910s than 1891. He was in a jacket and waistcoat in midnight blue, charcoal trousers, and a crisp high-buttoned white shirt with no tie. Sitting beside Jamie, Joan could see the resemblance—more in manner than looks. They both had an air of polite formality.

Ying's gaze stumbled again on Nick. He knew who he was, Joan realized. Who he'd been. Joan put down her cup and felt another wave of déjà vu. In another timeline, in a courtyard much like this, Joan had asked Ying how she could undo Nick's massacre. Did Ying remember that?

"So," Ying said again. "You spoke to Astrid. She told you of the coming calamity." He had a beautiful voice—a singer's voice—and he spoke with careful diction, making every word seem considered.

"It's true, then?" Joan said. Ying's resonant voice had made it all seem very real suddenly. She sought the others; they'd ended up in pairs. Tom and Jamie to the left of Ying, Ruth and Nick to the right, and Aaron and Joan opposite on the bench.

Ying nodded. "Some few among us have the ability to remember previous timelines." He met Joan's eyes; he *did* remember her. "But Astrid has a rarer power than that. She remembers what is still to come. And"—the sad lines of his face deepened—"she has seen a terrible future."

The end of everything that matters. He would have stopped it. But you stopped him.

As if he'd heard Joan's thoughts, Nick set his jaw. His expression was so determined that her heart stuttered.

It's inevitable now, Astrid had said. But how could that be true? Surely, if Nick could have stopped it last time, there was a way to do it this time. Together.

Joan refocused on Ying. "There must be *something* we can do." Ying regarded her without answering, and Joan felt a tug of unease. "We know who's behind it," Joan said. "Eleanor of the *Curia Monstrorum* wants to create a world where monsters rule."

"A world where monsters rule?" Ying looked puzzled at that—so puzzled that Joan's stomach turned over. "Astrid's memories of the future are not so clear as that."

"But . . ." Joan heard the word trail off. She'd *seen* the world Eleanor wanted to create. She'd seen the Court livery on a police van. A guard had killed a human in broad daylight. And then Eleanor had confirmed that was what she wanted. . . . "What did Astrid see?"

"Many deaths," Ying said simply. "The end of this timeline."

The sun was streaming down, pleasantly warm. Incongruously cheerful. There was something wrong here, Joan thought suddenly—something wrong with her own assumptions. It was a feeling she'd had before, when she'd blundered into Whitehall Palace. But now, like then, she had no idea what was amiss.

"You wish to stop this," Ying said heavily. He leaned over to refill their cups and sighed. "It is not possible to succeed."

Joan's heart sank. She had hoped that Ying would help them fight Eleanor himself. But his stiff posture reminded her of how Astrid had looked: resigned and matter-of-fact.

"I don't believe that," Nick said, his dark eyes resolute. "We have to *try*." Like Joan, he couldn't believe that all this was fated. But maybe that was a human trait—to doubt the concept of inevitability—because when Joan glanced at the monsters, she could see that they were all far less sure.

"You must know something of how this will happen," Joan said to Ying. Astrid had never told the Lius that she'd sided with Nick, but it seemed she'd shared her memories of the future with the other heads of her family. And Tom had said that the Lius were the scholars of the timeline. They'd surely figured at least some of it out. "You must have some idea."

"Of how the timeline will be changed?" Ying asked. He bowed his head, and Joan had the impression again of sorrow, of resignation. "Yes, we have our suspicions."

Joan sat forward.

"You understand the theory of change?" Ying said. "That something of significance must be changed if the path of the timeline is to be altered?"

"Yes," Joan said.

"The timeline resists change," Ying said. "But the Lius believe that there are certain places where the timeline is weak.

We suspect that when a significant event overlaps a weak area of the timeline, change is possible."

And now Aaron was sitting forward with Joan, a frown on his fine-boned face. "I've never heard of such a thing."

Joan took in what Ying had said. Had she been at a weak place in the timeline when she'd unmade Nick? She'd taken time from herself to escape from Nick's prison, but she didn't know what time period she'd landed in. And Nick had followed her there. . . . Had they ended up in a weak area of the timeline?

"These are only theories," Ying said to Aaron.

"Then theoretically . . . ," Nick said intently, "do you know where we can find these weak areas of the timeline?"

"No," Ying said, and Nick sat slowly back in his chair, disappointment tightening his mouth. "I'm sorry," Ying said. "I cannot tell you what you wish to hear—that you can stop this. The truth is, we are already seeing signs that this timeline is coming to an end."

A cold wind blew across the river, raising goose bumps on Joan's arms. "Signs?" she said.

"Signs of disruption to the timeline; signs of a breakdown. Signs we saw at the end of the previous timeline."

"*What* signs?" Joan asked.

Ying looked down at his tea, and shadows deepened the creases of his face. He sighed. "What do you know of fluctuations?"

Joan felt herself tensing, uneasy without knowing why. The term was familiar. Corvin Argent had spoken of fluctuations, and so had the gamblers at the Wyvern Inn.

Beside her, wool rustled as Aaron shifted his weight. She felt his eyes graze over her. Or thought she did—when she turned, he was sitting up, alert, looking at Ying.

"I don't know what fluctuations are," Joan said to Ying slowly.

"In general, they are a normal part of the timeline," Ying said. "They are created by us. By monsters. We time-travel, and that means that the timeline must compensate for us. For example . . ." He thought for a moment. "If I were to hail a hackney cab right now, I would likely take the place of a human who *would* have hailed that cab. Imagine I caused that human to miss a meeting. And now imagine that it was a significant meeting. I would have altered the timeline just by going about my everyday life."

It was how Aaron had described time travel at the boathouse— he'd thrown a stone into water and pointed out the cascading ripples. "But the timeline would smooth out your changes," Joan said. "It would arrange for the meeting to happen at another time, or for the cab to drive past you without stopping."

"Yes," Ying said. "A cab driving past . . . a rescheduled meeting . . . These are examples of fluctuations. The everyday corrections made by the timeline."

Joan swallowed. She *did* know that mechanism—only too well. It was why the timeline kept bringing her and Nick together. Jamie had explained it once: *If people belonged together in the true timeline, then our timeline tries to repair itself by bringing them together. Over and over and over. Until the rift is healed.*

Only for Joan and Nick, that rift could never be healed. Too much had come between them. . . .

"Why are we talking about fluctuations?" Aaron said. He was tense too, Joan realized then. He'd been wary at the beginning of this meeting, but the turn in the conversation had him leaning forward, fully attentive.

Ying put his cup back onto the tray. "The Lius remember what others don't. We, alone of all the families, remember both the original events and the corrected ones. The cab arriving and the cab driving past." He folded his hands together and sighed again. "At the end of the last timeline, we began to observe seemingly minor events—parties, appointments—shifting weeks, even months, from their original dates." He was silent for a moment, staring down at the fire-made phoenixes behind their metal cutouts. Then he said, "It is a pattern we are seeing again now."

Aaron whispered: "There have been rumors spreading among the Court Guards of unusual fluctuations . . ."

"Yes," Ying said heavily. "I think the timeline is struggling to repair itself."

Joan took a sharp breath. *Signs of disruption. Signs of a breakdown in the timeline.*

"I believe we are at the end of days of this timeline," Ying said. "We are in a cup riddled with cracks."

The words echoed in Joan's head. She saw again the gaping wounds in the timeline, and caught Tom's eye. His lips were pressed white. He was thinking of the same thing.

"We saw something," Joan told Ying. Ying tilted his head in question, and she hesitated. "We think it was a hole in the timeline."

There was a moment of silence while Ying took in her words. He didn't seem to know what to say. "I don't understand," he said finally.

"We saw a tear in the fabric of the timeline itself," Tom said. "It was concealed behind an Ali seal—we think the Court was hiding it."

Ying opened his mouth and then closed it again. Joan had met him twice. This was the first time she'd seen him lost for words. "Describe this for me." His face was carved stiff, but Joan had the impression that he was disturbed underneath.

They hadn't really talked about it since they'd left the café. Joan looked around at the others and realized that there was a reason for that. Ruth had folded her arms around herself, and Jamie's forehead was waxy—even the memory was making him sick. Tom's usually invisible freckles stood out, russet on milky white. They'd all been deeply shaken by the thing.

Jamie answered. "It was like the timeline had been ripped open by a force. We saw a hole in midair with ragged edges." He swallowed visibly. "We saw the void inside it—the black abyss of it."

Ying took a long moment to respond. "You saw the void that surrounds the timeline?"

Joan's skin crawled. The Monster Court had been surrounded by that shadowy nothingness. *There's nothing there,* Ruth had said. *It looks like there's something there, but there's nothing there.* At the time, Joan had had the feeling that if she were to step from the grounds of the Monster Court, she'd have been lost forever.

"We only saw it for a minute or so," Jamie said, "and then it was like—" He hesitated. Joan understood the hesitation. She still wasn't sure what exactly had happened either. "It was like we saw a different timeline inside it," Jamie said. "A timeline where monsters ruled."

Ying's face showed a hint of disturbance now. "You saw another timeline?"

"I didn't think it was possible either," Jamie said.

Joan bit her lip. Jamie had only mentioned the tear at Covent Garden. Hadn't he seen the other one? Maybe not. The library had been full of smoke when he'd broken in. "There was another tear at the guardhouse," Joan said.

And apparently *none* of the others had seen the tear at Holland House. Now they all looked dismayed. Ying actually frowned, and Joan's stomach churned.

"This didn't happen at the end of the previous timeline?" Joan asked Ying. "There weren't holes in the timeline?"

"I have never heard of holes in the timeline outside of pure theory," Ying said. "Outside of stories."

"What do you think this means?" Jamie asked his father. "I've only ever heard of it in *one* story." For a moment, his expression was almost childlike. "*Finis saeculorum.*"

Joan tried to translate that. *Finis*: Final? *Saeculorum*: What did that mean? All the monsters seemed familiar with it, though. Aaron made a soft sound. Ruth screwed her face up skeptically.

Tom reached for Jamie's hand. "You're worried about that? It's just a story."

"What is it?" Joan said uneasily. She'd once thought that the hero was just a story too.

She checked on Nick now. He'd turned to listen, head tilted, so that she could only see the edge of his face. His dark hair fell over his eyes.

It was Aaron who answered her. "It's called *the End of Ages.*

It's about a kid who tears through the timeline, trying to find his lost parents. But instead, he tears the timeline apart. He falls into the void, and so does everyone else—every moment in history, every person who'd ever lived, are lost."

Ying's hands rose in a calming manner. "It *is* just a story."

But Joan's stomach twisted. How had the boy torn apart the timeline in the story?

"We *did* see holes in the timeline, though," Nick said. "A fairy tale didn't cause that damage. So what did?" Joan's stomach twisted again. Nick added: "Do you think it confirms the theory that there *are* weak places along the timeline? That these holes have been torn in weakened areas?"

Ying took a breath, visibly trying to regain some equilibrium. "It's possible," he acknowledged.

"Then we just have to find other weak places in the timeline!" Nick said, sitting up. "We can narrow down where Eleanor might be. We can find her!"

For a moment, Ying's gaze was pitying and *old*, and Joan remembered something Aaron had once told her: *Everyone goes up against the timeline.* It was a lesson every monster had to learn themselves; every monster tried to fight fate at some point, and every monster failed.

"You can try to stop Eleanor," Ying said to Nick. "But Astrid is among the strongest of the Lius. If she says that Eleanor's success is inevitable, then it is inevitable."

"How can you say that?" Nick said. "*Inevitable?*" He didn't sound angry exactly, but at his raised voice, Ying's eyes widened very slightly. And Joan wondered suddenly if Ying had been at the Liu house during Nick's massacre. Did he remember it? Was some part of him as afraid of Nick as Liam had been? "Humans are going to suffer in that timeline, and we can still stop it! It hasn't even happened yet!" Nick said.

Those same words had come from Joan's mouth last time. And she *had* changed the inevitable. She knew it was possible. It *had* to be.

Nick was right. Joan's dad, her friends, her human family were *not* going to live in a world like the one they'd seen. A world of tangled bodies and terrified bystanders. "We have to do *something*!" Joan agreed.

"It is not that I wish it to be true," Ying said to Joan, to Nick. "It's that I know it to be true." He sighed. "We must take the long view—we may have more freedom to act in the new timeline. And I promise you that the Lius will remember what has been done. We will carry the knowledge with us."

"We *may* have more freedom to act?" Nick said. "You don't even know that! And you just said there'd be many deaths!" Ying's eyes widened more.

Jamie interjected. "Listen," he said heavily. "We all had a long night and not much sleep." To his father, he said, "We should get some rest."

Ying nodded slightly and stood. Tom and Jamie took that as their cue to stand too. Ruth followed and then Aaron. Only Nick looked reluctant to leave. His jaw was set tight. Joan could read his expression completely for the first time in a while. He was going to do something about Eleanor, even if that meant doing it alone.

Joan took a deep breath. Whatever happened, he wouldn't be alone.

She hesitated, though, as they all headed across the courtyard to the door.

"What is it?" Aaron said. When Joan had hung back, he had too.

The others were almost at the tea shop. "I'll meet you outside," Joan said to him. There was something she still needed from Ying.

THIRTY-THREE

Ying didn't seem surprised that Joan had lingered. "You already owe the Lius a favor." His tone was not unkind. "We do not allow people to owe two."

Joan should have expected that. The last time she'd been here, she'd had to bargain for information. And Ying had just given up knowledge for free, but Jamie had been present for that. Ying wouldn't require payment from his own son.

"There's something I need to know," Joan said to him. "Something unrelated to Eleanor."

Rather than answering immediately, Ying gestured for her to sit on the wooden chair opposite him. He poured more tea for her. The fresh-grass scent of it mixed with the less pleasant smokiness of this time.

"What is your question?" Ying said. It wasn't the promise of an answer, Joan could tell. Just an invitation for her to ask.

Some part of Joan didn't want to articulate it. "The last time I saw you," she said, "I offered you a necklace in return for information. You refused it."

Ying gave her a searching look—one that reminded her of their conversation in that other courtyard. She hadn't had his attention until she'd shown him that necklace, and then she'd suddenly had it completely.

"I remember," he said softly.

Joan touched her collarbone, where the necklace had once sat. "There were dark patches on the gold chain." *She'd* made those marks. As Gran had lain dying, Joan had clutched at the chain. It had been the first time her power had manifested—she'd reverted the metal to ore.

"I remember," Ying said again.

Joan swallowed. She shouldn't have been saying any of this to Ying, but she had to know. "Your expression changed when you saw those marks. You recognized them. They were made by a power, and I think you'd seen that power before."

"You have not yet asked me a question." Was there a gentle note in his voice?

If he were going to turn her in, he'd have done it last time. "It was a power outside of the twelve families," Joan said. She saw again Edmund Oliver's face, full of loathing. *You don't even know what you are.* Joan braced herself now. "My gran gave me that necklace. It was untarnished when she gave it to me, but after I touched it . . ."

"It was marked," Ying said. He *had* seen her power before. "Ask me your question, Joan."

Joan wet her dry lips. "We told you that there were tears in the timeline—in a café and at Holland House. But there was something we didn't tell you. Something that *I* didn't tell the others."

For the first time, Ying seemed puzzled by Joan's line of conversation. "Go on."

"Those tears in the timeline are in places where I used my power. I used it in that café—in the exact spot where the tear was. And I used it at Holland House—on Nick."

"You think you tore those holes in the timeline . . . like the boy in the fairy tale?" Ying's expression was hard to read.

Joan ducked her head. Ying wanted her to ask directly. A favor owed for a question answered. "Why is my power forbidden?" she said. And then she found herself blurting out too: "Why does the Court want me dead? What *am* I?"

"You say that as if you were some kind of aberration. Some creature that slipped out of the void itself."

Edmund had once called her an abomination. *You should have been voided in the womb*, he'd said.

"I tore open the timeline like the boy in the story," Joan said. "I damaged the timeline. I . . . I think Astrid's warning could have been about *me*. Maybe I'm the cause of the cracks in the world; maybe I'm going to tear the timeline open and throw us all into the void."

Ying regarded her. "Astrid's warning was not about you. I do not believe you have been damaging the timeline." He always looked sad, and right now melancholy hung over him like a storm cloud.

"How do you know?" Joan asked.

"Do you remember the children's chant?"

"*Olivers see. Hunts hide. . . .*" Joan started. Ying had recited it to her last time. It was the chant that monsters used to teach their children about the family powers.

Ying completed the chant in his resonant voice: "*Olivers see. Hunts hide. Nowaks live. Patels bind. Portellis open. Hathaways leash. Nightingales take. Mtawalis keep. Argents sway. Alis seal. Griffiths reveal. But only the Lius remember.*"

"The twelve families of London," Joan said, feeling uncertain. Why was Ying telling her this again?

"Yes," Ying said, "but there is a secret version of that chant. One that only the Lius know. It has a different ending."

Joan felt herself start to tense and wasn't sure why. "What ending?"

"*But only the Lius remember,*" Ying said in his beautiful voice, "*that there was once another family.*"

The hairs rose on the back of Joan's neck. "What?" she whispered.

"There was once a thirteenth family in London," Ying said. "*Your* family. The Graves."

His words seemed to echo through the courtyard, as if a gong had been struck. They seemed to echo inside Joan. *Your family.*

I'm not a Hunt, am I? she'd said to Aaron once. But confronted with Ying's words, she found herself saying, "No." Her families were the Changs and the Hunts. She'd had the Hunt power as a child.

Aaron had once said to her: *As we get older, the only power that remains is the power of our true family.* Still, she shook her head. "That can't be true." If it was true, Gran would have told her. Except . . . Gran *had* tried to speak to her before the attack on the bakery. *Your gran wanted to talk to you about something,* Dad had said.

"You reverted the necklace into ore," Ying said. "That is the Grave family power. They could unmake things; turn back the clock on things. And . . ." His eyes softened. "You have the look of them, Joan."

Joan had never even heard of the Graves. "I don't understand," she said. *There was once another family.* What had Ying meant by *once?* "Where are they now?"

Ying's eyes were still soft. "The strongest of the Lius remember fragments of the *zhēnshí de lìshǐ,*" he said. "The true timeline. Collectively, we have some idea of what happened to the Graves."

Joan stilled. *Happened to?*

"The ancient Romans had a punishment," Ying said. *"Damnatio memoriae.* Have you heard of it?"

"No," Joan whispered.

"Those punished with it were condemned to be forgotten by history," Ying said. "Their statues were smashed, their portraits destroyed, their letters burned. Speaking their name was punishable by death." His voice was gentler than his words. "But our King was more ruthless than that. We believe he erased your family from the timeline—he assassinated them, hunting down the earliest members of the family through history, so that their children and their children's children were never born."

Joan stared at him. She knew violent death. It looked like Gran covered in blood, her breathing hoarse; Lucien Oliver with a sword in his chest; Margie with her eyes wide open. "He killed them all?"

"We don't know why the King did this," Ying said. "We believe it was a punishment. We don't know the transgression."

Joan couldn't take in the scale of it. What possible transgression could warrant all those deaths, the erasure of an entire family? She answered her own question. *Nothing* could warrant a punishment like that. "You said they were all gone. I *can't* be a member of their family, then, can I?"

The deep lines of Ying's face made Joan think of wood carvings. Of sorrowful statues. "I don't know how you are here," he said. "But you *are* a member of the Grave family."

"Do *you* remember them?" Joan said slowly. The strongest of the Liu family remembered fragments of the true timeline itself. . . .

"I remember . . ." Ying wasn't quite looking at Joan now. He was inside his memories, his eyes distant. "I was married to a member of the Grave family. I don't remember her name. The Liu power is perfect memory, but I don't remember my wife's name. I don't remember my children's names."

There was deep emotion in his voice, and Joan felt as if she were seeing him for the first time. This was the source of his ever-present sadness. Like Jamie, he'd been born with painful memories.

"I'm sorry," she said softly.

"The Liu power has its burdens," Ying said. "I think you understand." He glanced in the direction that Nick had gone.

They were quiet for a time after that. The flame under the teapot flickered out. The weather was turning again. Storm clouds hung over the river, heavy and oppressive; the water whipped in the wind.

Ying leaned over to pour more tea into Joan's cup and then his own. "It is a lot to take in."

"I don't know *how* to take it in," Joan admitted. In a strange, guilty way, she felt worse for Ying than herself. Ying was grieving for the Graves, but Joan couldn't remember them at all.

But as she thought that, something roiled inside her, as if some half-lost part of her *did* feel it. As if something in her *did* remember.

On the Thames, the tide was rising, along with the wind. The tiny red sails of the Thames barges billowed violently. Joan watched a man wind a winch in fast movements, pulling his sail down. She ran a hand over her face, trying to ignore the turbulence inside herself, more violent than the rising wind. She was in the shadow of an apocalypse. She didn't have the luxury to feel this right now. To process this. And something else was worrying her. "What if the Graves were erased because they tore up the timeline?" she asked. "What if they were erased because they were a threat to the world?"

He *would have stopped it*, Astrid had said. *But you stopped* him.

What would Nick have stopped? Maybe he would have stopped Joan. Maybe that was how he'd have saved everyone.

Ying was silent for a long moment. "I do not believe that. There were no holes in the timeline when the Graves were here. No unusual fluctuations." He searched Joan's face. "You keep speaking as if you are some destructive force—some creature who deserves to be put to death by the Court. You are not. You are a member of a lost family."

Joan swallowed hard at the kindness in his tone. "Then what damaged the timeline if it wasn't me?"

"I do not know," Ying said. He tilted his head, considering. "You told me yourself that you reverted that necklace to ore. Where did that happen?"

Joan was thrown by the question. "In one of the bedrooms of Holland House."

"There is no tear in the timeline there," Ying said.

Joan took that in. She'd also used her power in the boathouse without apparent consequence. And at the Wyvern Inn. "Maybe the Alis came in after me and sealed up any tears."

Ying shook his head. "Only four Ali seals have ever been ordered by the Court."

"Four?" Joan said.

"The Chicago Café in Covent Garden was sealed in 1993," Ying said. Joan blinked at that. She'd used her power there in 1993. *Surely* she'd torn that hole in the timeline. Ying went on: "The former location of the library at Holland House was sealed in 2053." And that had to have been Joan too. "There is also Seventeen Rainery Road, Sheffield, sealed in 2003. And St. Magnus-the-Martyr Church on Lower Thames Street, sealed in 1923."

Whatever Ying believed, Joan *had* to have made those tears in Covent Garden and Holland House, but what was the one in Sheffield? What was the one on Lower Thames Street? She'd never used her power in either of those places. Then again, maybe she just hadn't done it yet. . . .

Joan bit her lip. She needed to figure this out. She needed something else from Ying first, though. She looked up at him. "I know that I already owe you a favor," she said.

"The information about the Graves requires no payment," Ying said gently. "I am sorry that the King did such a thing."

Joan looked at him.

"You need something else?" His eyebrows lifted slightly. "The Lius are never owed two favors from a single person," he reminded her.

"But this is a new timeline," Joan said, hoping. "One for each?"

Ying gave her one of his almost smiles at that. "What do you need?"

"Is there a trustworthy member of the *Curia Monstrorum*?" Joan asked. "Someone loyal to the King above anything. Someone unimpeachable."

"Conrad," Ying said.

Ice ran down Joan's spine just at the name. *Conrad.* Ying had been unhesitating in his answer, but Joan pictured a man whose gaze had felt like the cold bite of winter. A man with eyes as pale as the dawn. Last time, Conrad had come after her—intending to execute her—when he'd learned of her power. His name alone had shaken Ruth and Aaron to the core.

The others wouldn't like this idea, but the truth was, to fight a member of the *Curia Monstrorum*, they needed another member on their side. "Conrad," Joan said, nodding. "I need to send him a message."

Joan walked back out onto Narrow Street. It had started to rain in big heavy drops. The others were waiting just outside the tea shop, splotches falling around them. Tom had found an umbrella somewhere. He held it carefully over Jamie, but no one else seemed too bothered by the water.

"What was all that about?" Ruth said to Joan. She took a step closer then. "What happened?" Her forehead creased, and Joan wondered what her own expression was showing.

Of course Ruth could tell something was wrong—she and Joan had known each other their whole lives. *Your family*, Ying had said. *The Graves. No*, Joan thought. *This* was her family. Ruth was her family.

She shook her head. "Nothing," she said. But she found herself swallowing around a lump in her throat. *Keep it together*, she told herself. This wasn't the time to think about the Grave family. "I found out something that might help. Ying gave me some locations of Ali seals: St. Magnus-the-Martyr Church on Lower Thames Street, and Seventeen Rainery Road in Sheffield. Do they ring a bell?"

"Seventeen Rainery Road?" Nick straightened, looking disturbed and confused. "That's my childhood home. Why would he give you that address?"

Joan stared at him. She'd blown a hole in the timeline when she'd unmade and remade Nick—at Holland House. But Nick had been unmade and remade before that—in the home he'd grown up in.

That meant that three of the seals on Ying's list were accounted for. Only one was still a mystery. . . .

"What is it?" Aaron asked Joan.

"What's going on?" Nick said.

"I think I know where Eleanor is going to change the time-line," Joan said. "Where and when."

THIRTY-FOUR

"St. Magnus-the-Martyr Church," Tom mused as they headed back down Narrow Street. "What could Eleanor be doing there in 1923?"

"St. Magnus used to be the entrance to Old London Bridge, right?" Joan said.

"By 1923, though, it's just a church," Jamie said. He frowned, thinking; Joan guessed he was running through his mental archive. "I don't know how Eleanor could change the timeline there. Whatever event or person she's targeting, it's not obvious to me."

"Did Ying say anything more specific than 1923?" Aaron said. "Did he have a date?"

"March fifth," Joan said.

Nick lifted his head. He'd been gazing down the long street, tracking a man begging for coins, hat in hand; a little girl scooping something from the street into a basket. His 1890s outfit should have been nondescript—half the street was wearing the same style: shirt, waistcoat, trousers. Nick's physique, though, made his ensemble look unassumingly dangerous. "Why did your father and Astrid say this was inevitable?" he asked Jamie. "That doesn't make sense to me."

"I have some theories." Jamie glanced up at the thunderous sky from under the shelter of Tom's umbrella.

Tom noticed the glance. "Let's get a coach," he said.

They ended up jumping on an empty omnibus, drawn by two plodding horses and emblazoned with an ad for Borwick's Baking Powder: *The Best That Money Can Buy*. It was rickety and old, but fully enclosed, and Joan saw Jamie relax as he took a seat. There was just enough room for them to sit three abreast, and they ended up with Tom, Jamie, and Aaron on one side and Ruth, Nick, and Joan on the other.

Joan found herself pressed tight against Nick. When Aaron toed at the thick layer of straw on the floor, his knees brushed against Joan's. A tiny jolt went through her at his touch. She was still getting used to him being here, she thought.

"What are you doing?" Ruth said to Aaron.

"Checking for fleas," Aaron said, as if that should have been obvious. "What's the point of straw without strewing herbs?"

"Insulation," Tom said. It was a tight squeeze for the six of them, and Tom barely fit into his seat. Frankie stood on one of his knees, with the easy balance of a boating dog. She watched the rain-smeared street rattle by, huffing a yearning *whuff* as a horse passed them.

Aaron examined a frayed hole in the blue velvet of the seat with horror. "If you'd given me half an hour, I could have arranged for decent transport."

"As if we'd let you send for an Oliver coach," Ruth said. "Half the Court would arrive with it."

"I'm not going to turn you in." Aaron's tone was impatient, but his gray eyes turned to Joan as he said it.

"I know," Joan said to him. A vulnerable look flitted across

Aaron's face, followed by wariness. Even after their conversation, he didn't quite believe she trusted him. He still thought he might be hurt at the end of this.

Joan bit her lip. He *wouldn't* be safe if he went after Eleanor. None of them would be safe. She pressed a hand against her breastbone, trying to ease the tightness in her chest.

Nick shifted beside her. "So what's the plan?"

"First up, sleep," Ruth said. "You two were unconscious for most of last night. You need real rest."

As Ruth said that, the background ache of Joan's body throbbed to the fore. She *was* tired. She wouldn't be able to rest, though. Not with so much going on in her head. There was so much to plan.

Nick said what she was thinking. "I don't think I can sleep. There's too much we don't know. We have to figure out our plan of attack. And we'll need clothes for 1923. . . ."

"We need to understand what we're up against," Joan agreed. "What powers does Eleanor have access to? What resources does she have? And what are we going to do when we actually find her?"

"We're going to kill her," Tom said flatly.

"Tom," Jamie said.

Tom had never looked more serious. "If I get the chance, I'll do it myself."

Jamie took his hand. "She probably doesn't even remember me."

"That only makes me want to kill her more."

Looking at their clasped hands, Joan had a flash of Jamie's crooked, broken fingers from the previous timeline. Unlike Nick,

Jamie remembered some of his torture.

"Nothing's going to happen until 1923," Aaron said in an even tone that reminded Joan of Ying trying to calm them. "That's thirty-two years from now. There's plenty of time to plan *and* rest." He perked up as he said it. "Does this bus leave Limehouse? There's a decent place in Mayfair, run by . . ." He trailed off at the unenthusiastic response from the rest of them. He muttered to himself, "Or I suppose we could just stay here with the fleas."

Joan found herself staring at him.

"What is it?" Aaron said.

Nothing's going to happen until 1923. It hadn't worked like that last time, though. "When I changed Nick's life—" Joan felt Nick's eyes on her and faltered for a second. "When I changed him, it wasn't just the future that changed. The past changed too. All at once." Joan had unraveled Nick's whole life. She'd erased all his past actions and brought her family back. The new timeline had swallowed up the old in an instant, head to tail.

"What are you saying?" Aaron said, frowning.

"She's saying that we *don't* have until 1923 to stop this," Tom said. "This timeline could be replaced at any moment, without warning. None of us would even know, except maybe Jamie."

Nick sat forward at that. "When Eleanor spoke to us, I had the impression she was already on the cusp of doing something."

"She said it was already in motion," Joan remembered. She pictured Eleanor in 1923, making a change that rippled out along the timeline, supplanting all this in an instant with a crueler and more terrible world.

"Guess we don't sleep, then," Nick said.

As the bus rattled through Limehouse, they wrote down a list of essentials. Tom ran a finger down the page. "We'll need a pretty shady market for some of this." He read out a few items. "Clothes, weapons, surveillance equipment . . ." He scratched his neck. "And time," he added. "If we're all going to 1923, we'll need human time."

Joan felt sick suddenly. She'd known that they'd have to travel thirty-two years—*each*—to get to 1923, but she'd pushed the thought so far down that she hadn't let herself think about where they were going to get the time.

Nick felt it too. His breath hitched, just a slight jolt against her arm. Tom couldn't have heard it, but his gaze flicked to him; Tom had been suspicious of him since the boathouse.

"I've been meaning to ask," Nick said to Aaron. "You dragged me to this time with this golden tattoo. Is that the only way a human can time-travel?"

Ruth frowned. "Strange thing is, I didn't think humans could travel at all. Cuff or not."

Joan took that in. Nick had traveled in the previous time-line, but she'd never seen a cuff on him. He'd never disclosed the method, other than saying that he'd traveled in a different way than Joan. He hadn't stolen human time.

"How does the cuff actually work?" Joan asked Aaron.

"There's time embedded into the mark," Aaron said. "Much like a travel token."

"There's human life tattooed onto my *skin*?" Joan stared at her wrist in new horror. She'd been thinking of the mark as just a handcuff. She'd already hated it; now she wanted to take a knife to it. She wanted to tear it off with her nails. "How much life?" *Whose* lives?

Aaron's gaze was almost too penetrating for a moment. "I can't tell how much is left without the controller," he said. "But as I recall, neither of you had much left. We'll need to obtain more."

Joan turned her wrist over so she wouldn't have to look at the thing. Without the controller, she was still mired by the tattoo. Even if they managed to somehow acquire another one, though . . . She really did feel sick. The last two times she'd traveled—to the future, and then here to 1891—she'd been dragged involuntarily. This time, though, it would be her choice to use human life.

She could feel Nick's tension. Against her arm and thigh, his muscles felt like stone. What was *he* thinking?

They got off the bus at the Regent's Canal Dock, a chaotic throng of barges, sailing ships, navy uniforms, and dockworkers, all muscling in on each other for the limited space. Timber and coal and heavy stone moved back and forth from deck to dock as workers shouted instructions.

Tom headed straight for the colorful mess of Hathaway boats at the edge of the dock. Within ten minutes, he had a horse-drawn narrowboat named *Cornflower.*

The boat was bright blue and decorated with roses and castles, along with the more familiar double-headed hound of the Hathaways. The roses seemed to be a common motif on narrowboats of this time, but Joan thought uneasily of Eleanor's sigil—the thorned rose stem.

Tom hitched a placid white mare with huge dinner-plate hooves to a tow line. "Easiest route is up the Regent's Canal."

"I wondered whether the Hathaways kept a boat in every time period," Joan said curiously. She should have realized there was a pool of shared ones.

"The Hunts sometimes help us push our own boats through time," Tom said. "But usually it's easier just to borrow one—especially when you cross between horse-drawn and engine periods."

Ruth had been looking at the boat; now she did a double take. "Wait, *what?*" she said. "The Hunts do what? Who does that?"

"Just some of the Hunts in some of the times," Tom said, shrugging. "They charge a bucketload. Your family drives a hard bargain."

"Didn't even know we *could* use our power on anything as big as this," Ruth muttered, almost to herself. She sounded intrigued.

Joan boarded the boat. The space was comfortable, but tiny compared with the luxurious width of Tom and Jamie's barge. It was ingeniously furnished with hinged chairs and a table that could be flipped down after use. In one corner, a tiny potbellied stove radiated warmth.

The boat dipped as Nick made his way down the stairs. He sought and found Joan's gaze, and her breath caught. For as long as she'd known him, he'd searched for her instinctively as he'd entered every room. He was still doing it, even now.

Jamie and Ruth came down next, and then Aaron, who removed his hat as he entered. His hair shone in a stray beam of sunshine, and the boat's grandma-lace curtains and duck-egg paint suddenly glowed around him, as if his glamour were reflecting on them.

He looked between Joan and Nick, eyebrows rising. He still seemed to be the only one of the group who'd registered the tension between them. "Cold in here," he said wryly.

Ruth looked puzzled. "Is it?"

"Hmm," Aaron said. "Maybe it's just me."

Tom led the horse up the towpath, pulling them along the canal, with Frankie trotting ahead. The Victorian era rolled past: crumbling houses covered in climbing vines, smoke-billowing factories, towering brick chimneys, and then trees and more trees.

"Never been on a Hathaway boat," Aaron said, looking at the view. "Quite a pleasant way to travel," he added, a little grudgingly.

Between the speed of the horse and the traffic on the canal, the boat arrived around lunchtime. By that point, Frankie was asleep on top of the boat.

They took the stairs from the canal bank up to the Roman Road bridge. The smells of a street market floated toward them, a funfair mix of sausages and toasted buns and baked apples. Ahead, canopied stalls lined the street with tables full of produce—apples and pears, fresh eggs, golden butter. Farther up, more stalls offered secondhand clothes, shoes, furniture.

Joan almost missed the familiar slouched figure leaning against the wall behind the apple seller.

"We should get some food as well as the stuff on the list," Jamie said, and Joan nodded absently. But as the others walked on, she reached for Tom's arm to hold him back. She had no doubt who'd called in Owen Argent.

Tom waited obligingly until the sounds of the market were enough to swallow their conversation. They both kept their eyes on Nick. He didn't seem to register Owen as he headed to a pie stall.

"I know the Argent power has worn off him," Tom murmured to Joan. "His mind is free, isn't it?" He rubbed at his jaw. "Did you two make some kind of deal? Stop Eleanor first and *then* fight it out? Or are you planning to side with him in the aftermath?"

The questions jolted Joan. Side with Nick against *who*? Against him? Against *Ruth*?

Tom saw it in her face. "The former, then," he murmured. "So he's with us until we stop her. And then what?"

After that, our paths will diverge, Nick had said. Joan swallowed. "I should have told you he was free," she admitted. "I was afraid of what you'd do to him. Of how he'd retaliate." She was still afraid.

"What we'd do to *him*? What he'd do to *us*." Tom's gaze was too shrewd, although there was a hint of something considering too, as if he was wondering what he'd have done if Jamie had been in Nick's place. "And where would you be in all this? On the sidelines? In the middle?"

Joan didn't want to fight at all. But it didn't seem optional. How, she wondered again, had the original Joan and Nick made their relationship work? That Joan surely couldn't have known what she was. "He *is* on our side right now," she said. "I don't know what's going to happen after we fight Eleanor. But Nick and I agreed that stopping her matters more than anything else."

"He agrees," Tom said. "You and Jamie agree."

Joan was surprised. "And you don't? Tom, we saw that world through the café window. We can't—"

"We can't *what?*" Tom interrupted her. "We can't live in a world where monsters rule? Where Court Guards execute people at whim? Wake up, Joan! The Court already rules over all of us— human and monster. They already do whatever they want! Do you think it makes a difference if they do it openly or in secret? With or without the masquerade?"

Joan opened her mouth. She hadn't thought of it like that. And at the same time, Tom laying it out gave her a strange feeling that they were still missing something. *Monsters and humans will die in uncountable numbers*, Astrid had said.

"Jamie wants to stop this," Tom said. "And that means I do as well. I'd *like* Eleanor to die. I'd like to do it myself. But all that really matters to *me* is that Jamie is alive at the end of this. And that means protecting him from Eleanor *and* Nick. So you fucking bet I'll have Nick compelled. And that's only out of respect for you." The unspoken *I'd rather take care of it in another way* hung in the silence between them.

Joan swallowed hard at the implied threat to Nick. *The Argent power is wrong*, she wanted to say. It was what she'd told Liam Liu. But she remembered again washing Gran's blood from her hands—red lines streaking the sink—and the words died in her throat. What if Tom was right? What if Nick turned on them the moment they stopped Eleanor? What if he killed them all? Or maybe it would be the other way around. Maybe Tom would kill Nick just to make sure Jamie stayed safe.

"Jamie told me about Nick's massacres," Tom said. "Are you

really going to risk your cousin? The rest of us? In the *hope* that it won't happen again?"

Nick had told her that they were only working together for one task. Tom was right. Joan couldn't risk everyone else just because she cared about Nick. He'd killed all their families before.

"If we do this, I'd want a guarantee," she said. Even saying that much felt so wrong. All her arguments to Liam still stood. Compelling Nick would only make him hate and fear monsters more. It would only make him more dangerous. And it was just *wrong*. Controlling a person's mind was wrong.

And yet . . . *After that, our paths will diverge*, Nick had said.

A battle was looming between Nick and monsters. The battle lines had already been drawn. But maybe this would delay it—at least until they could all regroup. In the short term, this might be the only way to keep them all alive—Nick included.

"What guarantee?" Tom said.

"If we put the Argent power on him, I want your word that he won't be harmed. That no one will hurt him while he's helpless." And *helpless* seemed such a strange word to associate with Nick. Before Tom could even answer, Joan added, "You *owe* me."

Tom pushed a hand through his sandy hair. He was considering it. Joan held her breath. She wasn't holding any cards here. Tom didn't really owe her. Joan had gotten Jamie away from Eleanor, but that hadn't been her primary goal. And even if Tom *had* owed her, he'd repaid her three times over by rescuing her from the Wyvern Inn and then the guardhouse, by harboring her and Nick from the Court.

What could Joan even do if he said no? Shout a warning to

Nick? Start the battle right now?

"All right," Tom said finally. "You have my word that he won't be harmed while he's under Argent control."

Joan felt a burst of nausea and relief at the same time. And trepidation. Was this the right thing to do? Would it save them all or doom them? Would it prevent a battle with Nick or cause it? She didn't know.

"There's something else," Tom said before Joan could turn away from him.

They'd stopped just outside the first stall, where seemingly endless lines of people were buying eggs and butter, and fresh cheese curds scooped from a big saucepan into whatever container the purchaser had brought.

"We need to talk about Aaron Oliver," Tom said.

Joan felt herself tensing, defensive. "There's nothing to talk about."

A few stalls up, Aaron was examining a tray of hot apple dumplings. He looked stupidly posh in his beige suit. As always, his beauty had drawn the attention of the people around him, and as always, he seemed oblivious to the nudges and whispers, the double takes.

"We brought him back as a prisoner," Tom said. "Because we needed information from him."

"And then he and I had a conversation," Joan said, still defensive. "And now he's on our side again."

Tom laughed—just a huff of breath. "You can't actually trust him. He arrested you. He took you to a guardhouse to be executed."

"I told you. I explained to him that we knew each other. I told him the truth about the other timeline."

"*Look,*" Tom said seriously, "I understand why everyone else is going up against Eleanor. You, Nick, and Jamie think you can stop some calamity. I'm here for Jamie. I think Ruth's just here for you. But *him* . . ." Tom looked over at Aaron. "He's not getting anything out of this. Nothing I çan see, except the prospect of a reward if he flips back to Eleanor when we get there."

Joan swallowed. Ruth had warned Joan that Aaron was playing her. That he'd only said what Joan had wanted to hear to get out of that locked room. But Joan had seen the sincerity in his gray eyes when he'd given her his mother's brooch. His blooming shock when she'd described that brooch at the boathouse. The way he'd looked at her after that . . .

"Joan, he doesn't *know* you. You were bonded by a trauma that never happened to him. You feel things about him that he doesn't feel about you."

The words landed. Joan's chest tightened. "I know." She knew that Aaron didn't feel the bond that she felt. Just days ago, he'd been calling her *filth*; he'd wanted to watch her execution. "I know." But then they'd had that conversation. . . .

"You miss him," Tom said. "You miss him, and that makes you want to trust him like you used to."

Over at the stall, the owner had given Aaron some apple dumplings, and she was smiling at him, a little starstruck by Aaron's good looks. Joan would have bet he'd gotten those dumplings for free.

"I'm just saying," Tom said. "You need to be wary of them both."

"Where were you two?" Ruth asked as Joan and Tom rejoined the others. She handed Joan a thick Banbury cake, the pastry still warm. It smelled sweetly of currants and orange peel, but Joan's stomach was already hurting. In her peripheral vision, she saw Owen Argent push away from the wall, tossing aside a half-eaten apple.

Owen looked almost exactly as he had when she'd last seen him. His hair was the same gray-toned ash, his angular features a contrast with his soft mouth.

Nick turned, and *now* he registered Owen. His eyes widened.

Joan had observed the ripple of desire that had followed Aaron. Now she saw again what she'd seen at Queenhithe. Complete strangers reacted to Nick too. There was a shade of desire when they looked at him, but it was more than that. They turned toward Nick as if seeking the sun.

Nick stared at Owen. For a split second, Joan had a terrifying vision of Nick realizing his own effect on people, calling out: *To me! Rally to me!* She pictured all the humans in earshot falling into line behind him, following him as he raised an army, street by street.

But Owen raised his own voice, colored with the deep note of Argent compulsion. "Come here!" he ordered Nick. "Be calm about it! Don't fight!"

Nick's gaze leaped to Joan, and Joan read the clear belief in his eyes that she'd protest this. That she'd try to stop it like she had last time. Her stomach turned over as Nick obeyed Owen's order, heading over to him.

She *should* protest this.

But she couldn't see any other way to keep everyone safe. The Argent power would protect all of them in the aftermath of fighting Eleanor—whether by oath or compulsion.

Nick reached Owen, and Owen said to him, "Stand right there."

Nick stopped, still looking at Joan. He and Owen were in the middle of the street, shoppers streaming around them. But Nick only had eyes for Joan.

Joan walked over. She had to force out the words: "Make sure he can still fight Eleanor," she told Owen. "And make it as strong as you can. He broke your compulsion last time."

Nick's eyes widened in betrayal and hurt—and shock. As if he hadn't believed that Joan still had the capacity to hurt him. He stared at her as Owen gave him a series of orders. Joan could barely hear Owen's words. She forced herself to hold Nick's gaze while Owen made him verbally acknowledge the details of the new compulsion.

Joan hadn't understood until this second that Nick had still trusted her—just a little. In the carriage ride back from Holland House, she'd promised him that she wouldn't compel him. She'd just broken that promise *and* what was left of his trust.

"It's done," Owen said.

Nick's eyes stayed on Joan, expression hardening from betrayal to something far darker. Joan's heart pounded. She replayed the moment that Owen had said, *Come here!* Had there been a moment of hesitation before Nick had obeyed him?

Joan remembered suddenly something else that Nick had said in the carriage: *Truth is, I'm not sure the Argent power would work on me again. I can feel how I'd break it. I know how.*

She breathed in sharply. Had he been able to fight off Owen's compulsion just now?

Frankie barked at something, and Nick looked away from Joan finally. Beside Joan, Jamie and Ruth seemed relieved. Only Tom was frowning. Did he suspect, as Joan did, that Nick was still free?

An awkward cough from Aaron. "So," he said, "these stalls sell monster stuff? Just out in the open?"

Tom shook out of his reverie. "This isn't the market." He beckoned them to follow him up the road.

Joan walked behind Nick's straight-backed form. She wanted to catch his arm and explain: *You killed my family. I couldn't risk you killing more people I loved.* And: *This is just temporary. Just to give us time to go our separate ways after Eleanor.* But in her heart, she knew what Nick would say in reply: *You should have told me that instead of trying to control me by force.*

That was what she'd have said if someone had done this to her.

Tom went to a dodgy little shop with dirty windows and a white stencil on the brick wall: *We buy and sell anything.* Inside, there were no staff—just stacks of old pots and pans, a shelf of chipped cups, a bin of rags and other junk.

Tom whistled an unmelodic phrase. When he'd finished, a door opened silently in the back wall, apparently of its own accord, revealing a flight of rickety wooden stairs leading to a basement.

"*This* is the real Roman Road market," Tom said.

Joan tried to catch Nick's gaze again, but he avoided her eyes. She swallowed around the lump in her throat and followed Tom down the stairs.

THIRTY-FIVE

If Joan hadn't felt so uneasy, she'd have been awed as she descended into the basement. The market was a vintage shopper's dream, a ballroom-sized space packed with circular racks of clothes: suits, dresses, shirts, skirts, overcoats.

Natural light streamed in from a strip of Portelli glass running down the long length of the ceiling. It showed a sky so blue that Joan expected to feel the warmth of sunshine, but it was only light.

Aaron lifted a dark jacket from the nearest rack, waist length at the front and long at the back. It was pristinely clean, but slightly worn at the cuffs, and Joan thought he might sneer at it for being secondhand.

Instead, he murmured in shocked reverence: "Is this a Jonathan Meyer original?" He examined the stitching. "It *is*." He looked around the shop then, like a starving man surveying a buffet. "I didn't know this place was here."

"There's always been a market down here," Jamie said. "Doesn't get picked over as fast as the West End ones."

"Huh," Aaron breathed.

The left wall was all shoes, some velvet, some satiny with polish; a sliding ladder reached the highest shelves. The right wall was a rainbow of hats and gloves and bags. And the back held glass cabinets of jewelry. There was so much here that Joan could barely see a path to traverse it all. It would have taken days to look at every piece.

"This market is mostly clothes," Tom said, "but there's equipment from future periods in the offshoot room. We should be able to find some weapons among it all."

"Well, that's . . . illegal," Aaron said.

Tom shrugged. "And time is there." He nodded at the jewelry on the back wall.

Time? It took Joan a moment to understand that he meant *human* time. She folded her arms around herself. Nick's mouth curled down. As the others spread out among the racks, Nick strode straight to the equipment room. Joan's stomach churned as she watched him. Was there some way to test whether the Argent compulsion was active?

She bit her lip and looked around. She needed clothes for this time jump. She lifted a dress at random, long and structured, made of heavy gray wool. A bit of rough-cut cloth was pinned to the collar with a date: *c. 1936.* She put it back.

The racks seemed to be more or less in chronological order. Farther in, Joan found a plain black dress in some kind of crinkly fabric, labeled *1919.* It wasn't *1923,* but it was close enough. What else did she need? A hat? Gloves? Stockings?

"Joan." Tom appeared from the next aisle. He called Aaron over too.

Aaron had been efficient. It couldn't have been more than a few minutes since they'd spread out, but he appeared with brown and gray tweed draped over his arm. There was a gray hat on top of it all.

Tom dug in his pocket and produced a gold object. He tossed it to Joan. Startled, she almost fumbled it.

"What is this?" she said. It looked like a closed pocket watch with a hinged side. She turned it over and found a winged lion etched into the metal.

Aaron leaned to look at it. "That's a controller for Court cuffs." His mouth dropped open. "That's *my* controller!" he said to Tom. "That's the one you took from me!"

"You said you smashed it," Joan said to Tom, surprised.

Oh, come on, Tom's expression said. *As if I'd do that.* "Let's get that thing off you," he said to Joan.

As much as Joan hated the cuff, the prospect of removing it made her nervous suddenly. She'd been mired for days, and she hadn't realized until this moment how relieved she'd been that she couldn't travel.

She felt around the edge of the device and found a button that unlocked the clasp. She flicked the lid open with her thumb. It could still have passed for a pocket watch—or maybe a compass. Around the edge, nine black symbols stood at regular intervals. They looked like stylized letters from a non-Roman alphabet. In the middle, there were three gold clock hands of different lengths. None of them were moving.

Joan tugged up the billowing sleeve of her Victorian blouse to reveal the mark on her right wrist. The winged lion shone, bright and vivid in the Portelli sunlight. Now that Joan knew there was human life in the mark, she could hardly bear to look at it. She blocked her view with the controller, and as she did, the largest clock hand spun like a compass needle, shifting back and forth until it landed on one of the stylized letters—the one at the twelve o'clock mark.

Aaron peered down at it. "Almost empty," he said. "You'll need to buy a travel token to get to the twenties."

Joan didn't look at the back wall with its thousands and thousands of pieces of jewelry—all imbued with human life—but it seemed to loom behind them.

"Well, I'll leave you to it," Tom said. He called Frankie to follow him and ambled away.

The room was so big—and so packed with merchandise—that as soon as Tom was out of sight, Joan felt like she and Aaron were in a bubble of their own. The clothes racks on either side could have been solid walls.

Joan touched the tattoo. It still felt like her own skin. Like there was nothing there on her arm. "How do I take this thing off?" she asked Aaron.

"Just hold the device over the mark. There's a mental component. It should respond to your thoughts."

"A mental component?" That sounded like magic.

"It's a blend of future technology and Court powers," Aaron explained.

"Huh." Joan hovered the device over the tattoo. Nothing seemed to happen. The clock hands didn't even spin. She pictured the tattoo melting away. But the visualization didn't work either.

Aaron put his bundle of clothes down onto a small table between the racks. "It might be easier if I do it."

Joan hesitated. Tom would have told her to hold on tight to that device. Aaron had been able to control her body with this thing, as well as drag her through time.

Aaron winced slightly. "Or you could try—" he started, but Joan made up her mind at the same time. She handed him the controller. He blinked down at it, and then up at her, as if he hadn't expected her to just give it to him.

You need to be wary of them both, Tom had said. Joan swallowed. She'd betrayed Nick; it would serve her right if Aaron betrayed her now. Maybe deep down she'd given this to Aaron because she knew she'd deserve the betrayal.

But Aaron only stepped closer. "May I?" He mimed cradling the underside of Joan's bare forearm.

Joan nodded, and Aaron cupped her arm with a steady grip. It occurred to Joan that she hadn't often seen him touching people. When he'd taken off her glove at the masquerade, he'd had a guard hold her arm, and he'd only touched the fabric. As she thought that, though, she had a vivid flash of him fastening a pearl necklace on her. Of him brushing her cheek with his hand.

Aaron lifted his gray eyes to hers. "This might hurt," he said softly.

Even with the warning, Joan was shocked by the scalding pain—like the tattoo had turned to molten metal. She gasped. Aaron's hand tightened, steadying her as her arm spasmed. And then she was gasping again, in relief, as the pain faded.

"All done," Aaron said, and Joan stared at her wrist. Her arm was bare for the first time in days. And Aaron had a cylinder of lacework between his thumb and forefinger. He placed it into a slot in the controller and handed it to her.

"Thanks." Joan shoved it into her pocket. She hadn't thought there'd be any immediate difference without the cuff, but her sense of the timeline already seemed stronger: a steady breeze against her skin rather than a breath. She felt raw and a little jangly, like she'd just had three cups of coffee in a row.

"That's a mourning dress, by the way." Aaron nodded at the black dress draped over Joan's arm. "For someone grieving."

"What? *This* is?" Joan looked down at the crinkly fabric. "Oh." She should have realized. She'd liked it for its classic cut; she hadn't been thinking of the historical context of black.

"It's fine," Aaron said. "I mean—" He hesitated. And then, as if he couldn't help himself, he grabbed a pale plum dress from the rack next to him and offered it to her. "Just another option," he said. "If you don't want to look like a widow."

Joan lifted it to her chin and looked in the mirror at the end of the aisle. The dress hadn't seemed like much on the rack—she wouldn't have given it a second glance. But as she held it up, it seemed to transform. It was two dresses in one: a plum-colored underdress with near-opaque ivory gauze over the top. The plum provided a hint of color, and the gauze wasn't fussy—as Joan might have guessed—but mysterious.

She turned back to Aaron and was surprised again to find him looking at the mirror too—at her reflection—his expression curious, almost wondering. When she caught his eyes, though, he ducked his head.

"This place has a surprisingly excellent selection," he said. "If we were here under different circumstances . . . Well . . ." He neatened his tie, although it didn't need it.

"I like the dress," Joan said. "Looks like I just stepped out of the 1920s." As she spoke, she was hit with a sudden intense rush of yearning out of nowhere—as if her body had just realized that it wasn't mired anymore. She caught her breath, shaken with it.

Distantly, she sensed Aaron closing the gap between them, concerned, but she couldn't hear anything but the roaring in her ears. She caught sight of herself in the mirror again, the dress still under her chin, and that was all it took. The bright light from the Portelli window darkened, plunging the room into twilight. Aaron's voice cut off like a stopped recording. Joan tried to control her panic. She hadn't had a fade-out since Corvin had cuffed her wrist.

Focus on your senses, she told herself. That was what Aaron had taught her. But she couldn't feel anything at all—not the temperature on her skin, not the breath in her lungs. *Was* she even breathing?

In the darkening room, Aaron leaned closer. He was saying something to her. Joan tried to read his lips. Eyes wide and worried, he clasped her hand, and Joan concentrated on the curl of his elegant fingers around hers. She couldn't feel his touch, but she could faintly feel the warmth of him, like cold winter sunshine. She focused on that warmth.

Aaron's voice began to seep into the silence. "You're still holding the dress," he was saying. "Can you feel it?" He sounded calm but tight, as if he was suppressing some emotion. "It's cold in here. Can you feel that?"

Joan blinked down at the dress he'd picked out. It looked very soft—the gauze must have been silk. She could just barely feel the texture of it. She frowned, concentrating.

Slowly, the room brightened back to afternoon. Aaron's hand solidified over hers. He tightened his grip, and Joan felt an unexpected electric charge run through her as he did. A shot of desire. She swallowed. Her whole body felt jangled and confused.

"That's better," he murmured. "I can see you're coming back."

She found her voice. "I'm here," she managed, and was relieved to hear herself at normal volume. This was where she wanted to be, she told herself. Right here, in this time.

Aaron closed his eyes for a moment, and his shoulders went down too, as if he'd been scared. When he opened his eyes again, he searched her face. "Has that happened before?"

Joan should have told Gran, she thought again. As soon as these fade-outs had started. "Almost every morning before that cuff was put on me," she admitted, and Aaron looked shocked. "I'm still learning to control it," she explained. "You taught me how to focus on my senses. I've been doing that."

Aaron looked appalled. "*I* taught you?" he said. "You're saying this happened in front of me? And I taught you *as* it happened?" His hand tightened on hers, and they both realized at the same moment that they were still touching. Last time that had happened, Aaron had snatched his hand away like she'd burned him. This time, he released her gently. "You should have been taught control as a child!" he said. "*Before* you could travel!" He turned sharply, looking over the tops of the racks, and Joan realized he was searching angrily for Ruth. No one seemed to be nearby, though. Joan could distantly still see Nick in the equipment room, and Tom—a foot taller than everyone else—over at the jewelry cabinet.

Joan had forgotten how angry Aaron had been last time too. "The Hunt records said I *couldn't* travel," she explained. "Ruth didn't know. I didn't tell my gran when this started happening."

Aaron looked troubled. He swiped a hand over his mouth. He started to say something, and then seemed to think better of it.

"Thank you," Joan added. "For this time. For last time." She'd been using his lessons almost every morning for months. She had the weird thought then that this was a side of her that only Aaron had seen. She'd never have been able to admit to Nick how strong her craving for travel really was. For Aaron, though, the morality of time travel just wasn't a factor.

"If that's happening every day, then what I taught you last time wasn't enough," Aaron said seriously. He retrieved his clothes and hat from the table. "After this is all over, we need to do something about it."

After this? Joan opened her mouth and closed it again. She didn't even let herself hope. The truth was, whatever happened *after this*, Aaron would have to stay away from her. His mother had been executed for sheltering someone like Joan. And if Ying was right—that Joan was a member of an erased family—then the King himself would still want her dead. After this, Aaron would go back to the Olivers, and Joan would still be on the run.

Movement across the market caught her eye: Nick striding from the equipment room.

Aaron followed her gaze. "You know . . . when you were questioning me, I told you that I wasn't sure what I'd seen in the library. But I *did* see it. I saw the tear in the timeline."

Joan turned back to him. "You saw what I did?" She heard the crack in her own voice. She hadn't imagined she could feel worse about that moment, but knowing Aaron had seen it *was* somehow worse.

"I saw what happened in the previous timeline," Aaron said, tilting his head slightly.

Joan dropped her gaze. Aaron had seen her kiss Nick in the other timeline. He'd seen her unmake Nick. She'd already felt ashamed, and now the feeling redoubled. She'd betrayed Nick twice, and Aaron had witnessed it both times. She could imagine what he thought of her—the Olivers valued loyalty above everything else. *Fidelis ad mortem.*

"Joan," Aaron said. She forced herself to lift her chin, to meet his eyes. To her surprise, the disgust she'd expected to see wasn't there. "You told me that you and I worked together last time to save our families," Aaron said. "That we succeeded. . . . I saw the decision you made at the end. I saw how hard it was."

Joan swallowed again. Things had been so much clearer before she'd entered the monster world. "I think I made a bad decision with the Argent power just now," she admitted. "We shouldn't have done that to him." The more she thought about it, the worse it seemed. She'd begged Liam to take the compulsion off Nick the first time. *It's just wrong*, she'd told him. It was still wrong. And she'd warned Liam that compelling Nick would only make things worse for all of them. That seemed just as true now.

"I don't know about *shouldn't have* or *should have*," Aaron said. "But my mother always used to say: *From here on . . .*"

There was a shade of vulnerability in his expression. He'd barely spoken of his mother in the previous timeline. Joan knew what it must have taken for him to quote her now. She nodded.

Aaron took a breath. "I'd better get the rest of the things on my list."

Joan looked down at the dress he'd given her. She still had a few things to get too.

Joan found a jacket that matched the dress, an overcoat, a pair of shoes, and a cloche hat. Weapons next, she thought. But instead, she found herself walking over to the jewelry cabinets.

Three glass cases stood along the room's shortest wall. From afar, the jewelry had looked like a museum display; closer, the pieces didn't look cheap exactly, but they were eclectic: a statement necklace of enamel violets, a scarab ring, a milk-green jade pendant. Little handwritten stickers under each piece provided a price. The statement necklace had a small element built into the chain, next to the clasp: a gold rectangular frame with three rotatable numbers; it reminded Joan of a combination lock. The numbers read *100*. It took her a full second to absorb the meaning. There were a hundred years of human life in that necklace. As the wearer traveled, they could rotate the numbers to show the remaining time.

Like the clothes, all the jewelry was neatly organized. The bottom shelf had plain charm bracelets. The shelves above held the charms themselves: cute enamel birds, enamel skulls, sigils from each family. Even the Hunt fox was there. Five years each. Joan pictured, with a roil of nausea, monsters discarding the used charms like throwing out food packaging.

Joan stepped back. The next shelf up had chain necklaces. Above them were red pendants: ten years each. Then green: twenty years. Black: fifty years.

Then the statement necklaces: one hundred years, two hundred years, five hundred years.

Joan took another step back. For a second, the cabinet was so clearly a display of corpses that it was like she could see people splayed out in death.

She felt rather than saw someone slip into the space beside her. She glanced up, expecting Tom or Jamie. Her stomach turned over. It was Nick.

"Have you chosen a piece?" he asked her.

Joan couldn't suppress a shudder at the thought. He wasn't looking at her but at the cabinet. His eyes were clear of influence and hard as flint. She glanced over her shoulder. Only Tom was visible among the aisles. "The Argent power didn't work on you this time, did it?" she said.

He didn't react. He could have been a statue of himself. "I told you it wouldn't."

Joan's chest tightened. "Unforgivable?" It came out as a question, although she hadn't intended that.

Nick looked at her directly—for the first time since the failed compulsion. Pain crossed his face, almost too briefly to read.

"I thought you might kill us afterward," Joan whispered.

"I gathered." Nick turned back to the cabinet of corpses. "How much life is in here?" he wondered. "All these charms and pendants . . . Thirty charms times five years. That's a hundred and fifty years." His lips moved as he quickly calculated the rest. "There's nearly ten thousand years of human life on this wall, I'd say."

Joan hadn't done that calculation. Her stomach rolled.

"That's a hundred and twenty-five whole, long human lives

from birth to old age," Nick said. "A massacre. But monsters don't steal time like that, do they? You told me that they take it in small increments. So maybe we're looking at ten thousand people dying a year earlier than they should have." Joan heard her own indrawn breath. He looked at her. "Life means something," he whispered to her. "When my dad died—" His voice cracked. "After Dad died, I missed him more than I could ever have imagined. And I had fourteen years with him. My little brother, Robbie, only had two. Robbie doesn't remember him. And . . . Dad was such a good man, you know? Just *good*. Kind. Wise." He swallowed visibly. "I would give *anything* for Robbie, for my little sister, Alice, to have a year more with him. For them to remember him." His eyes shone wetly. "I would give *anything* to see him again."

Joan swallowed around the lump in her own throat. After her family had died, she'd had those same thoughts. She'd have given anything for a year more with them. For an hour more. Even a minute would have been enough to tell them that she loved them one more time.

"I can't do it," Nick said softly.

"Can't do what?" Joan said. But some part of her already knew what he was going to say: Nick would never steal time from another human. Her eyes were already wet when he answered.

"I can't take anyone else's life," Nick said.

Joan felt a tear fall. "*Nick*," she said. It came out with so much emotion that Nick seemed startled. "If you do this, you're going to lose *thirty-two years* of life."

He searched her face, as if trying to solve a puzzle. "I know," he said finally. "I understand."

Joan's heart hurt. The thing was, though, that he was right.

All the little numbers in the cabinet weren't abstract at all. These necklaces and charms carried the lives of people like Mr. Larch. Like Margie. People who loved and were loved.

Never again, Joan had said to Nick, when he'd asked if she stole human life. She'd meant it then. Did she mean it still?

She took a deep breath. "I understand too," she managed. He was right. Life meant something.

She'd taken life from herself before—to escape from him. About thirty years, she guessed. Had that been reset when the timeline had changed? Or was she already thirty years down? Would thirty-two more mean she'd have lost more than sixty years of life by the end of this?

And when she thought about it like that—in spite of her own vow of *never again*—a tiny voice in her head asked, *Would you have taken it from yourself again if he hadn't set an example first? Or would you have bought a piece of this jewelry?*

It took Nick a moment to grasp what she'd meant. He looked sick then too. He opened his mouth, and Joan could almost see what he was thinking: *I didn't mean for you to do it too.*

The reality of it hit her again. *Don't take it from yourself,* she wanted to say to him. *Take it from these strangers who I don't know.* "I did love him," she blurted. "You asked if I did." *I love you. I think I always will.*

Another flash of emotion on Nick's face, ruthlessly suppressed. He opened his mouth, and Joan braced herself for what he was about to say.

But as Nick drew a breath, Jamie called from the equipment room. "Come over here! Look at this!"

The equipment room was surprisingly big—maybe a quarter of the size of the clothes room. Near the entrance, there were tables full of secondhand phones: chunky nineties bricks, familiar phones, and—strangely—in the same trays, bracelets and rings in a rainbow of metallics. Could those be phones of the future? Joan slipped on a smooth rose-gold bangle with a black-agate stone. She was startled when a white square appeared on her palm with the word *Hello* in black, crystal sharp. Apparently, the stone was a kind of projector.

She took off the bangle and kept walking. Farther in, she found drawers full of knives and guns. She walked on, opening and closing drawers of cameras, microphones, drones, and, in the same section, black sticker dots on white sheets. Were they cameras as well? Trackers?

Farther still, there were drawers of sunglasses and little figurines on key chains and enamel brooches that lit up when touched. Joan could guess at the technology embedded in the sunglasses, but what about the figurines and the brooches? What period did they come from? What did that time look like? What might she see if she traveled two centuries forward? Maybe— She cut off the thought as she felt herself drift toward yearning. She *really* didn't want to fade out again.

"Holy shit," Aaron said from the doorway. "There's stuff from the next three centuries in here. If the Court knew—"

"How would they find out? You going to snitch?" Ruth said.

Aaron rolled his eyes. "Yeah, the second I'm out of here, I'm going to snitch about anachronistic sunglasses."

"Over here!" Jamie called from the far end of the room.

Joan found him with Tom, surrounded by boxy machines that could have been anything from 3D printers to espresso makers. They'd pushed them aside, clearing a square of bare floorboards.

Jamie pointed down. There was a piece of white plastic on the wood—it looked almost like a bread tag without the slot.

Ruth came over and peered at the thing. "Where did you get *that*?"

"Just here," Jamie said soberly. "Just among this stuff."

Aaron arrived then, Nick just behind him, and spotted the thing straightaway. "That is—" Aaron seemed truly shocked. "That is *illegal*. That is *far* future technology!"

Aaron's tone, more than his words, triggered the memory. Joan had retrieved a device like that from the Monster Court. Jamie had left it in his prison cell—it had contained the recordings of Nick's creation.

"It just looks like a bit of plastic," Nick said.

"It's a recorder," Jamie explained. "It takes images and sounds directly from your mind." He frowned down at the device, concentrating. A moment later, a window opened up in the wall.

To Joan's horror, the view was the gloomy street they'd seen through the café window. The dark, not quite Victorian buildings, the frightened people in drab clothes, the statue of Eleanor with roses at her feet.

"What *is* that?" Aaron said.

"It's the other London—the one we saw through the hole in the timeline," Joan whispered. It took her a moment to realize that the view was frozen: none of the people on the street were moving. And this wasn't an actual window; this was Jamie's memory of what they'd seen in the café. He was using the device to record and project what he remembered.

"It looks so real," Nick murmured.

It *did*. The café window could have been right here, in this room. Joan was awed again by Jamie's perfect memory.

And then the tableau unfroze. Joan held her breath. She registered more details this time: Eleanor's bronze statue stood on a plinth, a winged lion etched at the base. But it wasn't the usual lion of the Monster Court. That lion was always posed as if stalking the viewer. This one was outstretched in attack, its mouth an open roar.

Movement caught Joan's attention. It was the blond man, running from around the corner. Joan could hardly watch. It was somehow so much worse now that she knew the outcome. The hearse-black van pulled up, and the guard got out. The blond man's face contorted in fear and resignation. He *knew* he was about to die; he knew that no one was coming to help him.

And no one did. The frightened onlookers snatched glances at the scene and just kept walking.

The guard killed the blond man, and then wrenched open the back of the van. Joan gasped. Her mind had blurred it out—at the time, she'd barely been able to look. But Jamie's memory had perfectly captured it.

The corpses were stacked in undignified tangles, necks and ankles and elbows at unnatural angles. All the people looked so ordinary. They could have been Joan's own human family, her friends at school, her neighbors. Joan saw again the black shoe with the broken strap. This time, she made herself follow the person's foot to their leg, to their face. The dead woman had a sharply cut bob of black hair and a round face with kind lines.

"Seventeen," Nick murmured shakily, and Joan realized that he'd counted the number of bodies.

Joan put a hand over her mouth. It wasn't just the visceral horror of it. She'd forgotten how *wrong* this world was—it was evident even in a recording. Something deep inside her said that this shouldn't exist. It was a corrupted version of reality. An incorrect timeline.

Now a ripple shuddered through the market room, and the hairs on Joan's neck rose. It was like the timeline itself was trying to raise the alarm. As if it was as disturbed as Joan was.

"This is what you saw?" Aaron breathed, and Joan nodded. He'd gone very pale. "I felt the timeline react to it," he said, and Joan nodded again. "Like it couldn't abide its existence."

"It doesn't exist yet, and it never will," Nick said. He was so certain that he sounded eerily calm. "We're going to stop it."

They decided to leave from the south bank, within sight of St. Magnus. Close enough that they could access the church, but not so close that they'd accidentally run into any of Eleanor's people.

"And we can borrow a Hathaway boat from the wharf when we get there," Tom said.

They walked across London Bridge together, in the dim light of gas lamps. It was a cool night, and Joan was glad of that; they were all in overcoats to conceal their 1920s clothes. They'd talked through the initial jump already. If everything went to plan, they'd arrive on February 24 with plenty of time to surveil St. Magnus.

With luck, they'd find Eleanor before March 5—and with even more luck, they'd find out who was working with her. Aaron had warned that she could have allies with unusually strong family powers, and the more they knew about those allies, the better they could plan.

As they reached the south bank, Owen Argent pushed away from a warehouse wall, hands in his pockets.

"He's coming with us," Tom said.

"Tom," Joan said. That hadn't been the agreement. And if Owen traveled with them, it would cost another thirty years of human life.

Tom glanced meaningfully from Jamie to Nick. "Just in case," he murmured without apology. He checked Nick's reaction, but Nick's expression stayed blank.

"Nick." Aaron beckoned to Nick with an elegant curl of his fingers. "It's time."

Joan wet her dry lips. *Don't ask Aaron to do this*, she wanted to tell Nick.

Nick's cuff was still empty; only a Mtawali would have been able to embed more time into it. But the cuff had a backup function; whoever wielded the controller could use time they'd stolen themselves to drag their prisoner.

And Aaron was still the only one of them able to wield that controller.

Please don't, Joan thought again. *Let Aaron use a piece of jewelry instead.*

But Nick went to Aaron, stopping just within his circle of personal space. He was only a little taller than Aaron, but his muscled body gave the impression that he was towering over Aaron's narrower frame.

"You're sure about this?" Aaron said to Nick very seriously.

"I'm sure," Nick said steadily.

"Very well," Aaron said. He reached up and ran his hand over the back of Nick's neck.

Nick took one shuddering breath and released it.

"I have it," Aaron said softly, and Joan was torn between feeling sick and relieved. She'd been so afraid that Nick would drop dead like Margie had. And then the true horror of it hit her. Nick had just lost more than thirty years of his life. Just like that. It was gone. How much did he have left?

"I didn't even feel it," Nick said, eyes a little wide as new understanding dawned on him. Monsters stole human life so easily and secretly that humans would never know it.

Aaron was still staring at Nick, seeming off-balance. Joan bet he'd never looked a person in the eyes as he'd taken time from them.

"We're traveling from here?" Aaron sounded a bit shaky.

"No, just a bit farther up," Tom said.

They'd found a spot between two warehouses, with a view of the Thames. Tom and Nick led the way, and Joan let herself fall behind. She'd been putting off taking time from herself—she'd been too scared. She couldn't delay anymore, though. They were almost there.

Without letting herself think about it, she put a hand to the back of her neck and wrenched away what she hoped was thirty-two years—no more and no less.

Just like last time, it was agony—like she was tearing into her own flesh. Humans didn't seem to feel it, but Joan's body knew what she was doing to it. She heard a sound work its way up her throat. Last time, she'd screamed. This time, she clenched her teeth as hard as she could, holding it in.

"Hey," Aaron said, perhaps hearing her. His footsteps stopped ahead of her.

Joan found herself doubled over slightly, breathing too hard, trying to control the pain. "Nervous," she managed. It wasn't even a lie. She forced herself to straighten and was startled to see Nick standing just behind Aaron, staring at her. He'd been up front with Tom a second earlier. How had he gotten back here so fast?

Nick had guessed what she'd done. He took another step, putting him in front of her, and another, so that he was almost in her personal space. His hand twitched as if wanted to touch her, but he aborted the impulse. He stared down at her, eyes nearly black. His jaw was so tight, she thought his teeth might crack.

Joan found her voice. "We should catch up to the others," she said.

After a long, long moment, Nick nodded.

Aaron was clearly puzzled about their silent exchange. He knew something had just happened, but not what. "I'm nervous too," he offered, and Joan tried to smile at him.

They walked up the rest of the way together, Nick at Joan's back. She could feel his eyes on her until they reached the departure spot.

It wasn't an alley exactly—just a large space between warehouses. The ground was unpaved dirt.

They stripped off their overcoats and nineteenth-century hats, discarding them on the ground. Tom put Frankie into his knapsack. And then they were ready. Next stop, 1923.

Aaron took Joan's hand, his clasp weirdly reassuring. Joan didn't have enough experience to jump accurately without help, so Aaron was going to navigate for them both. He reached for Nick too, wrapping his hand around Nick's tattooed wrist, activating the cuff.

Joan gave 1891 a last look. It was nearly midnight, but on the river, people were rowing barges, scrubbing decks. And on the opposite bank, dockworkers at London Bridge Wharf unloaded crates from a schooner. London never slept. St. Magnus was a tower behind the wharf. In Joan's time, it would be overshadowed by new construction, but in this time, it soared above its neighbors. She pictured it as an oasis in the middle of London. Later in the day, people might sit in its courtyard in peaceful silence; maybe they'd have lunch there; maybe they'd read a book. She couldn't imagine anything happening on the church grounds at all. What was Eleanor going to do there to change the timeline?

Joan looked over at the others. Jamie seemed nervous; Nick determined. "Ready?" she said.

"Ready," Ruth confirmed, and Tom and Aaron nodded too. Owen shrugged.

Tom and Jamie took a step, and then vanished. A few seconds later, Owen was gone, and then Ruth. Strange to think that, if everything went well, they'd all arrive at approximately the same moment.

"Remember, you need to jump when I jump," Aaron said to

Joan. To Nick, he said, "The timeline protects us when we travel—we won't land in a brick wall or submerged in the ground. But be ready to duck down and hide. There might be people around." He squeezed Joan's hand. "On my mark."

Joan closed her eyes. To time-travel—to *jump*, as Aaron had called it—monsters had to evoke in themselves a feeling of focused yearning for another time. Joan had been suppressing that feeling so fiercely lately that the prospect of giving in to it felt terrifying and thrilling at the same time. And she was aware, too, that she was about to expend thirty-two years of her life.

"*Now*," Aaron said.

Joan opened her eyes and let herself *feel* it.

The world jolted.

And they arrived into chaos.

THIRTY-SIX

Someone grabbed Joan, tearing her from Aaron's grip. She kicked out, and pain burst through her foot as she struck someone's shin. But she'd hurt them too. They grunted, and their fingers slipped from her arm as they stumbled back.

Joan tried to make sense of the blurred bodies and shouts, the blunt thump of fists against flesh. She knocked away a grasping hand, and nearby Nick made a satisfied sound as a body thudded heavily to the ground.

What was going on? Who was attacking them? There were too many bodies pressed close, and in the near-dawn gloom, Joan couldn't see much of the attackers—they were just arms and chests and legs. Underfoot, the ground had more traction than a minute ago: it seemed to be brick rather than slippery mud. And Joan had the sense that the surroundings were more open; the warehouse on the right had lost a level, and there was more sky.

"That's enough!" someone called out.

Strangely, everyone reacted as if they'd heard a bell in a boxing match. The sounds of the scuffle instantly ceased. Tom swore under his breath. Joan looked up and saw why they'd all stilled; why Tom had sworn.

Their attackers had surrounded the top of the path—at least ten of them—and they were pointing guns. Joan's heart pattered. What was going *on*? Her eyes were starting to adjust now. The attackers were in 1920s clothes—a mix of suits and dresses, billowing in the breeze coming off the Thames. The guns weren't from the 1920s, though. They looked like the blunt black weapons of the future—the ones Joan had seen at the Roman Road market.

On the other side of the river, the wharf had been cleaned up and modernized, rotting wood replaced with fresh. St. Magnus was still visible, although surrounded now by cranes.

Joan risked a look over her shoulder. In 1891, there'd been a route out. Now her heart sank. A brick wall had appeared, turning the path into an alley with a dead end.

"Steady," Tom said with tamped frustration.

Joan felt it too. They'd all brought weapons, but they hadn't anticipated being attacked on arrival. How *had* they been? They were ten days early, and they'd deliberately chosen an obscure landing site, away from monster houses and way stations. They were supposed to spend the next few days scouting and planning.

"What's going *on?*" Aaron's voice shook.

"It's an ambush," Joan whispered. "But how did they know we'd be here? We're *early.*"

A familiar voice rang out then, low and sweet. "No, Joan." Eleanor emerged from around the corner. "What you are is *predictable.*"

Even here, surrounded by the ocean-rot stink of the Thames, Eleanor was regal. She walked in unarmed, her golden head held high. She wore heavy gold earrings in an intricate pattern that made Joan think of religious jewelry of the medieval period. Her dress was reminiscent of the medieval too—long-sleeved with a straight cut, the same style she'd worn at Holland House.

The attackers had made a semicircle outside the alley with

Eleanor at the center of it. Joan could feel their collective powers, so present that the air itself seemed to crackle with static.

Who *were* they? Other members of the Court? Joan couldn't see any family sigils.

Joan's group had been coaxed by the fight to the mouth of the alley. It was a big enough space for them to stand in a semicircle of their own. Joan judged the distance to Eleanor. Ten paces, maybe. A few seconds to rush her. If they did that, though, they'd be shot.

"Look at Tom Hathaway, wondering who betrayed you all," Eleanor said. She raised an eyebrow at Jamie, who paled visibly under her attention. "You married a man with such a suspicious mind," she said to him.

Tom's jaw worked. "Take your eyes off him."

"Or what?" Eleanor seemed mildly amused.

"Or I'll risk the bullets."

Jamie put a hand on Tom's arm, gripping so tightly that his knuckles whitened. After a long moment, Tom's chin lowered very slightly in acknowledgment of Jamie's unvoiced request.

A smile played over Eleanor's mouth. She looked at them all, one by one, and Joan viscerally felt Tom's rage as Eleanor's gaze roved over Jamie. Then Aaron, Nick, Ruth. Joan was furious too. Eleanor had killed their families. She'd tortured Nick over and over. She'd tortured Jamie.

"So who informed?" Tom said tightly.

"I didn't need an informant," Eleanor said. "Not when Joan is so predictable."

Why did she keep saying that? "What are you talking about?" Joan said.

"I told you," Eleanor said to her. "I *know* you, Joan. I know you better than you know yourself. I know how you think . . . I knew you'd be *here*, on the opposite bank, with a view of St. Magnus. It *was* your idea to land here, wasn't it?"

Joan stared at her, feeling suddenly off-balance. How could Eleanor have known that?

"Did you like the clue I left you?" Eleanor asked. "I had an Ali seal placed at the church. I knew you'd think it was a sign that the timeline was going to be changed there."

Joan glanced at the others. They all looked as wary as she felt. She was starting to realize that this wasn't an ambush—it was a trap. Eleanor had lured them here.

"Now you're wondering how I knew *when* you'd arrive," Eleanor said. "That was hardly a test at all. You and your cousin were trained by Dorothy Hunt herself. She has a rule of thumb: ten days' minimum from concept to job. You'd have preferred longer, but you were afraid I'd change the timeline first."

Joan swallowed. She and Ruth had figured out the schedule together, and the others had agreed. "Why did you bring us here?"

"Don't you remember this place?" Eleanor said.

Dawn had broken, and the sky was brightening. Joan looked around. The arches of London Bridge were just visible to the west. "Do I remember it?" She was familiar with the area, of course—Tower Bridge was just to the east. In a hundred years, the Shard would be built behind them.

"I'm talking about London Bridge," Eleanor said. "Don't you remember it?"

Joan felt a bloom of confusion. She could see it right now, the elegant arches rising and falling, serpent-like in the water.

"I'm not talking about *this* bridge," Eleanor said impatiently.

"This dull thing behind me. And certainly not the concrete monstrosity they'll erect later in the century. I'm talking about the *old bridge.* The one that was *here.* Two centuries ago, the entrance was right here, where we're standing." She turned her head, as if she could see the length of it now, stretching all the way to St. Magnus.

Nick twitched on Aaron's other side, tempted by the opportunity of Eleanor's distraction. Joan was tempted too. But the guns still gave her pause, and apparently the same was true for Nick. He held himself back.

Eleanor had spoken with so much emotion that Joan found herself answering truthfully. "I've never traveled that far into the past." She'd seen illustrations of the old bridge, of course. It had been London's longest-lasting bridge: built in the twelfth century and surviving until the mid-nineteenth. By 1923, though, all that really remained of it was the pedestrian archway at St. Magnus.

"It was beautiful," Eleanor said, for once without any hint of cruelty. "One of the wonders of the world." She sounded nostalgic as she gazed at the space where it had once been. "Nineteen arches with water roaring through them. The daring and the drunk used to fly through the rapids in rowboats, surfing the rising tide."

Aaron covered Joan's hand with his own. She blinked at him, and he curled her fingers gently into a fist. He squeezed once and then let go. It took her a second to understand that it was a technique for staying grounded in the here and now. He was helping her not to fade out. She nodded slightly, holding her hand in the fist Aaron had made.

Eleanor was still talking. "For more than five hundred years, people lived on that bridge. There were houses and shops . . . jewelers, booksellers, glove-makers, tailors . . . even a drawbridge to defend London from invaders. And the centerpiece of it all was a grand four-story mansion made completely of wood—not an iron nail in it." Eleanor's voice softened. "When I was a little girl, I grew up in that house. I still dream of it. The never-ending rush of the river like a hundred waterfalls."

Joan squeezed her fist even tighter. Her recent dreams hadn't been so pleasant. For months, she'd dreamed of Nick crying out at finding his family dead, of Gran's last breaths. "I don't *care* where you grew up!" she blurted. Eleanor turned to her, eyes distant as if she was still half in her memories. Then she focused on Joan, and for a weird second, she almost looked hurt. Joan couldn't believe it. *Eleanor* was hurt?

"You *ruined my life*!" Joan told her, fury rising to the surface. "My family *died* because of you! Aaron's family died! Jamie's! Tom's! Nick's!" She felt Nick shift at that, confused. He didn't know what Eleanor had done to him. What she'd manipulated him into doing. "You tortured Jamie," Joan said. Jamie had nightmares about *that*. "Do you think *any* of us cares about *your* life?"

"You really don't remember any of it, do you?" Eleanor said. "You don't remember the house?"

What was she talking about? "Why *would* I remember it? Why would I care about some house that hasn't been here for two hundred years?"

"Because it was *your* house," Eleanor said, and now she didn't just look hurt—her voice was thick with it. "It was *ours*! We grew up there together. And all this"—she gestured at the swath of the north and south banks—"all this belonged to our family! It belonged to the Graves!"

Joan stared at her. "What?" The word came out as a barely voiced breath. *Your family*, Ying had said. *The Graves.* Joan had hardly begun to process what he'd told her. And she really couldn't process this. She shook her head. "You and me are *not* family!"

"Yes, we are, Joan." The hurt still shaded Eleanor's voice. "Not like you and *her*." She jerked a chin at Ruth, who glared at her.

"You're wrong. Ruth *is* my family!" Joan said. There was no way she was related to Eleanor. Eleanor had brutally converted Nick into a killer. She'd set him on a path to massacring all the monster families—including Joan's. She'd taunted Joan about the Hunts' deaths.

"Who are the Graves?" Tom said.

Eleanor's jaw tightened. "There are twelve monster families in London now," she said, "but there was once a thirteenth family—the Graves." A gust of wind blew from the river, rippling the base of her heavy dress. "Our territory was *here*—in the vicinity of London Bridge. Our back gardens were Borough Market and the original Globe."

Joan stared. Ying had told her about the Graves, but some part of her hadn't wanted to believe it.

"A thirteenth family?" Ruth said. Aaron looked confused too. Jamie alone was unsurprised. *Only the Lius remember that there was once another family.*

"Ruth . . . ," Joan said. Monster families weren't sorted by blood, but by power. Joan had the Grave power, and in the monster world that made her a Grave, not a Hunt. But *Ruth* would still think of Joan as her family, right? Joan thought of *Ruth* as family. She thought of herself as a Hunt.

"I don't understand," Ruth said. She turned to Eleanor. "You said *there was once*? What does that mean? Why haven't I heard of them?"

"Some people call it *Damnatio memoriae*," Eleanor said, and Aaron drew in a sharp, shocked breath in response. "The King punished the Graves by erasing them from the timeline." Eleanor turned back to that empty space in the sky where the Graves' house had once been. "He pulled us up by the roots for the most part. He killed our earliest ancestors so that their children and their children's children and *their* children were never born. And he didn't just punish us. . . . He murdered people in other families who protested, loyal friends, those who sheltered us. . . . By the end of it, if anyone remembered us, they didn't dare whisper our name."

"How did *you* survive?" Joan asked Eleanor. How had Joan survived?

Eleanor just stared at her, and Joan felt her own breath shudder out. She hated Eleanor—*hated her.* But she couldn't help but feel horror for her too. She knew what it was like to lose your whole family.

But . . . this was *Joan's* family too. She'd have been grieving them if she'd remembered them. If Eleanor was telling the truth, the King's punishment had worked on Joan. And she couldn't get her head around that. She felt horror and sympathy for that lost family and for the people who'd tried to protect them, but it wasn't visceral. It wasn't anything like what she'd felt when the Hunts had died.

No. That wasn't quite true. There was a resonance in her chest when she thought of the Graves, as if her body remembered what her mind didn't. She was reminded of the suppressed feeling that always came when she thought about Mum.

And did all this mean that Mum had been—

Joan pushed away the thought. She couldn't handle that right now.

"Erased," Aaron murmured. Joan could guess what he was thinking. This was why *his* mother had died—because she'd tried to protect a member of the Grave family. And Aaron himself had the true Oliver power—the ability to differentiate family from family. He'd been unknowingly tasked from childhood with finding the last of the Graves. To finish the erasure that the King had started.

It struck Joan then that Aaron had seen Eleanor as a Nightingale. Eleanor must have disguised herself from him somehow. . . .

Eleanor turned away from the empty sky, her blue eyes darkening with anguish, and for a split second, Joan could see everything that Eleanor had been holding inside. It was like glimpsing the void itself—a bottomless well of grief. And Joan's understanding suddenly reframed. She'd thought that Eleanor had wanted to take power from the King, but she saw now what Eleanor was really doing.

"You want to create a new timeline," Joan whispered, "because you want to bring them back." It was what Joan had done last time for the Hunts.

Eleanor's hands clenched into fists. "I *am* going to bring them back."

Joan herself had said something very much like that when the

Hunts had died. *We'll undo it*, she'd told Ruth. *We'll get them back.* How had she missed the jagged edge of Eleanor's icy exterior? How had she missed Eleanor's grief when she'd felt those feelings herself? Joan had had a one-track desperation after the massacre of the Hunts. *Nothing* would have stopped her from bringing them back.

Or would it have?

She saw again the tangled bodies in the van. The terror on the bystanders' faces.

There had to be a way to explain to Eleanor what Joan had seen. Eleanor wouldn't be bringing back the true timeline but ushering in something horrific. "You've been working to create a world where monsters rule," Joan said to her. "But if you just want to bring the Graves back, then—"

"What I want," Eleanor said, hard, "what I'm going to *take*, is a world where *no one* can hurt my family again. No human and no monster. I'm going to make a world where they'll survive, no matter what."

"Eleanor—" Joan said, and Eleanor's face crumpled a little. Joan hesitated, and then realized that she'd never said Eleanor's name in her presence.

"Do you really not know me?" Eleanor whispered to her. "Do you really not remember me at all?"

Joan was thrown by the non sequitur and by the momentary note of truce. She searched Eleanor's pretty face—a face from a fairy tale—trying to find *something* she recognized. But she didn't feel anything but distrust. Was this how Aaron had felt when Joan had told him that he'd once known *her*? The thought broke her heart.

And had Eleanor always been like this? She kept talking to Joan like they'd once been close. *It was* your *house*, she'd said. *We grew up there together.*

But . . .

Joan and Nick had been together in the true timeline, and Eleanor had torn them apart. She'd had Nick tortured and orphaned by a monster. She'd made him into a monster slayer, and then he'd led the massacre of Joan's family.

Eleanor *had* to have known that the timeline would keep forcing Joan and Nick back together after that. She'd broken the two of them so much that they'd keep hurting each other until one of them died. It was too cruel and too elegant to be an accident.

A shot of anger went through Joan again. "I know enough," she said. "I know you tried to destroy all our lives! I know you're still trying to!"

Anger flashed over Eleanor's own face then. The moment of softness was gone. "You never change," she snapped at Joan. "You always side with the wrong people." Her jaw tightened. "You think *I* ruined *your* life?"

"You *did*," Joan said. Why was Eleanor even questioning it? "You *know* you did."

Eleanor took a step toward her, and Nick twitched again. He wanted to make a move. His eyes flicked between a red-haired man behind Eleanor and a dark-haired woman. Both had guns focused on him.

"Do you know why the Graves were punished?" Eleanor asked Joan softly. "Do you know why the King erased our family from history?"

Ying hadn't known. Joan shook her head. She'd only just

learned that the Graves even existed. She felt herself tense up, though.

"It was because of *you*," Eleanor gritted out. "You and *him*." She looked at Nick. "Everything I'm doing now is because of *you*."

"What are you talking about?" Joan said, shaking her head. How could she and Nick be responsible for something that the King had done?

Eleanor's fists clenched. "The two of you convinced our family that there could be peace between humans and monsters. You convinced them to pursue it."

Joan felt her mouth drop open. Nick's forehead creased; he hadn't expected to hear that either. Even so, the truth of Eleanor's words rang through Joan like a bell.

Just before the end, Nick had offered Joan peace. He'd suggested exactly this—and Joan had rejected it. She'd unmade him.

Joan swallowed. She'd speculated that the Joan of the true timeline hadn't even known that she was a monster. How else could she have made her relationship with Nick work? But maybe *this* was how. Maybe she and Nick had tried to bring monsters and humans together. . . .

"*You* wanted to stop monsters from traveling," Eleanor said to Joan, and Joan tried to absorb that too. "The arrogance of you! Convincing our family to go against their own birthright!"

"They agreed to it?" Joan asked, shocked. From the flash of rage in Eleanor's face, they *had*. Joan couldn't imagine it. Could an entire monster family really have been persuaded that peace with humans was possible?

Who had the Graves *been* that they'd listened to Joan and

Nick? Joan felt a thrum again in her chest. An echo of the grief she couldn't consciously feel. The memory of the body.

"*You* disagreed," Aaron said to Eleanor. Joan blinked at him at his unexpected interjection.

"Monsters are *supposed* to travel in time," Eleanor said to him, chin lifting.

"It's no one's birthright to steal life," Nick said, just as hard. Eleanor's eyes darkened even more; Joan felt a thrill of fear. There were still guns trained on them all.

"So you informed on them to the King," Aaron said to Eleanor. And Joan was surprised by that too. She wouldn't have made that leap. She wasn't even sure it was true until Eleanor's expression turned defiant.

Aaron gazed at her coldly. He hated disloyalty.

"You told the Court?" Joan said to Eleanor. "You informed on us?"

"I got word to the King that there'd been peace talks with humans," Eleanor said. "I assumed he'd intervene and stop the talks. But—" Her voice failed. She made a visible effort to force more words out. "*You* put that idea in their heads," she whispered to Joan. "Our family would *never* have considered treating with humans if it wasn't for *you.*"

Joan opened her mouth, but nothing came out. She could picture it all too easily now. "The King didn't stop the talks," she said. She didn't even remember it happening, but she felt a sick rush of horror as if she had.

"The King saw only treason," Eleanor said. "He punished our whole family for something that *you* started!" Her feelings were naked on her face now. She blamed Joan for this; she *hated* her. "The King killed our family because of the two of *you*."

Joan had a flash again of Nick's torture: his broken nose, his broken arm. *Again*, Eleanor had said with relish. *Again*. Nick had been tortured over and over. *This* was why. This was why Eleanor had chosen Nick to be the hero, why she'd taken such pleasure in his pain.

"I wish I'd been there when Nick massacred the Hunts," Eleanor said to Joan softly, and Joan shuddered. "I wish I'd seen your face when you had to run for your life from him."

Nick made a soft noise as if he'd been stabbed. "That's why?" he breathed. Joan knew what he meant. He was asking if that was why she'd unmade the hero.

Joan couldn't even bring herself to nod. She could hardly take in what Eleanor had said.

Eleanor's eyes were like flint now as she stared Joan down. "This started with the two of you seeking peace between humans and monsters, so I turned you against each other. I made him into a slayer. Someone who'd hurt you—who you'd hurt—until neither of you could bear it anymore. So that you would feel a *sliver* of how I feel every day of my life." She gave Joan a small, furious smile. "I made him into a slayer because you loved him and he loved you. Because if he killed the people you loved most, you'd never trust him again. Because when you fought back, he'd see you for the monster you are. He'd never trust *you*. And it worked, didn't it? You'll never be able to seek peace again. You'll never really feel the same about each other again."

Joan was plunged right back into her worst memories: Gran's

rasping breaths; Gran's blood sinking into the carpet; the look on Nick's face when he'd seen his brothers and sisters, his parents, dead.

Another sound from Nick. This one deep in his throat.

"I wanted to hurt you, but that wasn't the only reason I made him into a slayer," Eleanor said.

Joan's throat was so tight that swallowing was painful. "*Why*, then?"

"I told you." Eleanor's voice sounded as tight as Joan's. "I'm bringing back our family."

Joan shook her head. She didn't understand. How could any of this bring back the Graves?

"Why would a monster create a monster slayer?" Eleanor's tone was almost mocking.

It was the question Joan had kept asking herself. It had never made sense to her. Nick hadn't killed monsters in targeted assassinations. He'd massacred monsters indiscriminately. How could that be part of any plan?

"After the King erased our family," Eleanor said, "I went looking for *him*." She nodded at Nick. "He didn't remember me, of course." To Nick, she said, "I had someone beat you up. They broke your nose. It was more satisfying than you'd believe."

Nick's expression didn't change. "Brave of you."

Eleanor shrugged. "I used my Grave power to undo the beating. At the end of it, you were unbruised and your nose was unbroken. That was *less* satisfying, but it was proof."

"Proof of what?" Joan said.

"That the timeline would allow her to make a change." It was

Tom who'd spoken. He'd figured it out first.

"A very small change," Eleanor agreed. "An insignificant change. I had to do it slowly to make sure that the timeline didn't figure out what I was really up to. I broke Nick's bones over and over. Fixed them over and over. I killed his family and brought them back." A flinch from Nick at that. "And then I did it all over again."

Joan had a flash of Nick again with a broken nose. Nick crying. Nick screaming. Nick begging for his family's lives. *Again*, Eleanor had said. *Again. Again.* And Nick had been tortured in a whole new way. *Again.* Eleanor had hurt him and reset him and hurt him again.

"Why?" Joan ground out.

"I had a theory," Eleanor said, "that if I could change someone's personal history over and over, the timeline would eventually lose its grip on them. I remember the first time that he killed a monster without the timeline trying to fix it." She laughed. The note of triumph made Joan shiver. "That was when I knew I'd done it. I'd made a weak point on the timeline."

Ying had said that events could be changed at weak points on the timeline. *Nick* was a weak point?

"I'd made someone who could change the timeline at will," Eleanor said. "And I made him *perfect*." She turned to Nick again. "You were *perfect*. I had a monster kill your family so that you would hate us. Hate *Joan*. And then I had you trained into the perfect monster slayer. The perfect human hero. My work of art." She wasn't even mocking this time; it was sincere. Some part of her saw him as her masterpiece.

Nick stared Eleanor down, as cold as Joan had ever seen him.

"You went after monsters with a righteous fury," Eleanor said to Nick as if she hadn't noticed his expression. "Every time you killed a monster, you became even more detached from the timeline. Even more capable of change."

"It didn't matter who he killed," Joan said slowly. "It was the killing that mattered. You only wanted him more and more free of the constrictions of the timeline."

Joan thought of how Aaron had thrown a stone into the canal and told them to watch the ripples fading. She imagined Nick now as a ripple that couldn't be smoothed over. The changes he'd caused stayed changed. She shivered.

It hit her then that *she'd* changed the timeline by unmaking Nick. Was that why she'd been able to do it? Because Nick was special? Because he was a weak point on the timeline?

"What did you make me *for*?" Nick said, jolting Joan from her thoughts. "What change did you want me to make? You need me to bring back the Graves? *How? What am I supposed to do?*"

Eleanor's smile was small and private like she was laughing at an inside joke.

"Why did you bring us *here*?" Joan said suddenly. She'd been expecting Eleanor to try to change a significant event. To change *something*. But she'd just been standing here, talking to them.

"Honestly?" Eleanor said. "I could have done this anywhere. But I thought it would be poetic to change the timeline where the King did it. To bring our family back here—on our own territory—in the very place where he killed the first of us. And when I create the new timeline, no one will touch our family again. Not the King. Not humans. Not anyone."

Joan's next breath shook. She saw Eleanor's full vision now.

The timeline they'd seen through the window wasn't a mistake. Its horrors weren't a terrible by-product of Eleanor's plan to bring back the Graves. That world would be *exactly* as Eleanor wished it to be.

Eleanor wanted to create a world where the Graves would never again question what she'd called their *birthright*: a world where monsters would steal life with impunity; where humans and monsters would never imagine coming together in peace; where nothing like the past would ever happen again.

And maybe the Graves would live again, but it would be a nightmare for humans. Joan pictured that terrible street: the blond man's terror and his resignation. He'd known that the monster would drain his life; he'd known that his body would be tossed into the back of the van like rubbish.

"We won't let you create a world where monsters reign," Nick said to Eleanor, anger thickening his voice.

He was right. "We can't let you do it," Joan said.

Eleanor's mouth twisted. "You really do always choose the wrong side, Joan."

Before Joan could even think of the next step, there was a blur of movement to her right. Nick rushed at Eleanor, and Tom was just a moment behind. They'd been in quiet communication while Eleanor had been talking.

Almost as fast, they were both thrown violently back into the alley by an invisible force.

"Tom!" Jamie said, reaching for him.

Joan scrambled to Nick unthinkingly. He was already getting to his feet. Tom had fallen on his side to prevent Frankie from being crushed. She jumped out of Tom's knapsack, her stubby tail wagging as if Tom had been playing a game.

Tom glared at a dark-haired woman standing behind Eleanor with her hands raised.

"Quite the master of the Ali power," Tom growled at the woman.

"I don't want to kill you, Tom Hathaway," the woman said to him. "I know your sister is an Ali."

"That's your one warning," Eleanor said to them matter-of-factly. "Try that again, and someone gets shot." She looked meaningfully at Jamie and then Joan, and Tom made a rumbling sound at the back of his throat. Nick glared at Eleanor like he was going to kill her.

"There's no point in fighting me anyway," Eleanor said. "The change is already in motion. It started when you brought him here."

"What?" Joan said.

In answer, Eleanor took a step back from them and lifted her eyes. The sky had lightened to dull white. Shouldn't it have been brighter by now, though? It hit Joan that she hadn't heard any background sounds for some minutes: the river and the docks had gone silent. Near St. Magnus, a steamship had been pulling from the wharf. Now it was unmoving. Gray smoke stood above its chimney in a frozen swirl.

Eleanor saw Joan staring. "You are so far out of your league in this timeline," she said almost gently. "Have you even figured out your own powers yet? What you can do?" She swiped at the air, the gesture almost dismissive. And as she did, the familiar, unbearable buzz of dissonance hit.

Joan gasped as she realized what Eleanor had just done. There'd been an Ali seal above them this whole time. Eleanor had opened it as easily as wiping steam from glass. She was *so* much stronger than Joan had understood. And, by opening the seal, she'd revealed a vast tear in the timeline above them.

Aaron groaned with nausea. Jamie and Ruth bent double next. Even Nick paled.

The tears at the café and at Holland House had been tiny in comparison. This one rent the sky—a scar of blue among white clouds.

Eleanor's hands were up, and Joan could almost see the power streaming from her, ripping open the seal to reveal more and more of that torn sky.

"Close that seal back up!" Tom said. "Close it *now*, before that tear gets bigger!"

Could Joan do something? She focused on the flame of power inside herself, and she hurled it at Eleanor's hands, trying to undo her stream of power at its source.

"Stop that!" Eleanor snapped at her. "*Stop it!*" Her tone reminded Joan weirdly of Ruth's when they'd argued as kids. The irritated tone you'd use on family.

She was so annoyed that Joan realized with a jolt that her own blast of power must have done *something*. She concentrated. Eleanor's power was almost visible, like heat distortion in the air.

Joan hurled her power again at Eleanor, and this time she

tried to keep up a steady flow of it.

"Stop it!" Eleanor said again. Maybe it was working.

But then Eleanor's power roared to life—a wall of fire to Joan's flame. Joan gasped—she could almost feel it as real heat, and her own power couldn't compete.

"You'd really fight me on this?" Eleanor said to her thickly. "After you sacrificed everything to save the Hunts? If you remembered your *real* family, you'd be doing anything to bring *them* back!" Her expression crumpled again for just a moment. "God, look at what the King did! *Our whole family is gone.* And you don't remember them at all! You don't miss them at all! You don't feel anything!"

That wasn't quite true. Joan did feel something—pressure thrummed deep in her chest again. Maybe Eleanor was right. Maybe if Joan *could* remember the Graves, she'd have been fighting for them too.

But she could only act on what she knew. "*You* need to stop!" she said to Eleanor. "That world is *wrong.* I *saw* it! You'll make people suffer!"

"It's going to engulf us!" Tom said. Joan looked up dizzily and saw that uncanny blue sky bearing down on them.

A rumble rippled through them all suddenly—more earthquake than thunder. It reverberated through Joan's bones in a long, long bass note.

Eleanor's head snapped up.

"What was that?" Ruth whispered.

"What was what?" Nick said, and Joan realized that it hadn't actually been a sound. Only the monsters had sensed it.

"No," Eleanor breathed.

The air in front of Joan blazed. She flinched away, shielding her eyes, and then realized that the brightness wasn't something she could actually see. It was an interpretation by her monster sense.

A man was stepping out of the air. He exuded so much power that looking at him felt like looking into the face of the sun.

Joan's eyes watered with the effort of trying to see him. He was handsome, but she couldn't make out much more than that. Her perceptions seemed to be oscillating. He seemed old and young at the same time; terrible and benign; cheerful and grave.

The man spoke. Joan had expected his voice to match his presence—to be a rumble of thunder—but he sounded surprisingly human. He addressed Eleanor. "Did you really believe that I'd allow this? Did you believe I wouldn't know? I am aware of every moment, every ripple, in the timeline."

Beside Joan, Aaron drew in a sharp, shocked breath as if he'd realized who the man was. He collapsed to his knees and dropped his head into a bow. He wasn't the only one. Eleanor's allies were lowering their guns and falling to the ground, prone, their arms outstretched.

"Joan," the man said. "You sent a message to the Court. You sent for Conrad to save you." He lifted his hand, swatting lazily at the sky. And the timeline responded like an obedient pet; the blue gash above vanished as if it had never been there, zipping itself back into white sky. Joan gasped at the immense power of it.

"You sent for Conrad," the man said again. "But I rather think you need a king."

THIRTY-SEVEN

The King stood outside the alley, his back to the river. He was a bear-like figure, taller and broader even than Tom. Or was he? Joan's perceptions of him kept changing: he was old and young, his face lined and smooth; he wore prehistoric furs or maybe a futuristic suit. And Joan had thought that Eleanor and her allies were strong, but the King's power spilled from him like sunshine. It was difficult to look at him directly; Joan's eyes kept sliding away.

"What have you *done*?" Eleanor whispered to Joan.

Joan couldn't answer. She'd asked Ying to get a message to Conrad, saying that Eleanor had turned against the King. She hadn't imagined that the King himself would arrive. This man hadn't just murdered the Graves—he'd erased them from memory. His presence here was even more frightening than Eleanor's.

"Those on their knees may rise," the King said in his oddly human voice. "And then you will all stay where you are." It was conversational, but Joan felt it as a press of power, an order impossible to disobey.

She started to shift her weight, and then realized with a wave of horror that she couldn't lift her feet from the ground. It didn't feel like mind control; it felt like her shoes had melded with the wooden walkway. She tried to slip her shoes off and couldn't make them slide at all. Trying not to panic, she lifted her arms just to see if she could. A rush of relief ran through her. Only her feet were trapped.

Was this what the Argent power felt like to humans? Was this what it had felt like to Nick? She turned to him, but he just looked grim as he tested his own feet and found himself stuck too.

Between them, Aaron stood shakily. As he settled, Joan saw his feet freeze too. He shuddered. The bare skin of his neck was a pale line above his shirt collar. He turned that collar up now.

Joan was halfway through flipping up her own collar before she recognized the unconscious need to protect her neck too. Looking down the line, all the others were doing the same thing. Did they all feel it? The spine prickle of primal danger from the King? Joan's body thought she was too close to a predatory animal. She could almost smell a musk scent. And she couldn't run.

"Sweet Eleanor," the King said, and Eleanor stared back at him defiantly. She seemed more able than Joan to look the King in the face, but her feet were glued to the ground just like everyone else's. And that sent another pulse of fear down Joan's spine. Eleanor was the most feared member of the *Curia Monstrorum*. She'd brought allies here with the power to freeze the world around them, to wield the rare Ali power like a weapon, and who knew what else. And yet just a few words from the King had subdued her.

"Did you truly think that your sister needed to send for me?" the King said. "I see every event on the timeline, every fluctuation. I knew the moment you sought to betray me."

Sister?

For a long, long moment, the word didn't make any kind of

sense. *Joan* had sent for help. Why had the King referenced Eleanor's sister?

Eleanor saw Joan's confused expression, and her lips pressed until they whitened.

And then Joan could only stare at Eleanor's pretty face, her waves of golden hair, her cornflower-blue eyes. Why wasn't Eleanor contradicting this? They *couldn't* be sisters. They looked nothing alike. And . . . some part of Joan would have remembered her. Surely.

"I rewarded you for your loyalty once," the King said to Eleanor. "I granted you life. I granted you membership in my Court."

"You call that a reward?" Eleanor said. "Keeping me alive after you erased my family from existence? Bestowing me with this sigil? The Graves were the most powerful family in London, and now no one even remembers our name." She turned to Joan, and her expression was so full of emotion that Joan couldn't look away. "My own sister doesn't remember me," Eleanor said hoarsely.

"I'm not your sister," Joan blurted, and Eleanor took a visibly shaky breath, as if Joan's words had actually hurt her.

They really couldn't be sisters. Eleanor had done things Joan would never understand. She'd tortured Nick and Jamie. She'd hurt the people Joan loved most. She'd trained Nick and set him loose on the world. He'd massacred hundreds and hundreds—maybe thousands—of monsters. Joan's own family included.

Eleanor had taunted Joan about it. She'd locked her up in a cell.

"We grew up together," Eleanor said to Joan. Was there a shake in her voice? "You're only here because I am."

Joan was aware of the others listening—even the King. But she could only look at Eleanor. Stuck fast in place like the rest of them and dwarfed by the King's bulk, Eleanor seemed smaller than she had before. The world was still frozen around them, and without any breeze, her straight-cut medieval dress hung limply.

"I don't believe you," Joan said honestly, and *again* Eleanor looked as if Joan had hurt her feelings.

"The King rewarded me with life," Eleanor said. "To grant me that, he had to preserve my entire line—every ancestor down to my mother. *Our* mother."

"My mum was Maureen Hunt."

"*Our* mother was Maureen *Grave*! She was marked for assassination as soon as I was born. But . . ." Eleanor's voice faltered for a moment. "Mum was always clever. There were rumors that she'd escaped—that a Nightingale had saved her. That she'd gotten out through a series of safe houses."

Joan found herself turning, shaken, to Aaron. His mouth parted slightly, and his eyes widened. His mother had been a Nightingale, and she'd been executed for helping someone like Joan. A member of the Grave family, Joan knew now.

Aaron's mother had had a safe house in Southwark. . . . Had she saved Joan's mother? Joan pictured the two of them cowering there in the dark, knowing the King was hunting them down. . . .

"Mum must have found your dad again after she escaped," Eleanor said to Joan. "They'd belonged together in the *zhēnshí de lìshǐ*, and so the timeline would have brought them back together. And then . . . I suppose she sought refuge with the Hunts. I should have guessed. Or maybe I shouldn't have—she and Gran never really did get on."

"Gran?"

"Dorothy Hunt," Eleanor said. "She's my grandmother too. To be honest, though, I never got on with her either. Mum used to say we were too alike. Spiky peas in a pod."

She didn't sound like she was lying, but Joan couldn't process it. *Nothing* about Eleanor was familiar. Not her precise, mannered way of speaking; not her doll-like features; not her casual cruelty. And at the same time, Joan had a flash of Nick introducing himself as if they'd never met. Of herself standing in that little airless room with Aaron, begging him to believe that he'd once known her.

We grew up together, Eleanor had said. And she'd known things about Joan—she knew how Joan thought. And . . . "You knew how Gran planned jobs," Joan said slowly. "You said it was a ten-day minimum." How could Eleanor have known that? Gran didn't share secrets like that with anyone but her own blood.

Sisters. Could it be true? Joan shook her head, trying to clear it.

As Joan stood there, blankly, the King turned toward the north bank and waved a casual hand. Around them, London leaped back to life, the water of the Thames lapping again at the foreshore, a ship's horn faintly sounding. On the other side of the river, the steamship pulled farther from the wharf. The buggy-like cars and unwieldy buses of 1923 rolled along the bridge.

With the King's back to Joan, the sensation of staring into the sun wasn't as pronounced. Even so, her perceptions of him were still shifting from moment to moment. Who *was* he? What family had he originally been from? What abilities must he wield that Aaron and even Eleanor's allies—with all their powers—were staring at him half-fearful, half-worshipful?

Joan had been experiencing the timeline as a force lately. Now, though, it felt more like a great beast, leashed by the King's presence but not tamed. Aaron had once told her that the King and the timeline were one and the same. But, in the King's presence, Joan sensed some stubborn core of rebellion from the timeline. It didn't like being tethered and, every now and then, there was a faint jolt in the air, as if it were tugging at its leash.

"An interesting choice of location," the King commented. "I must admit, I'd quite forgotten that the erasure of the Graves started here." He turned back to them, and Joan's eyes watered as she tried to keep looking at the glare of him. "Follow me." His cheerful tone felt sinister.

The word *sister* kept echoing in Joan's head as she was forced with the others to shuffle out of the alley, eastward along the river. She registered, vaguely, that the wharf was cleaner than it had been in 1891. A wooden walkway had replaced the mud of the foreshore. Creepily, the dozen dockworkers they passed seemed unaware of the strange procession walking by them.

Nick caught her eye. She could see how much he wanted to speak to her—away from all this. His expression was wary, though, and Joan thought about what Eleanor had said. *I made him into a slayer because you loved him and he loved you. Because if he killed the people you loved most, you'd never trust him again. Because when you fought back, he'd see you for the monster you are. He'd never trust you. And it worked, didn't it? You'll never really feel the same about each other again.*

"We can stop here." The King phrased it as optional, but they all stumbled to a halt, their feet sticking again.

They'd ended up near where City Pier would one day be. Rowboats and barges bobbed in the water.

Joan tested her feet again but couldn't move them. What did she have on her? There was a knife in the inner pocket of her jacket. She undid a button, and then felt a flare of too-hot attention from the King and the impression of brief amusement.

"No," he said simply.

Joan saw then a scatter of guns and knives along the path they'd just walked. Eleanor's people had dropped their weapons along the way.

An ancient god-king, Nick had called him. Joan had thought Eleanor and her people were powerful, but the King did seem more god than man.

"In the original timeline, the old bridge lasted somewhat longer, didn't it?" the King said to Eleanor conversationally.

"Up to the twenty-third century," Eleanor said tightly. "It was rebuilt a few times along the way."

"What are we doing here?" Joan dared to ask. Why had the King moved them up the river? Just as he was still alternating between old and young, he seemed both capricious and considered. Joan couldn't figure him out. Was he going to kill them all? Spare them? She'd never felt more off-balance; more powerless.

"There's a better view from here," the King said. He barely looked at Joan as he said it, but again his brief attention was a flare of light. Joan flinched, closing her eyes automatically.

When she reopened them, the King's back was to them all. He pinched at the air, and Joan had the impression that he was tearing away a swath of wallpaper. Barely pausing, the King reached into the air again, and made another tearing motion.

Eleanor half gasped, half groaned. Joan stared.

Old London Bridge suddenly stood upriver—a palatial street of carved and gabled Renaissance buildings, more beautiful in life than any of the illustrations Joan had seen. The structure beneath was breathtaking too—a huge stone span with nineteen arches, each supported by boat-shaped wooden piers.

"There it is," the King said, as if Eleanor hadn't just made that agonized sound. "The Graves' territory, as it once was."

"We're looking at the true timeline, aren't we?" Tom whispered. "The *vera historia*."

Joan understood then. The King had torn a hole in the timeline. There was no feeling of dissonance, though; no jagged edges in the air, no shadows from the void. And maybe that, more than anything, was a hint of the King's true power.

Eleanor's eyes shone with tears, and then Joan understood too why the King had brought them *here*. This spot offered a perfect viewing angle. *In the original timeline, the old bridge lasted somewhat longer, didn't it?* he'd said.

The window had no visible edges. The illusion that the bridge still existed was almost perfect. The only discontinuities were cars vanishing as they reached the north and south banks. If Joan hadn't known better, though, she'd have thought that she could walk to the bridge in just a few minutes.

Her chest constricted at the thought. She'd told herself that she didn't remember anything of the Grave family, but there *was* something familiar about Old London Bridge, about the close-built configuration of the houses. She somehow knew the red-gabled roofs and white walls.

From here, she could just make out the carved arch that ran through the ground level of all the buildings so that vehicles and pedestrians could get across the bridge. And she couldn't see what was inside that arch, but she had a vivid memory of walking under it, past shops with swinging signs charmingly illustrated with parasols and books and gloves, past slow-moving cars; being held up by wandering tourists; looking up to see balcony gardens, bright with overhanging flowers.

Now her gaze hit the mansion in the middle of it all. The Graves' house. Her heart stopped. It was taller than the buildings around it. And the other houses were traditional, but this was a tiny exuberant castle with square turrets and meringue-shaped cupolas and huge arching windows. Joan didn't know where to look—at the gilded columns or at the walls and trims, brightly painted in red and green and yellow.

"Remind me," the King said. "What did the sundials on the roof say?"

"Time and tide stay for no man," Eleanor said shakily, and Joan felt another thrum of resonance at those words. Eleanor's gaze stayed yearningly on the house. "It's not really here, is it?" she said heavily. Her eyes shone with unshed tears.

"This is just an echo of what was here," the King agreed. "An afterimage on a screen. The original timeline is gone. I erased it." He pretended to think. "What do you blasphemers call it? The *zhēnshí de lìshǐ*? The *vera historia*? The *true timeline*?" He added, mock-gently, "But what have I been thinking? You won't recognize anyone here—this isn't your time. You and your sister were raised in a later age." He snapped his fingers, and the view inside the window darkened. Joan finally saw the extent of the window—it was bigger than she'd realized. The size of a house. Inside it, the moon rose and fell, followed by the sun rising and falling too, the cycle quickening, until the image was a blur. Then the King snapped his fingers again, and it all stopped. Joan felt her mouth drop open.

The view still showed the true timeline—with its elaborate bridge—but the date seemed to have advanced to sometime in the twenty-first century. Modern cars crawled across the road.

"*Oh*," Eleanor said, hard and breathless, as if she'd been punched.

On the walkway, people had appeared too, strolling up and down: tourists with shopping bags labeled *Bookshop on the Bridge* and *Bridge Bakery* and *Drawbridge Gifts*. Among them, locals walked their dogs and carried fruit and vegetables in market bags. Eleanor stared openmouthed at a man hurrying in the direction of the Tube station. Then her eyes flicked to a girl with pink hair. Then to a man in a tailored suit. Realization jolted through Joan. These were members of the Grave family. People Eleanor had once known. People Joan must have known. They all wore the same sigil, as a pin on a lapel, a tattoo on a bare shoulder, a motif on a shirt: a silver rose.

Bestowing me with this sigil, Eleanor had said, and Joan understood then Eleanor's strained tone. The King had given her a new sigil: a thorned rose stem without the flower. A reminder, always, of what she'd lost. Of what had been done to the Graves.

Beside Aaron, Nick shifted, and Joan realized that while she'd been staring, Nick had been subtly struggling with the King's bonds, trying to free himself.

But just as she observed that, Nick froze. His face was blank, but his eyes were suddenly alight, like he was trying to keep a handle on some strong emotion.

Trepidation curled inside Joan. She followed his gaze to the walkway. To the lost people from the true timeline.

She gasped.

It was Nick. The *original* Nick. Through the window that the King had made, he was strolling casually up the walkway, his pace and posture relaxed.

Joan was hit with a feeling of bone-deep recognition. His dark hair was long enough to make soft curls. Joan had never seen it that length, but she somehow knew what it felt like to push her hands into the thick silk of it; what it felt like to have his hands cup her waist at the same time.

He was holding hands now with someone who seemed familiar, and it took Joan a weirdly long moment to recognize herself. The original Joan.

They both looked *so* different. Joan's hair was shorter than she'd ever cut it, floating just above her shoulders. But it was more than that. Their other selves seemed easier somehow. Comfortable within themselves. Unconflicted.

The original Joan said something to Nick that made him laugh. He leaned down to kiss her, soft and intimate. When he pulled back, he and Joan smiled at each other, open and trusting, and so in love that Joan's chest hurt with yearning. They were looking at each other as if nothing could ever go wrong. As if no one could ever hurt them.

As Joan watched, their heads turned away from the bridge. Someone had called to them, she guessed. And from the way they lit up, from their open postures, it was someone they'd been waiting for, someone they were eager to be with. Joan glanced back over her shoulder to see who it was, but the window into the true timeline wasn't visible behind her. The only person in her line of sight was Aaron, in his 1920s suit, pristine and perfect, as always, amid all this chaos.

The King snapped his fingers then. Joan turned back fast, but he'd already closed the window. She heard herself make a shaken sound.

It was all gone. The Graves. Old London Bridge. The original Joan and Nick. All that remained was 1923, with its boats and cranes.

Joan could still see the other Joan and Nick in her mind's eye, though. How happy they'd been. . . .

She turned instinctively now to *this* Nick. His eyes were still on the walkway too. And . . . Joan's breath caught. He looked cracked open and *raw*. It lasted for just a moment. By the time he turned to meet her eyes, his expression was closed again.

His name started in her mouth, but the King spoke over her.

"A last gift for you," the King said to Eleanor. "And now, come here." He beckoned her over.

Eleanor had been looking on the span of the water where the old bridge had stood. Now she was forced to turn away from it; to shuffle to the King. He stopped her, with a raised hand, a few paces from him.

Joan's heart stuttered. Eleanor and the King had ended up in the center of a loose circle of Joan's allies and Eleanor's. What was about to happen?

Joan had come here to stop Eleanor—even if that had meant killing her. But . . . having seen that lost family, the thought of watching Eleanor die right here, right now, seemed too much.

Eleanor had been cruel and vengeful. She'd done things that Joan would never forgive. But at the same time, Joan knew what it felt like to lose your family, to want them back so badly that you lost yourself.

Joan had lost herself last time. She'd been thinking of Eleanor as alien, someone whose actions and cruelty had been incomprehensible. But was she so different from Joan, really? Eleanor had gone to extremes to bring her family back, but so had Joan. Joan had stolen decades of human life. She'd dragged Ruth and Aaron from danger to danger—into the Monster Court itself—in the hope of bringing her family back. And at the end . . . she hadn't thought about it consciously, but some part of her must have known that bringing monsters back—her family back—would cost human lives.

And maybe that was the real proof that Joan and Eleanor were sisters. Maybe it ran in the family.

"I was never loyal to you," Eleanor told the King, her voice tight. "I've been working against you since the moment I woke up in this sick timeline."

The King emanated paternal indulgence. "You never had a chance against me. You must have known that. You should have tried to forget them."

"I guess it's not in my nature to let things go."

Something in her tone made Joan pause. Eleanor was on the cusp of death, and yet . . . she was unafraid. Her chin was up; her expression was calm. She had the air of someone at the end of a long journey.

Eleanor seemed to feel Joan's gaze. She looked over at her and smiled. There was a shine of triumph in her blue eyes, and Joan thought suddenly about how Eleanor had ambushed her. How meticulous she'd been in crafting Nick into a slayer.

"You're so predictable, Joan," Eleanor said softly.

What? Joan felt a curl of unease.

"I know how you think," Eleanor said to Joan. "You always have a backup plan. To defeat someone like me, you'd want another member of the *Curia Monstrorum*. So you sent for Conrad."

Joan wet her dry lips. She didn't nod, but Eleanor was right. It was disconcerting to be known so thoroughly by someone who'd been using that knowledge against her.

Eleanor turned to the King. "And I know *you*. I've had a long time to observe you. You'd never trust any member of the Court with a job like this. Joan called for Conrad. You should have let him come in your stead."

"And why is that?" the King said.

Eleanor leaned closer. She was still pinned to the ground like everyone else, but she didn't seem to care. "Why do you think you're here?" Eleanor said to him. Behind her, the tide was rising. Tied-up rowboats rocked with the waves.

The King still emanated amusement. "You know why I'm here." He looked at each of Eleanor's allies. "Mariam Ali," he said. "Joseph Nightingale. Adriana Portelli. Shalini Patel . . ." He named all of them with the heavy note of a death sentence. "You should have kept your oaths to me."

"You think you came here to execute us," Eleanor said.

"Of course," the King said.

"No," Eleanor said so seriously that Joan shivered. "I'm going to undo what you did. I'm going to bring my family home. Right here, on our own territory."

Joan stared at Eleanor. She was starting to see it now. Eleanor had lured the King here, just like she'd lured Joan. She was going to unmake him, like Joan had unmade Nick.

Eleanor guessed what Joan was thinking. "No," she said to her. "Unmaking him would bring our family back. But I want more than that. I want to create a new timeline that will keep them safe *forever*. And for that, I need what he has." She looked the King dead in the face without any hint of discomfort or pain from the glare of his presence. "Complete control of the timeline."

A feeling of indulgence from the King. He didn't seem to have realized that Eleanor was serious. "You'd have to kill me to take control," he said.

"Yes," Eleanor said. "You're here for *your* execution."

THIRTY-EIGHT

"Really?" the King drawled as Eleanor drew a knife from her belt. Joan had the impression that he'd allowed her to draw it. Maybe he had so much power that he thought this mild excitement was worth entertaining. "What are you going to do with that?" he said. The feeling of bright light was so intense now that Joan flinched from him and saw the others wincing too. Even Eleanor looked away. "The truth is," the King said, "I can't be killed. Not by you and not by nature. I'm so entwined with the timeline that we're essentially the same entity."

Were they? Joan's impression was still of the timeline as a separate creature, unwillingly leashed to the King.

"I can't kill you by my own hand," Eleanor agreed. She held up the knife. It was exquisite: silver-bladed with gold roses worked into the hilt. More roses and leaves curled up the flat of the blade. "Only someone unbound from the timeline can do it."

Joan drew a sharp breath at that. Eleanor threw the knife on the ground. It lay gleaming, close to Nick, but just out of his reach. Nick took an unthinking step toward it.

"Nick," Joan said uncertainly.

Nick's eyes widened as if he'd only just realized that he'd taken that step. He tilted his head, clearly unsure how he'd overcome the King's compulsion. Then, very slowly, he bent to pick up the knife.

The King stared at Nick, disturbed, as if he was looking at something uncanny. He lifted a hand in a lazy gesture—to disarm Nick, Joan guessed. When Nick didn't drop the knife, the King took a step toward him and repeated the gesture. Still, nothing happened.

"I couldn't kill you by my own hand," Eleanor told the King again. "So I made someone who could. Someone who'd be free from the timeline; free from *you*. I made a monster slayer to kill a monster king."

The King shot her an alarmed look. He gestured again. This time, Joan felt him drawing power from the timeline. It didn't come easily—the great beast dragged at its leash. The King gathered what he could and threw it at Nick.

"No!" Joan strained, trying to free her feet.

But the King's power washed over Nick without effect.

The King stared, clearly taken aback. He was so perturbed that his radiance actually dimmed. For a moment, Joan could almost see his face. He was handsome, younger than she'd expected, and strangely familiar. Where had she seen those features before?

"What did you *do*?" the King said to Eleanor, shaken.

"You can feel it now, can't you?" Eleanor said to him. "How Nick's proximity alone weakens the timeline around him." She smiled slightly. "And since you and the timeline are one and the same, he weakens you too."

The King started to move toward her and then gasped. He dragged at his foot but couldn't seem to move it from the walkway.

"I brought some powerful people with me," Eleanor said. "To

keep you under control while Nick kills you."

"No," Joan ground out. Nick *couldn't* kill the King. Eleanor couldn't create that timeline, even if it meant bringing back the Graves.

"I know," Nick said to Joan, his gaze steady. Joan took a relieved breath. They were on the same page about that, at least. "We saw the world that you want to create," Nick said to Eleanor seriously. "None of us is going to help you make it."

"Well, I didn't expect you would," Eleanor said to him. "Not without an incentive." She bent to pick up one of the discarded guns. The King snarled but seemed unable to stop her now.

"I think you need me alive more than you need me dead," Nick said.

"True," Eleanor said. "But I don't need *her* alive." The muzzle of the gun moved to Joan. "I brought you here for a reason too, Joan."

Joan didn't even have a chance to react, to feel scared. Nick hurled the knife—not at the King, but at Eleanor—lethal and accurate.

It should have struck Eleanor in the chest, but it stopped in midair, the hilt quivering like the shaft of a shot arrow. It had hit an invisible barrier and stuck there. Behind Eleanor, the Ali woman had her hands raised. She'd been ready for it.

Eleanor had barely flinched. "Oh, Nick," she said softly. "You're rather predictable too."

Nick stalked up to the barrier, his dark eyes on her. He looked as dangerous as any of the powerful people Eleanor had brought with her.

Eleanor only smiled. She put her hand on the barrier, where the point of the blade was. "You know," she said, her tone nostalgic, "I had you for a long time." Joan felt her own eyes narrow at that. "Not just our three weeks together at Holland House," Eleanor said. "I had you for years last time. We got to know each other *very* well. I know what you're like when you're pushed to the limit. *I* pushed you to those limits." Her intimate tone made Joan's stomach turn. "I pushed you beyond them. I know everything you're capable of. I know you stripped to the core and raw."

"I don't remember you at all," Nick said coldly.

Eleanor seemed to react slightly to his tone. She shrugged it off. "You don't need to remember. I know *you*. And I know you're going to take that knife and kill the King." Her mouth twisted slightly. "Or I'm going to kill my sister."

"You *can't* kill him," Joan whispered to Nick. To her relief, Nick nodded slightly in acknowledgment. Joan released a breath she hadn't realized she'd been holding.

Joan glanced at the King. Trapped in place like the rest of them, he seemed more beast than man now, growling and struggling like a bear.

"I'm going to count to three," Eleanor said to Nick. "And then you'll choose." She put her other hand on the gun, steadying her aim.

Ruth said something to Eleanor. She sounded desperate, but Joan couldn't make out the words; couldn't really hear anything but her own pounding heart. She took a ragged breath. She wished she could move. Her feet had stuck down a little too close together, and her left calf was starting to cramp.

"*Nick*," Aaron said. "Don't do this!"

Joan turned to him. Aaron's gray eyes were just like they'd been at the market—thundercloud dark. He usually dampened his visible emotions, but Joan could see anger and helplessness—and something more.

"It's okay," Joan whispered to him. She wanted to tell Aaron how glad she was that they'd reconciled in this timeline; how glad she was to have seen him again. How much she'd missed him. But she couldn't find the words. "It has to be this way."

Aaron looked like he wanted to argue, but instead he reached for her hand. Joan closed her eyes and held on tight, grateful for the comfort of his touch.

"One," Eleanor said.

Joan gripped Aaron's hand. Nick wasn't going to kill the King. He'd never usher in a timeline where monsters ruled. He'd never allow humans to suffer. And the knowledge of that was weirdly calming. Joan took a deep breath.

"Two," Eleanor said.

Nick would have stopped Eleanor in the previous timeline— that was what Astrid had said. And he was going to stop her now too. Eleanor had picked the wrong person for this role. She didn't understand that Nick *always* chose the greater good. Always.

"Three," Eleanor said, and Joan opened her eyes.

With a growl, Nick wrenched the knife from the air. He threw it viciously, and Joan flinched away from the anticipated pain.

But there was no pain.

The knife flew past her to the King.

For a long, long moment, Joan was frozen. The wash of water filled the silence.

She couldn't understand what she was seeing. The knife was embedded in the King's chest, blood blooming across his shirt.

The King collapsed to his knees, forehead dropping to the ground in a strange parody of the cowering bows he'd received when he'd arrived here. He might have seemed like a god at times, but apparently he was man enough to bleed; man enough to fall.

Joan shifted, and only realized that her foot had moved when she heard her heel scrape against the wooden walkway. She looked down at her foot and then back at the King.

Slumped over, he seemed smaller and more ordinary suddenly. The bright emanation of light had left him, and the oscillating effect was gone too. He wore a black suit—maybe twenty-first century in style. Blood pooled around him, dripping through the gaps in the wooden walkway.

Joan took a testing step. Her foot lifted clear of the walkway. She wasn't pinned anymore. And her freedom could only mean one thing.

The King was dead.

Nick had killed him.

Joan turned to Nick, and his eyes locked on hers, hard and dark. Joan stared. He'd thrown that knife without hesitation, as if he would never have made any other choice. She couldn't take it in. It went against everything she knew of him.

She opened her mouth—to say what, she didn't know. But before she could speak, a blinding light flared, making her wince. She flung up a hand to shield her eyes.

A glaring golden ribbon streamed from the King's body. It paused in midair; Joan had the impression that it wanted to fly free, but instead it rushed toward Eleanor like lightning to a rod.

Like Eleanor was the most powerful person here, and it was helplessly drawn to her.

It twined around Eleanor, over her arms, over her torso. Eleanor's face contorted in pain for a moment, and then she began to blaze as brightly as the King had.

Joan struggled to look at her. Had Eleanor just taken the King's power? Because if she had . . . The full implication hit Joan in a wave of horror. With power like that, Eleanor could mold the timeline to her will. She could create the hellish timeline they'd seen.

Every human Joan loved was in danger. Dad, the rest of her family, her friends, her neighbors, everyone at school. *Everyone.* They could all be dead in the new timeline. Even if they survived, they'd all be under monster rule.

"You can't do this!" Joan blurted to Eleanor. "*Please!* Don't bring them back like this! Don't make humans suffer!"

"*You* can't stop me," Eleanor told her, her voice filled with relief and triumph. "You were already too late when you first arrived in 1923. You saw the hole in the timeline forming then. It was emanating from *here*. From *this*—" Eleanor dragged her hands apart in a tearing motion.

"*No!*" The word burst from Joan. She looked up and shuddered. The sky had split open. Like an echo of the Thames below, there was a slash of blue. The sky of another timeline.

The earth trembled, and the buildings of 1923 creaked and swayed, the sounds rattling and guttural. On the river, the steamship rocked precariously from side to side. In the distance, people screamed.

Joan struggled to keep her feet. She threw herself at the Ali barrier separating them from Eleanor. She poured her power into it, and was distantly aware of Nick punching at it; of Ruth trying to use the Hunt power on it.

Just behind Eleanor, Mariam Ali stood with her arms raised. Maybe *she* would listen.

"Did she offer you power in the new world?" Joan asked Mariam, already breathless with effort. "Is that why you're helping her?"

"Power?" Mariam looked insulted. "*No.*" She had thick dark hair curled in a bun, and now that Joan was closer to her, she could see that Mariam was older than she'd realized—maybe forty. "My father was a Liu," Mariam said. "I had the Liu power as a child. I remember the Graves." Her gaze hollowed. "What happened to them was an atrocity! I'm doing this for them! For *you*, because you can't remember them yourself!" She nodded at the rest of Eleanor's people. "We all have a connection to your family!"

"Look at St. Paul's!" Aaron blurted.

Joan searched for it—in 1923, the cathedral's dome was the tallest point on the skyline. As she watched, it narrowed and soared even higher, becoming a towering spike before shrinking back again.

"The timeline's changing!" Tom said. He was straining against the invisible wall with all his strength. Trying to get to Eleanor.

Joan concentrated her power on the barrier, trying to break it open. They had to stop Eleanor before it was too late.

"Stop fighting me!" Eleanor snapped at her. "When I'm done, our family will be back! You don't remember them now, but you will!"

Joan looked up at Eleanor, blazing now with the King's power. "But then I'll forget what you did to bring them back!" Joan told her. "I'll forget that there was once a better world than the one you're making!"

"This is *not* a better world!" Eleanor said.

"Jamie!" Tom shouted suddenly, voice thick with terror.

Joan spun around. To her horror, Jamie flickered out like a snuffed candle. "Jamie!"

And then Jamie was back. Tom grabbed his hands, tight enough for Jamie to gasp.

"What just happened?" Tom demanded desperately. "What the hell was that?"

Joan's heart thundered. In the true timeline, Ying had been married to a member of the Grave family. Would Jamie exist if Eleanor brought the Graves back? Was Eleanor erasing Jamie right in front of them?

As if in answer, Tom was suddenly holding on to nothing. Jamie was gone.

"Stop!" Joan screamed at Eleanor. "Look what you're doing to him!"

Jamie reappeared again, looking off-balance. "What's going on?" he asked unsteadily.

Tom turned and put his shoulder against the barrier, bull-like. "I'm going to kill you with my bare hands!" he gritted out at Eleanor.

In response, Mariam made a shoving gesture, and the invisible Ali wall became a weapon again, throwing them back along the walkway. Joan stumbled, trying to stay upright.

Tom brute-forced his way back up and ran at Eleanor again, but he wouldn't be able to break through that barrier. He didn't have the power.

Above, that unnatural blue sky began to swallow up the world. Panicked, Joan did the only thing she could think of. She gathered everything she had left, the last dregs of her power, and threw it, not at the Ali barrier, but around herself and her friends. She made a shield against the changes.

Around them, the world transformed, the dome of St. Paul's spiking back into a spire. Buildings shivered and rose and fell. In the distance, people vanished from the walkway, and new people appeared.

Eleanor's power battered at the shield. A storm. Inexorable. Joan struggled to hold it and pushed back against her. Her hands shook. She couldn't catch her breath. She couldn't keep up the stream of power. Eleanor was too strong. Had Jamie vanished completely like the people on the walkway? Joan didn't have the strength to look back.

Eleanor made a furious sound. "Let go!" she screamed at Joan.

Above Joan, the alien sky bore down, and Joan's power sputtered like a doused flame. The shield cracked. She fell to her knees, black spots covering her vision. As darkness closed in, she had a single thought.

It was over.

EPILOGUE

Joan groaned. Was she dead? No. Surely your body didn't hurt this much when you were dead.

"Joan?" A hand on her shoulder. "*Joan?*"

She opened her eyes. She was lying on the ground, her cheek pressed against something gritty and hard. A pavement? She turned her head and found Aaron bending over her, his fine features tight with concern. His thumb hovered over the line of her cheek for just a moment. Before Joan could even react, he blinked and seemed to catch himself, pulling his hand away. "Are you all right?" he asked.

"What happened?" Joan managed. She shifted, and Aaron supported her to sit up. Joan winced at the new ache in her head as she moved. Images flashed in painful sparks: the King's bright light flowing to Eleanor, St. Paul's dome rising to a spire as London changed around them . . .

Had Nick really killed the King?

Had Jamie—

Joan breathed in sharply. She turned, searching. But it was okay—Jamie was here, getting to his feet a few paces away, eyes bleary. And the others were just beyond him. Joan took another breath and closed her eyes, overwhelmed with relief. They'd survived.

A soft rustle beside her. Joan pictured Aaron removing his

jacket and shaking it out. "Look at these wrinkles," he said, sounding a little disgruntled—and more like himself. "I'll never get them out."

Joan opened her eyes again. They seemed to be in an alley. Dark buildings had risen around them, narrowing the view of the north bank. Across the river, a bland skyscraper stood directly opposite. Far too tall for 1923. It took Joan a long, long moment to understand what that meant. "We're back in the twenty-first century?" she said slowly. "We're home?"

But as she said *home*, her stomach turned over. She'd been feeling uneasy since she'd woken, she realized. Her body thought that something was wrong.

"No." Nick's voice was horribly blank. He'd gone to the mouth of the alley, and now he stood with his back to Joan, staring at the city. Joan's unease flared to life. "We're not home," Nick said.

Joan's heart started to pound. With trepidation, she walked up the alley. The view opened as she did, and she gasped.

Under a thunderous sky, Old London Bridge stood to the west, its arches straddling the water, rapids rushing through the gaps. And at its center was the mansion of the Graves, beautiful and terrible, and *wrong*. A discordant note in a song.

With growing horror, Joan followed the skyline. There was St. Paul's—not the familiar dome, but a spire like a sharpened stick. There was the architecture she'd glimpsed in the tear in the world: not quite Victorian black brick. And the dark skyscraper she'd dismissed as *bland*. Now, light caught the side of the glass, revealing a tint in the windows, a design that ran up the full height of the wall. Joan recognized the image with a jolt: a sea serpent engulfing a sailing ship. The sigil of monsters.

"*No*," Joan heard herself say. She could see signs of monsters everywhere now. More sigils emblazoned on buildings: a griffin; a burnt elm tree. And on the walkway across the river, people strolled by wearing dark tweeds and gauze, Roman tunics, medieval dress.

Nick met Joan's gaze. His eyes were dark—almost black. "This is the world we saw. Eleanor's world."

A world where monsters ruled.

Joan swallowed hard. This world existed because of *her*, because Nick had chosen her.

And this new Nick was hard to read, but Joan could guess what he was thinking. He had to be regretting his choice to save her. He had to wish he'd chosen to kill her instead. Now that he'd seen all this . . .

Nick's gaze dropped to the ground, and he frowned. He bent to pick something up—a knife etched with roses. The knife he'd used to kill the King.

The blade shone, clean and new—as if it had never been used to stab anyone. It struck Joan then that the King's body wasn't here. Owen wasn't here. And . . . someone else was missing. Her heart thumped.

"Where's *Tom?*" she blurted. When she'd woken, she'd assumed that Tom had been around the corner from the alley, but now she was standing right at the mouth of it, and she couldn't see him anywhere. Frankie and Jamie were alone.

"He isn't here," Jamie said hollowly.

"*What?*" Joan saw then what she hadn't seen when she'd first woken. Jamie was barely holding it together, leaning heavily against the alley wall, his legs shaking.

"Tom isn't here," Jamie said again. "He was outside that protective dome you made."

Joan opened her mouth, but no words came out. *Oh God.* She replayed the last moments before she'd blacked out. She'd thrown a shield up in desperation, trying to protect them all from Eleanor's changes. Now, though, in her mind's eye, she saw Tom brute-forcing his way to Eleanor. Moving beyond the scope of the shield. "*No,*" Joan whispered.

Jamie pushed away from the wall. "We have to find him." He usually projected a gentle calmness, but right now his face was granite. "He's somewhere in this world. I know he is."

Joan managed a nod. "We'll find him." It was a promise.

"Owen's missing too," Ruth said, looking around. "Was he outside the protection as well?"

"No," Aaron said. "I saw him when I woke up. He ran off." He grimaced. "All the Argents are cowards. I just—" He froze.

They all heard it at the same time—an engine on the Thames.

A hearse-black boat was making its way down the river with the menacing pace of a slow patrol. A golden sigil shone on the black of the boat: a winged lion. Not the familiar Court sigil Joan knew, but the version she'd seen through the café window: the lion roaring in attack.

Joan and the others drew back into the shadows of the alley instinctively. And they weren't the only ones afraid. On the other side of the river, people watched the boat pass, wary and tense.

Nick's hand tightened on the hilt of the knife. Was he thinking, as Joan was, of the last time they'd seen that sigil on a vehicle? Was he thinking of the tangled bodies in the van? Of the human murdered in broad daylight by a monster guard?

Joan looked across at the looming skyline again. This world was wrong. She could feel it like the thrum of her own heartbeat. And people she loved were out there. Dad, her family, her friends . . . They might even be— No. Joan shied from the thought. They *couldn't* be dead in this world. They had to be somewhere. Like Tom was.

Like Eleanor was.

"She'll know we escaped," Aaron said softly. "She'll be looking for us."

Nick's knuckles whitened around the knife's handle. "I'll be looking for her too," he murmured.

Joan watched the patrol boat disappear behind the bridge— the heart of this new, corrupted London. "We need to get out of here," she said. They needed to regroup.

And when they did . . . Her jaw tightened. They were going to fix this world. They were going to make it right.

ACKNOWLEDGMENTS

The last few years have been such a strange mixture of whirlwind and stasis. I wrote the first draft of this book during a series of long lockdowns where every day felt the same. And, just a few months later, it was so exciting, and such a dream come true, to see my first book, *Only a Monster*, out in the world, on shelves and in unboxings.

Thank you so much to everyone who read and supported *Only a Monster*: family, friends (and friends and family of friends!), booksellers, bloggers, bookstagrammers, booktokkers, event organizers, panel organizers, podcasters. It means the absolute world to me.

Thank you, always, to my family for all your love and encouragement, especially to Dad, Jun, Ben, Moses, Lee-Chin, Wennie, Zaliyah, and Nina.

Thank you so much to my critique partner, Cat, for reading every iteration of every scene of this book at least ten times and making every version ten times better.

Huge thanks for all your encouragement and support to: Shelley Parker-Chan, Rose Hartley, Lilliam Rivera, Mike Reid, Evan Mallon, Alison Laming, Susan Trompenaars, Jessica Boland,

Sharon Brown, Kathryn Lindsay, Kelly Nissen, Noni Morrissey, Amanda Macdonald (and Tamlyn!), Emma Durbridge, Leanne Robertson, Madeleine Daniel, Kate Murray, Anna Cowan, Belinda Grant, Katya Dibb, Liana Skrzypczak, Leanne Yong, LinLi Wan, Naomi Novik, Amie Kaufman, Jay Kristoff, Astrid Scholte, Ellie Marney, Jess Barber, Pip Coen, Bernette Cox, Nathan Hillstrom, Becca Jordan, Travis Lyons, Eugene Ramos, Sara Saab, Melanie West, Tiffany Wilson, Elaine Cuyegkeng, Kat Clay, Aidan Doyle, Emma Osborne, Sophie Yorkston, and Suzanne Willis.

To my brilliant agent, Tracey Adams, at Adams Literary, and the team—Josh Adams and Anna Munger—thank you for performing miracles for this series!

To Christabel McKinley, thank you for all your amazing work in the UK and Australia.

Thank you so much to Vera Chok for your incredible performance in the audiobook.

At HarperCollins in the US, a huge thank-you to my wonderful editor, Kristen Pettit, for your insightful feedback and guidance, and to the whole brilliant team: senior editor Alice Jerman, associate editor Clare Vaughn, marketers Audrey Diestelkamp and Sabrina Abballe, publicists Lauren Levite and Kate Lopez, designers Jessie Gang and Alison Klapthor, cover artist Eevien Tan, production editors Caitlin Lonning and Alexandra Rakaczki, copyeditor Erin DeWitt, proofreaders Jessica White and Lana Barnes, and production managers Allison Brown and Meghan Pettit.

At Hodder & Stoughton in the UK, I'm so grateful to my incredible editor, Molly Powell, and to Sophie Judge,

Callie Robertson, Kate Keehan, Lydia Blagden, copyeditor Alyssa Ollivier-Tabukashvili, cover artist Kelly Chong, and the whole amazing team.

To the incredible team at Allen & Unwin in Australia—Kate Whitfield, Jodie Webster, Eva Mills, Sandra Nobes, Liz Kemp, Simon Panagaris, Yvette Gilfillan, Anna McFarlane—and everyone else who has worked on and supported the book. Thank you so much; it means the world to me to have had so much local support.

Thank you so much as well to the amazing teams and translators at Alta Novel in Brazil (translator: Giovanna Chinellato), CooBoo in the Czech Republic (translator: Petra Badalec), Lumen in France (translator: Mathilde Tamae-Bouhon), Anassa Könyvek in Hungary (translator: Ádám Sárpátki), Eksmo in Russia (translator: Olga Burdova), Vulkan in Serbia (translator: Elena Milosavljević), Montena in Spain (translator: Elena Macian Masip), and Olimpos in Türkiye (translator: Yasemin Bayraktar). As I write this, the book is also coming soon from Piper Verlag in Germany, Mondadori in Italy, and Wydawnictwo MAG in Poland.

It has been a dream come true to see special editions of *Only a Monster*, and I am beyond grateful to the incredible book boxes that featured the book and brought it so many readers. Thank you so much to Anissa and the FairyLoot team, to Korrina and the OwlCrate team, to the Bookish Box team, the Librarian Box team, the Fabled team, the Duality Box team, to NovelTea Chest, and Lovinbookscandle.

Thank you so much, also, to the amazing authors who blurbed

Only a Monster: Hafsah Faizal, Stephanie Garber, Chloe Gong, Adalyn Grace, Cindy Lin, Natasha Ngan, Lynette Noni, Naomi Novik, C. S. Pacat, and June Tan.

The 2021 and 2022 debut groups have been a huge support. I learned so much about every aspect of publishing, especially marketing, from you. Special thanks to Deborah Falaye, Jessica Olson, Akshaya Raman, Kylie Lee Baker, Lillie Lainoff, Leslie Vedder, Sue Lynn Tan, June Tan, Judy I. Lin, Emily Thiede, and Lyndall Clipstone.

Finally, I would like to acknowledge the Traditional Custodians of the lands on which I wrote this book, and to pay my respect to their Elders, past, present, and emerging: the Wurundjeri Woi-wurrung, Bunurong Boon Wurrung, and Dja Dja Wurrung peoples of the Kulin Nation.